# HURRICANE SWEEP

# SAMANTHA HARTE

**DIVERSIONBOOKS**

Also by Samantha Harte

*Cactus Heart*
*Timberhill*
*The Snows of Craggmoor*
*Kiss of Gold*
*Vanity Blade*
*Sweet Whispers*
*Autumn Blaze*
*Summersea*
*Angel*

Diversion Books
A Division of Diversion Publishing Corp.
443 Park Avenue South, Suite 1008
New York, New York 10016
www.DiversionBooks.com

For more information, email info@diversionbooks.com

First Diversion Books edition March 2015.
Print ISBN: 978-1-68230-088-6
eBook ISBN: 978-1-62681-657-2

To Art and June Johnson…
gentle critics, best friends.

The mighty wind comes from the sea, relentless, merciless, absolute. Wind and sky become a screaming, grinding, whirling fury born of heaven's passion and hell's delight. Nothing is left untouched.

Then comes the peaceful, silent blue eye of calm. Deceptive and seductive, it drifts by like a caress, a promise of respite.

Caught unaware, anything left standing begins to tremble. The wind turns, suddenly delivering an all-powerful blast so devastating those few who have survived call it a hurricane sweep.

—J. Roebling, 1869

# Roebling - DeMarsett - Mercedes Family Tree

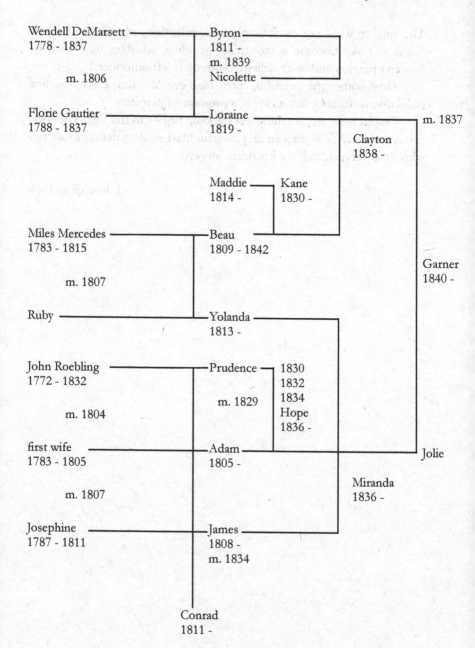

Wendell DeMarsett
1778 - 1837

m. 1806

Florie Gautier
1788 - 1837

Byron
1811 -
m. 1839
Nicolette

Loraine
1819 -

m. 1837

Clayton
1838 -

Maddie
1814 -

Kane
1830 -

Miles Mercedes
1783 - 1815

m. 1807

Ruby

Beau
1809 - 1842

Garner
1840 -

Yolanda
1813 -

John Roebling
1772 - 1832

m. 1804

first wife
1783 - 1805

Prudence

m. 1829

1830
1832
1834
Hope
1836 -

Adam
1805 -

Jolie

m. 1807

Josephine
1787 - 1811

Miranda
1836 -

James
1808 -
m. 1834

Conrad
1811 -

# BOOK ONE

## Florie

# PART ONE

## 1806

## One

From the steamy recesses of the cookhouse to the seamstress's cobwebby corner in the attic, Gautier Plantation readied for the wedding.

In the many upstairs sleeping rooms, guests languished in the thick dawn heat. More flatboats arrived by the hour. Already the cook and her dark army of serving girls had placed before the hungry travelers an array of foods befitting the occasion.

It was to be the first wedding among the honey-haired Gautier girls. Eighteen-year-old Florie had risen with the first cock's crow and now sat silently before her dressing table. Her sisters fluttered and buzzed behind her, and Lusey, her mammy, labored over her gleaming curls.

"Perk up, child," Lusey whispered close to Florie's ear. "It's your weddin' day. You're the luckiest gal in these bayous. Luckiest in this house, that's for sure."

Florie met her mammy's creamy eyes in the looking glass. She wanted to please her old protector so she forced a smile. When she caught sight of her own reflection, however her eyes darted away.

She blinked and drew a deep breath. Everything would work out. Soon she'd be happy. For six agonizing years she'd dreamed of this day. Mama had promised she'd be happy and find a great love. Florie clutched that long ago promise to her heart.

"She looks mindless with fright," Dulcine whispered to her older sister Lalange. "Whatever is troubling you, dear little sister? Can it be your intended is not to your liking?"

Dulcine and Lalange leaned toward each other, wearing mutual simpers, their rouged cheeks and frog-colored eyes flashing. They looked like two crooked candles, white and waxen, dripping hot little remarks upon the polished floor.

Watching from the corner of her eyes, Florie felt her stomach curl. They looked like elegant ghosts. Fringes of curls tickled their foreheads. A snarl of coils hung down their backs. Their morning gowns of tulle over rose-colored satin clung damply to their torsos and thighs in a most revealing and scandalous manner.

Lalange, being twenty-five, wore a chemisette tucked in her décolletage. It wasn't seemly for her to expose her bosoms so early in the day. Dulcine, however, was still young enough to show all that propriety allowed. Her arms were bare and her slippers showed all the way to the tops of the laces.

Their eldest sister, Fabrienne, would thrash her for such brazen exposure.

Florie sighed. It didn't matter what they wore. Until that day the Gautier sisters had been considered unmarriageable. The gentlemen from New Orleans and neighboring plantations remained uncharmed in the face of all that exposed white flesh.

Florie lowered her eyes. She tried to loosen her grip on the edge of her dressing table. Lusey tugged her hair into place and secured the shining mass of sausage curls with a tiara trimmed with precious gems. Across her forehead, Florie also wore fringed ringlets that framed her skimmed-milk face like a garland of spun gold.

Urging Florie to her feet, Lusey steadied her. "You don't need this hardly," Lusey whispered. She reached for the corset and wrapped it around Florie's slim body, crushing Florie's ribs and hip bones into an even narrower silhouette.

Florie felt as if she was disappearing into herself. While Florie's older sisters snickered, Lusey tied the laces and fetched the satin underskirt.

Dulcine's giggles erupted. "Skinny."

Lalange fanned herself. Her face was a perfect mask of controlled delight. "I don't know what he sees in her. She surely does need those forms."

Lusey's coffee-colored cheeks began to glow. Her glossy lids lowered. Florie began to pant.

At that moment Fabrienne walked into the bedchamber like a queen into her court. At twenty-seven she was mistress of the Gautier house. Since their mother's death ten years earlier she had reigned supreme, and she carried that responsibility with a stiff and impenetrable hauteur.

She too had fringed forelocks, but the rest of her dull gold hair hid under a mop cap. She'd been up since before dawn supervising the breakfasts, including the bridegroom's. Her gown hung on her like moss from an oak; she was far too removed from marriageable age to take pains with her appearance.

Presenting a large tissue-wrapped package to Florie, Fabrienne silenced the smothered and dimpled mirth of her sisters. "Put this on!"

Florie saw her sister's eyes, the cold gold gleam that murdered any hope for happiness on this day. Her thank you came out small, and then she caught her breath. Her neck grew hot. Nestled in the rustling tissue was a breast-form of cotton and wax.

Florie wanted to throw it down and stomp on it. She wanted to put it on Fabrienne and laugh, but as quickly as her anger rose, she denied it life. She would never be like Fabrienne, cruel and cold, venting rage with a terrible violence whenever it suited her mood. Florie would be like her mother.

Lusey lifted the cups from the tissue and clucked her tongue. "She don't need this. How's her gowns going to fit?"

Fabrienne raised her brows.

Ducking her head, Lusey fell silent.

Fabrienne's gold eyes drooped with malice. "Mr. Wendell DeMarsett is a Yankee. Such people like endowments, and surely you recall that is what caught his eye years ago. We've waited a long time for him to make good his troth. I don't care to have him turn his back on our dear little sister at this late hour."

Florie's chest emptied of air. Turn his back?

"Put the forms on. Your gowns will fit. I saw to it myself."

Florie's head was shaking.

"Your Yankee betrothed will find you...irresistible. Hopefully, that'll spare us the scandal of having him reject you."

Florie edged closer to Lusey. Reeling, she tried to recall the evening before. Wendell had clung to her hand, a most ardent suitor.

Her breath came in sharp gasps. The room rang and began to whirl. She must not faint. She must survive this day, just as she had survived all the previous ones. She must go through with the marriage.

She'd seen Wendell for the first time in six years when he arrived the week before. Stepping from the flatboat, he'd croaked a hello and staggered toward her. She stared. She'd raised a shock-limp hand...

It hadn't occurred to her he might be disappointed in *her*.

Cringing behind Lusey's bulk, Florie lowered her camisole and watched with straining eyes as the cups went into place over her breasts. Her sisters looked like a trio of cats. Their eyes missed nothing, and Florie felt their gaze touch her like claws.

The pink satin felt cool and confining. Florie cupped the unyielding mounds bulging from her chest like overly risen loaves. The mirror grew dark, the hand-painted wallpaper sporting scenes from the French countryside, dimmed. She felt like the dressform in the seamstress's attic room, immovable and helpless.

Lusey's reassuring touch faded. Florie felt herself shrinking, fading, growing invisible. It was as if Lusey was tying ribbons around someone else's back, closing the camisole over vulgar mountains on someone else's chest.

Insinuating snickers still penetrated Florie's trance. Her sisters' eyes were on her like hands. She could not let go, she told herself. She must survive just one more day.

Teeth aching, Florie lifted her chin. Her chest rose and fell, but she would not allow the hate heaving inside her to erupt.

She would marry the Yankee because he was the only man who wanted her, who could take her from this hot, languid hell. She would go to the altar wearing the forms, naked if it amused her sisters, and escape the clinging stench of this place called home.

Six years before she'd seen her freedom shimmering on the young sweating face of Wendell DeMarsett. She'd been twelve and blooming before the astonished eyes of her sisters, then the belles of New Orleans.

After he sailed, she kept his desire for her alive in letters. The years had passed, and her sisters soured like overripe peaches. When she'd turned sixteen he couldn't sail for her, and still her hope burned, hope for escape, for freedom.

Now he had come, Wendell DeMarsett, Yankee sea captain, plump and red of face, still sweating, still panting. He wanted her. She knew that as surely as she knew death awaited her here with her sisters.

Wendell was her salvation. He'd prospered in the years she waited. His ships carried much trade about the American ports. He lived in a fine house, ate at a generous table it was obvious and at last he had come to take her away with him.

She would go with him. She'd sail away with a man she knew only through letters, a man who had matured so beautifully in her imagination, but in reality was just a foppish dandy in green satin and pumps, who talked too loudly and looked at her too long.

At half past two that spring day in 1806, the sun stood in the sky hot and yellow. Assembled on the front lawn were all the friends and neighbors of the Gautier family.

The massive red brick house surrounded with shrouded live oak cast a verdant shade over those seated on gilt chairs. The land flowed away in green waves of heat. Fields of cane, marshes, and the curve of muddy river, broad and sluggish, slipped away to meet the sky.

Garlands of magnolia, lilac and peach blossoms burdened the altar. Father Jacques stood nearby nodding with the relieved father of the bride.

"From America, you say," the priest said for perhaps the hundredth time. His black frock tugged with the breeze as if signaling to be away. "Of good family?"

"Good enough," Pierre Gautier said, his narrow eyes traveling the gathering. "I'll not look a gift horse in the mouth about now, Father. My little ladies are chaffing at the bit, and longer than this one man can stand. Yes, sir, Father. I say let the girl go to the Yankees."

Pierre, a compact man in his late fifties, held up his cigar with a womanly hand as he squinted at the priest.

"Never expected she'd go first," he said, flicking his ash into the breeze. He sucked on the rolled tobacco a moment. "Like a river rat, she was, when she was born. Didn't expect her to live. Then she was always ripping about, getting into trouble. My other three, they were always proper. Pink as shoats, they were. Docile. Can't abide unbridled females."

"A good Christian though," the priest muttered.

Pierre cocked his brow and then nodded. "Like her mother in some respects. Can't say I mind losing her though, troublesome as she's always been. Now, if Fabrienne was to marry, I'd be a helpless fool. That's just what I'd be. Couldn't run the place without her. Ah, there he comes now. Reminds me of a..."

"Afternoon, my boy. Father Jacques, this is my future son-in-law from Union Harbor, Massachusetts."

The priest offered his pale hand. He connected with Captain DeMarsett's palm and his nostrils flared. "We're about to begin," he said, swallowing.

Wendell took his place beside the altar. He stood first on one foot and then the other, cursing his snug pumps. Wringing his hands, he found them damp and cold and wiped them again and again on his pink claw-hammer frockcoat.

Ducking back out of the sun's reach, he hoped his thinning hair didn't show too much. The heat made him breathy and uncomfortable. The pale green breeches were too tight about his belly even when he tightened his muscles.

Wendell liked the plantation. It spoke of enviable wealth and undeniable power, but he hated the gathering guests. They kept eyeing him, making him feel like an ox. He shifted his weight and sighed.

Violins began a quiet lament. All eyes turned to catch the first glimpse of the bridal procession which appeared from the parlor doors.

Wendell felt his frockcoat dampen under his arms. Since arriving, he'd hardly had time to talk to Florie. What a treasure she'd turned into. His heart skipped when he thought of that lovely creature soon to be his wife. He could hardly believe she was willing to go all the way back to Massachusetts with him.

A union with the venerable Gautier family would certainly serve him well in this newly acquired territory. Pierre would profit from Wendell's contacts in the north as well. Wendell supposed the marriage would never have been allowed otherwise.

Fabrienne, the sharklike maid of honor, lead the procession toward Wendell. He threw back his shoulders, pleased with himself for having had the wisdom to make them wait. The other two brittle-eyed sisters followed; he couldn't remember their names. A troupe of cherubic girls in ruffles and flounces stumbled after them, flinging rosebuds.

Then, wearing a gossamer gown trimmed with pearls, came the floating bride. Dainty honey-colored curls and a veil of handmade lace framed her face. He'd never seen such large sparkling dark eyes. They reminded him of expensive bonbons, and the thought watered his mouth.

As she drew near, Wendell felt his eyes begin to strain from their sockets. He'd been so nervous and impatient since arriving he'd failed to notice the truly amazing curve of her bosom. His plump fists squeezed the humid air.

How tender her narrow shoulders were, how soft and slim the arms. He recited the appropriate words, slipped a band of gold on Florie's finger that reminded him of the shackles on a slave's ankle.

Then, waking as if from a dream, Wendell realized the ceremony was over. He wanted to snatch Florie up and carry her away. As his thoughts raced ahead to the marriage bed awaiting them, his chest heaved and his heart sputtered in his chest. When they turned, she tucked her dainty hand into the crook of his satiny elbow. He groaned.

Florie kept her face turned away. "Put him on the divan."

Two uniformed black footmen hauled the breathing pink mountain of satin reeking of champagne, rum and whiskey, and dropped him across a divan in the corner of the bridal chamber.

Florie flinched as the door closed. For a moment she stood staring at the carpet, feeling the day's tension run out of her like muddy flood water. Across the gentle French colors in the carpet stood the bed, a monster of mahogany covered with satin comforters and lace-edged ruffles.

Forcing herself to move, she turned and twisted the key in the lock as if with the last of her strength. Leaving a trail of costly embroidered silk, satin slippers, gossamer stockings and lacy underthings, Florie dragged herself across the room. While her newlywed husband snorted and sighed, looking like a glob of breathing pink lard, Florie sank to one knee on the bed and struggled with the detestable breast form.

She began to giggle. When the tangle came away, she dashed the form against the bedstead. Wiping away tears with her fists, she wept with sharp silent gasps, ever mindful of a house filled with fervid ears.

Turning, she looked at the fat man and her head fell back. She closed her eyes, moaning in the back of her throat. Thank God for liquor.

She stood, looking for a likely hiding place for the forms and then, wandering toward the man she'd married, looking at him in a most unladylike and curious way, she draped the forms over his rumbling chest.

Convulsed with rigid, shaking laughter, Florie went and flung herself across the bed. Her ears still rang from all the music and talking. Her feet throbbed from the hours of dancing. Oh, to run away...

She stared at the plaster mouldings covering the ceiling in intricate squares and garlands. She was free at last. She had freed herself from her sisters' eyes and words and terrible secret ways of hurting her. *I'll be all right, Mama*, she thought, having not the energy to cross herself.

Florie could picture her sisters lying in their beds now. Listening. Did they hope for some sigh of wedded passion or tortured scream? She considered orchestrating a delicious sequence of fake sounds, but lay still, breathing in the hot night air feeling it press on her like the damp hands of that man.

Lying there, safe, Florie thought of her mother's lovely pale face. She felt as if she'd just come from her mother's bedchamber, from the foot of the vast plump bed where her mother had lived from the moment of Florie's agonizing birth.

Together on that bed they had whiled away Florie's childhood— eight years of songs, private games, kisses and stories.

Florie drew herself up and sat staring at her narrow shadow on the floor. The lamps had been turned low. Moonlight streamed through the tall windows and fell across one corner of the bed.

She padded to her husband and lifted the forms. He grunted and stretched, slipping closer to the edge of the divan. Florie couldn't bring herself to push him back.

He looked small, lying there with his arms flung out to each side, his mouth open and slack, plump cheeks like those of a boy. There was pain in the tilt to his brows. Florie understood pain, and regretted the harsh thoughts she'd had since he'd arrived to rescue her. She would be good to this man.

Somehow.

Hiding the cups under her next day dress, Florie crawled into the soft bed and curled into a ball. She shut her eyes and her heart and her mind to thoughts of Fabrienne, willing herself a peace-filled night.

If she was quiet, obedient and good, no one would ever hurt her again...

An hour before dawn, morning birds twittered in the oaks outside the window. Lavender light filled the bridal chamber, tinting the painted wallpapers, frosting the white linens with dreamlike hues. Still unable to fall soundly asleep for the alien presence of the man on the divan, Florie turned yet again, slapping at the lumps in her pillows. The bed felt made of rocks.

The sharp pink faces of her sisters welled in her mind, and with them came the lifetime of pain-filled memories that always haunted Florie's night hours. Smothering, Florie flung away her pillow.

She thought she heard a thud. For a frozen moment she lay listening, straining, too terrified to sit up and see if he had awakened.

Hearing nothing more, she clutched the coverlet to her throat.

The embroidery threads felt rough under her fingertips. The cool linen touched her fevered skin, reminding her that this night was...

The darkness behind her eyes deepened into an image of sooty clouds drifting close to the mud and marshy ground. They were standing around her, three naked ghosts with faces undulating in the swampy mist. Wiggling like reflections in black water, the ghosts surged close and then drifted back. Close. Back. Florie tried to move and found her feet held by sucking dark mud.

She was naked, and her breasts were so large they floated before her like nippled soap bubbles. The ghosts began laughing, for they had long spears—or were those things pins? She felt the points pricking her, pricking and pricking until the pain became penetrating, thrusting, deeply dull and aching violation.

Florie tried to call her mother. Her mouth was filled with mud. Mama was long dead. The happy days of her childhood were long dead.

The ghosts were chanting now. Their voices rose in a hissing chorus. "You killed her. Killed...You were wicked." Pain stabbed into Florie from all sides. "You drove her away."

She was eight years old again, standing behind Lusey's calico skirts. Her mother's tomb rose gray and cold in the mists, and her sisters were weeping. Her bodice swelled and suddenly her newly born breasts bulged from the rents in the fabric.

Looming, receding, relentless as the tide, Florie's sisters jeered and laughed, spinning her around so that the pins of their tortures began slicing her to ribbons. Then a great wind came, silencing her cries. A long white switch whistled through the air. Florie looked down to see a red welt rise from her hip bone across her thigh to her other knee.

"You took Mama away..."

Welts sprang up in a crosshatch of pain on her tenderest skin.

Seizing the comforter, squirming to avoid more blows, Florie thrashed upon the bed, moaning deep in her throat. She hadn't meant to kill Mama. She hadn't meant to smile at the sea captain. "Take him if you want him!"

Flinging herself to a sitting position, Florie opened her eyes. Her breath rasped in her throat. She nearly stuffed a corner of the comforter into her mouth to silence the harsh sounds she was making.

Mama had died of a fever like many that year.

She closed her eyes, weeping into the comforter. Yes, Mama had died. Because she had died, Dulcine and Lalange had little hope of finding husbands. Who would remind them to be sweet and charming?

Who would prevent them from making scandalous mistakes?

Fabrienne had turned her face from her beaus immediately. Her duty lay in helping Papa…

Florie jerked as if she'd been struck. She threw herself back down, now tangled in the linens and bound by them. She lay listening to the wild hammer of her heart. It didn't stop even after she had calmed herself, certain Mama had died of that fever. She heard nothing but her own heart, nothing but the cries frozen unforgotten and unhealed in her memories.

Wendell peeled his tongue from the roof of his mouth, licked his lips and swallowed. Panting, he pressed himself upright, waited for the room to stop whirling and determined it was nearly dawn.

He rubbed his stubbled double chin, pinching and plumping the soft folds. Then he ground his knuckles into his burning eyes.

Belching with a sign of satisfaction, he stumbled to his feet and lurched across the room to stand at the foot of the bed. The linens were torn asunder, twined about a pair of shapely slim legs like white snakes.

He licked his lips again.

She turned, moaning, twisting, exposing her hip.

He swallowed another burp and thumped his chest. Had he done that damage to the bed?

Rubbing his hands down over his belly, he found himself still dressed, his waistcoat gathered like fetters under his sodden armpits, watch fob dangling against his thigh. He plucked at the tied laces but couldn't free himself. Then, at last he ripped them free of the holes, releasing him so that he could breathe once again. Scratching at his sparse curls, he looked about for a chamberpot.

Glancing in likely corners for a suitable receptacle, he sidestepped the bed. His bride's pretty face was nearly buried in the pillow. Her curls splayed across the shining folds like golden rivulets. Her lips swelled full, and parted as if about to taste something. Her eyes were clenched, her brow knit, and she mewed as she clutched at the coverlet wrapped about her neck.

What a prize. Wendell knelt beside the bed where he could see her childlike face. He hadn't known a woman in a long while. The last had been ugly. He still remembered her scream.

Thrashing, exposing a shoulder, arm and bare side, Florie whimpered in her sleep. Wendell's hand slid across the linen, feeling the warmth where she had lain moments before. As he scaled the tender recesses, she threw back her head.

"I did not!"

His hand closed over her breast. It fit his palm perfectly. Didn't she have the largest breasts he's ever seen?

As if in pain, she writhed, mumbling a jumble of words he neither understood nor cared about. Tearing the coverlet from her little hands, he vaulted himself upon her.

Bulging with terror, her eyes opened, dark, bottomless and unfocused a scant inch from his. Oh, that was nice. She filled the lavender air with a scream that nearly split his eardrum. Arched against her in his own pain, Wendell ejaculated against her hip.

He felt her scramble from under him, but didn't bother opening his eyes. He urinated across the mattress and lay motionless, panting, reeling, dazzled by the intensity of his satisfaction.

# Two

Florie watched the hazy outline of New Orleans shrink and fade into the distance. A gray mist soon swallowed the twisted shoreline, the huddled buildings and jumbled rooftops, and the memories that now belonged to another time.

Easing into the river from the landing a few days before, Gautier Plantation had been much like that. The world Florie had known since birth had been eerie with mist, humid and languid, all contrasting Florie's sharpened perception. Her body tingled, then and now.

Clutching her red wool mantle tightly over her pale blue gown of spider net and embroidered muslin, Florie smiled as her husband emerged from the cabin door of the old square-rigger. Thanks to Wendell's worrisome nature, they'd set sail a week early. Some disturbance in the city had him fearing for his ship.

Her father had talked of a take-over—Florie paid no attention. Their farewell had been stiff, lacking even hypocrisy. She'd hoped at least one member of her family regretted her leaving. Only Lusey's sad smile followed her, and Florie knew she'd never see her mammy again.

She lifted her face to the salt wind and blinked.

Wendell intended to sail along the coast, trading at various ports and then dashing for home waters when his holds were filled. When he wasn't leering at her, he looked for quick fortunes by talking loud and long with whomever he cornered.

During those last days at the plantation Florie had never known such deference. Her dawn scream had set her above and apart from her sisters. Now she was married, privy to secrets they'd never known.

Florie pitied her successor in the order of things, poor Dulcine. Perhaps even Lalange would bear Fabrienne's torment. Her concern for their future, however didn't dilute her sense of victory.

Wendell looked green as he showed her into his quarters. His was not a large schooner nor well kept. As she slipped inside out of the yellow haze, his crew peered at her from under low sunburned brows. When Wendell latched the door, Florie's heart lunged.

He'd been solicitous since their wedding night. She wondered if he was now afraid to approach her for his husbandly due. She felt ashamed of that scream and anxious in Wendell's massive presence.

The chamber closed around her, dank and rotting and odorous of spoiled cargo. The sails far above caught the wind with resounding whacks. The DeMarsett Gulf Packet got underway. The surge and swell of the ocean moved the deck under her feet. Her stomach began to pitch and roll.

She grabbed the rough edge of Wendell's narrow bunk, and as quickly, snatched her hand away again.

"What ails you?" Wendell asked, his voice too gentle for the shadowed look in his small eyes.

She reeled, casting her eyes into murky corners, seeing movement where there oughtn't to be movement, hearing whispers and scratchings and feeling breath. "This room is so close," she breathed, unable to look at her husband or force a smile.

Sometimes Wendell's muddy brown eyes burned through her like embers. As quickly they'd soften. She'd reassure herself she had married a man who loved her. He'd make an agreeable smile in his round cheesy face and beg her to have patience with him. She'd twist at the hem of her mantle until the threads broke.

Leaving her swaying and gulping, Wendell found work at his great scarred black desk bolted to the pitching deck. He made himself look busy and important. Florie loosed her mantle, forcing herself to give no regard to the deckhead looming above her or the bulkheads drawing in like the sides of black lungs. The days would be long in this ship.

The hours began flowing by, marked by the risings and settings of the moon and sun. The weather turned rough and the sea high. With each roll came the awful rise and crash as the ship's hull fought the waves. Squalls and showers beset them, and shadows of strange ships lurked near pale horizons.

Florie slept, her dreams always breathless struggles. She found the bunk solitary comfort, vaguely damp and odorous, a dreamworld of boredom without end.

In all that time Wendell didn't approach her. His attention focused on guiding his crew south around the keys and then on for home. Florie's fears rose and fell with the sea. Her worry, guilt and relief twisted about in her head like tropical storms.

Her nights she spent alone, safe, virginal in the salty cabin.

Wendell ate little and talked less and less. When the sea was high he remained topside for hours, sometimes days. When the great waters grew docile and the sails pulled them ever northward, he sometimes sat at his desk.

Florie thought he'd forgotten her. No lust fevered his dwindling cheeks. His sober-hued captain's cloak and straining trousers began to droop. When she asked, he said responsibility kept him from her. In truth, his belly gave him no mercy.

Just north of the Virginias, Captain DeMarsett took to his bunk, a shell of the plump goose Florie had married. Might he die? Then she would cross herself.

Summer heat baked the decks white as the first mate guided them into Union Bay at the wretched end of their journey. A high odor rose from the holds. The masts and shrouds slung about in disorder. Wendell lay below, barely able to take water, his eyes sunk to hot points of humiliation.

Only Florie DeMarsett, bride, stood at the rail that blistering day, watching the few rooftops of Union Harbor draw near.

The air smelled crisp there, tart and salty like clean wet beach sand. Gautier Plantation had always smelled of stagnant mud. Here a thousand fishing boats cluttered the green water. A few East Indiamen stood rocking at anchor, masts nodding toward the docks and then out again to open sea as if urging the men back.

A conglomeration of building slips and warehouses cluttered the wharves. Shanties crouched along narrow dirt paths that snaked up the sharp rise to a lime green meadow overlooking the bay. There was a look of tranquility about the town. Its white houses and wood-lined roads gave way to a few officious two-storied buildings in the middle of town. Above the chimneys, a church steeple pointed the way to heaven.

Florie sighed. Perhaps the Yankees wouldn't be too different. She laughed to think she'd imagined them like savages.

As the ship came about, Florie first saw the bluffs. Beyond a rocky arm curving and jutting into the bay, a perfect long silvery beach stretched. The dunes spread away until she saw them no more. The bluffs rose from the golden grasses like white petticoats, and atop them perched magnificent white houses.

Each looked out over the sea with solemn windows and sobering widow's walks. Set apart from the rest, and up the coast on the far side, sat an even more grandiose house. It slipped from her sight as Wendell's ship lumbered close in. The first mate and ship's surgeon helped Wendell walk jelly-legged toward the gangplank.

Florie strained to see that grand house a little longer, but it was gone. Gone.

As she disembarked and followed Wendell to a waiting closed carriage, Florie saw darkies working the wharves. They moved about without driver or overseer. In fact, all manner of hard-eyed men lurked in the shadows. One face stood out. Though nearly hidden in the doorway, a face harsh and twisted with interest smiled at Florie as she climbed inside the carriage opposite her husband.

The carriage clattered across hollow-sounding planks. She steadied herself. I'll die here, she thought.

# Three

"You've taken a chill," Wendell said a week later. He looked down at his bride nestled in her cloud of colorful quilts. She couldn't even sleep in his bedchamber so fierce were her shivers and coughs. Like a sickly child she lay in this chamber with its faded wallpaper, and sloping ceiling.

Florie looked at him with red watery eyes. "Forgive me, Husband. I'll be well soon."

He nodded with wild annoyance. He'd known he would recover from that rough voyage *she* had weathered so easily. Already he could eat and drink his fill. But now, little Florie with her face the color of a winter sea, lay abed.

She sniffed and sneezed, smiling with great weariness that annoyed him, and coughed. "Will the doctor come again soon?"

"Soon," Wendell said though he didn't like calling for the likes of Thomas Baines. The day before, that homely fool had fawned over Florie as if she was visiting royalty. Wendell, however didn't intend for the northern air to kill his bride after all he'd gone through to get her. So he sent for the physick—whatever was necessary—so that Florie wouldn't return home to a kinder climate.

Longing for the feel of her soft flesh, Wendell fidgeted at Florie's bedside aching for release. An impotent rage began to build in him. Did he dare take her as she was?

"Don't fret so," she said.

"Was I wrong to bring you here? I wouldn't harm you in any way." His words tasted as sour as they sounded.

"Have no more thoughts about it, Husband. I'm here to stay, and gladly." She looked as if she meant it. He dared believe she did.

Wendell's housewoman tapped at the door. "Doctor's here," she called, casting a jaundiced eye toward the maker-of-so-much-work idling among the quilts.

Young Doctor Baines blustered in, tall hat in one hand, black bag in the other. He brought the fresh scent of the sea with him. "You look better this morning, Mrs. DeMarsett," he said, his voice a pleasant tenor and full of good cheer. "I knew you'd conquer this cool weather. Just no more walking, especially in our cold rain." He clucked his tongue and shook his curly dark hair. He was perhaps thirty-five, with a high broad brow and mouth too sensitive for one of his trade. Though he seldom smiled, in his eyes dwelled the very depths of kindness. They could be haunting, too, as if he had seen too much and yet wasn't afraid to look.

Wendell scowled by the door. "I was at my office, good sir, and didn't know she went out." Wendell's voice was just an edge away from a defensive whine. "I certainly wouldn't have allowed her out alone."

"You'll get used to our Yankee climate," the good doctor said, giving Florie a wink. "Off with you now, Captain. I want to examine my new patient thoroughly." The doctor plucked off his threadbare gray frockcoat and opened his bag.

Wendell slunk out. He hated physicians. Too much knowledge, especially of the body, made him feel stupid and weak. And he hated being ordered about like a boy. He plodded down the stairs to his study and poured himself a hefty rum. Mrs. Worley, his housewoman, duly avoided him; she knew his expressions. Wendell gulped loudly and poured another. He wondered how soon Florie would be well. Then, with a curse, he threw the mug across the room.

Dr. Baines kept up a steady prattle about his wife and young son as he examined Florie from her dark cocoa eyes to her slender white hands clutching the quilt. He looked for signs of early pregnancy, but found none and was glad. She was too young. He decided she carried only the change of climate in her chest. With care she wouldn't succumb to lung fever.

"May I?" he asked beginning to pull back the quilt for a more intimate examination.

With a terrified shake of her head, Florie held on more tightly.

Dr. Baines then bid her good day. As he escaped the house, his heart felt sore. Thin sunshine greeted him, lighting the exterior gray stones of the massive two-storied dwelling making it appear only slightly less foreboding.

What an ugly place it was, he thought, casting his eyes from the only stone-built house in Union Harbor. It had been built close to the bluff more than twenty years before by a rather notorious sea captain who wanted a place able to withstand anything the sea could muster. Wendell DeMarsett bought the house—Dr. Baines couldn't remember how long ago—after that first captain went down with his ship and all hands in a gale off the coast of Britain.

He was glad to quit that gloomy assemblage of rooms. It gave him a great pain in his head. He resolved to stop home for a powder before going on to visit the new infant at the Roebling estate.

There, too, was a place he didn't like. The Roebling house was too big, too alien in its old English dignity for the humble town with its shingled and clapboard cottages. Thomas could have said the same for the builder John Roebling. John Roebling also built ships, bringing fame and wealth to Union Harbor, but he paled every other man in town by comparison. Less than six months before he had brought his Boston bride home to bear a son. And then he buried her. Though the boy child, Adam, was handsome and robust, his mother's death cast a shadow over that great white house overlooking the sea.

Losing that little woman to childbirth still preyed on Thomas' mind. She'd slipped away like grains of sand through his fingers. Sand. That was the color of pretty Florie DeMarsett's feathery curls. Sun-drenched sand. How very glad he was that she as yet carried no child.

Thomas wanted to examine her without the shield of so much heavy linen. If that fat little man was mistreating her...Dr. Baines lifted his narrow chin and smiled at folks passing him on the sun-dappled, tree-lined road.

He cared too much, he told himself. He forced thoughts of the young bride from his mind. He couldn't cure the world. He could scarcely keep these few people in town entrusted to his care from succumbing to the myriad ills nature so generously provided. His father had once warned him his heart was too soft for the rigors of physicking. The old gentleman had been right. Already too many cares etched Thomas Baines' face. He scarcely had time to worry about one more sickly young woman. Yet, as he walked, a vision of her pleading eyes drifted before him.

He felt compelled to comfort and protect her. Leaving her in that dark stone house so far up the lonely road lined with scrub, cut only by an occasional rocky wall nearly buried in leaves, gave his heart a sound twist. She was at the mercy of a man Thomas knew frequented taverns and whores, and in some way was connected with the slave trade. He knew that to be true, for nothing else accounted for the wealth of such a lout. Dr. Baines felt quite out of sorts by the time he reached his cottage. Before continuing on, he gave his jolly wife a stout hug and kiss that knocked her ruffled cap askew.

The days grew shorter. The nights fell cold. At last Florie ventured from her chamber at the head of the stairs to the shadowy lamp-lit parlor below. With lap robe, shawl and woolly cap, she took tea with her impatient husband.

"How soon again will you go to sea, Wendell?" she asked, his name falling strangely on her tongue.

"To sea?" He looked startled. "I vowed after that last voyage to retire. I thought I told you. I'm quite well off and need not labor if I choose, my dear." He waved his arm to indicate the large richly paneled room and furniture that looked miniature in his presence. "I've already opened an office near my warehouses. I shall conduct my business there, never to leave you for a single moment."

Florie closed her eyes. So. There would be no more delays. She needed only to think of her sisters, however, to refresh her resolve. She was there to stay.

From her tall narrow window trimmed with aged brown and gold brocade, Florie could see far beyond the rooftops and the tangle of tottering masts in the harbor to the glittering open sea. In silvery moonlight, it lay motionless and cool to the horizon, a vast and empty place of peace. She breathed in the salty night air, a strangely moist but not heavy atmosphere. No cough lingered, she thought. She was well.

Hearing Wendell stumbling about below, Florie quickly dressed in a high-necked white sleeping gown of downy flannelette and crawled into her marriage bed. Her wedding day seemed impossibly remote, spring's sunny warm hand but a memory. Now winter's cold breath left the oaks stripped—a phenomenon she'd never seen—and it was almost embarrassing to see those naked black branches waving in the heavy winds that often buffeted the house for days on end.

Wind howled in the eaves like a lover's cry, and sometimes Florie thought the house answered with groans of its own. Tonight

Wendell would have her, she thought. Tonight he would…Mother of God, tonight…

His footsteps fell heavily upon the staircase, drumbeats in half step with her heart. Wheezing, he opened her door and filled it with his shadow. "Are you asleep?"

How odd it must feel to push around that great quivering belly and stand upon such stout legs. She watched him undress by the fall of moonlight upon the bare floor. Each time he lifted a foot, the narrow boards creaked. "I'm awake," she said.

When he crawled in on the far side of the four-poster, the ropes in the frame groaned. Florie rolled against her husband and the whole bed listed to the left!

His hands were on her at once. He kneaded her breasts with fingers as plump as sausages and explored swiftly and with breathtaking accuracy places she considered solely her own.

Florie wondered if he noticed the change in her bosom's size. Somewhere out on that great black sea floated cotton and wax forms that had made a mockery of her vows. Florie fixed her mind on that image. The silliness of it helped her blot out the grasping touch of this man she had wed.

She was expert at journeying within the comfort of her mind. Sometimes she wished she could stay forever. Twice, she'd tried. Then she hadn't heard her sisters. Even when they switched her legs crimson or locked her in the musty wardrobe she hadn't cared.

Now her bed rolled like a ship in a tempest. Florie kept herself from throwing her husband overboard by slipping deep into her mind. It was a place so safe and serene. There lay Mama in her wonderful bed, her eyes as gentle as love itself.

He worked frantically at her buttons and pushed at the hem of her gown. His breath felt like gusts in her face reminiscent of all he had eaten that day. Florie was oblivious, sinking, sinking, as if descending into an inner sea. The sensation of his hands upon her faded to a bearable—

"Get up, damn you, and take off those fetters!"

Reeling, Florie scrambled from under the bed linens. She was dizzy from returning so abruptly from her trance-like state. She'd never heard that tone from him before. In front of his wide eyes and wet lips she shed her night dress and stood shivering. He got up and rounded the bed in a thunderous charge. Florie was amazed at his height. He had, until that moment, seemed like such a short man. When he took her in his arms she found beneath his fat a layer of alarming muscle.

He seemed ready to swallow her with kisses, for indeed, his kissing noises were not so unlike his eating noises. He fell back to the protesting bed and dragged her atop him. When his touch became rude, she thought surely she must faint. This was all so very different from what she had, in her innocence, imagined. So swiftly did he teach her his husbandly ways she couldn't find the entrance to her secret world of inner silence. With eyes clenched, and fingertips digging into his shoulders, Florie tried very hard not to cry out. "Husband, please..."

Her eyes popped open! Not that! Dear Lord, let him stop! Not that, too! Did he leave her no dignity?

She found Wendell's little eyes fastened on her face. A little smile showed the unevenness of his little teeth. He wrenched her against his chest and pressed the breath from her. "You're mine!" he breathed, fingers possessing her. His eyes fairly glowed! She couldn't twist free. She couldn't take her eyes from his face. She couldn't drift away...

She decided later, lying alone in her bed feeling the fresh sea air wafting across her hot cheeks from the open window, that Wendell had deliberately made her scream again. It had been a quiet scream, one she regretted, but enough to satisfy him. He hadn't penetrated her, and indeed, hadn't seemed to want to. He had just stared at her, spilling his seed upon her breasts.

The first winter in Union Harbor was unimaginably harsh and kept young Mrs. DeMarsett indoors. Wendell could be seen lumbering down snowy roads to his office on the wharf, his rotund person strangely robust compared to his neighbors with their lingering ailments.

In the spring he looked even better.

Summer found the formerly bad-tempered captain a truly jovial man.

Little was seen of his bride and even less known of her. Gossips in the shops along Wendell's morning route wondered just how well the poor dear from the South was doing. If one judged by Wendell himself, she was a remarkable wife to have transformed him.

Even Mrs. Worley, his house woman, could give no clue as to how well the marriage was working. Gray-haired and hard of hearing, she cooked and cleaned for the DeMarsetts and made a fair wage, "Though I deserves more," she would say to her friends. "The little missus likes Frenchy food. Says my stews and breads don't suit her."

"But do you ever *see* her? Is she well?" would come the questions at the shops where Mrs. Worley would buy eggs and fresh fish.

"She sleeps overmuch for one so young. Don't have no friends but that young physick Baines—aye, he's tatter-worn and bony. I see m'lady at eventide. She's always in the same gown, rightly out of date and shameful at the hem. She paces the afternoons away. A restless sort, you know. She ain't bought nothing new since she come here. Don't you think that's odd? She hasn't plumped up much yet either. I don't see that there's a child expected, though the captain is at her half every night. The good doctor comes often enough, too."

And so the talk went.

Wendell would sit in his office next to the warehouse poring over his daily manifests with a certain relish though no good news was contained on the lists. Britain's new war with France was cutting severely into his trade. Though he'd invested in a second schooner and hired on two able captains, he'd lost one already to the crown. It seemed not to affect him. He'd sit back smiling over his pipe, his newly grown brindled side whiskers making him look more prosperous than he was. His assistants would look at him and wonder what his mind's eye saw. Had they known, they perhaps wouldn't have felt so easy around him.

Autumn once again filled the muddy roads with red and yellow leaves. Wendell took himself home earlier than usual that particular September day. He smelled rain on the air but unlike former years, didn't cast his eye seaward to scan the horizon for an impending tropical blow. Thinking about Florie undid him. He would have at her again before supper, he decided, stopping for a tankard at the corner tavern.

King's Horse Tavern was silent at this hour, a hollow-sounding gray shack filled with greasy trestle tables and scarred benches.

He couldn't get enough of the girl, Wendell thought breathlessly. He sat sucking at his ale and smiling to himself. The brute near the kegs kept staring at him.

"Be on with your business," Wendell snarled at him suddenly, tossing down a tarnished coin. "Let me drink in peace."

"You come in often, Captain DeMarsett," the ale-tender said, betraying a recent kinship with the London slums. He filled Wendell's tankard again.

He was a big man, as big as some wharf blacks. His cheeks were pitted and hard, his nose blunt and depressed as if a fist had laid waste his profile. Wendell didn't trust those dangerously smiling black eyes, and the accent shriveled the fullness he'd been savoring in his groin.

Wendell glared at the ugly devil dressed in a poorly cut dark vest and pantaloons, and swallowed his ale. The man had called him captain. Wendell longed for the sound of that.

"My little woman, Ruby's her name, she tells me you used to frequent some of the wenches up the road from the rope walk. Have you need of one today?" the ale-tender asked, smiling, revealing a gap in the side of his otherwise perfect white teeth sharp as fishes'.

Wendell eyed that broken face.

"Oftentimes…" His deeply set eyes twinkled. "A wedded man needs a change of diet."

"What is your name, sir?" Wendell asked.

"Miles Mercedes, Captain, sir, proprietor of 'er King's Horse Tavern, a place no finer than my own dear dad's. At your disposal, anytime."

"I'll remember that." Wendell belched and rose. "I've no need of a strumpet these days. I, sir, am a married man, and happily."

Miles Mercedes grinned, touching the edge of a dark knitted cap he wore on his low forehead.

Wendell pushed on toward home. Beast, he thought.


She was in the parlor playing the pianoforte he'd had shipped up from Boston the month before. Her hands froze over the keys when he entered. She turned and smiled with her mouth, her eyes large and richly dark and moist. "You're early, Husband."

He smiled.


She waited for him in the bedchamber by the time he'd finished a generous rum in his study. He still couldn't believe his luck. Ungodly luck! After that first night with her he had been certain she would leave him. She had looked so lovely, so fragile, so helpless…he had forgotten himself. Such satisfaction he had never known!

In the cold dawn light he had been certain no decent woman would tolerate his ways. But perhaps, Wendell thought with a smirk, she liked his touch.

So the weeks had passed.

All the nights passed.

Wendell satisfied himself with a passion, and meekly Florie submitted. Even if he got impatient or rough, she submitted. He was captain of his pretty little vessel, his wife. It seemed not to matter what he did. No matter how he frightened her, she didn't contemplate returning to her father or sisters.

Ungodly luck, he thought, entering and bolting the chamber door. She lay curled on her bed, her slender body covered only by the bed linen. He knew she was naked because one night he had slapped her in his impatience with fabric and buttons.

Wendell whipped off the linen with a flourish, his mouth working at the waters rushing around his tongue. He didn't see her face now, only plump breasts, sleek thighs, rounded ass so very tender…She made sounds appropriate to please him, so he didn't need to see her eyes. Consequently he didn't see the absence in them.

She looked as if she had stepped out and away for a while, or rather, inward and away for a pleasant hour within her own impenetrable world. He reveled in his own pleasures with her flesh and his, and she was still a virgin and blessedly free of her sisters.

# Four

Dr. Baines dragged a spindly chair close to Florie's bedside and sat. "That wasn't so bad now, was it?"

Florie opened her eyes slowly and looked at him with a puzzling softness.

Thomas pulled at his chin, undone by her wide-eyed look. "Now we must talk," he said, unaccountably nervous before her. "I expect you to answer with the truth."

Florie's knuckles whitened as she clutched the edge of her quilt.

"You're still not pregnant, Florie. In fact, I can't see that your husband has..." Thomas cleared his throat trying to word his question delicately. The very thought of that mountainous man atop this waif made him shudder. "Do you deny him?" He made a fist. He was graceless, and now she looked shocked.

"I thought Wendell was satisfied. Has he complained?"

"Are *you* satisfied—happy, Florie?"

"Don't concern yourself with me, Doctor!" Her eyes grew dark and immense. "You have others to see today."

"I'll spend as much time with you as necessary! A girl your age shouldn't spend so many hours in bed. It isn't healthy, or natural. You need air, sunshine, friends!"

"Wendell doesn't want me to wander about. He says I'll take ill."

"And so you have, right in your own bed." Thomas forced himself to lower his voice. "I'll not say a word to anyone. Forgive me, but I must ask—where did you get those marks on your legs?"

Florie squirmed, but Thomas caught her unwilling gaze. For a moment she looked terribly frightened, but just when he thought he would have to leave her again, his concern and curiosity unquenched, she seemed to sag. A look of relief softened her mouth. He felt as if he had just won a great battle with her reserve.

"My oldest sister raised my sisters and myself," Florie whispered, looking about the darkened bedchamber as if someone might overhear her. "My mother died, you see. A fever took her when I was only eight. Fabrienne didn't know the first thing about running such a great household, and my father was a stern taskmaster. She came to be harsh with us against her better nature, I'm sure. I was youngest and made the most mistakes. Sometimes I deliberately ran away from her to avoid a punishment. I had been spoiled by my mother, so I had to be disciplined. After a time…I began to obey Fabrienne. It was wise that I should."

"She beat you?" Thomas was somehow shocked, though the evidence on her narrow thighs was unmistakable. He wanted to take her hand and kiss it, for he could see she was becoming upset. Her eyes filled with tears, and Thomas felt cruel for making her remember. He couldn't bring himself to touch her though. It would be out of place, and mean far too much.

"It matters little now, Doctor. Don't you see? Wendell doesn't mind the scars."

Thomas had to look away quickly lest she see the hate for Captain DeMarsett he knew showed plainly in his eyes. He took up his bag and pretended to be searching for something. "Have you ever been happy?"

"Oh, when I was young…" She smiled suddenly, a blessed thing to see. "I was always with my mother. Always happy. She cared for me from her bed. It was like our own little world."

"What about your father?"

"He had much work and was often away. My mammy was wonderful. I would have liked for her to come here with me, but I wouldn't have dreamed of taking her away from her little boy…" Florie's face twitched. "Lusey couldn't always protect me, though. I don't know what my sister did to silence her, but it worked well. Since marrying Wendell I've been much better off. This is a fine house, and Mrs. Worley is becoming a good friend."

"Then you never loved him." Thomas sagged with relief.

"I liked him when we met." She laughed a little. "I was only twelve, and lonely. Dreams of coming here helped get me through many empty days. And I wasn't mistreated all the time."

"A beautiful girl's life should consist of more than that!"

"In time…" Florie said blushing, "I'll have a baby. I've been content so far with Wendell's apparent decision to put it off."

She blushed again. Thomas suddenly got the unreasonable idea she was lying!

"Will I prove too small?" she whispered.

"That has certainly been on my mind," he said.

Thomas looked hard at Florie. "What, then, about the bruises?"

Florie suddenly shrank into her pillow. "I've always marked easily! I'm clumsy as well."

Thomas stood. "I thought you trusted me. Tell the truth. I won't have that man hurting you."

"Whatever Wendell does is nothing compared to...Surely you know the mind is more fragile than the body. If you truly care about me, you won't interfere. I'm begging you." She half rose and grabbed his fist. Her eyes blazed with an emotion Thomas would have thought impossible. "I'd rather be dead than go back!"

For a moment she looked truly alive, amazingly strong. Then Thomas watched her veil her eyes. Her face fell back into docile innocence. She began to look distressed.

"Perhaps he's angry I haven't yet given him a son. I'll...see to it, Doctor. Please, let's not talk of this again. I'm very tired."

Thomas turned stiffly, his mouth painfully tight. "When the weather warms, I want you out walking every day."

"Wendell would prefer I stay home." For a moment the chamber echoed with her soft words.

"My blood boils to think you accept this so willingly," he said turned away from her.

"Thomas," she said gently. "I'm much stronger than you realize."

He turned back to see her dark eyes flash.

"I have to be."

Scarcely six months later, in the spring of 1810, Dr. Baines came down from Florie DeMarsett's bedchamber. Wendell rose from the groaning wing chair behind his desk in the great dark study. He shook the doctor's outstretched hand damply. "The news, sir?"

"Your wife is with child, Captain DeMarsett. Due in January. She'll not have an easy time. She's small-boned and frail. Such women shouldn't even attempt childbirth. You must see to it she eats properly and enjoys pleasant surroundings."

"A son," Wendell whispered. "I'm to have a son!"

"I must warn you, sir, any disturbances to her person..." The doctor eyed Wendell and felt duly understood when Wendell squirmed. "I'd take extreme care these next months. She could miscarry. I must be off now.

John Roebling's second wife is expecting again."

"I'll look after Florie, sir. You have my solemn word."

"See that you do. In fact, now that you're to be parents, you should make a place for yourselves in Union Harbor's society."

"Indeed, I will, sir! Good day." Wendell looked pained again.

"I'll take it upon myself to tell Mrs. Roebling about your little wife and her happy news. Josephine might invite Florie for tea. That would do them both a world of good. You know how superstitious pregnant women get. The new Mrs. Roebling is afraid she'll die in childbed as did her predecessors."

"I don't want my Florie going up there then."

"Nonsense. You'd do well to get on good terms with Roebling. John's ships are the best in Union Harbor. Friendship with him might profit you. And you have your son's future to consider. Who will be the boy's friends? Where will he go to school?—that sort of thing. When a man starts a family he must widen his horizons. Don't you agree?" Thomas hoped his eyes didn't betray him.

Wendell nodded sullenly.

"I'll have an invitation sent to Florie soon. You'll see. She'll perk up, and you won't have to worry about losing her." The doctor strode away from the portico wearing a smug smile.

The rickety back stairs of King's Horse Tavern trembled under Wendell's weight. He stumbled into the common room adjusting his frockcoat, a sour look on his face. He stopped at his corner of the table for a tankard before going into the afternoon rain. The harlot had been ugly and fat, he thought, the memory of her yellowed smile giving him a shudder. She'd laughed at him. Florie never laughed.

He swallowed too large a gulp and his throat ached. Damn the pregnancy! No sooner had Florie shown him a wonderful new pleasure, and now he couldn't enjoy it!

Wendell called for another tankard.

Those few women he'd paid in the past hadn't laughed. Had marriage changed him, or was it true? All this time he hadn't been doing what other men—normal men—did?

Wendell drained the tankard, dizzied by the thought. That new pleasure had been unbearably delightful. Why had he never guessed *that* was how it was properly done? Why hadn't those whores shown him?

Why did it have to be Florie? How had *she* known about it?

Wendell went on gulping. Sometimes lately he caught Florie looking at him. He suspected she didn't like him. And she hadn't become pregnant before because he had never planted the seed correctly. Why then, had she encumbered herself with his child? Why now?

Shortly after she guided him into her secret recess, crying out with what he supposed was desire or pain, or both—and he had enjoyed that immensely—he had begun to feel like a fool.

Had she gotten pregnant to rid herself of him?

Wendell drained another tankard and asked for a fourth. A sick lump of fear lay in his belly. He wanted to hit someone. He saw that Mercedes wretch watching him and rage boiled in his brain like thunderheads on a horizon.

She had shown him the way to shame him. He knew that now. She had done it to show him he was ignorant of the ways of sex. She had done it to get with child so he couldn't touch her.

He wanted to punish her. He knew women screamed during childbirth. As the ale slid down his throat, he smiled. She had shamed him, but she would suffer for it.

He looked about the dank tavern filled with men of many stations. Wendell didn't truly like being seen there. The place was below him, but at times he needed to get away. No one in Union Harbor knew he came from just such a place, that at a tender age he had watched men wallow in their ale, vomit it upon the street and carouse with their women into early dawns.

Wendell didn't often let himself think back to that. The town had been farther north, small and decaying even then. His father had been a whaler, but lost a leg and so had had to content himself with tales of whaling in an alehouse so like this it could have been the very same.

Wendell's mother and father had had roaring battles that often left them both bloody. Wendell's first memories were of such battles culminating on a dirty cot nearby.

At fourteen he had run away and neither knew nor cared if those two people still lived.

Eventually he took the name DeMarsett, which sounded proper and high class, and decided he wanted to be a sea captain. The few boys he knew on the wharves told him to sign on as cabin boy aboard a whaler or fishing boat. Wendell chose instead a British trader.

Though he had been sorry to the depths of his soul once to sea and at the mercy of the men, he learned his trade well. Later, when he was older, he found being big gave him an edge, that being selfish, cruel and swift ensured survival.

After a time he had enough money for his own bark. Union Harbor knew not of his background, and so he chose it for his home port. Most thought he was of good Boston stock and treated him accordingly. Florie had made his social position unshakable.

His anger swelled again. The little whore. She had known something he did not and had shamed him. He had known only the ways of drunken sailors, ways taught to him screaming in the darkness of a ship's hold on a vast and merciless sea where there was no escape, only endurance.

He had gone to a harlot later to prove to himself he could also be with a woman—thinking that the only proof necessary to his manhood. He had used her as he had been taught. She hadn't questioned his desires, but now he understood why her price had been so high.

He had wanted to use Florie in the same way, but his instincts had told him she couldn't endure it. He had contented himself with gentler amusements.

Still, he had married her in ignorance, used her in ignorance. All along she had known. He would get her for that. He didn't know how, or when, but someday she would be sorry.

And so Wendell DeMarsett, not so wealthy as he had been when he married the pretty honey-haired Gautier girl, bided his time. He sincerely hoped his wife survived her confinement. And his son? His son would be his ally. No terrors would tarnish *his* boyhood. No sailors would rape him. Wendell DeMarsett's son would know only wealth, power...and women. Many, many women.

He looked up to see Mercedes leering at him like always.

"The rain's let up, Captain. Going now?" Mercedes asked.

Wendell debated whether he should have another tankard. His brain wasn't numb yet and he longed not to think. He wanted to avoid Florie when he got home. He silently cursed the harlot he'd just paid. The sow hadn't satisfied him. Nothing satisfied him, nothing except..."Another tankard," Wendell said belching and dropping coins onto the table.

"You're not so happy these days," Mercedes said, his eyes to either side of that crushed nose sharp and mocking.

"Get a decent cunny upstairs, or I'll take my coin elsewhere."

Mercedes smirked, his chuckle low in his throat.

Wendell dragged himself to his feet, drained the last tankard and lurched out. A fine mist clung to his face and turned all the shacks a soft dripping gray. He wandered home muttering, shaking his fist at unseen foes, vowing revenge on all who crossed him. When he drew near his house he saw two black carriages standing under the portico.

His house looked like a rock poised on a lonely point. It neither had fence nor garden, only a few outbuildings. He didn't even have a horse. There might be a war soon. He could lose everything he'd worked so hard to get...Did she care?

There she sat in her parlor all day with his son swelling her belly, threatening her very life, making her off-limits to his touch. And now, as if to shame him still further, she took tea with "ladies" who talked of their trips abroad. He knew London, Paris, Glasgow...Yes, he knew the taverns and alleys, not opera houses or grand hotels.

Florie was comfortable among those females, though she sometimes complained they would never truly accept her. She was French Catholic, as different from them as horses and cows.

Wendell saw a young matron emerge from his front door and duck into her carriage. She didn't even turn and nod good day. He was of no consequence, a man of low birth, a wharf rat with a cripple for a father and a whore for a mother.

He should go in the side entrance, he thought. He was master, and could come and go as he pleased. Florie couldn't go out without his consent. She had visited that woman up at the Roebling estate a few times, but her sudden vitality had alarmed him. He told her she couldn't go anymore. It wasn't proper for her to be seen in public pregnant. He remembered how she had looked like she might choose to defy him!

How long had she been inviting the ladies she'd met through Josephine Roebling into his house? He didn't remember her mentioning that she had invited them before. He didn't remember giving her permission to do so on this day.

He pushed his way through the front door past Mrs. Worley. Her plump hand went over her mouth. "Good day, sir! You're early," she said backing away. "Should I get you some tea?"

He cast her an evil look that shriveled her ingratiating smile and sent her scurrying back to the safety of the kitchen. *There* was a crone he'd like to thrash!

He heard soft voices and laughter in the drawing room. *Who* was in his house? He went into his study slamming the great door. His study was dark and dusty. He didn't allow Mrs. Worley to clean it. His desk was littered, his bookclosets jammed with materials he never read. He poured a great glass of rum and swallowed it down. Now his belly felt full and churned like a hurricane sea. His eyes slid around in their sockets like cold fish eggs. He couldn't focus on anything except a pair of ornate duelling pistols he kept on a table under the window. The inlaid gold handles caught even the dim light of the rain-wet glass, pleasing Wendell.

The laughter seemed very loud, very near. They were laughing at him, laughing because he didn't know how to properly bed a woman. He had been used. He never learned the proper way from whores, to their utter and everlasting damnation. He would see to them all!

Wendell found himself suddenly teetering in the doorway of Florie's parlor. Three pairs of pretty round eyes stared up at him. He felt vaguely surprised. He didn't recall returning to the hall. He didn't recall opening this door.

"Good afternoon, Husband," Florie said in a distant meek voice.

Her pale face swam before his eyes. Yes, he decided, she had been talking about him, and the ladies had been laughing.

"Wendell, you remember Mrs. Longford. Her husband owns the chandlery. And this is Josephine Roebling. She was just telling us about her husband's boatyard."

A wary "Good afternoon, sir," met his ringing ears. The other woman whispered good day and rose.

"What's going on here?" Wendell said, his tongue far too large and lazy to obey him.

"We're having tea. Have you taken a chill? Shall I call Mrs. Worley to turn back your bed?"

"My bed? Don't you mean our bed? Do we not share the same bed?"

The other woman, great with child, rose, her face crimson.

Wendell wanted to hit her. He moved toward her with that thought and heard her whimper.

"Please sit down, Wendell! You don't look well! I'll send Mrs. Worley for the doctor."

"Close your mouth, slut."

The parlor rang with his words. No matter what he'd done, he'd never seen her look like that. He hadn't known he could do that with mere words.

Florie urged her guests to leave. With her voice hushed and strained, her eyes round and wet, her swollen body awkward as she skirted Wendell, she fairly pushed the women down the hall.

"Don't come back, you bitches," Wendell said before the ladies were out. "I'll not have you in my house."

Florie's hands flew to her hair. "Stop it! Stop it!"

Wendell moved toward her, his hands flexing, his mind gone mad with rage. He put his fingers around her soft arms and jerked her up so he could look straight into her eyes.

She began shrieking like he had never heard in his life. The shrill sound split his head. He'd never known such piercing agony. As Florie's nails raked his cheeks, he didn't hear Mrs. Worley running out the front door. He wasn't conscious of climbing the stairs.

When Wendell came to, he was sprawled in the upstairs hall. Dr. Baines had him by his shirt front and was jerking him to his feet. Wendell saw a fist coming toward his eyes. Then his entire face exploded with blinding red pain!

# Five

A month later Florie was still recovering abed when Dr. Baines brought the news of Josephine Roebling's death. Florie had fainted back into her pillow.

With that tragic news between them, Florie forgot the shame she had felt in the good doctor's presence since Wendell's attack on her. Her bedchamber felt cold this gray morning. Florie sat up, testing her strength. Her body felt limp, but her resolve was unshakable.

She slipped her feet to the floor and stood. The wardrobe seemed so far—she wondered if she could make it after so many weeks in bed. Surprisingly she managed the chilly distance and began dressing. She pulled her petticoat high over her swollen abdomen and sighed with gratitude. Dr. Baines had been certain the attack would bring on an early delivery. She had feared it, too, but still the child within her lived and thrived.

A killing wind howled outside her window. Florie shivered, stopping periodically to say a prayer for her friend Josie who had been only twenty-six. They had barely gotten to know each other. Florie remembered the first time the grand Roebling carriage called for her—it had been even more grand than her papa's.

She remembered how Josie had looked tucked into a chaise in the great parlor of that magnificent white house. Both had been embarrassed to be seen pregnant, but they had become fast friends.

She could scarcely lift her wool skirts into place now, but Florie wouldn't consider returning to her bed. Today Dr. Baines was taking her to Josie's funeral. The only reason he dared allow her such a trying journey was because she couldn't be dissuaded, and at eight months into her pregnancy, she might now safely go into premature labor and have an easier delivery.

Wendell didn't know of her plans. He remained in his study as he had for days, eating, drinking and sleeping in his own squalid privacy.

He had neither spoken to Florie nor crossed her threshold since that afternoon Dr. Baines broke his nose.

Florie smiled, though she tried very hard not to. She wished no one harm, not even Wendell. But the anger she felt was a powerful force and hard to dispel. Mrs. Worley had told her a man from the wharf had had to set Wendell's nose because Dr. Baines refused. She hoped it had pained him a little.

Mrs. Worley tapped at the door and stuck in her head. "Why, Missus! What are you up to?"

"If you've forgotten," Florie said softly, her voice sounding a bit edgy, "I'm going out. Help me finish dressing. I feel as weak as a baby."

"I'd hoped you'd come to your senses." The old woman shuffled across the floor with uneasy glances. "He won't like it, the captain won't."

"No, but he'll say nothing. I want you to go out today and have a pleasant afternoon with your friends while I'm away. I don't want you here alone. Have you yet located a nurse?"

Mrs. Worley sighed as if the whole of the world's troubles rested on her bent shoulders. "Not many is willing to works for the captain, Missus. I'm sorry."

"Offer more in wages then. I must have a nurse to help care for my child."

"Aye, Missus." She helped Florie adjust the skirts over her abdomen. The gown hid her condition well. Florie's beautiful black-brown eyes had grown ever larger and beheld the world with a luminescence that gave her an ethereal quality, an impression of untouchability that made Mrs. Worley wonder at her.

The old woman felt uneasy draping the heavy mantle about her mistress' shoulders. She remembered that awful night the captain came home soused and insulted Florie's young guests. When she returned with the good doctor, the house had been more silent than a burying ground. Watching from the lower hall, she had seen the doctor drag the captain into the hall and strike him! She had never seen the likes of it before in her life!

An hour later the doctor had allowed her to sit with Florie. "Don't leave her for even a moment," he had told her, his face a mask of anguish. Her bruises were covered with plasters, and she had been given a sleeping powder. But when he returned in the morning...

Mrs. Worley still wasn't sure why she hadn't told him about the young missus' dreams. Oh! the things she'd said and screamed as she thrashed upon the feather tick. The poor child! The poor dear child crying for her mother like that! Mrs. Worley had held her little hand and kissed it all that long night.

She didn't know why she didn't tell the doctor. Maybe she didn't believe in such things as ghosts with spears. Or perhaps she just thought it was all a horrible nightmare.

Now she watched Florie and wondered. The little missus seemed perfectly all right, but for three days following that awful night, Florie DeMarsett hadn't been of this world!

Upon the bed she had lain, her bottomless eyes sightless. "She was beaten," he had whispered as if Florie might have heard, lying there pale as death and limp as wet linen. "Her body's been shocked, perhaps even her mind. That animal of a husband ought to be hung!" the doctor had said.

Mrs. Worley had never seen the doctor look so angry. She had thought such a gentle, sensitive man incapable of it. The swelling on Captain DeMarsett's face was mute testimony to the good doctor's limits.

Then one morning Florie awoke as if nothing had ever happened. She seemed just like before; timid, sweet, friendly. Mrs. Worley and the doctor silently thanked God that she was "back."

"You're wool-gathering again," Florie smiled. "I asked if I look all right."

"Lovely, Missus. Are you sure you're up to this? It won't be easy, your friend's funeral and all."

"You're good to worry. See if the doctor's coming. I'll not go down before he's here."

"Don't forget your muff. The rain's freezing now, and the wind's bad. There'll be snow by morning."

Wendell wasn't aware of anything unusual taking place until he noticed his housewoman going again and again to the front door. When he appeared in the hall, she shrank from him, glancing uneasily up the stairs.

"Get out of my way, hag."

Wendell swung at the woman, missed and then attacked the stairs at a drunken turtle's pace. The door to Florie's bedchamber trembled on its hinges as he burst in.

His shirt hung half out of his straining pantaloons and was stained with rum and many suppers. His eyes burned and felt sunk deep into his skull. "Where do you think you're going?" he puffed.

Florie straightened her shoulders, clutching her red mantle over her belly. She met Wendell's gaze and looked unafraid. "I'm going to Josephine Roebling's funeral."

Wendell bared his teeth and took a step toward his wife.

"You'll not stop me!" she said. "You hurt me, Wendell. I was too afraid for my life to stop you, but I'll not endure it again. There's talk about town that your insult caused Mrs. Roebling to deliver too early. Some say you killed her."

Wendell froze, his chest and belly empty and convulsing with the effort to get breath back into his lungs.

"Dr. Baines would need little provocation to bring you before the court, Wendell. One more bruise could send you to the gallows."

"I was drunk," he said in a low voice. "The woman took herself into the rain that day. It was well known she was frail. Her own husband killed her! Her death is not on my head!"

"To me, it is! You should have been called out! I don't know why you weren't. Go back to your rum and your sty, Husband. I'll be home by dark. The good doctor will see to my care."

"The good doctor be damned!"

Wendell watched Florie slip trembling hands into her muff. She started toward him, her head back and shoulders straight like a brave little bird. Her face was white save for two bright red spots on her cheeks.

Inclining her head to look into Wendell's eyes, she smiled a smile of such loathing Wendell shivered. He edged back from her.

"Dr. Baines thinks I don't remember," Florie whispered. She looked past him into the hall obviously afraid to let anyone learn of what he had done. "As long as I don't remember, you're safe. Thomas tended me so he knows what you did. If you should ever have occasion to discuss such a matter with a lawyer, you might learn some acts are considered crimes against God and are punishable…by *death.*" The word hung on her tongue. "I was young when you married me, Husband. Very young and very desperate. Now you are desperate. Take comfort in it. You can't send me away and I don't intend to go. Ever."

Every word she spoke caused him to shake harder. What did she know of innocence? What did she know of acts against God? "You forget who you're talking to, slut."

One of her hands flew from the hiding place of her muff. He found himself jerking back to avoid a slap. She merely covered her mouth.

Wendell had wondered those past weeks if he had only beaten her. Now he knew the worst. He hadn't thought he would ever do it, not to his little wife.

She looked ridiculous gazing up at him with those large shining eyes that still held such a curious fascination for him. He realized that he feared her. Hated her. And damn her, he was afraid he loved her. She would not beat him! He had endured before. He would endure again.

He watched her pick her way down the stairs ever so carefully. He would triumph, he thought, watching her push outside into the sleet. She would be sorry.

Then Wendell kicked her door. It crashed against the wall and something small and fragile fell to her carpet in shiny pieces. He tumbled down the stairs, staggered, righted himself and then flung his bulk into his study.

His crashing, grunts and thuds echoed throughout the house, but no one heard. When everything about him lay in ruin, Wendell, who had been an ugly fat little boy and was now an ugly fat little man, sank into a corner and cried.

Such weather transformed the town of Union Harbor into a dream world. The gray sky sank to the sea swallowing ships and rolling inland to obliterate buildings, trees and roads. As the doctor's carriage rounded the bend, Florie marveled at the forest. The road turned into a dense thicket of barren trees jutting up like masts from a leafy sea. Here and there boulders rose up from the earth, gray wet faces in a tunnel of branches nearly blotting out the sky.

Only the steady suck of the horses' hooves in the mud kept Florie from thinking backwards to Wendell's livid face, or ahead to Josephine's funeral. Her shoulder bumped against the doctor's. It was comforting to be so near him. It almost frightened her to think how she depended on him now. He was the one bright spot in her world.

For a time she had thought she couldn't go on. She had come to this alien coast to find happiness. Was that happiness and great love to be found in a doctor's kind face and healing touch? He was not hers to love.

She knew now she had been wrong to escape Gautier Plantation. Escape wasn't enough. She must conquer those who hurt her, but how? She had been bred to her times, meek and obedient. She had grown up within a culture of masters and slaves. She had seen her family and her own life a part of that. Florie knew no other way.

She couldn't slip away to her half-world either. She carried a child who would soon need her, and with this new love grew new hope that she would find happiness—or at least give it. Yet how she longed for the repose, the half dream world where time passed painlessly and the visions she saw were of beauty and love.

For a few days she had tried. Oh, it would have been easy to stay that time. But that dear old woman with too many questions and too few teeth, who pampered and petted her so, and Thomas, dear, dear Thomas, they had willed her back to them, and so there she was to face whatever more fate had in store for her.

"If you feel at all tired, you must tell me," Thomas said, startling her from her thoughts as if he had sensed she had been thinking about him.

"When I first came here last spring," Florie said wistfully, "everything was in bloom. Reds, yellows, blues. Heaven must look as beautiful. And so much green, it hurt my eyes! I hope someday to have a garden at home. Have you ever seen the Roeblings' garden, Doctor? Josie and I walked there every time I visited, and I was sick with envy."

The flat planes of Thomas's face looked grim. "I've come to this estate only to attend and deliver the two Roebling wives. Three times I delivered John a son. Fever took his first wife and now I've lost another. This land must be cursed."

"I didn't think you'd be superstitious," Florie said saddened by the pain etched around his eyes.

"I should never have suggested you come to this place. I shouldn't bring you here now." He put one reddened fist to his lips and blew to warm his fingers.

"What causes the fever?" Florie asked, watching the great stone gates emerge from a primeval forest.

They turned into the arched iron gateway and traveled up a mud-slick brick drive toward the main house. Compared to her own house, a boxy Georgian as robust as her husband, this house looked to Florie to be elegant and refined. The main structure was flanked by matched wings. Across the front were massive pillars—it indeed looked out of place if compared with the town. Taken alone, as the Roeblings were, it was a place of magnificence and grace.

Josie had told her the house had been finished only ten years before. She had given Florie a tour of the main floors and wings, the drawing rooms, sitting rooms and upper bedchambers. The rooms had been filled with the finest, from the imported carpets and damasks at the large, light windows to the furniture which spoke of another age, a time of elegance and wealth going back to the Old World.

"A foulness in the blood," Thomas said, reluctantly answering Florie's long-forgotten question. "Leeches don't cleanse as they should. Nothing I know of does—and I studied with the best in London!"

"Each time you treated Josie and that first wife the same?"

"Yes, to the best of my ability. The infants *were* overlarge. John Roebling is a big man, you know. If that is what caused their deaths, then any woman bearing him a child will die. Yet, even in death those women were proud to have given him a son. Their love staggered my ability to understand them. I did everything known to medical science, even a few practices not yet accepted. Josie survived the first time—but not this time. Perhaps I tried too hard."

"Do the midwives in Union Harbor lose many to fever?"

Thomas turned, his eyes wounded. "Do you trust me to deliver you?"

"Do you?"

They had followed the drive lined with young oaks misty in the growing fog. The grounds of Roebling Estate looked sleepy and unreal.

"When I first saw this place it was alive with spring's color. Now it looks…dead." Florie's fingers knotted within her rabbit fur muff. She thought the house should be bathed in sunlight, white and sparkling as a jewel in the gentle wood. Now it stood gray and lonely in the drifting mist, resolute.

The wind was bitter. Every branch and blade of winter-yellowed grass glistened within a coating of ice. It was as if the house was sleeping under death's cold hand, but that life was still there. Come spring the beauty would bloom anew.

Thomas helped her down and guided her up the treacherously icy steps. Even the fluted columns were encased in ice.

"I never had occasion to meet John Roebling," Florie said as a raw-boned footman ushered them into a grand reception hall. "What do you think of him?"

"I hate the man. If he marries again, I'll not come!"

The drawn parlor drapes shut out the weak November daylight. Black bunting hung from a massive white marble chimneypiece. In a far corner, away from flickering yellow flames in the hearth, stood the coffin. The rich red mahogany looked as if it was suspended in a night sky, for the base was also draped with black and shrouded in shadows.

Florie and Dr. Baines stepped into the hushed parlor. They were late. Florie declined to give up her mantle. Shivering, she pulled the wool tighter, reluctant to look upon the young face nestled in the satin-lined box.

Perhaps after all she had been wrong to come. To look upon death so near the birth of her first child would surely bring on a tragedy. Feeling a deepening sense of foreboding, Florie edged closer to Thomas. She should leave this place. Here she would find only sadness and heartache.

Moving like a specter, a young nursemaid with severely knotted black hair and an equally severe black uniform brought in the Roebling sons. As if mesmerized, Florie stared at the little boys. The eldest and youngest had entered the world on the last breaths of women who had had the misfortune to marry the wealthy and powerful John Roebling, founder of the Roebling line. Only the middle son had known his mother a little while.

Envied by all, rivaled by none, John Roebling's ships sailed to all corners of the sea. Through those young boys the Roebling name would move into the mists of the future. In the darkened corner lay the second woman whose blood and breath helped found the empire.

For a moment Florie, too, hated John Roebling. How could a man marry again knowing his seed brought forth life *and* death?

The oldest boy was nearly eight, tall and painfully thin. He wore a frockcoat and breeches so black and severe he seemed to melt into the shadows surrounding the coffin. Only his white face remained visible.

He took a seat on a straight-backed chair and didn't move. He looked at some point above the coffin, perhaps where the highest garland of greenery reached. His face held the promise of awesome masculine beauty, for his cheekbones and jaw were classic and sharp.

Florie's breath caught as she stared at the boy Josie had told her was called Adam. She had seen Adam only once before, on a summer day so very remote it couldn't possibly have been a few short months past. He had been playing in the garden with his younger brother, and he had been smiling. Florie had thought then he'd someday make a magnificent man.

He had looked the picture of boyhood in scuffed knickers and a torn dusty shirt. He had shaken her hand when Josie called him in from play, firmly, like a little man. He had looked directly into her eyes, startling her. His eyes had been as clear and dark as a summer sea, only with fire, intelligence, with mischief.

Florie could hardly stand to look at him now. Her heart ached. He had come to love Josie. Now he could only sit and stare blindly at some spot above her coffin, his bony hands knotted in his lap.

Without warning, young Adam Roebling turned. His eyes didn't search the faces collecting by the door, or those already seated. He looked right at Florie, his eyes wide and full of anger. She wondered if he knew or understood what had killed his pretty young stepmother.

The little boy seated next to Adam turned when Adam looked again at the spot above the coffin. He was perhaps five, his hair a fair contrast to Adam's black curls. The boy was average compared to his older brother's already extraordinary height. His face was plump and innocent. His eyes moved curiously about the room, watching the mourners, catching their surreptitious looks and making some weep.

For a moment Florie became the object of his attention and she saw that his eyes were brown, almost the same warm color as his hair. Round and quick, no grief clouded his eyes, for he was too young for sorrow. Florie was glad.

When his wiggling became noticeable, his brother made a slight movement with his head and the boy froze. Several minutes passed before his eyes again began to stray. Josie had named her first son James.

Had Josie time to name the newborn before she died?

He lay in the nursemaid's arms swaddled in a black blanket, a hideous gesture, Florie thought.

Florie longed to be in a church suddenly. Union Harbor had only a small Catholic population. She hadn't been to mass in years. She longed for God's unseen hand to touch her as it had sometimes in those dark and terrible times imprisoned in her sisters' sleeping room. Protect me, protect my child, she prayed. Bring me peace. Tears suddenly welled in her eyes.

She hadn't cried after her wedding night, nor after that night she resigned herself to bearing Wendell a child. No tears had touched her cheeks those hours and days following Wendell's attack.

Florie had chosen her fate and would bear it willingly. She thanked God she was no longer subject to Fabrienne's cruel tongue. But now? Now a small life stirred within her. What had she been thinking? How could she sentence a child, not only to this uncertain world, but to be Wendell DeMarsett's own son?

She would have a daughter then, she decided. How wonderful it would be, the two of them always together laughing, playing, kissing. That would be her happiness!

Thomas's arm went around her. She realized she was openly weeping. Several people had turned to look at her. She drew in a breath so deep no sound could escape her lips. She did it well, for there had been times when a single sound would have brought Fabrienne's wrath down upon her.

Florie sat motionless until her lungs demanded air. Her cheeks blazed. She banished all thought and fixed her eye on that same spot young Adam found so fascinating. She felt dazed and dizzy, slightly removed, as if someone else was sitting there in the circle of Thomas Baines' arm.

Eyelids heavy, face brilliant, Florie couldn't know how beautiful she looked. The tears made her lashes dark. Her eyes glistened luminous and black. The twist of her lips and the angle of her brow made anyone looking at her want to gather her up and banish her sorrow.

That was exactly how Thomas felt as he pulled her close. He hoped with all his heart that those watching would think he was only comforting a patient bereaved, not offering his arm as a token of a love he could no longer deny.

Silently, Thomas begged his wife's forgiveness for the faithlessness in his heart. He feared she already sensed he felt too strongly about the little DeMarsett bride, who was, unfortunately, bride no more. He had to look away from Florie because he wanted to kiss her.

Suddenly everyone in the parlor grew quiet. Only the sound of the hissing fire and soft sniffling met Florie's ears. The baby began fussing. All eyes focused on the writhing black bundle. All hearts hurt at the sight. Momentarily the mourners seemed suspended. The only sign of life came from the curling flames beneath the white marble and the infant swathed in black.

Into this unreal scene John Roebling strode. Towering above ordinary men, his expression said he was used to looking over others to things beyond. His hair was black and curly like young Adam's, who looked up at him with open awe. John Roebling held his head high, almost belligerently so, and didn't look like a man grieving.

Like everyone, Florie looked up at him and the room suddenly filled with a mysterious expectant force. She could feel the air crackling, feel the rush of breath into her lungs as if a bolt of lightning were about to strike.

He wore black from frockcoat to boots. Only his neckcloth was white, and centered in its snowy folds was an onyx stone. Before turning toward the coffin, he observed every person attending. His eyes lingered on Florie only a moment.

In that moment separated from time, Florie saw deeply into his eyes. Instantly she knew his pain as if it were her own. She touched his soul.

Somehow he, in return, touched hers.

Tears suddenly spilled from her eyes so furiously she didn't bother to stanch the flow. She cried from the pit of her being, shamelessly, joyfully letting the tears splash upon the red wool of her mantle, the only color in the parlor save black. She shivered and her hands went protectively over the kicking bulge under her shirts.

She wanted to run! She wanted to shout and throw herself into the sea. Florie wanted to be anywhere but in that room looking at that tall man's broad back as he bent over the coffin and kissed the cold lips of her friend, anywhere, anyplace but there to see him sit and fold his wide hands as the minister stepped up to the altar.

Mother of God, Florie thought, unable to stop crying. For this very moment she had lived! For this very moment Florie Gautier DeMarsett had already been punished by a jealous and all-knowing God.

Now she understood why her mother had died, why her father hadn't loved her, and why her sisters mistreated her. She accepted it all with an open and justly humble heart.

She was going to sin, and gladly.

Florie looked at the widower now casting a careful glance her way, blasting her with the dark spark of his tormented eye. Her breaths came faster and faster, dizzying her, alarming the doctor protecting her with his trembling arm.

God forgive her, she, a married woman soon to bring a new life into the world, had just fallen in love! God forgive her, Florie was happy.

# PART TWO

## 1813

## Six

Florie sat at the cherrywood parlor desk composing a letter to her sisters and father though the effort left her aching with irritation. She was sorry to hear Lalange was ill, but could find little sympathy in her heart that would sound genuine.

Wendell finally went out; she heard the thunder of his tread in the hall. In his wake even the house seemed to relax. Florie laid aside the quill and rested her head in her hand. She stared dreamily out the windows at the meadow across the road, tenderly green and gold, as inviting as a lover's smile. How good it would be to get out again.

Mrs. Worley crept in smelling of soap and hard work. "I'll be airing things a bit now that the captain's off," she said wrinkling her nose at the lingering odor of cigar smoke.

"Will he be back for supper?"

"He weren't in a talking mood this morning." The housewoman threw open the sash letting the summer heat pour in with the morning sun. "Young Byron is awake if you was thinking of going up."

Florie rose straightening her high-waisted blue cambric daygown. It was comfortable and she liked it though it was out of style.

"He loves playing with you," Mrs. Worley went on.

"I wish that were so," Florie sighed. "I've been thinking of sleeping this afternoon, so you could rest. I can tell your foot's bothering you again. A parlormaid would be such a help to you."

"Don't put me out 'fore my time, Missus." The gaps in Mrs. Worley's smile looked cunning. "I can manage the house just fine with Aileen in the kitchen and Martha upstairs. I knows the captain can't afford more."

Florie gave the old woman a hug. "What would I do without you? But do have a rest. It would please me."

"Yes, Missus, but if you don't mind me saying, I think you should get out in the air and sun today. Go on down to the beach again. You seemed to take to that sketching the doctor suggested last week. You was good at it, too!"

Florie smiled. She was tempted but shook her head. When Mrs. Worley limped away in disappointment, she wished she hadn't. She just wasn't sure she could go to the beach again. It was so hard to force herself back!

Upstairs, Florie hovered in the nursery doorway unable to make up her mind. The nursemaid was playing on the carpet with little Byron, a stocky child of two years and eight months. His name still sounded odd to Florie—Wendell had chosen it.

Byron, her son. He seemed to grow up before her very eyes. Two years...almost three, Florie thought in amazement and still...She thought back to the day Josephine Roebling had been buried. The young woman's face didn't fill Florie's mind, however. It was *his* face, his name that haunted her still.

Florie drew a ragged breath.

The nursemaid looked up, her merry eyes a startling contrast in her sun-darkened broad face. "Morning, M'lady! I didn't hear you come up. May I take the lad out a while? The sun looks so nice today." Martha's voice was as uncultured and unlovely as her face, but Florie liked and trusted her.

She was something more than twenty, Mrs. Worley's niece, and said to be a bit slow by some of her kinder relations. She worked tirelessly and had brought a note of cheer into the otherwise gloomy house when she came to care for Florie's newborn son.

"He'd like that," Florie smiled holding out her arms to the round-faced tot in an embroidered white dress. His fawn-colored curls were the same shade as Wendell's. A thick fringe made his large dark eyes quite pretty, and Florie hoped he would one day be handsome. He couldn't exactly be called that now.

He scowled at her reaching hands, his cheeks flushed and his pink lips in a pout. Beginning to whine, he nuzzled against Martha's ample bosom. Florie drew away. She wished the little fellow would let her mother him. She couldn't understand why he didn't. For a woman thirsting for love, a smile from Mrs. Worley and an occasional hug from Thomas was precious little.

"Come out with us, M'lady," Martha said, her eyes shining. "My ma says the sun's good for beauty." Then she giggled. "It's plain I've always worked under a stout roof!"

"In your case..." Florie said kneeling and shaking a tiny wooden ship near her son's pudgy fists, "...the sun comes from within."

Martha's eyes glistened. She gathered up the chubby baby, her cheeks very red, and lumbered down the back stairs beginning to sing.

A while later at her chamber window, Florie watched Martha settle Byron on the grass behind the house. Without reason or warning, her heart began hammering. At first she tried to ignore it, but it kept up until she was sweating with heat.

She recognized the breathless madness born of dark, inescapable places. Leaning against the window frame, she wished she could tell Thomas about this. She wasn't sure why she couldn't.

Except for this, her life had settled into a comfortable pattern. The letters came from Fabrienne yearly. Wendell avoided her for the most part. She could count her servants as her friends—her only friends.

What, then, drove her heart to such dangerous speeds?

She knew, but could hardly admit it to herself. She was still wondering when Wendell would resume his nightly visitations. Ever since Byron's birth she'd waited, vacillating between the decision to silently submit or violently resist. She wondered if a wife had the right to turn her husband away. She stood there panting, her chest filling to an unbearable tightness and feeling as if she was dying breath by breath.

With that thought Florie snatched a bonnet from her wardrobe shelf and tumbled down the back stairs. She wouldn't stand quietly by and listen to herself die!

She called a hello to Byron and Martha as she hurried around to the road. Near the massive stand of oaks at the end of the road called Atlantic Avenue, Florie looked back. Perched indifferently on the rise, her hip-roofed house looked like a forgotten headstone.

She must escape, even if just for a while. Escape was all that was left. Halfway down the steep winding path cutting between rocks and brambles, Florie realized she'd forgotten her drawing paper and nubs of charcoal.

She laughed suddenly and ran on, hairpins raining on her shoulders as she tore off the bonnet and tossed it aside. The ocean breeze caught her hair and spun it out like a shining wave. She felt like a child again!

Across the sand dimpled with pebbles and tufts of tall waving grass, the waves advanced and receded, playing a provocative game with Florie until she sank exhausted to a low rock just at the farthest reach of the water. She wasn't so bold as to shed her gown and run into the cold, clear sea, but she could imagine how luscious it might feel, as cool and gentle as a lover's caress.

Lulled by the pounding surf, Florie let herself think of John Roebling again. She tipped back her head to feel the breeze on her hot face. She opened her mouth to the salty spray—and moaned softly. The longing was like a hunger never satisfied. The desire was something she knew instinctively but didn't truly understand.

She ached for the sight of his face again. She tried to imagine how he might sound speaking to her, but she'd never heard his voice because Thomas had feared for her health that day and had taken her home early.

Her labor had started a week later. Four days of uncertainty and nagging pain followed. She had promised God she wouldn't think of John Roebling again if He'd let her child live.

On the fifth day God answered her prayer.

For six months she lingered in bed and, though she still prayed, the memory of John Roebling's eyes lived in her mind, malignant. She loved him. How she loved him!

"There you are, John!" Max Reardon called, marching down the deserted wharf, the sun glaring off the bleached planks under his boots and making him squint. As always the sight of his friend surprised him. There was something about John Roebling's eyes, the way he stood that set him apart from other men.

John came down the narrow ramp alongside the half-finished schooner standing in the cradle. He tossed back his curly dark hair and smiled. "Max! How are you?"

They shook hands and Max felt, as always, proud that John was his friend. "I'm feeling my years," Max said uncomfortably aware of the six years that separated him from John. He craned his neck at the awesome swell of the hull and rubbed his eyes. "I thought you gave up manual labor."

John pushed up his sleeves. He still dressed like a shipwright, loose linen shirt, brown trousers and gleaming black hessians. Max had never looked that good at forty-one. John looked like a boy, really, a cocky one to be sure. No one but Max, however, knew of the loneliness, the longing that filled John Roebling's days…and nights.

"When I'm restless," John said, "I come here. I designed this one, you know."

"And it's a beauty. I was up to the house," Max said. "I saw the boys. They're growing fast. Isa said I'd find you here. I wanted to tell you I've secured the sight for your new mill. Want to ride out this week for a look?"

John shook his head.

"Well, then…" Max didn't know what else to say.

"I'm sorry, Max," John said sitting on the edge of a pile of timbers. "I appreciate all you've done. You know how I get when work suddenly isn't enough. I look at my life and begin asking questions that have no answers. Am I mad, Max?"

"No more so than I, John. At least you have your boys. What do I have?"

"But I'm no good as a father. What do I know of children? Adam stares at me—expecting what? James badgers me with questions and jabs at my ignorance. And Conrad? He cries. I wish Josephine had lived…"

"Still blaming yourself?" Max asked. Then he wished he had exercised more tact.

"If you're about to suggest I take another wife," John said softening his eyes with a short laugh, "Save your words. Isa takes good care of my boys."

"But such a woman? You were meant for better faces!"

"Isa's face is female enough for my needs. Either I endure her or take up with some rosy wharf wench. I'm ashamed to say such an idea stirs me not at all. If it did I'd be a more pleasant friend."

Max moved off shaking his head. "Wenches aren't the only way. My wife's been dead nearly ten years, John, so it's not as if I don't know your needs. I do, and that's the rub. You're a restless man. And you're human."

Like himself, Max thought. The two shook hands again and Max headed back to the road. It was a crime such a man as John should be alone—any man for that matter. Max nursed his own loneliness and turned toward town. They were only human. Too much so.

• • •

John Roebling watched the man, his friend and adviser, disappear beyond the timbers. Silence closed around the cluttered deserted shipyard save for seawater lapping on nearby pilings and the sharp call of gulls. The war had idled the yard almost a year now. Already the smell of cut lumber and tar was fading.

Like himself. Fading. And restless? Yes!

He mounted his chestnut horse tethered nearby and angrily jerked the reins. Abruptly, the horse thundered down the dock past the warehouses where loitering shoremen stood in tavern doorways. An ale might take the edge off his mind, John thought, but he preferred his pain distinct. No man could witness the death rattle of two wives and ever again feel life in his loins.

Yet John did.

On and on he rode, paying no heed to his course. Along dusty lanes cluttered with gray shanties to the open shore he tore. Golden splashes of sand flew back under the attack of his horse's hooves. He pounded across sodden sand and through curling waves blue and silver in the sun. The wind felt refreshing in his face.

At length the horse tired. Coming within sight of the southern bluffs, John slowed to a plod. The beach was especially beautiful there. Being so far south of town, it claimed few visitors. The rolling dunes were cut here and there by boulders, low marshes and sleepy coves protected by the bluffs. John liked it there though he usually rode to the north nearer his estate.

He came to a stop unexpectedly. There, upon a dark rock several yards away, sat a vision. Her hair looked like sunlight playing on the wind. When she turned, he saw dark eyes, fair cheeks and lips which spoke silently of hurt and love.

For a while they just looked at each other.

Softly the cry of the gulls, the urgently whispering waves and his quickened heartbeat came again to his ears. John felt as if he had just taken a hard fall from the saddle. That was the woman! He felt suddenly uneasy, as if he had conjured her up!

She looked nearly the same. He had never learned her name, but he hadn't forgotten her. That woman had lived in his dreams so long he almost felt as if he knew her, that he could ride up to her and speak, as if they had just parted an intimate conversation only moments before. Maybe she was a dream still. That was all she could be, he thought.

Blinking, John knew the woman sitting stiffly on the rock was dangerously real.

She looked as if she had been waiting—that she had known he would come this way. The thought alarmed him. Then he almost laughed. He had never ridden there before and never would again. He wished, however, that he hadn't once vowed before God to seek only riches. Crying at his dead mother's feet so many years ago, could he not have chosen love?

Unfortunately, in that terrible moment, he had seen poverty, not loneliness, his only foe and set his life's course. Losing two wives was proof God had answered his prayer. John Roebling was meant for wealth, not love.

Would that he had been a wiser boy, John thought, turning and riding away with her eyes on his back.

# Seven

Florie stood before the looking glass and held up still another gown. The pale rose crepe with the deep rose-colored satin sash livened her pale cheeks, but oh, her eyes! She looked demented, in need of chains!

No one must suspect, she thought, pushing at her curls sticking damply to her forehead. She was just spending another few hours sketching along the beach. And she had proof—several hastily rendered seascapes and the sun's rosy signature on her cheeks.

She listened at the door, waiting for Wendell to go out. Her heart danced in her breast with impatient anticipation. Every day for a week she had gone to the beach and waited, and every day John Roebling walked his glossy chestnut steed along the water's edge. As if ignoring her, he never came close.

Even so, Florie found she could eat again. She played with little Byron and he didn't cry! She slept among dreams so erotic she wished for eternal night. Waking was a painfully delicious terror. Her body told her secrets she never guessed existed, that deep within her was a place of pleasure yet untouched and waiting...waiting for the promised love.

Unable to wait another moment, Florie grabbed her sketching paper and tiptoed out into the hall and down the servants' stairs. Aileen, red-cheeked over the steaming wash tub, looked up briefly as Florie crept out the service door waving her fingers with a little smile.

She was later than usual that day and so ran down the road to the path. She was down the slope so quickly her slippers filled with sand. Just beyond the bushes, she saw him! He stood by the rocks looking out to sea as if wondering what she did there each day.

He made a wonderful dark silhouette against the sparkling water, a hard-looking yet graceful man who now haunted her every moment. She could live on the memory of his face. She could dream on his sudden appearance the week before—and yet something within, that awakened beast of pleasure in her loins, drove her to come each day inviting perhaps discovery and ruin. Or perchance they might...

Florie broke into a hobbled run. Suddenly her sketch book fell from her grasp and her drawings scattered in the blustery wind. She snatched a few from the weeds. She hated to lose them for they did please her, as foolish and hurried as they were.

When she looked back, he had gone!

"No!" she cried, pressing her fist to her chest.

The drumming in her ears began to run together in one thunderous pulse. She crushed the sketches to her face and fell to her knees. He mustn't go yet! She needed to see him.

She bowed her head to the noise her heart was making in her ears. She clenched her eyes, fighting the sense of panic. She *must* tell Thomas about this! She would. She would! Thomas! John! Wait!

Florie pounded her breastbone. Damn her heart! She had missed her love! He might never return! Pity me, Lord, she wept. Deliver me of this pain. Let me see his face once more, and I swear on my mother's soul I'll not sin. Her throat contracted with pain. Just one more glimpse...

She heard soft hoofbeats. Softly John Roebling dismounted. She heard his boots in the grass and looked up with surprise to see a broad calloused palm thrust toward her. Above it was the delicate new blue of the sky.

This was only a dream! He wouldn't come so close! But her nose told her of sun-sweetened cotton, horse and fine leather! Such a sweet dream.

"Are you all right?" he asked with a deep, warm voice hinting of cockney. She felt so delicious...so hot...She wondered if she would faint.

Crouching, John leaned into Florie's line of vision.

Could a man who looked like that be real, she wondered?

"Hello," she said. Then she laughed. It was a silly little girl laugh lingering from another age. "I was afraid I'd missed you today."

She felt suddenly as if she had just leapt into a chasm. There was no use pretending. He knew why she appeared each day and she accepted why he did, too. The current between them was as bright and hot as the sun. They had no time for coy games of sparking. This was the beginning of her sin, and she gave up her prayers and vows as easily as shedding a binding gown. To this sinful freedom she smiled and let him help her stand.

As he gathered her papers, she laid the hand he'd touched against her cheek and relished a shiver of pleasure. "Thank you, Mr. Roebling," she said saying his name aloud for the first time. A surge of warmth reached to every point in her being. How she did adore this tall, squint-eyed man!

John's eyes swept over her and left her burning. His mouth looked tight, as if he was annoyed, and she wondered at that. Then unexpectedly he swung back into the saddle and wrenched his horse around. After a few halting steps he twisted in the saddle. "I swore I wouldn't come this way again. I swore I wouldn't speak to you. Yet here I am, and speaking."

Florie tipped her head back. Her hair tumbled across her shoulders, cool and feathery as she imagined his kisses would be. Dear God, let him think me pretty, she said to herself. Let me have this one moment in time to know I am a woman fulfilled.

"May I ask your name?" John asked still looking annoyed.

"Florie...DeMarsett. I live up there." She turned and pointed. Then realizing she was in full view of any back window, she snatched up her sketches and ran across the beach. The horse followed.

"Beyond the rocks is another beach," he said pointing. "It isn't visible...from that house."

Florie turned eagerly to see the place and wondered how she would climb over the barrier of water-smoothed boulders nestled among a host of slippery pebbles.

John edged his mount away. The sun caught his face and lit it. "I was only going to suggest a more sheltered spot where you might sketch a sunrise."

Then the horse and rider moved away and Florie smiled. The next morning she would watch the sun lift from the ocean like a giant glowing red eye. She knew he would be there, too.

Climbing over the rocks was nearly impossible in the pale morning darkness, but there Florie finally stood on the far side, alone.

All was quiet at that hour save for the relentless waves rolling and slipping up over the sand with frothy edges, and then sliding back leaving the shore dark and wet, the color of her mother's hair. Florie wondered if her mother had had a happy life and the thought startled her. Those years in the bedchamber began to look empty, and Florie felt sad.

She shook herself. She didn't want to think of the past now. Here the sea lay dark, a mirror to the changing sky. Behind her rose a rock bluff coming alive with gulls. A nearby hollow afforded her shelter and there she waited.

Spilling its crimson glow across the water like blood, the sun crept up. It peeked over the horizon first brilliant yellow, then orange and then painfully red, overlarge and so very slow as to hypnotize her. When the glow faded to pale morning, Florie felt weariness overtake her. She had scarcely slept the night before and was now almost too tired to think clearly.

As the sun climbed higher, she smiled. He would come. He would. But gradually her hopes melted with the morning fog. Her legs grew weak and her heart heavy. Her love was only a dream. John Roebling wasn't going to join her.

She climbed back over the rocks glad she hadn't seen him, and yet...

Mrs. Worley looked horrified when Florie stumbled in the back door toward noon that day. "Missus! Where have you been?"

Florie didn't want to look at her. Instead she mounted the back stairs letting her dampened mantle smelling of the sea fall behind her. She said nothing as she climbed into her bed and turned toward the wall. She wrapped another cloak about her, a cloak old and familiar of guilt and sin and wouldn't shake it off. She had been wrong to want John.

Soon winter storms began to beat the shore. Florie spent her days reading, drawing sunrises or staring into space. She felt herself growing old, like a flower left to dry in an autumn wind. In the spring Dr. Baines was frantic with her.

"I won't go out, Thomas," she said as always. "It's too hard." Outside her open window the spring morning was green and enticing.

"Last summer you had sun on your cheeks and a special sparkle to your eyes," Thomas said leaning close. "You'll get your strength back if you leave this room. Don't look away, Florie. Listen to me! If you want a divorce from him, I'll summon a lawyer."

"A divorce?" Florie laughed a little. "Wendell isn't my problem. Go home, Thomas. You waste your time on me. I can't divorce my husband. I've sinned enough."

"Don't be absurd. What could you have done?" Thomas looked hurt.

"Can it be I've been married to that man almost eight years?" Florie looked vaguely amazed. "Sometimes it seems like a matter of weeks. Other times it's a lifetime."

Thomas pulled her up from the permanent depression in her pillow and shook her, his fingers sharp on her shoulders. "If you confess this sin, will you let it stop killing you? The war's almost over, Florie. Times will be better and Wendell will have money again. You'll have your garden…"

"You do try too hard, Thomas."

"I'm *trying* to make you well. You could have more children—to occupy your mind and heart. At least Wendell is a devoted father."

"Is he?" Florie said shuddering at the thought. "How is my boy? I've forgotten how old he is. Am I going mad, Thomas? Sometimes I feel… mad." She felt uncomfortable with his eyes on her and looked away.

"My God, Florie! I stay away from you for my own foolish reasons and…No more of this. Get up! You're not ill." Thomas shook her harder, until his knuckles were white and his eyes full of anger.

"It's too hard," she said again wearily.

"I'll *make* you go to the beach. The sun will smile on your cheeks again. Florie, my dearest," he whispered. "Do it for me."

"I don't deserve your care, Thomas. Let me alone."

"No! I've lost enough patients."

"Another Roebling wife?" Florie's heart twisted. She hadn't thought John might take another to his heart if she stayed away!

Thomas looked puzzled over her words. "John Roebling hasn't remarried. What brings us to him? All I've heard is that he opened a textile mill inland. Why do you look at me so?"

Florie reached for his hands. "Dear Thomas. I can't go to the beach. It's too hard on my heart. Those who should love me, do not. And those who should not, do. I feel…cursed."

Thomas jerked her against his chest. "Silly fool! If you could know love for just a while you'd realize how you were meant for it."

She shook her head feeling the rough nap of his coat against her cheek. He was warm and solid and she clung to him.

"Let me show you how wrong you are!" he whispered.

Florie lifted her face to look at him. He had such a sweet and gentle soul, she thought, but his words, his touch, his eyes didn't burn her. Tears sprang to her eyes. She was glad because it was so hard to cry and she needed to so much. "I found my life on the beach, Thomas, and turned from it."

He stroked her hair and rocked her. "If you love, it's with God's blessing."

Florie threw back her head suddenly angry at his incessant probing. "But if I sin, I'll deserve to die!"

"You're dying as it is! If you must, die for love!"

Florie felt stunned at his words. She stopped a moment and stared at Thomas. Could it be what her heart wanted was right and good? She threw her arms around his neck. "Oh, Thomas! Thank you. You're so good. You've given me back my life!" She had never seen his eyes so bright. She kissed his lips lightly and watched him lean closer, his eyes growing tender. "It makes me so happy just to tell you. Thomas...I love John Roebling!"

The shine faded. His smile became wooden. He pulled back.

"You don't approve!" she cried.

Thomas let out a breath. "I'm only surprised. If there's any way I can help..." He swallowed visibly.

"You already have! Help me up now. I've wasted far too much time. It will be all right—if you say it will. I'll go to the beach and remember all the beautiful days when I saw John. He's forgotten me by now I'm sure, but I'll enjoy my memories."

She put her white feet to the smooth cool floorboards. Thomas' warm hand cupped her cheek as she stood feeling so small and weak before him.

"Not memories, Florie. Seek life. For me."

For me, his lips moved silently.

John was stooping over a beached dingy that bright spring day when he heard a noise and turned. He watched Florie clamber over the rocks stopping now and again to look up and search the beach. When she saw him her face lit with wonder. John's own heart swelled with joy—for he had come to the beach every day, waiting through the rains and winds of winter to this day.

He had known she would come, though the months were long and lonely. He knew because he had seen a great light in her eyes that day they met and he spoke to her. He had felt it kindle the embers in his own heart. And because he wouldn't quit his vigil, he knew she wouldn't forget him.

He watched until, with painful care, she reached the nearest rock. Then he walked to her with an outward calm that belied his leaping heart. With hands that trembled, he helped her to the sand.

"Hello," she laughed, her cheeks bright with excitement.

"Hello," he said smiling at her.

• • •

The next day, and the next, John and Florie met at the rocks. John rowed her around to the secluded beach where they talked of the unusually early spring and fine weather. The fishing was good. Mr. Madison's war was nearly over. John spoke of his sons, and she of Byron. John confessed he hadn't forgotten her, that just going to the beach had pleased him these past months.

Florie wept with delight. She was always sure these moments were only dreams. She didn't know happiness and felt awkward and timid with it.

They grew easy with one another as the days passed. They began to smile as if it came naturally. When they talked, they walked. And when they walked they gradually closed the charged space between them.

Days went by. Weeks. They weren't aware of time. Then one morning John assisted Florie from the dingy to the wet sand and didn't let go of her hand. Florie felt small and pretty and...happy!

"Does anyone know where you go each day?" she asked at length.

"I tell my housekeeper I'm working," he laughed. "I'm a good liar."

Fingers laced with his, Florie still couldn't believe this man appeared every morning to be with her. "Do you always work?"

"When I'm not with you. I have nothing else."

John led her into the shelter of the hollow. Thunderheads were boiling in angry colors on the horizon that morning. The whole sky was a caldron of blues and blacks. "It's a compulsion founded in fear," John said telling some of his past.

Lightning danced from sky to sea. Moments later thunder blasted them and John turned to her. "I love you," he said as a chilly breeze pulled at his hair.

The world suddenly vanished from under her feet. Florie relished the dreamlike falling, the wonder of her heart pulsing with anticipation.

John shielded her from the wind and then lifted her chin. "I know of your husband. If I really loved you, I wouldn't come. This must mean I'm selfish, but I need you, Florie."

How she had longed to hear him say those words. Love! Real love! Selfish, unreasonable, demanding and commanding love! She looked into his face falling in heavy shadows that stormy morning and suddenly saw another dark day appear in her mind.

"I see Josie's shadow between us!" she cried.

"You're a lovely liar," John said. "But a poor one. There's no shadow between us. Don't you think I've tried to conjure up a ghost as well? I've tried every way I know. I've said to myself, you're a fool to love this woman. You can never have her. You'll hurt her. Yet here I am. It's as if that storm has driven me to you. We've pretended long and well, Florie DeMarsett, but now it's done."

"What is?"

"Our pretending. Look at me. Are you terribly unhappy loving me?" His lips looked soft and vulnerable. She felt herself drowning in his eyes, eyes that promised the delights she longed for.

"Terribly," she said. Then she laughed. All thought of Josie vanished.

John lifted her hand to his lips and kissed each fingertip. "I wouldn't lie to you. I cared for my wives, but never loved them. I met Marie in Boston two years after arriving in America. My mother and I came over after my father died in debtor's prison. Mother died aboard ship. I swore then I'd never be poor again. I impressed Marie's parents and so married her money. She married the house I had built. She wanted to be mistress of a founding family like her grandmother." He watched the clouds rolling north, his face suddenly as stormy as the sky.

"Josie was British, visiting her aunt here in Union Harbor. She was a quiet girl, pretty and intelligent. I think she had been jilted. I needed a mother for Adam, and she was willing...After James was born, I thought all would be well," John sighed. "I can recall a gown, a snatch of conversation, but the faces have faded."

Suddenly John turned on her. "Tell me something to bring me to my senses."

Florie began to shake. Must they fight what they felt? He had his curse and she her promise. They mustn't give in to a love born of hurricane winds.

"Wendell was the first and only man to court me, and I married him even though after six years he had changed...for the worse." She met John's anguished eyes. "I tried to be a good wife. I bore a son..."

"...and welcome him now to your bed as dutiful wife..."

Florie's lips trembled. She wanted to lie and say yes so that would be between them and hold them apart, but she couldn't. "I would die rather than accept him. Yet I can't leave him. I have nowhere to go." Her voice broke. "My father thinks nothing of me. My sisters...I have three... when my mother died they said...they said she went away. I waited and waited for her..." Florie pressed her cold fist to her chest. She didn't want to go on. John moved close but she held him away and took a deep breath. "I once ran into the swamp looking for Mama," she said. "My sisters found me. They laughed when they told me Mama had left because she hated me. She was tired of me, ashamed of me. She didn't want me. They laughed…"

His arms slipped around her.

"If I ran away, they caught me. They knew all my hiding places. I couldn't get away from them! Fabrienne had a switch…If I wet my linens or vomited my supper she would beat me…and laugh! I have scars!" Florie found herself screaming and tried to stop. She'd said more than enough. "When Father was in the house," she panted on as if to ruin their happiness, as if to drive John away with the horror of her past, "I was tied or hidden. I got so sore, so sick, so hungry! My sister hated me and beat me especially if she lost a beau. They all hated me because…I killed my mother!"

"Stop!" John shook her. Now he looked furious. "Stop."

"And then…Wendell came! I had a beau and they didn't. They stripped me and…and…I can't tell you! Dear Lord, Mother of God, how I hated them! I couldn't get away! I was like a slave and I hate them still."

Florie burst into hysterical laughter. She felt herself crushed to John's chest.

John had never heard a woman cry so. Similar sounds began to come from his own throat. Suddenly he pulled her reddened face from his shirt, looked into her eyes mad with terror, and kissed her! He couldn't leave well enough alone. No vow was sacred before this. He loved her and was helpless.

He kissed her with a tender violence, with no sense of himself, only of some deep inner place black and open where he, too, lay stripped and bleeding. His lips moved over her salt-stained face, swollen eyes and mouth, the convulsing throat and heaving breast. "Florie," he whispered brushing back the curls stuck to her cheeks and forehead. He wasn't sure if she could see him.

She drew a ragged breath. "I am mad. I promised God Himself I would not love you."

John kissed every inch of her face, eagerly, bittersweetly, feeling tears in his own eyes.

"I hope," she said caressing his cheek, "that you will think of me sometimes and perhaps pity me a little. I don't want you to hate me completely."

Had she taken leave of her senses? "I love you!" he shouted. "I must have you."

Florie looked at him with horror, shaking her head, pulling away. "But I've told you…They…They…"

"I'll make you forget all that. Don't say no, Florie! I love you. Say you'll meet me where we'll be safe. Soon. We must be together."

"It'll never be!"

"But it will," he said. And then he smiled softly and kissed her. "It will."

# Eight

The white clapboard cottage on Melrose Avenue was surrounded by a white picket fence and neglected shrubs. In back was a small carriage barn, wood pile and shed. It wasn't unusual for John Roebling to be seen going in and out of the cottage, for he often visited with his friend, the lawyer Maximilian Reardon.

On a hazy May morning in 1815 passersby saw nothing unusual about Mr. Reardon's cottage. The faded blue shutters were closed and latched, the sprouting grass tall and tender and tulips standing with uplifted faces, for he was inland attending to the Roebling mill in Saxwell.

That a horse stood in the closed carriage barn, and an anxious male face appeared now and again in a dormer window surveying the quiet dusty lane below, drew no one's attention. Those who may have seen a young woman hurry beneath the elms and gain entrance to the cottage later that morning probably forgot Mr. Reardon was out of town. He had a good many clients whose comings and goings seldom concerned his neighbors. His own visitations about the town and surrounding villages seldom concerned them as well.

But on that morning the man peering between the crack of a half-closed shutter was certain every eye in Union Harbor was trained on that fair cottage. Every sort of suspicious conclusion was being reached when the woman knocked and slipped inside panting, nearly crying with tension. Only when they were in each other's arms did they forget the outside world.

"I was afraid you wouldn't come," John whispered, leading Florie into a dark, musty-smelling parlor. "Did you have trouble getting away?"

Florie allowed him to help her remove her red mantle. Then she sank into a chair. She looked about nervously and then met John's anxious eyes. "Wendell lingered today, all talk! Why am I suddenly of such interest to him? For months we don't speak, and now, when I want to be on my way, he must tell me all his news from the office. He insisted

I tell him all about how Byron is doing, when he knows full well I've been spending my days on the beach, sketching. Then he had to see my progress. I thought I'd go mad!" She laughed suddenly and too loudly and clapped her hands over her mouth.

John chuckled and went to a lowboy for a bottle of champagne.

"In the middle of the morning?" she giggled.

"We must enjoy today with no thought for any tomorrow," John said coming to her then and kneeling at her feet. Their eyes locked and their pulses raced a twin beat of impatient desire.

"You're very romantic, John. How do you come by it?" Florie whispered.

"It's because I love you."

"Drinking so early in the day again, Captain?" Miles Mercedes put a dripping tankard on the slimy plank table.

Wendell bolted his ale and belched. He wiped his mouth on his sleeve and cast his eyes toward the stairs. "What do you have available for me today? Not Darla. I can't abide that slut. Have you no young and pretty wenches about? I've plenty of cash today. My business is recovering." He rubbed his lips, avoiding Miles' eyes. Wendell was sweating in his new frockcoat.

"For a bit of coin I'd offer my own Ruby for your pleasure, sir, but since the last brat birthed, she's grown as fat as the rest. Surely with your eyes closed Darla is as good as the next."

Wendell eyed his questionable friend. He downed more ale and considered taking the squash-nosed man into his confidence. "What *would* you do if your woman earned a bit on the side?"

Miles chuckled wickedly. "I'd count my blessings. Like I said, Captain, I could use the money. Ruby, unfortunately, won't be harnessed."

"You seem to know much of women," Wendell said slyly.

"My share, Captain. It hasn't escaped my notice the happily married man of a few years past spends more and more time tipping his tankard here—and visiting Darla upstairs. Could it be you're no longer so happily married?" Miles slipped onto the bench across from Wendell.

Wendell leveled brimstone eyes at him. "My troubles with my wife have nothing to do with you."

"Might be I could help in some way. I might have some advice or a service I could perform for you. If your little wife is giving you grief

I could…"

"Shut your mouth before I shut it myself."

"You wouldn't want to silence me if I could help you." Miles' smile was crooked and unnerving.

"What could a lout like you do for me?"

"There's only one reason a man is happily married, and that's when he's got a tidy piece in his bed. That being true, it stands to reason he would be unhappy if that piece were no longer available—as evidenced by your visits above with the massy Darla."

"Lower your voice!"

"I'm aware your wife birthed you a son. I'm a family man and know the hazards. If the lady can no longer service you…That's your bad luck. But if my guess is right, the gentle Mrs. DeMarsett has simply turned her thoughts to other things."

"I did neglect her during the war."

"Yes, the war was handy for much." Mercedes' black eyes gleamed. "Now that it's over I need new ways to keep myself in pleasures. Could be your wife has found new ways, too."

"What are you saying?" A large drop of sweat rolled between Wendell's eyes.

"I'm saying, if the rumors hold water, she does a lot of visiting these days. She requires a great many gowns. My wife should know, she knows the seamstress…and your house woman. And it's come to my attention your wife goes to the dunes behind your house…"

"Your brain is sogged, Mercedes. Beds and gowns have nothing to do with each other."

"Ah! But they do. Captain, when the gowns are for another and the bed at home is empty."

Wendell reared up and caught Mercedes by the throat. "I'll make you eat that lie, bastard!"

"Bastard I may be, sir, but I speak no lies. You don't know where you darling bride is even now. She must not be at your side come cock's crow, otherwise you'd not be here now."

"I'm a man of many passions. I require more than she can give."

"Indeed! It could be she requires…"

Wendell enjoyed only a moment's pleasure sinking his fist into Miles' already indented profile. In seconds he lay sprawled backwards on the tavern floor feeling the dirt grind deep into the weave of his new coat. His chest was empty and fear crawled in his heart.

Miles wiped his bleeding nose on his sleeve. He was grinning and the grin was ugly with little sharp teeth flashing. He brought his muddy boot down on Wendell's belly. "The time will come, Captain, when you'll fill my pockets to know where she goes. Women crave the same ways of the flesh as men. When they're not in one bed, and not dead, they're in another, alive and smiling. Think on that, Captain, sir. Smiling, naked and opening willingly to one far, far better than you. It'll take a lot to fill my pockets before I forget what a pig you are and feel curious enough to find out who your wife does open her legs to." He threw back his head and howled with laughter. Then he fell silent and evil-eyed as Wendell scrambled out the door on his hands and knees to a chorus of sneering laughter.

With the shutters tight against the noonday sun, the little cottage on Melrose Avenue grew hot and sultry. To Florie it felt much like a summer day on the plantation. Her head felt swimmy. The champagne had slowed her blood and dulled her brain.

She and John had eaten and talked, always their eyes drinking in the special private secretness of being together. Now he had gone upstairs and was waiting for her. She felt drawn to the narrow stairs and could almost hear his heart beating in concert with hers. She sat stiffly, breathing deeply to clear her head. There was still time to repent and go home. The thought of leaving, however was almost absurd. She belonged to John, heart and soul. She had from the moment they set eyes on each other. Perhaps she had even before that, paired by fate to love this grand man!

She longed to join him, to love him as a woman could only love a man, and so she rose a bit unsteadily and faced the oaken stairs. Her heart shivered in her breast. Her palm dragged wetly up the banister. She lifted her face to the faint glow above and watched motes of dust dance in narrow shafts of sunlight. She came to the top of the stairs feeling faint with excitement. She saw that one door stood open.

The chamber within was lit by slatted sunshine, golden and ripe like a summer day. The heavy furniture looked lazy, almost liquid in the heat. A massive bed stood in the middle of the room.

He had laid his clothes upon a nearby chair whose curved mahogany arms held them tenderly. How tall his black boots looked there legless upon the floor. How white his shirt...

She dragged her eyes to the bed. He lay propped on one arm watching her, his shoulder sun-dark and mysterious against the snowy linens. She couldn't see his eyes concealed in shadows. Was he real?

She closed the door, her hand trembling.

How sweet was this sin, how welcome and quiet. He was smiling at her and she felt unafraid. She wanted him to look at her electrified body, skin tingling with life, belly quickening with desire, and so she let her blue silk gown fall to the floor in a heap. Her fingers trembled over the tiny buttons of her camisole—she had left her corset at home.

She let her underskirts fall and stepped out of her slippers. Her delicate knitted stockings came down like feathery fingers upon her legs. A sudden unwelcome memory flashed across her mind; Wendell's hands had once touched her so.

She tossed her head to cast away the thoughts. She pulled the pins from her hair and dropped them. Her curls fell in cool folds across her shoulders, like kisses.

With breasts rising and falling under the sheer embroidered lawn of her camisole, Florie approached the bed, its posters rising up from the counterpane like stout masts. The rough nap of the carpet tickled her naked feet. Her skin felt moist and smooth from the soft warmth of the lazy air.

He held out a wide opened palm. She held out hers and when they touched, her throat tightened with unbearable joy.

She seated herself gingerly on the edge of the soft featherbed and watched as if dreaming as his hands moved to her shoulders. As he slid one lace-trimmed strap down, she caught her breath and held it. The camisole fell back exposing her breasts to his full gaze. How delicious his eyes felt upon her. She hadn't known she would love it so. It was too very real, intense, breathtaking, blood-tingling!

His warm palm brushed against her breasts and her nipples immediately twirled to tiny points of desire. The fire of desire spread to her legs, softening her caution, forcing her to forget everything except John and the love flowing from his eyes to her face.

Warm and sure, John pulled her against his chest. She felt as if she was sinking into that wonderful private place within her mind, that place no one else could enter, that place where she was safe, loved and treasured. This place entwined upon the bed with John, however, that smelled richly of summer sun and bed linens scented with the love of a man, was alive. She gave herself up gladly to drown in it.

# Nine

Florie stared at her plate as her supper grew cold and saw *his* face. Her finger traced the stem of her spoon, and she felt the warmth of *his* body. Her heart pounded to twice, three times its size, and she felt still his hand upon her breast.

"...enough gowns to clothe ten wives," Wendell was muttering.

Florie forced herself to look across the dining table at her husband. She found it faintly amazing that she could sit there in front of Wendell thinking of the man she'd made love to that very afternoon.

Now that the deed was done, and often, Florie felt no guilt. Whether she was wicked or not, sinning or not, damned or not, she no longer cared. She was happy. Never would she let go of it. She had waited too long for her mother's promise to come true.

"Are you going to fit for still more gowns?" Wendell asked gulping a mouthful and wiping grease from his lower lip. "Where will you wear them all?"

Florie felt puzzled for a moment. Oh yes, she had told Mrs. Worley she would be visiting the dressmaker again that afternoon.

That meant Wendell had asked about her whereabouts! To Florie's knowledge Wendell hadn't cared where she spent her time in...in years! Was the end of the war to change that, too?

"Answer me!" The table rocked when Wendell stood. He glared at her and his eyes bulged. Gravy oozed down his chin and dripped onto his neckcloth. "Are you determined to bankrupt me? First servants. Then gowns. Parties..."

"Parties?" she squeaked, feeling suddenly faint.

"Where else do you intend to wear all your new clothes? Are you perhaps...planning a trip?" He leaned his fists on the table edge and tilted it. Her goblet fell over. A watery stain spread across the cloth.

"I've been following Thom—Dr. Baines' advice. I must go out in good weather. I sketch..." Florie hated the tremor in her voice. She wanted to sound strong.

"Thomas now, is it? *Thomas*. He says you must get out—for your health. Does he tell you to commission dozens of gowns as well? I saw your bursting wardrobe! What more could you need?"

He had gone into her room!

To keep from screaming Florie folded her hands in her lap and kept them rigid. *How* could he know? Had she been seen? How *could* he have guessed so quickly?

She felt terrified, and furious. She had only just found the breath of her existence, and now Wendell had guessed! She felt suddenly small and helpless in the face of her rage. How sudden it came upon her now!

If only Wendell would leave her alone! That wonderfully ugly hold she'd had over him for so long was gone now. She shuddered, remembering. Dear Lord, she had thought she had buried that day so deep in her mind it couldn't possibly surface. Yet there it was, fresh as blood, Wendell's hands upon her, her cheek pressed against the cold, rough floor, the flash! flash! of inhumane pain…

As she stood reeling, her chair fell backwards. She didn't make it a foot before the few morsels she had managed to swallow erupted, a splash of watery bits upon the faded carpet. She staggered in the doorway, retching. He wouldn't humiliate her again! She would die first.

The floor came up and met her in a smack of defiance. Only in sickness could she battle Wendell and win.

"I said *nothing* to upset her!" Wendell whined, fumbling for another rum.

Dr. Baines grabbed his forearm and that hurt. "Your wife fights for her health every waking moment, but a single word from you sends her back to her bed faint and sickly. What in God's name is the matter with you, DeMarsett? She's frail! Do you enjoy hurting her?"

Wendell cringed back from Thomas' wild eyes, flinching from his touch. He shrugged, voicing half-spoken excuses, and then peered at the doctor with burning, tired eyes. "I think you tell her to go out too much! Where does she go?" Wendell felt his breath go out suddenly. His boldness surprised him.

"She goes to fresh air and clean surroundings." With his upper lip curled, the doctor cast a look around the study. "If this was a shanty and you an out-of-work shoreman I wouldn't find this stench and filth surprising. But you're supposedly a respected shipping merchant. I thought you were going to make a place in society for your son. A proper nurse is necessary. Well-made clothes are necessary. Florie is trying to do these things for you. She cultivates ladies from the right families. You know the value of appearances, DeMarsett."

"All right!" Wendell shouted, ashamed before the doctor, and afraid, too, that the doctor had guessed his true background. "I'll hold my temper with her, but she could ruin me! I'm only just recovering my losses."

Wendell watched the doctor snatch up his frockcoat. "If you want her to stay here," Thomas said pausing as he went out into the hallway, "I suggest you make this a place she can stomach. I remember her once saying she wished she had a garden. If you can't tolerate her walks, perhaps you could permit her a few trees and flowers."

"Yes, yes, a garden!" Wendell said already visualizing a high brick wall to confine his little wife. "I can afford that! But, Doctor, you must do something for me as well." Wendell tried to hold back a little smile twitching nervously at the corner of his mouth. "Tell her she's too weak to travel."

"Travel? Where? A walk to the Longford's or Peltine's is no great journey. Exercise is…"

Wendell chopped the air with his swollen fist. "I mean a sea voyage, to New Orleans! That's why she ordered up so many gowns, isn't it? She visits the dressmaker every day. My housewoman tells me so. Every day, Doctor! She means to leave me!"

Thomas snorted a laugh. "I've never understood why she has stayed this long. And considering the way you treat her, I wonder why you wish her to stay. I must be going, DeMarsett. This house harbors foul vapors, it's no wonder Florie lives from her bed. To think you begrudge her a few gowns! Count your blessings, man! She's too weak for a long trip, though I doubt she was thinking of one in any case." Thomas swallowed noticeably. "Her life is here, with her son."

"My son," Wendell whispered looking around at the shadows, feeling as if thieves were closing in on the one person who would *always* belong to him—little Byron.

For a moment Thomas looked at Wendell until the blood rose to Wendell's cheeks, and discomfort twitched along his backbone.

Then the doctor went out.

Wendell fell into his chair rubbing his groin where it ached most and kept his cheeks tight below his eyes so that the tears wouldn't spring free.

From the beach Florie could hear the brick masons and their laughter. The tumble of bricks and the scrape of mortar upon the growing wall came faintly upon the wind. The prospect of a garden should have made her happy, but Wendell had insisted on a wall. A wall!

Scrambling over the rocks, she quickly found silence and peace on the far side. The sight of that wall brought Florie to a panic. Soon it and the garden would hold her fast to that stone house and that man she had wed.

Ignoring her gown—new, fashionable and carefully sewn—Florie sank to the sand, her heart pounding. She shook out aching fists and flexed tired fingers. Her life had become a storm. Each day she endured this torture, the sweet terror of escaping Wendell's house, and the unnerving fear that she would be caught in a lie. Yet she could think of no other way to be. For two weeks she had known enough joy and passion to fill a lifetime. A bit of treachery seemed a small price—when John was the prize!

Above all Florie had to be with him. All the worry over her eternal fate didn't sway her. Now the sun stood high filtering through a haze of stirred-up thin clouds. She saw beautiful square-riggers on the horizon again—John's ships launched after three long years of war. (Wendell's little ships scurried about for trade like hungry rats.) America had survived cannon and fire. Union Harbor had survived the blockade and now bustled with trade. A lone woman hurrying to a lawyer's private residence or sunning wind-blown and barefoot along the beach seemed unworthy of note.

Now Max Reardon had returned to his house. Florie wondered if he sensed a change—she didn't know if John had told him they had been lovers there.

Lovers! She was a lover!

Florie giggled. She pulled her knees up to her chin and hugged them. Little birds were diving into the shallow water for food. The gulls were crying and soaring. The waves surged back and forth like the world's own heartbeat.

She wondered if her reborn spirit lingered in that dark hot bedchamber on Melrose Avenue. Perhaps her joyous scent still clung to the linens where she had lain in John's arms naked and gasping. She indeed wondered if her cries echoed within those walls—a faint call of thanks to the maker of her fate. Maybe someday she'd go back and hear the laughter—the *laughter*—of two people entwined and moist with desire.

Dear Lord, she hadn't known love would be like that. What she had known with Wendell had never been love. It wasn't even lust. It was perversion, an abomination on her, and she shuddered to think she had ever endured it.

If what she knew with John, however, was sin, she feared greatly that God was mixed up.

She traced John's name in the sand. Then she pulled off her stockings and got up to run to the hollow. Maybe John was coming to the beach from there. The sand gave under her slight weight leaving dainty footprints. Did the prints of John's kisses linger upon her face? Was that why, after years of indifference and punishing neglect, Wendell now watched her?

For whatever reason, Florie had become calmly, expertly deceitful. She could lie into anyone's eyes, even Martha's who thought her a most impeccable lady.

To Thomas she didn't lie. As yet she hadn't been forced to tell the truth. To him she merely wept, clinging to his wise shoulders as if he were the papa she should have had, but never did. To Mrs. Worley she took strength as from the mother long dead. And Martha, she was a sister! A *real* sister.

Florie had a whole family of gentle people who loved her, and she lied to them. "I'm off to the dressmaker's..." No new gowns were delivered. "I want to sketch the ships..." More often than not she forgot her sketching paper.

Now Wendell had ordered the garden built. She had designed it: banks of bright flowers, stands of fruit trees, winding paths in stone, ornate little shelters with white iron benches and marble fountains raining into glassy pools...She had sketched it all out to the last marble statuette the day Mr. Reardon came back to town and she couldn't meet John for the first time since she took sin and adultery so joyously to her breast.

Now drays lumbered up to the portico by the hour. Wendell had warned her the garden's construction would take months. The whole adjoining lot was to be dug up to suit her whim, her physical *need* to get out-of-doors in obedience to her physician's orders—contempt had fairly dripped from Wendell's words.

And inside the great stone house?

Mrs. Worley had not one, but two new maids! They were sweating, brawny girls of fourteen who gawked at "the Captain" and scrubbed until the oaken floors shined nakedly.

New brocades hung at every gleaming window. Colorful thick new carpets all the way from the East of Persia graced the shining floors. Florie could scarcely move for fear of tripping over some carpenter or paperhanger. Perhaps, she thought, falling back in confusion on the shady sand within the hushed hollow, she should vomit in front of her husband more often!

"Florie!"

She leaped to her feet so fast her head spun. Before she could draw a surprised breath she and John came together like stormy sea to rocky shore, a splash of frothy laughter and kisses.

"You're here!" she wept pulling away to gaze up at his face. She searched every crag and plane as if it had been centuries, not days since she last saw him. "It feels like a lifetime since…"

"Sh-h-h," he smiled, lowering his mouth to hers.

She let him take possession of her lips in one long sweet kiss that rendered them both weak. "I don't care if anyone sees us," she panted. "I love you so!"

"Have you been ill?" John looked worried and tired. His face was dusty from the steep climb around the south side of the bluffs.

"Do I look it?" she laughed, delighted by his concern.

"No! You look beautiful, but when the doctor was up to check on little Conrad he mentioned…It's not important now. I can see for myself you're all right.

"I have special news! Yesterday my boys left for Boston. Adam's grandparents wanted him and the others to spend the summer there. Even my housekeeper, the sad-faced old crow, is gone with them! God is with us, Florie. I can take you home with me. Today!"

Florie hung back from his eager tug toward the tumble of sand and boulders knotted together by bushes and grass. "It's too far. I'd get home too late!"

"I left my carriage just above hidden in the woods. No one will ever know." He kissed her and smiled.

"I'm afraid Wendell already knows!" she cried, clapping her hands over her mouth to quiet herself.

"How?"

Florie balled her fists. "Perhaps he senses it, or sees it in my face. I don't know, but he's changed! I feel his eyes on me even now." The hair rose on the back of her neck.

"Then we must be off quickly." John didn't look the least bit afraid.

"But John. Wait! Wendell's building my garden. He's having the house decorated. Nothing I've asked for has been too much! Soon I'll have to stay there. He won't let me go! What will we do?"

John stopped pulling at her and took her hands. Pressing his warm lips to her palms he said, "In time I'll know. I intend to ask Max for advice. No—don't shake your head. We must face this. We need to be together. We can't go on skulking about like this. *I* can't. I'll go mad."

"I have already to be acting this way."

"Do you trust me?" John looked into her face, his eyes gentle, his lips tender.

She stood on tiptoe and kissed those lips. "You know I do."

"Then tell me one day soon we'll be together—always. Man and wife."

"It can't happen!"

"It *will* happen," he said looking fierce, his eyes blazing. "If I can face marrying again, you can face your husband."

"Do you expect Wendell to die, or will you murder him?"

John grinned, and his whole face changed as if the sun had come out after a sudden violent squall. "He'll give you up. I promise it."

John pulled her up the impossible slope although there was no path. She stumbled and tore her gown and laughed at their insanity. "John. John! Stop, and tell me how," Florie panted, pressing her fist into her bosom.

"Wendell DeMarsett has always wanted one of my fleet schooners," John said. "He's asked many a time, and always I refused. I've never liked him. Now more than ever he'll want new ships, and I like him far less. What more he might want from me I can only guess, but I'll make a friend of that most detestable man. I'll learn what he wants. Then I'll make him an offer only a fool would reject. I understand a man who wants wealth and power, as he does. You'll make a poor second next to schooners and gold. That much I learned listening to the good Dr. Baines the other day. He laughed as he talked, but I was listening closer than he knew. You'll have your freedom, my love. Everything you deserve will be yours."

John's hand slid around her waist sending shivers of desire over her. She fell against him, drunk on his words. Love *and* freedom? She couldn't bear it!

Though brambles tore her gown and dirt smudged her face, Florie followed John up the bluff. His closed carriage waited in a grove of oaks. Once inside they sat silently, hand in hand, wearing little smiles. All the way through town Florie thought of the heaven her lover had described. Freedom *and* love. It sounded too good to be true.

The great house overlooking the harbor stood silent except for the ticking of a massive tall clock near the door. A collection of doors to chambers she might never see met Florie's wondrous gaze. She tiptoed inside behind John's confident stride remembering a few of them. Josie had shown her about that long ago summer before she died. Now the hollow echo of footsteps were only hers and John's. The house was theirs now.

John led her up the curved staircase, a flight of amber and brown carpeted steps that put Wendell's stairs to shame. Most of the tables and chairs in the upper hall were covered with linens against summer's dust. Only Silvers, John's manservant, remained to look after household affairs. He lived in a small cottage beyond the garden. Florie and John were alone—more alone than they had ever been in Max Reardon's house. There were no other houses nearby, no passing wagons or distant voices.

The vast grounds, the solid walls, however didn't make Florie feel as safe as she had in town. This place smelled cold and new, like an empty cathedral. This house belonged to Josie, to three small boys not hers—even to Isa, the housekeeper.

Florie flung herself into John's arms suddenly weeping. "I don't belong here!"

"Don't be afraid," he said holding her tightly. "We'll find only happiness here. Don't you want happiness? Can't you enjoy it?"

She looked up at him puzzled. She wanted only to make John happy, and yet it seemed when they were together—and not making beautiful love—he spent far too much time frowning. "I don't know happiness well."

"It's yours any time you want. Against all my better judgment, I love you, Florie. And because I do, I mean to have you. Do you mean to have me? If I don't matter that much to you…"

She silenced those awful words with her lips. Could he possibly matter more?

Then suddenly his arm was behind her back, the other arm scooping behind her knees. He lifted her up and carried her, lips locked together, to the second flight of stairs and at last to the third floor and a small room where he laid her upon a little bed. "As far as I know this room has never been used," he said opening a small dormer window. Sunlight lit his face and spilled onto the floor in a golden shaft. "We have loved in darkness," he said. "And now we shall love in light."

He pulled his shirt over his head and came to her, his broad chest graced with dark curly hair, his skin fine and shining, darkened by the sun. She could never have enough of looking at him.

When the narrow bed groaned with his weight, she laid back, closing her eyes. Stealing into her bodice were hands of fire and life. How beautiful was love. It made her forget everything in the past. One thought filled her being: John.

Warm hands freeing her, warm lips freeing her, warm body freeing her...Take me, she thought. Make me whole.

Wendell stood in his study swallowing rum, his head cocked as he listened. The carriage that had just stopped out front rolled away. Quiet footsteps sounded in the hallway outside his door. A whispered hello to his housewoman lurking somewhere in the shadows raised the hair on his neck.

Beyond the closed drapes dusk lay hushed and warm. Wendell squeezed the tumbler in his hand and then, with care, set it down next to the case of duelling pistols. He had come home early that day to tell Florie he had found the certain tree and shrubs she required for her damnable garden. The crone had said Florie was sketching along the beach, but Florie's drawing papers were still in her desk.

Wendell had taken the time to search her drawers but found no clues among the letters from the bitch in New Orleans or the *good* doctor's exorbitant bills. He wasn't even sure himself what he was looking for. But he was looking.

Something about Florie had changed: the way she stood with her head up, the way she walked with greater purpose, the way she would look at him with a sudden and penetrating surprise...Somehow she had changed.

She was no longer the helpless little bird he had married—if she had ever been truly helpless—he was even questioning that now. She looked strong, sure and unafraid. It made him sick with apprehension.

He found no clues in her bedchamber either, nothing to say where she went each day or why. Good Dr. Baines insisted she was so frail that she couldn't stomach a single question from him. She fainted when he scarcely approached her. Why, then, did she look as healthy as a bloody horse? Wendell wondered as he clenched and unclenched his fists.

He looked down at his still sandy boots. He had wanted to follow her for some time now but hadn't had the energy. Now he had done it.

How did she climb down and up that bluff, to sketch, he thought with another swallow of rum, no sketches? *He* was exhausted!

He had followed her until her footprints disappeared by some rocks. For a moment he had actually feared she had come to harm!

He finished still another rum and laughed a little. What a beautiful little bitch she was. He had only just decided to summon help when she arrived home. Hours late. In a carriage.

Whispering.

He couldn't abide whispering. He peeped out his door. Florie and Mrs. Worley were standing in the upper hall—whispering. He stepped into full view.

Silence.

Florie slipped into her room. Mrs. Worley disappeared from his sight. Moments later he heard her back in the kitchen.

He climbed the stairs to his room, to listen.

After a time, Aileen carried a supper tray to the mistress of DeMarsett House. Wendell heard the cup rattling against the china plate. He smelled apples and cinnamon. Coffee. Starched linen. She carried it away again later.

By then he was drunk. His aim at the chamber pot was poor. Mrs. Worley would have to clean the mess because he'd fired the maids upon returning from the beach that afternoon.

All these luxuries—maids, gardens, fine new gowns—and still the little whore didn't stay home. He would teach her a lesson she'd never forget. Take his son away to New Orleans, would she? He'd kill her first.

That scourge Baines insisted Florie wasn't planning to desert him and wondered why he cared. Wendell cared, all right. God, he cared, and wished he didn't.

The rumor that she was seeking the advice of a lawyer was untrue, so Miles said. The lawyer had been out of town then. The woman seen going into his house the past few weeks was taller...and had been seen running.

Florie was small. She couldn't run!

She wasn't planning to leave him.

But she was up to something.

That dog Mercedes...Wendell laughed as he pressed his ear to his door. A hollow silence echoed through the cold oak panels. That dog thought Florie was whoring! Florie! Wendell shook his head at the absurdity.

She'd made a fool of him once. She would not do it again. If she ever dared...He couldn't begin to imagine his cold, lifeless little beauty with another man.

Wendell crept into the dim hall and was struck suddenly by how ugly it was. He heard muted voices in the nursery and cursed under his breath. The nursemaid must still be awake. He ducked into a shadow at the head of the hall when she came out unexpectedly and thundered down the back stairs. Byron was crying.

His son...

The only proof of his manhood.

Wendell's hand went protectively to his crotch. The pain was always there now, worse on some days than others. He wished he trusted a physick enough to examine him, but as yet he feared anyone's diagnosis.

Maybe Florie had poisoned him, he thought. The sores first appeared some time after Bryon was born. And now even Darla wouldn't have him. Florie gave him a son and then robbed him of his potency—an erection was a near impossibility now.

He pressed his ear to her door. Silence. His fists ached. His teeth hurt.

Owing to her bulk, Martha started up the back stairs more slowly. Before the nursemaid passed in the hall, Wendell slipped inside Florie's bedchamber. He let his breath out in a soft hiss, proud of his graceful, silent entrance.

He threw off thoughts of the nursemaid's tempting backside and turned cautiously, afraid Florie would hear or smell him.

She lay in her bed, a white embroidered coverlet clutched to her neck. Her windows were opened to the cool night air! Was she mad? Did she invite disease with open arms? Was she trying to kill herself?

The thought startled him.

Where had she gone that day?

He crossed the chamber and pulled the windows closed. She stirred and moaned. More than ever, he wanted to take her, but at the thought his pain increased to a throb.

Damn her! He'd need more rum to dull it. His hands shook as he watched her. He wetted his lips, and his tongue felt hot.

In the next room Byron's cries quieted. Wendell edged closer to the bed. He wanted a look at his little wife. He hadn't seen her naked in a long while. His hand hovered over her small white fingers clutching the coverlet. She couldn't possibly be...

Shaking his head again, he withdrew his hand. Not Florie. She took no pleasure in the flesh. He was sure of that. Whatever he had done as husband, she had hated. Even the proper coupling had pained her. The thought of her body bared to another man made him want to laugh.

But she stirred suddenly. She arched her head back and made a sound low in her throat so like pleasure, so like torture, his hair rose all over his body. And agonizingly his loins swelled.

He decided to talk to Mercedes in the morning.

# Ten

"Just make sure he pays," Ruby Mercedes said rubbing soapy water over the face of the girl-child seated on her knee.

"He'll pay, now and forever," Miles said. "We're set for life."

"I don't trust the pig."

Miles rose from the table and kicked at the young boy playing at his feet. "The brat hangs on me like a dog," he muttered. He went to his wife and slid his hand deep into the neck of her shapeless dress.

She slapped his arm away. "Pinching bastard! Go do your dirty work. I want a new gown."

"You're too ugly for a new gown," Miles laughed.

"Not too ugly at night. Not too ugly to give you brats to hang on you." Then she twisted the plump pink face of their daughter so he could see it. "Not too ugly to birth this little treasure."

The two-year-old child was indeed beautiful.

Miles cuffed Ruby on the side of her head. "You're still ugly. Next time DeMarsett complains about Darla I'll send him here. *You* make him pay."

She swung a wet rag at him. He caught it, pulled and upset her onto her back. The tot, Yolanda, naked and dripping, got up and waddled away to the comforting arms of her big brother.

"Got a fine ass, that one does. It'll bring a pretty penny soon."

Ruby leaped to her feet and came at Miles all teeth and nails like a screaming witch.

Miles finally pinned her with a vicious twist to her once beautiful blonde hair. He bent her backwards until he saw surrender in her eyes. Then with a slap he sent her flying and laughed as he walked out. She hadn't always been ugly.

She was strong though.

He patted at some blood rising in the scratches along his neck. He blinked and shielded his eyes as he stepped into the sunlight.

Couldn't it rain?

Though the roads looked unfamiliar in daylight, he found the stone house easily. It looked like DeMarsett, he thought, cold, ugly and too big. A brick wall was going up beside it. Miles stationed himself across the road in a clump of bushes and spit when he saw Wendell come out. The captain looked around and then went off to his office leaving the house to Miles' careful eye.

Miles wandered across the road and looked on the other side of the wall. The "garden" looked more like an uneven pit of mud. With a disdainful sniff, he slipped around the side of the house and took up a place just beyond the steps to Wendell's private entrance.

There he could hear carriages or guests arriving. He might also hear any interesting activity in the back of the house. The morning passed with him watching a fat old woman and a fat young one hanging wash back in a small kitchen yard.

What did DeMarsett's wife look like? Was she fat, too? Miles was longing for an ale when he heard the private door open. He sank soundlessly against the foundation and watched a slender vision in pale blue silk appear. She looked around and then dashed down the stone steps to the road.

Miles followed in time to see her enter a closed carriage nearby and speed off in a hail of clattering hooves and rising dust. The fat old bastard was right! She was up to something!

The next day Miles Mercedes borrowed a horse. Before noon he knew where DeMarsett's wife was spending her time.

And it made him laugh.

He could have reported to the pig right then; he would have liked being paid so quickly. But Miles smelled more coin. And from what he'd seen scurrying to and from the closed carriage, Florie was quite a pretty piece. If he waited…who knew? He could be rich and pleasured, too!

At the tavern that second night he told Wendell some of what he learned, that Florie went here and there on her daily visits. And she did. What he didn't mention was that she always found her way to the vast estate north of town, to the great white house facing the sea.

About town Miles learned the Roebling boys were on holiday. A visit to the Roebling yard produced a view of the famed shipbuilder himself. Perhaps there was opportunity for a few coins there as well!

Miles lay awake nights thinking over the possibilities. As the summer ebbed he knew he must act soon. He sensed something in the air, a tension he could almost taste that made him even more short with his brat son and plump daughter and most especially with his faded hag of a wife.

When the day finally came, Miles knew it.

The weather had been bad a long while. He watched little Mrs. Florie DeMarsett run out to meet her lover's carriage. He was prepared to get inside the great white house this day to catch the lover in the act. He knew DeMarsett would want to hear the details. DeMarsett was that kind of man.

He tethered his horse near the stone gate and walked like always to the house. He knew the third floor room the wantons occupied each midday—he'd often seen John at the window. He'd heard *her* laugh.

Stationing himself in his usual spot, Miles was thinking about getting inside when he heard them talking—their window was open and the wind was right.

She was weeping. He was being very earnest. Miles cared not at all what they were saying. He cared only that he should see them. He was lifting a nearby unlocked sash when they appeared unexpectedly from a set of rear doors, hand in hand.

Yes! Miles thought crouching behind a hedge, smiling at his good fortune. Perfect!

They walked eternally slow through the garden. "…be in harbor tomorrow at the earliest. I'll meet them and…" They moved out of Miles' hearing.

Judging his best route, Miles scurried to a new shelter like a rat under the wharf, quick, sure and evil.

Beyond the garden they sat in a shady grove within view of the sea. All about them were bushes, hedges and banks of flowers in full and final bloom. The September air was soft and silent, still warm yet blustery, hinting of the coming fall storms.

Miles thought of the flags he'd seen coming into port over the past few days—tropical force winds moving north—two schooners had gone down off the Virginia coast…

This would have to be the day he saw all. Wendell had grown tired of waiting.

Miles' legs cramped as he watched and waited. He kneaded the muscles and peered through the hedge at the pair in the grass. They were lying down now. Roebling kissed the adulteress as if he had an eternity to enjoy her. Miles wondered at the length of their kisses. Did rich men get more value for their pleasures?

And she *was* beautiful.

Milky white skin showed under her petticoats. Her little feet were pink on the soles. Her hair looked like Ruby's should have. And she had round full breasts...

"After he and your wife were naked," Miles whispered savoring every word, "they lay kissing and laughing as if there was no hurry." The tavern was quiet for late afternoon. Miles smiled at the sight of DeMarsett sweating over his empty tankard, clutching it with flattened sausage fingers.

"Who was the *man?*" Wendell croaked, teeth clenched, eyes fixed on Miles.

"Couldn't see him very clear at first. Captain," Miles said leaning back and smiling though he was trying not to. "I'd recognize the ass anywhere, but the face...I was about so far away, you see, and looking through a hedge, a thick one." He drew an invisible map on the table. "They was laying like so..." He cupped his hands together "...and then like so. And damned if they didn't do a lot of rolling and groping like a couple of frigging dogs all over that grassy knoll!"

Wendell slammed his tankard on the table. Ale flopped into the air and plopped onto the table top. "Who was he?"

"You've a beautiful wife, Captain, sir, if I may say so. Like a goddess, she is. Golden hair and white breasts big enough to fill the biggest of hands..."

Wendell grabbed Miles Mercedes' throat. "I've got an important meeting with John Roebling, and I'm late. Name the man and your price, you son of a bitch, or I'll eat you bite by bite."

Miles flung off Wendell's hand. He whispered his new price and watched DeMarsett's face drain. Leaning very close, he described in detail just what he had seen the pretty little wife do that day before God and the open sea.

"And when the man was done with her, Captain, sir, I saw him stand. It was none other than John Roebling himself laying out your sweet missus! I knew you'd want to know first off having your meeting about the ships today, so I rode down here fast as I could. For all I know they're still up there."

The pewter tankard handle actually curved under Wendell's trembling white fingers. Then he stood.

Miles watched the fat merchant drop coins upon the table. Once outside they saw thunderheads boiling on the horizon. A brisk wind began to pull at them. "I'll be taking that purse now, Captain, sir. I earned it," Miles said.

Wendell extracted a bulging wallet from the breast pocket of his flapping frockcoat and handed it over without ever meeting Miles' glittering smile. "Kill him."

"This is the happiest day of my life," Florie whispered stretching under the warmth of the sun filtering through the overhead leaves.

Leaning on his elbow above her, John traced Florie's lips with his finger. When he kissed her, his hand slid between her breasts to the rounded mound of her belly. "Forgive me," he whispered against her mouth.

Florie swallowed back tears. "When you've made me so happy? What must I forgive? I've already borne one child. This one won't kill me. It belongs to us, John, to our love."

"I'll speak to your husband today," John said. "I would have anyway; he bid on two of my ships and I was going to accept. Now we'll bargain a new price. I'm ready to offer anything. Do you think he'd want this land, this house?"

"John, no!" Florie cried grabbing his arm.

"You and I can be happy anywhere. My sons will love you..." He paused and closed his eyes. "Dear God, let no harm come to you from this." He buried his face between her breasts. His breath felt warm.

The sun slipped beyond the trees leaving them in a cool shadow. Florie held John's head to her breast and gazed up through the leaves, feeling a healing peace go through her. For this day she had lived. For this love she had waited!

Her throat ached with the joy of it. "To my last breath I'll treasure this day and our love fulfilled."

John lifted his face. She looked into those wonderfully dark eyes. She could see the specks of brown in the blue and the outer rim of black. Then he closed his eyes to kiss her again. How full were his lashes and tender his eyelids. She rubbed her fingertips over the whiskers along his jaw. She traced the fine lines near his eyes and the small gray curls marring the perfect black waves along his temples.

"I love John Roebling," she whispered.

John got up then and pulled on his trousers and shirt. "I want you to stay here tonight. The weather's turning. I'd feel better leaving you here while I talk to Wendell. We need to be careful now that you're pregnant."

"Don't tempt me," she smiled, gathering her clothes. "Of course I must go back. I'll go straight to bed. He won't bother me." She laughed a little. "Don't look so worried. What can he do to us now?"

"You know him better than I."

"He can't steal what he doesn't understand. Come! Take me back before he misses me. I'm hungry!"

John caught her in his arms. "Soon we'll be together always."

"Yes!" she smiled. "Oh, yes. Bargain well, my love."

Wendell had had enough to drink that he hardly minded the tall man fouling the atmosphere of his study. He was glad he'd let the hag clean it. He felt no shame before this wife-stealer. "I accept your offer, Roebling," he hissed enjoying the torment racking Roebling's face.

"A wise decision," John said. "When do you want the ships?"

"Now."

Roebling didn't flinch.

Wendell felt disappointed. He knew, though, that he'd get the two just completed, the best schooners north of Boston. He'd be rich before the end of the year. Nothing again would ever shake his wealth.

"And the cash settlement?" John asked.

"I'd like that when you come for her, if you please, sir," Wendell said holding back his laugh.

"When may that be?"

Wendell grinned. This was so miserably easy. He could have sold the little bitch long ago. "You should deal in slaves, sir. You've a head for it. Once the goods have been examined," he said pausing for effect. "Delivery can be anytime."

John swayed.

Wendell enjoyed every emotion playing on that horribly handsome face.

"On Monday then," John said. "As soon as I come from the banking house."

Wendell shook his head. "By night, sir. I don't intend for my son to suffer as a result of this transaction. If you want the little…lady, take her by night."

The two nodded but didn't shake hands.

When John Roebling had gone from DeMarsett House, Wendell sank back in his chair and lifted the rum bottle to his lips. He took several long throat-burning swallows that brought sharp tears to his eyes. Sell her, he thought? She would wish he had.

The house grew strangely quiet as Wendell sat in his study drinking into the long hours of the evening. His lamp was out. His head felt as if it was floating somewhere near the ceiling.

If all went well, he thought, John Roebling wouldn't live to see Tuesday dawn. Wendell would be rich. Florie, sadder and far wiser, would still be his and Miles would have earned his fair pay.

How distressed his little wife would be to hear her lover was dead of some clever accident, he thought climbing to his feet. Perhaps *good* Dr. Baines could meet with one, too!

Miles Mercedes had turned out to be the best friend he'd ever had. Wendell giggled.

Staggering to the stairs, he wondered if he'd ever been this drunk. When he took himself up to the nursery, Martha looked up with surprise and stabbed her finger with her mending needle. The dim illumination from the bedside lamp lit four-year-old Byron's sleeping cherubic face.

"Yes, Captain?" Martha whispered jumping up and nodding an awkward curtsey. She sucked her bleeding finger in a way Wendell wished she wouldn't.

"There's bad weather to sea," he said. "You and Worley best take yourselves and my boy inland 'til it passes. Pack tonight. Missus and me will be staying to tend the house. It'll stand the blow. I've hired a coach for you. It'll be here by dawn."

"Yes, sir, but where…"

"On with your work, or I'll toss you out like the others!" Martha shrank from him. When he didn't move, she went to the highboy and began gathering the little master's dresses from the drawers.

With his brow dampened and his groin throbbing, Wendell left the nursemaid and stopped to listen at Florie's door. Hearing nothing, he crept in. She was in bed and looked asleep. Wendell closed her windows and dragged the drapes over them.

She didn't stir.

For a moment he stood over her, remembering, curling his tongue back and forth behind his teeth. Then he took hold of the coverlet and yanked.

Florie made a little cry as she scrambled for the cover.

He held it out of reach so that she had to sit up. "Don't be afraid, my dear," he whispered. "I'll not hurt you. I've come to tell you I've sold you."

She looked blurry, as if underwater. Wendell moved closer. She didn't look as frightened as he wanted.

"You've seen slaves on the auction block before," he chuckled. "Stand up and climb upon this chair for me."

"Get out!" she said with a harsh but trembling voice.

"Come, come, dear little Florie. One last look for your old master. Up on the chair. Lift your hem so that I may inspect…"

"Get out!"

He lunged and covered her mouth. Her eyes swelled above the breadth of his hand as he pressed her back into the pillow. "Just one last look. That's fair, isn't it?" His free hand darted to her thighs and caressed the faint scars. "How does it feel to be a slave, Florie? Do you like it?"

As his hand slid higher she squirmed violently and wrenched free. She looked so pitifully ridiculous in that dainty night dress with all its little tucks and laces.

"You'd best not scream so near your child's bedchamber," he hissed. "Do you want to frighten him to death?"

She scrambled off the bed into a corner.

Wendell followed.

"I'm sorry. Husband," she whispered, her eyes sparking like fire. "I know I've hurt you, but…"

Wendell lifted her from the floor and spit in her face! He'd have none of her groveling, or her defiance.

A peculiar transformation came over her little face. Her teeth were gritted as hard as his. Her eyes bulged with hate. With astounding speed—almost grace—she raised her knee and brought it up squarely between his legs.

Instantaneous, blinding, unbearable pain exploded and radiated up from Wendell's groin! He let out one high cry and then doubled over clutching himself with one hand while dragging Florie down with the other. Holding his breath, Wendell silenced her with his forearm across her throat. He remembered, somehow, not to break her.

Blood began to trickle from his cheeks where she scratched him. He scarcely felt the pain. Then he realized her teeth must be almost to the bone in his arm and was amazed that she would actually bite him! Still he held her down. "Up on the chair," he said pushing her to her feet. He dragged a chair into the middle of the floor and ripped her night dress half off before she climbed up. At last she was crying, through her teeth, looking furious and terrified.

Moments later, an eternity later, he wasn't sure, Wendell found himself standing over Florie's body.

What was she doing on the floor?

He knelt and ran his hand over her swollen breasts. He pulled away the rest of her torn gown, puzzled now rather than pleased. Florie moaned and shuddered but didn't awaken.

Wendell slid to the floor beside her and sat for a moment trying to remember what had happened. Absently he caressed her as she lay so still, breathing as if she needed only a whisper of air to stay alive.

How lovely she was with her lips parted like that. He fingered her golden curls and felt sad. Little wife…little whore…

Miles' voice came to him. "…like this…and then like this…" and an impossible picture of little Florie and John Roebling filled Wendell's mind.

What was she doing on the floor?

He rubbed his eyes. Then abruptly he swiveled his head and saw the chair lying on its side nearby.

She must have fallen.

With an impatient sigh, Wendell pushed himself to his feet. She had been nothing but trouble since the day he first laid eyes on her. Cunning little bitch and her gigantic falsies. He turned away in disgust. Then he took himself out into the hall, locking the door behind him.

The next morning, Wendell watched Mrs. Worley, the nursemaid and his son disappear down the road toward town in the hired coach. Though his raw cheeks smarted, he smiled. Everything had been so miserably easy. The stage was set for the great drama. So before Aileen could set foot on the stairs with the missus' breakfast tray, Wendell stopped her.

Aileen drew back looking as if she smelled something.

"Gather your things and be off," Wendell said blinking his burning eyes. "You're dismissed."

"But, sir!" she said, that sour look quickly gone. When she saw he meant what he said, she burst into tears.

"Be off, and don't go wagging your tongue to my housewoman. She told me what you did!"

Wendell chuckled as she ran back to the kitchen. She had done nothing he knew of, of course, but it was the best way for ridding himself of her and silencing her at the same time.

He almost laughed as he listened to the woman clatter out in a wail of scarcely veiled criticisms. When she had gone the house was so silent Wendell felt as if he were standing in a tomb. Laughing harder, he lumbered upstairs and unlocked Florie's door. By dawn it would be.

Florie still lay naked on the far side of the bed where he'd left her hours before. What was all that? He rubbed his eyes. She lay in blood! He didn't remember it!

He fell to his knees and pulled her up. She wasn't dead! He could feel the quiver of life in her cool limbs. Wendell lifted her into his arms and shuddered because she was actually dripping. He didn't remember hitting her. Could it be the fall? Damn fragile bitch.

He staggered back and then saw it, pearly amid the pool on the floor. What was that small mass, curled, almost fishlike...

He took several steps closer feeling his skin crawl with foreboding. Florie felt very heavy for one so small. He shifted her weight and bent over the small bloody thing on the floor.

A jolt went through him. He nearly dropped Florie. That was...a baby!

He staggered back. Looking down at the limp naked body in his arms, his chest heaved.

The little whore!

Wendell burst into horrified laughter. The sound of it startled him. The house echoed with it. Outside the growing wind carried it wailing over the treetops like a death cry.

That bastard Roebling had made her pregnant!

The final unbearable insult.

He had been about to lay her on the bed. Now he turned. The whole of his plan, the inevitability of its outcome came suddenly clear. He had intended for Miles to kill John after John delivered the titles to his two best schooners. Now Wendell realized that never would have worked.

Miles was going to have to do more.

A violent chill went down Wendell's back. A queer kind of energy raced through his veins. He looked down at Florie and felt as he had many years ago aboard a merchantman far to sea. He had looked then upon the world with new and bitter eyes. How different everything seemed to him as he grew cold and sure.

How best to manage this?

He knew Florie would be able to escape her room. She was a clever bitch and had outsmarted him all this time. Where could he put her that she'd best suit Miles Mercedes?

Several moments passed. Then he knew.

The stairs to the attic were almost too narrow. He carried Florie sideways up the treacherous flight and at last lay her upon a cot in a room with one small gable window overlooking the unfinished garden.

He left her there while he ate and drank and slept. The wind grew fierce and the sky ominously dark. Wendell lit his lamp and sat over his cluttered desk trying to think. He was out of rum.

Florie was still unconscious when he looked in on her. She looked more like a drowned rat than a harlot. She didn't even spark the remnants of his lust. He brought her a clean night dress; no use giving Mercedes more than his due—and he brought up some food. Even a condemned criminal got a last meal.

Wendell stood several moments looking down at her trying to conjure up some emotion. He felt nothing save loathing, pure and simple. Perhaps if she had loved him...

He curled his lip, sniffed and belched. All women were whores. He knew that at last. He hadn't *really* believed all Mercedes said she had done, but lying still and cold on her chamber floor was proof that left him no room for doubt, no vestige of pity and certainly no trace of what he had once feared—that he loved her.

Now he wanted only to be rid of her as surely and absolutely as he had once clung to her. He had no more delusions. He'd strike first, swiftly, through the well-coined hand of one, Miles Mercedes, and be rid of honey-haired Florie Gautier once and forever.

Goodbye, dear wife, Wendell said silently as he found his way to the little door. He closed and latched it and walked down the dark attic corridor to the stairs.

Within an hour Wendell DeMarsett could be seen staggering into the wind toward town, a grimace on his face of pleasure and pain. Appearing at King's Horse Tavern at that hour, he looked like a cur. His stubbled cheeks were raked and raw all the way down to the tender flesh under his chins. And his eyes burned slick and red.

Even Miles recoiled from the sight. "Met your match in females, Captain?"

Wendell flashed him an ugly look. He grabbed Miles' sleeve and pulled him into a corner.

"Off with your hands," Miles snarled and jerked free.

"Would you take twice what I offered?"

Miles' lips tightened with satisfaction. He'd sensed all along he'd get more! "Roebling's worth double if you say so, Captain."

"What do you say to killing a woman?" Wendell hissed, his eyes cast aside as if seeing beyond the gray walls to another place.

Miles' back twitched. He felt suddenly full and throbbing. "I'd say yes to that pleasure, sir."

# Eleven

Florie rose to consciousness like a body bobbing to the surface of a cool, black sea. For a long time she lay staring at roughly hewn rafters, puzzling out the deep shadows of the strange chamber echoing with a raging storm.

At first she wasn't sure of just where she was. It could have been Gautier Plantation or DeMarsett House. She didn't know.

Then, suddenly, with a small cramp in her sore, empty womb, she knew! It was Wendell's house, and she was...

Her hands flew to her mouth, then her shallow belly. She curled onto her side with a silent scream. In a wicked flash she remembered Wendell awakening her and forcing her upon the little chair. She remembered their struggle and how he tried to abuse her.

She remembered nothing more, but it was plainly evident. She had fallen. The child was dead. Gone. After a time her tears dried. She lay staring at the crude plank door, too tired to think. Then she slept.

When she awoke, the tremors shaking her body were violent. She had been in strange, cold places before. She'd been sick before, but something about this dank room, these raking chills and the storm told her death lurked very near.

At that thought, a flood of heat went through her. She pushed to her feet, her head reeling. The sound of her heart was loud, yet reassuring. Wendell hadn't killed her.

She shook back damp curls. He hadn't quenched the fire in her heart. There would be other babes. A fresh, unbidden memory fueled Florie's faltering progress toward the door. "So you would marry a Yankee, dear little sister," Fabrienne and her sisters had hissed so long ago. "We'll show you what a bride can expect..."

Florie's breaths tore her throat raw as she chuckled a little. If only they had known. Though her legs felt buttery, with each step her resolve grew stronger. Escape. Escape!

The door stood fast.

For a moment Florie sagged against it. How easy it would be to slip to the floor and let life drain away...

She jerked herself upright. There was the window...

As she moved toward it, her heart grew quiet and her head stopped pounding. She rubbed a place on one of the lower panes clean. Through the spotted glass she could see only the pouring rain. The sound of it drummed against the rooftop and lashed in sheets the stone house alone on the hill.

She clung to the sill straining to see some means of getting out. Only the sheer gable wall met her frantic eyes. Undaunted, she crept back to the cot, laid down and curled herself tight against the damp. She'd think of something.

She couldn't begin to guess how long she'd been in the attic. She recognized the chamber as belonging to a former maid. Across from her inside a small wardrobe of plain oak hung an apron. Next to that was the door. In the middle of the carpetless chamber stood a table with one short leg. Some rags, apples, and honey-crusted biscuits were on it.

No wood lay in the box by the little grate set in the stone chimney. She had no blankets, only her hate and the warming hope that John would soon come to keep her alive.

Thinking of him, Florie pulled herself up again. She must be ready.

The chamber grew black and the wind began to shriek. The very bones of the house started to tremble. Florie could see the rafters shifting. The stone walls took the gale's blows with deep groans.

Aching, Florie stumbled to the table. She found a fresh nightdress there and put it on. The biscuit tasted good though she couldn't finish it. She leaned against the door, listening, one hand pressed to her belly.

She wished Wendell would come. She'd push him down the stairs! She could almost hear him falling. Picturing that made her smile, and she shuddered.

How could the house be so silent in such a storm? Didn't Mrs. Worley, Martha or Aileen wonder where she was? Was she alone?

The wind tore at the house like a beast shaking its prey in flashing teeth. Florie tugged at the locked door. John, John, come to me, she wept, slapping the door, her anger draining with her strength.

• • •

King's Horse Tavern was nearly deserted as the hurricane hit Union Harbor. Most folks were home behind barred doors, or inland. The tavern walls shivered in the blasting wind as if ready to take leave of the foundation.

"It's late, Captain," the blonde woman tending ale said, eyeing Wendell DeMarsett miserably. "Another ale before you shove off?"

Wendell's eyes stayed fixed on the quaking door. It looked like someone was trying to get in. He listened to the rising pitch of the wind as if it were a far-off scream. His tankard stood full. Since sitting down and watching Mercedes slink out into the wind he hadn't once lifted it to his lips.

The howl of a small child came from a back room.

"I got to see to my daughter, Captain," the alewife said, looking as if she was glad to part his silent malevolent company. "My little Yolanda doesn't like this screaming blow. Can't say I like it much myself. Will you be needing anything?"

Wendell just watched rain seeping under the door. It looked like blood.

"Beau!" the woman snapped as she went in the back room. "Get the mop."

A handsome lad of six or so darted into the common room and pushed some rags under the crack in the door. He was small for his age, thin as a wharf rat. His clothes were ragged and dirty, too small yet hanging on him. He looked sharply at Wendell, his remarkably good features tight, his clear blue eyes unsettling.

Then the boy's mother came back with a blonde toddler on her hip. "We're taking water in the back now, too, Captain. I should close up."

He didn't move.

Suddenly one of the windows burst open. Rain rushed in drenching a nearby table and the floor. The little girl began crying again. Her spindly-armed brother pressed the window closed and came away dripping. They glared at the fat man hunched over the corner table, his fat arse anchored as if he'd never move again. His hands stayed wrapped around the tankard as if it was a throat—and his knuckles were white.

Another child was crying.

In the great white house overlooking the sea north of Union Harbor, Conrad Roebling cringed from the storm. Isa held him to her cold flat bosom and sang a loveless lullaby. She watched the master donning his rain slicker, his face tight and white. She'd seen him change far too much since spring. Now she knew why. Another woman.

Isa turned away, her mouth feeling bitter and dry. Could he not see he was meant to live alone? She could care for him as well as any lacy lady, if not better.

"I won't be gone long," John said, jamming a hat on his head and flinching as the storm slammed against the house shaking the windowglass.

He should've gone earlier, he thought going into the library. He took a heavy leather purse from his desk and tucked it securely inside his shirt. He and Florie could be upstairs now, safe before a blazing fire oblivious to the hurricane trying to level the land.

Unfortunately he had had to help his man Silvers and the gardener latch all the shutters. He'd sent the stable boys to Saxwell with the horses, secured everything in the carriage house…

Then James begged him not to leave. Conrad wailed. Adam stared with those bottomless dark eyes so full of strength—shaming him.

All through supper John sat with his sons. Every increasing blast of wind drove him mad with impatience. As long as Florie was with that man she wasn't safe. He'd been a fool. The afternoon when she told him about their child, he should have kept her. He laughed and rubbed at a knot of worry in his neck. She'd scarcely had to tell him. He'd noticed the bloom of her belly for weeks. He'd hoped…

God, he was despicable. For a moment he imagined her beautiful face drained, a smile on her lips too haunting to bear. Let it not come to that again, he prayed. He'd gladly die in her place.

Isa had put the boys to bed early even though they wouldn't be able to sleep. Outside heaven and hell battled. From their windows the boys could see waves crashing upon the bluffs in explosions of white foam. Trees bent to the storm's will, stripped. Now and again a branch would give a mighty crack and sail away like a witch's broomstick borne upon an evil wind.

John felt uneasy now reaching for the door. As soon as he turned the handle, the door wrenched free of his hands and slammed against the wall.

Isa only watched, her face as solid and immovable as marble.

John felt suddenly elated. He'd soon be rid of her. How could he have ever let such a woman rear his sons? Florie was the mother for them, tender and loving. His heart swelled at the thought.

He put his hand on little Conrad's streaked cheeks and smiled. The boy was handsome, though thin and high-strung. They all were. To this boy and the two cowering in their beds above, John silently said, I wouldn't leave you now except that I go to fetch you a beautiful new mother.

And I a wife, he thought using all his strength to pull the door closed behind him. Immediately the torrent threw him against one of the pillars, soaked his face and plastered his hair into his eyes. The wind took his hat. He couldn't bring Florie back through this, he thought practically falling down the steps. She'd catch her death. Would this ill fate never loose its hold on him?

John could scarcely follow the lane to the gate. The wind fought his every step. He rested a moment by the stone pillar at the gate. Wiping the rain from his eyes he could see nothing but gray. Everything leaned with the wind. Branches whipped and snapped. Debris soared across the road like sodden birds.

He set off, head ducked, leading with his shoulder. His feet slipped as if the mud was ice. Often he struggled straight into a ditch. When he reached the stretch of road open to the bluffs the wind wouldn't allow him to stand. For nearly a mile he crawled, concentrating on each impossible inch.

When he reached the stand of oaks, he rested a while in a muddy hollow. His muscles cried for relief. He began to wonder if he'd make it all the way to Florie's house.

Rearing up, he staggered back to the road and pushed on harder and faster than ever. Not even a hurricane would keep him from reaching her. He lifted his face to get his bearings. Ahead, the wind tore the roof of a small house free and spirited it away, leaving the shack to fall in on itself. So fascinating was the sight, John didn't pay heed to a vicious crack just behind.

Wind screaming, rain blinding him, John felt an oak fall. The earth trembled beneath his feet. The branch that struck him and pinned him to the muddy road came as a surprise.

Darkness swallowed him, blotted out the wind's howl and the rain's sting. John Roebling lay still and dark beneath the tangled branches. And the hurricane whirled on, triumphant.

The streets were deserted. The wind came ever faster, white now, rather than gray. One lone man struggled through the fury, stopping occasionally beside a house to gather his strength. At last he reached the stone house at the far end of Atlantic Avenue belonging to Captain DeMarsett. Shielding his ugly face from the stinging rain, he paused to look up at the broken windows. Some lace-trimmed curtains snapped out into the wind like a lady's giant kerchief signaling a frantic hello.

Then he disappeared. The only evidence that he had entered the seemingly deserted stone house was that the front door, which had been closed, now slammed back and forth, a fitting answer to the curtain's signal.

The gale whistled through the house like an evil spirit set free. Broken dishes and fallen paintings littered the slippery oaken floors. Fireplaces smoldered and hissed as rain ran down the chimneys. The man made his way through each chamber casually opening cupboards and drawers, filling his roomy great-coat with all manner of valuables.

Climbing the stairs, he smiled and his eyes glittered. He left a muddy wet trail upon the carpets. Soon he was so laden he could carry nothing more. He turned his eyes toward the ceiling and pulled a knife from an inside pocket.

Every few steps he stopped to listen. Never again would he be so lucky as to be paid to ransack a man's own house. Then, to finish the job...

The howling wind pleasured him. He couldn't have asked for prettier weather to muffle the screams soon to fill these dingy halls.

He'd come to admire Florie DeMarsett's spirit and nerve. He admired still more the curve of her young breasts and the slope of those open thighs.

How nice it was that the Roebling bastard was late. Miles would have plenty of time to enjoy the lady of the house. Luck was with him this tormented night.

The captain had said he would find the adulteress locked in an attic room. Miles found the back stairs and climbed into the creaking gloom. He moved cat-like down the blackened corridor and pushed the first door he found open to emptiness and silence.

At the end of the hall he looked outside at the hollows of the walled garden. The newly planted trees lay uprooted on their sides. Where they had stood were great pits of water and mud. The storm had turned the acreage into a burying ground. He laughed at the captain's hapless attempt to turn this stone shack into a fine dwelling. DeMarsett House would always be a sorry excuse for quality. Even Miles could see that.

Door after door swung open to his touch. At last Miles reached a locked one. Taking a thick key from his pocket, he twisted it in the lock. He stood back grinning, breathing heavily, his loins quickening to the task ahead.

Inside the chamber he heard a cot creak. Her footsteps scarcely made a sound. Slipping back out of sight, he watched the door swing open. She leaned out looking much smaller than he remembered.

"John? John, is that you?" Florie could see nothing in the attic corridor.

John wouldn't hide, she thought. It must be Wendell.

The house vibrated now as if it had taken on a life of its own apart from the storm. Through the far window she could see the trees at the end of the road bent nearly double in the screaming white wind.

Suddenly the shadow of a man's head and hulking shoulders passed the window!

Florie had moved several steps down the hall, but now threw herself against the wall. She slid to the floor, her heart shivering.

That wasn't John or Wendell! A stranger! She could smell him; sweat, sour fish, and something odd, evil, tightening her chest, squeezing her throat!

"Hello, Mrs. DeMarsett."

Such a voice! So low and husky, the very sound of terror!

Who was it?

Florie's heart almost leapt from her throat as she pressed her hands to her mouth. If she didn't get a breath soon, she'd die! Who was it?

He didn't seem to be moving, but she could sense him there in the lightless hall, watching, waiting. Suddenly she did breathe and the sound of the little gasp she made brought forth a sinister chuckle from the intruder.

She began to creep toward the stairs blindly determined to get out of the house and away. How did he know her name? Who could he be? One by one she slid down the steps like a child sneaking away into the night.

"The captain told me I'd find you up here," came that awful voice so near. "We have some business, you and I. You'll save yourself a lot of pain if you submit quickly and quietly, as you did so prettily on the knoll a few short days ago. Yes, I was there. I enjoyed it very much."

She couldn't believe her ears! Wendell sent this man? She had been watched...

She felt suddenly ill. Where was John? She had to get out of this horrible place!

"Come, come, Mrs. DeMarsett. There's no use hiding."

Florie flung herself headlong down the remaining steps. She mustn't fall! She mustn't faint!

When the wind ebbed suddenly, the house sagged. Outside, the banshee wail ceased with a sigh and the gaping windows filled with watery gray light.

Florie paused and wiped sweat from her brow. Her fingers felt awkward and numb. If she could just rest a moment and think…

The man appeared at the head of the attic stairs. She turned and stared into his eyes. He was taller than Wendell, heavier than John, wearing a lumpy, clanking great-coat and a low knit cap. "My name is Miles Mercedes, my lady," he said in a calmly evil voice. He pulled a knife from the folds of his coat and smiled.

Florie screamed. She couldn't believe this was happening! It wasn't possible. Wendell sent this monster to…

"It's no use, Florie," he whispered. "I mean to earn my generous pay." He wiped the blade on his leg and tested its edge with his thumb. "You've had your pleasure with Roebling. Now I mean to have mine. Shall I kill you first, or would you like to watch my blade sink into your lover's heart? It matters little to me."

Wildly, mindlessly mad with terror, Florie gathered up the hem of her nightdress and bolted toward the staircase leading to the first floor. The front door had slammed shut. Florie nearly fell as she reached it. She pulled at the handle. It was stuck.

Looking back, she saw the man, Miles Mercedes, following, each step slow and sure as if he knew she couldn't escape him.

She ran toward the back of the house kicking aside broken crockery. The kitchen floor was wet and slick. She dragged the back door open and ran out into the cold gray light. The wind hung suspended like a frightened breath.

Tree limbs, odd boards and debris littered the muddy kitchen yard. She struggled through the mud around the side of the house hoping to get to the road and find John. A few frightened clouds skittered across the clear black sky. Then bigger ones, dangerous and heavy, gathered once again.

The wooden gate in the garden wall hung by one bent iron hinge. Crying with relief, Florie pushed it open. John! John! He must be there! She was so tired, so afraid. She couldn't take anymore! She just couldn't.

With a choked scream, she came face to face with the black eyes and lecherous smile of the man her husband had sent to kill her and John!

Florie laughed.

She stumbled backwards clutching her bosom, screaming with laughter! She couldn't tear her eyes from that satanic face, those piggish eyes ugly with intent, the bent, pushed-in nose…

Her heart squeezed up so tight the pain made her dizzy. He held the knife so casually in that powerful hairy hand. He was no raging woman, and no fat fool. He was a beast, the embodiment of every enemy she had ever faced.

A monstrous tide of anger welled in Florie's breast. She couldn't hold it back. It grew like the hurricane clouds, boiled, swirled, enveloping her in a force so great she couldn't resist.

When the man slipped his knife back inside his coat and came toward her, hands outstretched flexing, Florie felt strength flow into her arms. Her eyes narrowed. Her lips moved back over her clenched teeth. She ceased to be afraid. Thoughts of John fled. She faced her murderer with one thought: death.

He came closer and closer. His fingers barely touched her shoulders and suddenly she was the very essence of the hurricane, a whirling, driving fury of teeth and nails.

She opened Miles Mercedes' face and neck with her hate. He was her father, Fabrienne, Wendell…Her hate couldn't be contained. If the man didn't take his knife quickly and be done with her, she would put out his eyes!

She would take his own knife and carve out his heart. She would make him writhe in agony…

"You're a little hellcat!" he panted, still smiling. He had her now, and it was hard to do more damage to his face.

She felt his lips tearing under the attack of her nails and she enjoyed hurting him. She wanted more! More!

A white-hot pain exploded in her head and she fell.

Stars burst behind her rolling eyes. He had hit her! He hit her again! She tasted mud…blood. He was on her now. His hands were on her legs, his mouth on her face. She couldn't stop him…couldn't stop him…

She felt as if she was floating in a thick cold sea. She seemed to have all the time in the world to think and could gaze at the animal grinning over her exposed breasts with calm and calculating hate.

The wind began to rise again.

Its low howl grew like the revulsion in Florie's belly. Like a massive wave, the new wind blasted them with such force Miles was thrown aside. The storm had turned, and if possible, the wind was even stronger than before.

Florie tried to shield herself from the driving pellets of rain. Mud oozed into her mouth and ears. She wondered if she could drown and the thought made her so much more angry she began again to lash at the man.

Miles threw himself across her, driving out her breath. Her chest ached. Her belly convulsed and she felt vomit rising in her throat. He would not do this! Of all the degradations she'd ever endured, this would not be one of them.

His mouth opened for her breast, and the sight drove her mad with denial. She erupted with her whole body. Her thumbs found his eyes. She felt them sink deeper, deeper! He screamed. His eyeballs felt soft and wet, and she pushed with savage, teeth-gritting glee.

His howling reached the pitch of the wind. Suddenly she was lying backwards in the mud. She tried to get up and kept falling back. Her lungs were empty and felt flat, dead, helpless. The warmth of her own blood on her legs afforded her a little more strength but it was going fast.

This time there was no escape. This was a battle to the death. Miles lay on his side turned away from her, one hand over his eyes. Before he looked up, Florie kicked his shoulder with both feet and sent him toppling into the deepest mudpit beneath an uprooted tree.

She scrambled after him and threw herself onto his back. He reared up like a stallion and pulled the knife from the tangle of his heavy coat.

"Now I've got you," he roared, falling back, crushing her into the soft mud.

There was no time to think, no moment to judge. Florie just lay still as he rolled atop her. He pinned her throat with his free hand and raised the knife.

As his lips crashed into her jaw, she clamped her eyes shut. Her nose stung where his forehead struck her, and she thought it must be broken.

Then she drove her own forehead into his nose. He lifted up his face in a howl of pain. Florie grabbed the hand holding the knife with both of hers and felt a flash of pain as the blade slipped across her palm. She twisted and bit into his arm. He jerked away, dropping the knife.

Together they grappled for it. His breath was hot on her face, his body heavy on hers. A surge of triumph soared through her veins when her trembling fingers closed around the slim knife handle hidden in the mud.

Without hesitation, she jabbed blindly. The knife sliced deeply into the side of his throat! She pushed harder and felt resistance. Die! she thought, delivering all her strength into another mighty push.

They hung suspended.

He looked surprised.

His life quivered through the blade like a slender thread of lightning, so tiny, yet so vital. And draining like the hot river of blood pouring onto her hand.

The ugly gurgle of his silenced cry told Florie she'd done the impossible.

His eyes bulged. Then he sagged, fell upon his face, arched up so that Florie was able to slide out from under him. Then he fell heavily with a little splash.

She sat a moment watching him. He didn't move. The mud rose gently over his cheeks and forehead as if trying to swallow him.

Florie let the wind lay her back. The rain tasted like tears. Her eyes felt like sore suns. Every inch of her body ached.

When she looked, the body was half-submerged. She began to kick at the soggy earth and soon he was completely covered.

With her hands, her feet, her whole body, she pushed more and more mud into the watery pit. Let hell take him! Let him be gone forever!

Then she lay still. The storm washed her. The hurricane had been her enemy. Now it was her friend. She had become one with the wind and rain and crashing waves. The force of them had been her fury and now was her respite.

So far. So far she had come. She had stood fast, and won. Now she would sleep, sleep in the peaceful lands of her childhood, in the place where storms couldn't reach.

Crawling to a muddy patch of grass near the wall, Florie curled herself into a comfortable ball. With eyelids heavy, she looked across the watery pits and hillocks of mud until they faded from her sight.

When the wind stopped and the rain softened, Florie closed her weary eyes. As the land quivered in the light of dawn, she stole away home.

Sunlight fell through the clouds in golden shafts. John reached Atlantic Avenue and stopped a moment waiting for the dizziness to pass. His hand went to a huge knot on his crown and he winced.

People were stirring now, picking among muddy debris, surveying demolished homes and soggy shacks. He didn't bother looking to the harbor where his yard and ships would be in rubble. He could see Florie's house now, mute on the rise, windows shattered, shredded curtains limp over dripping sills.

A carriage thundered past. Clods of mud flew up and struck John in the face. He cleared his eyes with his wet sleeve.

The longer he staggered, the farther DeMarsett House looked. At last he reached the door and found that same carriage stopped ankle deep in the mud before the portico. Anxious voices called from beyond the glistening brick wall. Young trees lay against its upper edge, their bedraggled, broken branches hanging over, leaves shredded.

John stumbled through the crooked gate and saw Dr. Baines, an old woman and a servant girl holding Florie's child on her hip, standing near the wall. Wendell stood apart from them looking winded and confused.

"Get back," the doctor shouted, taking a blanket from the old woman. Then he lifted what looked like a slender body from the mud.

When John saw the doctor's face, his heart grew cold. He threw out his hand and followed the doctor to the kitchen yard. He couldn't seem to speak. A shaft of pain was splitting his head, and he was afraid.

Great pools of murky water reflected the fragile morning sunlight. Everything smelled fresh and earthy, new like spring, and surprisingly clean.

John's eyes began to hurt. His throat ached. Oh, Florie, he thought. My love…

Dr. Baines carried his delicate burden up the leaf-littered back stairs. When he saw John, he stopped, looking vastly irritated.

The old woman holding the battered kitchen door open rubbed at her swollen eyes with the corner of her shawl. Wendell had already gone inside. Briefly he met John's eyes but looked as if he didn't recognize him.

Like one beaten to insensibility, Wendell looked around shaking his head.

"Roebling," Dr. Baines demanded. "Are you hurt?"

"I was felled by a tree," John said coming closer, one hand on his welt, the other outstretched. "Is she…"

"The poor child was here all alone during the hurricane," Mrs. Worley wailed. "We shouldn't have left her! I told you we shouldn't have left her!" Her cry was directed toward Wendell who was now moving out of John's sight, drifting from one ransacked chamber to another. He didn't seem to hear the old woman.

Dr. Baines climbed to the top step. He looked down at Florie hanging limp in his arms. Her head lolled against his chest and her eyes came open. She made a soft mew.

"We don't know what happened," Thomas said swallowing. "We...
don't know."

John stopped at the bottom step. After a moment of looking up
hoping, hoping, his hand fell to his side. He watched the old woman lean
close to Florie and pat her white cheeks. "She don't see me, Doctor! I
don't think she knows we're here. It's like before," she added in a secretive
whisper. "The storm unhinged her." Mrs. Worley pressed a red knuckle
to her mouth. "And all this blood..."

The word drove through John like a harpoon.

"I didn't know she was pregnant again," the doctor said as they went
inside. The door creaked shut. "I think she must have miscarried. Maybe
she was trying to get to me..." He threw back his head, his cheeks lumpy
with tension. "I'll see to your head later, John. Right now I..." He called
back but John had turned away.

John's lips began to twist to one side. He took several uncertain
steps toward the gate, glanced back once toward the kitchen door, then
moved on.

Now his head tilted a bit to the left. His shoulders had rounded. As
he turned onto the road he seemed to sink into himself.


Thomas laid Florie upon her wind-ruffled bed. Mrs. Worley stood just
outside her door making brave little smiles for young Byron. She touched
a stray curl behind his protruding pink ears. "I'll bet the lad's hungry,"
she crooned, closing Florie's door. She and Martha went down to tidy the
kitchen and start the hearth fire.

Within Florie's sunny chamber Thomas sank suddenly to a chair
beside her bed. He had sat beside her far too often in the past years. She
had a welt on her temple, bruises both old and fresh along her jaw and
arms. A deep cut, perhaps from a broken windowpane, opened one palm
and would require sewing.

And the soul-wrenching evidence of a very recent miscarriage...

He covered his eyes a moment, gathering strength. She had already
lost so much blood he could scarcely hear her heart beating. He mustn't
use the leeches to draw out any poison in her system. If she lived, she
would do so on her own strength.

Without thinking, he slipped to his knees beside her and clasped her
cut palm with his thin white fingers. The sight of her empty eyes, her
steady shallow breathing, the unmistakable absence of her being, was

too much.

After a time he stood, his face set in a professional grimace. He opened his bag and began to minister to her wounds. He paused only once to wipe his wet cheeks.

Below, in the study, Wendell stared at a bag of coins laying in plain sight upon his desk. So much was missing. Why not this? Where was Miles? Why had he failed?

They lived! Both of them. Wendell blinked as if he, too, had gone mindless. The weeping throughout the house was maddening. He kicked his door shut and sat down.

After a moment he looked up, his brows knotted. His eyes rolled from one shadowy corner to the next. Ghostly thoughts walked along his spine. He felt as if someone was watching him, and he wanted to hide.

# PART THREE

## 1819

## Twelve

Her mother's hand always felt so warm. Her bed was a soft cloud of white linens and lacy coverlets, a haven of plump feather pillows. Her mother always smiled, and together they would laugh and sing. Together they drank mint tea and ate sweet cakes. All around was the song of birds, the heat of perpetual summer, the gentle rush of wind through live oaks.

How quiet was this world with her mother. Florie felt so safe, so small and pretty and special. No other world existed. She was forever six years old, petted, pampered, cherished. The bed was a vast beach of comfort that faded into a misty baby blue sky. Here no trouble existed. She and Mama needed only to decide which game to play next, which cheek to kiss next, which hand to touch hers forever and always.

Sometimes her mother's misty bedchamber could dissolve into a stretch of golden sand. There, in the heavenly bed which stood in the sunshine, Florie and her mother would watch a magnificent horseman ride along the water's edge beyond. He'd move beside the rolling waves which nibbled at the edge of her misty dream world. Florie would feel a longing to follow him.

She would rise from the bed. When her feet touched the sand and carried her away from her haven, she would grow tall and beautiful. Her breasts would tingle and swell with the desire for this man. She would call to him and begin running.

Then she would stop and look back at the bed growing hazy behind her. Her mother looked so beautiful against the pillows, but her face would grow pale as if she was suddenly, inexplicably ill.

Florie would always run back, her woman's body shrinking into that of a child's again. Her desire would fade and once again she'd feel the warmth of her mother's hand on hers, the soft safety of the misty bed and the soothing caress of being cherished.

The rider would fade into a distant shadow, but Florie would feel happy there with her mother and they would begin again to laugh and play.


Florie found herself running through the sand toward the rider as often happened. This time, however, the forever summer sun wasn't hot on her back making her feel sensuous and full of longing for the man on the great chestnut horse.

This time she felt cold.

She couldn't remember when she had last felt cold.

She knew only comfort, only happiness, and occasionally desire. Now? Now her shoe-pinched feet met a hard surface. She moved through a cold space shivering in a penetrating wind. She heard not the rush of waves or her mother's laughter but rustling branches and birds singing a different song.

Florie felt as if she was falling.

A savage corset crushed her ribs. A heavy mantle rested on her shoulders. A voice as repulsive and hissing as a water snake's rankled her ear. Ahead was a wide stone path lined with nodding tulips and blades of tender green grass. The stones were damp with dew.

Florie resisted the sharp urging hand of someone walking beside her. She tried to close her eyes to the sight of trees waving budded branches in the chill spring wind.

Wind.

She wanted to return to the warmth and safety of the bed, but nowhere could she see her mother. Nowhere lay the vast pale sea, nor the rider who never spoke but always rode by beguiling her.

Where was this place she was walking? Who was this person pulling her arm? Where had she seen that great stone house before?

"Are you tired so quickly? Sit then."

The voice was familiar. Florie shuddered.

The back of an iron bench bit into Florie's shoulder blades. She twined her fingers in the cold lace-work, painted white. The place felt unfamiliar yet somehow she knew she had been there before.

She knew this garden, that stretch of red brick wall softened now by tendrils of ivy snaking along the pale lines of mortar. The trees, hedges and stone paths were new.

Why couldn't she find her mother's bed? She tried to call out, but her lips didn't move.

"What did you say? Did you speak? Martha!—Where is that worthless, ugly girl? Martha! Fetch the doctor! Florie spoke!"

No, Florie thought. She had tried to speak.

For a great while now she hadn't been aware of this woman's body. She'd lived most often as her child-self, laughing with her mother on the soft bed. Only when the handsome rider rode by did Florie grow tall and slender—and she never spoke, not to him.

She had tried to speak now, she thought again, but her lips hadn't moved. Had they? "Mrs. Worley?" she whispered with what felt like a thick tongue.

"Oh, you mindless thing! Can't you see I'm not that hag? Oh, my lord! You did speak! Martha, fetch the doctor at once!"

Florie turned to the woman speaking beside her. She drew back in horror.

That face! That cold, white face! That honey-colored hair!

Florie was falling, spinning, gasping…

"What's wrong with you today? Sit up and take your sun, or I'll pinch you again, and harder. Sit up! I didn't believe for a moment you were mad. You nearly fooled me, but I know your tricks. You're still an awful, willful child. I wouldn't have come to this horrid cold place except your husband couldn't manage you. That hag must've led you about like a baby. Sit up, I say!"

"Mama?" Florie whimpered with a constricted throat. "Take me back…"

The woman with the pale hair laced with years stared at Florie with wide amber eyes. Then she drew back, her thin lips curled.

Martha trotted up the stone path from the direction of the house. Florie recognized her, though the nursemaid looked thinner and older. Florie would've told her how pretty she looked, but suddenly her attention was taken by a boy beside her.

He wore a dark blue velvet riding habit with a wide lace-trimmed collar. He slapped a little riding crop against his dusty thigh and stared at her with open suspicion. His curls were soft brown like…His eyes were little and hard like…His face was soft and round like…

Wendell!

Florie softly voiced the name. A wave of surprise swept over her. Her brow grew moist and her heart began to race.

"She's indeed speaking!" Fabrienne exclaimed clutching at her own heavy mantle and coughing. "Stop gaping, girl! I told you she was faking—speechless all these years—ridiculous!"

"Mrs. DeMarsett?" Martha breathed, creeping close so that Florie could see her. Martha ignored Mademoiselle Gautier's mutterings. "Can you see me, M'lady?"

"See you?" Florie whispered.

"Lord have mercy!" Martha wept. "She's back!" She stood and clapped the tubby boy's hands for him. "Your mama's well again, Byron! Praise God! Say good morning and give her a little kiss. Oh, Missus! If only Auntie could know…" Her face ran with happy tears.

The boy hung back. He looked so tall, Florie thought. He must be seven…eight…

"She was faking!" Fabrienne snapped. Her fingers found Florie's thigh hidden under many skirts and pinched, smiling through her teeth. "You don't know her as I do. She was a wild child."

The blackness that had begun to fill Florie's mind again instantly evaporated.

Pain…

Other places on her arms and legs ached as if she had been pinched recently and often. A white light of anger blotted out the swelling darkness. Florie watched Martha race out the garden gate calling a man's name, a name that pleased Florie. Thomas.

The boy took one more suspicious look at Florie and darted away.

Through the gate.

In the brick wall.

The trees. Pain. Wind and rain…

Florie leaped to her feet. The dreamy mist-world faded. The sweet memory of her mother's bed faded. The handsome rider disappeared one last time into the distant shadows of her mind. All that remained was this garden with trees arranged in pretty rows and groups. There, beyond a perfect hedgerow dusted with pale green buds, was a stone fountain spitting a fine silvery spray into the pool.

Names and faces flashed through Florie's mind. Her garden. Her house. Her sister. Her husband...

There he was now waddling red-faced around a stand of slender birches shimmering in the wind.

Wind. Trees. Rain. Mud...

"No!" Florie took a few clumsy steps back along the path. Let the mist return, she begged of her mind. Take me back to the soft light, the warm hands, the love. Let me stay there, please dear Lord! Let me stay where I'm happy. I don't belong here!

The mist began to come just as it always had for Florie when the real world became unbearable. In her mind the sun began to shine. The wind-ruffled sea appeared and stretched to the horizon. And there, beyond the sun-drenched sand was the bed and her mother waiting, smiling.

How good she looked, so beautiful, so loving, the only person in Florie's life who mattered. The cold wind faded. The hated voices, the hard surface of the stone path that led to death! It all faded.

She stood very still, her vision growing vague...and yet she felt puzzled.

Suddenly her hands spread across a gentle bulge in her belly.

She blinked. Her hands cupped tender swollen breasts, patted cheeks cooled by a spring wind.

She felt movement! Under her trembling hands was a special turn and flutter of life!

Behind her she heard hasty footsteps. Large, gentle hands closed over her shoulders, caressingly warm, cherishing hands she knew well.

"Florie?" came a voice deep and familiar, a voice she hadn't heard in a long, long while. The voice made her feel safe there in the real world. "Are you back with us?" Thomas whispered.

Was she?

Florie felt the call of her misty dream world, but her hands clutched at her skirts, spreading the muslin until she could feel the whole of the new life cradled in her belly.

Dear God, she thought, she couldn't go back now!

A child lived within her, a child she thought she had lost, a special wonderful fulfilment she could cherish and protect unto death.

"Florie?" Thomas whispered turning her around. He, too, looked older, not by much but enough to further mark his face with care.

A brief memory of the rider crossed her mind, but Florie couldn't remember his name now. Besides, he was only a fantasy. She blinked, searching Thomas' face. She knew she'd been away. Still, she'd never been alone. Mrs. Worley had protected her nights…

"Mrs. Worley?" she said, her fingers spread over her belly as if defending it already against this world to which she had just returned.

"Do you remember, Florie? She became ill. Then…" Thomas paused. Florie wished she could erase those lines in his broad forehead. "She died, dear, I…stayed with you then…until your sister arrived from New Orleans a few months ago. You were never alone…I didn't think she'd be much comfort to you, but Wendell insisted. Come. You look exhausted. And you must take great care. Do you hear me, dear?"

Florie looked at him.

Though a sharp-eyed spinster watched and the husband approached with caution, Thomas put his arms around Florie and pulled her close.

"Welcome home, my dearest. Forgive me for what I've done. I couldn't seem to help myself. I wanted so to bring you back. Do you remember you lost the other baby? This one is…" His voice was nearly inaudible. "Ours."

"What's going on now?" Wendell called, glancing at Florie with a sour grimace. He consulted a heavy gold watch suspended on a chain across his belly. "Is she better or worse?"

Dr. Baines pulled away from Florie and let Wendell see for himself. Visibly Wendell twitched at the sight of her.

She stood erect, her eyes clear, her face calm and commanding. Pulling her mantle tightly across her breasts, she walked toward the house. "I'd like to be called by my given name from now on," she said. "Floris. I'm not a child any longer." As she passed her sister, she looked up into the cold suspicious eyes and said, "I hope you enjoyed your visit."

Fabrienne opened her mouth. She turned to Wendell, enraged.

Thomas loped after Florie, his face split with a grin.

Wendell turned away, sucked in his flaccid cheeks and spit into a hedge.

Four months later, in September of 1819, Floris DeMarsett gave birth to a beautiful, healthy daughter.

Thomas Baines assisted a capable midwife. As Floris lay recovering that warm afternoon, he kissed her rosy cheek. Their eyes shared the secret joy of the moment. Then Thomas suggested she name the infant suckling at her breast Loraine, after his mother.

She liked the name. Loraine Gautier DeMarsett. She would someday be the belle of Union Harbor. And she would be very happy!

Wendell DeMarsett wasn't at home that day, and his eight-year-old son, Byron, threw a tantrum when he was taken out for a day-long ride in the country.

Captain DeMarsett, no longer called captain and sometimes not even sir, lingered at King's Horse Tavern drinking himself into a stupor. Always he looked to be waiting for someone.

Ruby Mercedes, mistress of the tavern, tolerated his presence only because he overpaid; she knew of a physick willing to treat his secret ague. She was generally a bitter woman having been deserted by a husband of shiftless character.

Soon after Loraine's birth, Floris, now thirty-one, rose from childbed to take charge of her household.

She was unable to win over the love and trust of her son, and so reluctantly left him to Martha, the nursemaid. The household accounts seemed in fine order. She hired a new parlor maid, raised the cook's wage and went about her daily duties as if she hadn't spent four years oblivious to all.

In time she'd give teas and dinners. She acted as if she didn't remember those blank years. Indeed, she didn't. She lived as if she had never set foot on the beach. Neither did she express any interest in sketching. When, one afternoon, a message arrived by private courier she read it with a puzzled frown.

"What does this mean?" she asked Thomas who was there for his visit with the new infant. He was bending over the draped and ruffled cradle making silly faces. "Should I invite this gentleman or his wife to dinner? Does Wendell know him through business?"

The handwritten note read: Florie, will you see me now? It was signed, John Roebling.

Thomas looked at her with alarm.

Her eyes were clear and innocent. She didn't remember! Maybe she didn't understand what was between them, either! Could she know of his love or those sultry nights they spent together while she was ill?

She seemed to remember nothing more than she wanted to remember. Her only concern was her lovely child. Their child. Now that Thomas thought about it, Florie acted as if Wendell were Loraine's father! She did, however keep him at a healthy distance.

One day Thomas suggested they take a short walk up the road to see how Union Harbor was growing. He insisted on a particular time and seemed unduly nervous. He talked of going all the way to his own house to visit his wife and sons.

Florie—Floris, however tired easily. Though she enjoyed the sight
of the expanding town, she seemed uneasy for the first time since spring.
They had just started back when a man approached on a winded horse.
He came to a dusty stop beside them and jumped down.

Their conversation was stilted: Good day, sir. Fine weather. No signs
of tropical storms brewing…

Thomas felt sick when John Roebling greeted Floris and peered into
her reserved eyes.

John had fared the worst of them. His hair had gone heavily gray
since last they met. The spark and zest were gone from his eyes. His
health was fading, and around his mouth was a network of creases
bespeaking bitterness and an ever-consuming preoccupation with work.

After only a few moments John rode away, his mouth twisted so
severely Thomas wondered if he had suffered a small hemorrhage in
his brain.

Then Thomas and Floris returned to DeMarsett House talking
of unimportant things. Floris' eyes were still blessedly free of any past
knowledge. She seemed relaxed again, and Thomas vowed to leave her
that way.

"I'll be going now, dear," he said with his throat tightening. "I'm
afraid I won't be able to call as often. I don't think you'll be needing me
much anyway. My patients increase with my age and reputation."

Floris laughed. The sun shimmered in her hair. She was so beautiful,
so fragile. Impossibly, she was happy!

He could see that. She breathed in the rich autumn smells, her
face aglow. Then she opened her eyes, dark, deep, hypnotic. She looked
down the road. A faint line appeared between her brows. "Who was that
gentleman, Thomas? Why did he stop us? Why did he look at me so?"

Thomas swallowed. "That was John Roebling, the widower."

"Did I once know him?"

# BOOK TWO

## Loraine

# PART ONE

## 1837

## Thirteen

Beau Mercedes paused at the low stone wall. He puzzled out the letters burnt into the small wooden sign hanging from the post: Dr. James Roebling. Then he peered through the leafy darkness at the small red brick house.

So, this was Yolanda's place. He pushed back his cap. It looked like she was damned close to her dream. She was living on the Roebling Estate only three miles from the main house. Give her a little while longer and she'd have that, too.

He rounded the wall and found his way behind the blooming lilacs to the back. One window glowed with a faint light. He knocked, expecting to wait. The hour was late, the woods dark and silent. His sister would be sleeping...

Only seconds later the door swung open. Yolanda, in a yellow silk dressing gown, recoiled in shock.

The lamplight nearly blinded Beau. "Have I changed that much?" he asked laughing.

Yolanda's studied poise fell away. She threw out her arms. "You old wharf rat! Where did you come from? Come inside before you're seen!"

She kept her voice low and then fairly yanked Beau inside. Shushing him, she looked out across the moonlit yard and then closed the door.

She drew him along a shadowy hallway to a warm kitchen.

"James is out on a call," she said. "I'm glad to see you again, but you can't stay here!"

Beau took a straight back chair from the corner and sat in it backwards. "I can stay and intend to," he said watching her search her pantry shelves for a quick meal. Then she poured a goblet of wine. She kept glancing at a clock standing on the mantle over the huge stone hearth.

This easy life as doctor's wife hadn't softened her. Beau had forgotten how Yolanda's blue eyes could flash.

"James may not shoot you on sight," she said dispassionately. "But Adam will if he learns you're here."

"Would you betray your own brother?" Beau held her gaze until she reddened and looked away.

She pushed the wine at him. "I should! I've lived in hell these past five years. Did you have to murder the Old Man?"

Beau closed his fist around the goblet's stem. He bolted the wine and then snapped the stem between his sunburned, work-scarred fingers. "The Old Man pushed me to it. He laughed at me. He said I'd never captain a ship until I could read logs and charts."

"Fool!" she hissed flowing around her kitchen in her whispering yellow gown. "*Killing* John Roebling! Then off to sea without a word to me. I thought you dead! Now I live in the midst of the Roebling bitterness. Adam hates me. I'll never forgive you."

Beau's jaw tightened. "You have your wealth. What have I? All I've ever wanted was to captain a ship."

She pulled another chair close and sat. "And you still haven't learned to read. You'd best learn to make do, Beau. Like me. Let's stop this friendly chatter. You didn't walk all this way from the wharf to bid me hello. You've come for money. What trouble are you in this time?"

"Don't bother your head. I need money, yes, and I'd like a new coat. Boots, too, if you can spare them."

Yolanda laughed and touched his hand. Her fingers felt cold.

As if afraid to break the silence, the clock chimed midnight. The moon cast long shafts of white light across the lawns outside the windows. Yolanda had enough of her dream, Beau thought. He felt shamed that he still searched for his, and had to hide in shadows everywhere he went.

"I missed you," she said. "I'm so alone here."

"I'm sure James still worships you," Beau said as if he hadn't a care.

Yolanda pushed herself away. "You know he never did. I tricked him just as you *tried* to trick Old Man Roebling. We've made a mess of things, we have. Don't look about my kitchen like that. James is a poor second. I've got about as much hope of getting Adam now as you that ship. You ought to know second best is nothing. Oh, be on your way! You haven't changed."

"You're in a ripe hurry to be rid of me."

"I don't need more of your trouble."

Beau wiped his mouth and leaned back. "Would you deny this weary sailor a bed for one night?"

Jumping up, Yolanda ran to her back door. A rider dismounted outside.

With his smile falling away, Beau rose and slipped into a shadowy corner. "Is it James?"

"Hide yourself in the parlor. Hurry!"

A thin young dandy burst through the back door and swept Yolanda into his arms.

"Unhand me!" she cried to the grinning man kissing her.

Beau slipped his dagger back in his boot and met his sister's discomfited eyes. Then he laughed. Like all the Roebling boys, her lover was tall, but he wasn't James. No wonder Yolanda had been so surprised to see him outside her back door—and eager for him to leave!

Conrad Roebling, youngest of the clan, stood lean and charming-looking in a gray full-skirted frockcoat and pinstriped trousers. Seeing that Yolanda had a visitor, Conrad removed his gloved hands from her waist. "You're back," he said grinning at Beau with languid dark eyes.

"My, my, dear sister," Beau smirked looking at the quality and cut of Conrad's coat with envy. "Do you aim to conquer all the Roebling men?"

"I didn't know he was coming back," Yolanda said to Conrad. "You'll have to come some other time."

Beau chuckled. "Does your husband approve of this match?"

Yolanda's lips compressed into a thin line. A few well placed words from him could end her marriage and liaison with the Roebling wealth and power.

"I've no desire to hurt you," Beau said at last. "I'm going back to sea as soon as I can. Union Harbor isn't the only town where I'm no longer welcome. Conrad, maybe you can help. I want my own ship."

Finger by finger Conrad tugged at his gloves. He had his father's dark eyes though now they twinkled with amusement. He put his fine boot on the chair and flicked dust from the polished toe. "*I* have no ships, though if I did it might amuse me to give you one. I had no great love for the Old Man's cold heart. I'm glad to be free of him. A DeMarsett packet might hire you, though. Offhand, I know of no other way."

"DeMarsett?"

"The fat old jock—surely you know of him. Most of the time he's drunk as a lord. He sails a few ships to Africa. Enough to live well. Not enough to get caught."

Beau nibbled the cheese and bread Yolanda set before him. "I want to captain my own ship."

"Then you'll have to steal such wealth. Or marry it. You know, of course, old DeMarsett has a choice young daughter ready for market. Loraine's her name. I've been invited to her coming out ball next week. I ordered a fine new coat from my tailor. Forest green serge." He made a charming smile.

Yolanda glared at him.

"Such cat's eyes," Conrad chuckled. "Are you jealous of an eighteen-year-old babe?"

"Take your horse and be gone," she hissed.

"Such a dreadful face, Yolanda. Would you deny me a wife? Oh, I see you would. I'm flattered you care so deeply. *I* must endure your lusting after my eldest brother and the warming of the marriage bed of my other brother yet *I* cannot hope for such daily comforts."

"Enough!" Yolanda snapped. "You both best be gone before James gets back." She stalked to the hall. "I have some money, Beau. And I'll hunt up a coat James won't miss. You can't go about town like that." She sniffed at Beau's bell-trousers and seaman's shirt. "But you'll have to leave tomorrow." She disappeared in a whisper of silk.

"So," Beau said smiling at Conrad. "Have you been at my sister long?"

"Long enough to know she still wants Adam. Don't tell her, but I mean to marry that kitten, Loraine DeMarsett. For the daughter of a pig, Loraine is a surprise indeed. And said to be fresh as the dawn."

"I take it Adam still wants my heart."

"On a stick," Conrad chuckled.

The coat Yolanda found pinched across the chest, but Beau liked it. He felt less conspicuous about the streets of Union Harbor the next morning.

It was a fine spring day, green and fragrant. As he headed for the wharf and the offices of Wendell DeMarsett, he thought of the curious events that led him to this man at this particular time.

Returning to his port of call had already dredged up much of Beau's past. The memories of his childhood at King's Horse Tavern held a tender spot in his otherwise calloused heart. Yolanda had been a pretty, spoiled child. His mother had always worked hard. Now she was dead.

He thought, too, of the night his father left. Few hurricanes ever came so far north. When one did, a boy of six didn't forget.

For years Beau had wondered what became of his father. Had he drowned in the storm, or had he, as some suggested, just gone away?

Beau reached the wharf and DeMarsett Shipping's door. He paused, puzzling out the sign. Wendell DeMarsett had been in the tavern that particular stormy night.

The door opened to a frown of clerks hunched over ledgers. The place looked prosperous enough. "Is DeMarsett in?" Beau demanded, the sound of his own full voice a pleasure.

"I'm Wendell DeMarsett," came a gravelly noise in a side doorway.

The man filling it was as large as a whale. His cheeks were red and veined, his nose like a root. He wore a fine coat for one so large, though it was rumpled.

"May we speak privately, Captain?"

Wendell's small eyes opened as if seeing Beau with greater interest. He stepped aside. Beau entered the private office and waited until the door was closed.

Wendell seated himself behind a cluttered desk. He spent several moments licking and lighting an impressive cigar. When he glanced up, Beau knew he was unsettled.

"Remember me, Captain? I served you many a tankard of ale before I went to sea."

Wendell's lips trembled as if he couldn't quite bring himself to speak. "*Beau* Mercedes?"

"Aye, Captain. I'll get to the point. I hear you have a packet to Africa. Is it the Black Trade?"

"One leg of it. I might consider hiring you if..."

"No, thanks, Captain, sir. It's not that I care what I do or where I go. I just want to captain a ship of my own. I'm here to persuade you to give one to me."

"I give nothing away!"

Beau smiled.

Puffing on that wick of leaves, the fat old man looked suddenly confident.

"In time, maybe? After your daughter's ball? I'd like to meet her. I hear she's lovely. I may not be what you'd want in a suitor, but I'd be content with a dance or two. I see you object. I had hoped you'd issue me an invitation just because you were once friends with my father."

Wendell DeMarsett's eyes sharpened. "What do you know of that?"

"I remember you were the last to talk with him before he disappeared. The night of the hurricane, it was. September 1815. I remember it well, Captain. Don't you?"

Wendell pulled out a desk drawer. Beau moved his hand nearer his boot. After much fumbling, Wendell tied a leather thong around a small brown paper packet. "We might do a little business," he said leaning forward.

Beau licked his lips. His palms itched as he took the captain's offering.

Before letting go, Wendell made a piggish smile. "I expect a return on this investment."

"I knew it was only a matter of discovering what service I might be to you," Beau said smiling.

Wendell released the packet. "You'll have no ship now, Mercedes. Times are hard and grow harder by the day. I do have a plan, though. It would be to your advantage that my plan succeeds."

"Would it?"

"I might have a ship for you then."

Beau tucked the unopened packet inside his coat. "For a ship I'll do anything, Captain, sir."

"Stay clear of my daughter then. I'm arranging her marriage. If I get the settlement I want, you might get a ship."

"Have I your word?" Beau enjoyed Wendell's jowls trembling at the tender insult.

"Have I yours?"

"I have no need for a maiden, Captain, not even one as fresh and lovely as your Loraine. It seems only right, though, to know your plan since my ship rests on it. Who is she to marry?"

"I'll be offering her to Adam Roebling," Wendell whispered. "I mean to merge with his line."

"You aim at the moon, sir!" Beau grinned. "His young wife died only months ago."

"That doesn't concern me. I want a merger and will have it. Roebling will want my girl. I'm belly-deep in debt to be sure he will." He expelled a billow of white smoke. "Where are you staying, Mercedes? Not at the tavern."

"No, with my sister."

Wendell's eyes opened even wider. "At the estate?"

"None other. Of course, I keep myself small. I did hear, however that Conrad has set his sights on your fair flower. Does that interest you?"

"You've already earned that packet. Next week, after Loraine's ball, come to me again. I'll have more money for you. I'll be planning DeMarsett-Roebling Shipping by then."

Beau gave a little salute. "Good to see you again, Captain."

Outside, the sun seemed hotter. Shoremen and cargo crowded the wharf. Beau walked out to two DeMarsett barks being unloaded of Cuban rum. He smiled up at the tangle of yardarms and lines. He'd take that newer one, thank you, sir, you old fart.

He perched on a bale of cotton destined for an inland mill. His luck had turned at last. When he saw two of his mates from the last voyage, Beau went after them for a bite and a drop at the nearest tavern. As he ate and talked and laughed, he thought of Loraine DeMarsett.

His curiosity was up indeed. He'd never seen her. She was almost ten years younger. Was DeMarsett a fool, or was she really enough to interest Beau's illustrious brother-in-law, Adam Roebling, heir to the Roebling Line?

Wouldn't such a marriage fry poor Yolanda's adultering heart? Beau chuckled. Then bidding his mates farewell, he was off to see for himself. This maid best be the most ripe of fruits, or he wouldn't get his vessel.

Towering oaks reaching protective branches over the hump of cobblestones lined Atlantic Avenue. Beau followed a walk of field stone and ran his hand along white wooden pickets. The houses were magnificently large. It was like when he was younger and wandering the streets dreaming of the rich people behind the glistening windowlights. The biggest houses had been built by famous sea captains. Beau wanted one.

Just before he reached DeMarsett's house, he ran his rough hand over a brick pillar connected to the next by black ironwork topped with spikes. Now *there* was a house!

Up the shallow crescent drive that curved under the portico, he could see a stooped gardener laboring over some climbing pink roses. The rest of the harsh gray stone wall was lost under a cloak of glossy ivy.

Beyond was a high brick wall, also alive with ivy. The old toad was better off than he remembered. Beau plucked a pointy leaf and moved on down the street.

The garden wall extended for nearly a block before angling off to enclose the acre of trees. The cobbles ended at a wood of oaks and from there the road curved on southward following the coastline. It was said to meet Boston Path.

Because houses had been built across the street, the best place to observe DeMarsett House was from the wood. There Beau sat for nearly an hour fingering the bank notes Wendell had put in the packet. He watched a maid airing linens out an upper window.

Through the branches Beau could see beyond to the bluffs. Growing bored, he walked a ways and discovered two paths to the beach below.

Tumbling down one, he came upon a cove and sheltered beach. One side was separated from the rest of the shore by a broad line of low rocks. He climbed over it and sat a while where he could enjoy the sweep of the sea.

Already he missed it. The sea was a fickle mistress, fitted with storms and calms, and as deep as death, but he wanted her. He wanted his hand at a helm taming the wind, cutting waves to distant shores, and wealth. He wanted so much. His mother had often said such ambition was a curse.

Looking back he could see that stone-built house on the far side of the wall. He suspected that hurricane of his boyhood had eaten away much of the bluff. Someday another storm might swallow that house and its fat old master. Beau chuckled. His fine house would be farther inland and protected by trees—like the Roebling mansion. Then he shook his head. He wanted the same things his sister wanted. But Yolanda had her beauty to bargain with. What did he have?

Beau noticed a small door set in the nearest corner of that far brick wall. When it opened his breath quickened. A young girl crawled out. She ran the length of a path skirting the bluff. Then with reckless speed she plunged down the path cut between brambles and boulders to the dunes.

Without pausing she hiked up her skirts and ran to the waves. She stood like a figurehead, the sea breeze pulling her fall of curls into a swirling deep-gold tangle. Her skirts snapped high like bluebird wings revealing a layer of snowy petticoats underneath. Beau wanted to reach out and snare her.

He needed no introduction. That was Loraine DeMarsett. And, even from that distance, he could tell she was the prettiest girl he'd ever seen.

Quickly he descended the rocky jumble and started across the beach. He put himself between Loraine and her possible retreat. Before long she heard the soft sweep of his boots in the sand. She whirled. They stared at each other. Warmth rushed through Beau's veins. She was more than pretty!

Her hair was the color of sunset, deep and golden. She wore it parted in the center. It framed her creamy oval face with gilt. Her eyes were large and dark, not coffee brown, more sweet, like mocha.

She looked as graceful as waving beach grass, and as provocative. How buxom she was, he couldn't tell by the cut of her droop-shouldered gown. He hated the style, though it did give him a pleasant view of her shoulders and throat.

He expected this hothouse variety of beauty to make a little cry of alarm and run. When she didn't, he paused. Before his eyes her face softened. Her eyes grew large, darkening to a depth and warmth that made him just a bit sorry he'd forsworn a claim on her.

"Afternoon, my lovely," he called, amusing himself. "Bid me hello."

Her cheeks began to glow. When she didn't speak, Beau took a few theatrical steps toward her. "She does not speak. Perhaps she is a vision. How fair she is. How young and comely."

Loraine DeMarsett giggled.

Then she darted away across the sand.

Beau followed and cornered her where the rocks fell into the waves. Standing several paces away, spread-eagled as if still on a pitching deck, he folded his brawny arms.

She was panting, her cheeks aglow and her slender arms akimbo. Her eyes sparkled. She wetted her lips. Beau was sorry, indeed!

"Who *are* you?" she whispered.

With a fanciful bow, Beau introduced himself. "Gracious darling of the beach, I am Beau Mercedes, at your feet. I'm your humble servant and worshipper from afar. And who," he asked just to be certain, "might you be?"

"My name…I'm Loraine DeMarsett!"

And, covering her mouth, she giggled again.

# Fourteen

"It's perfect, Mama! Really it is." Loraine twirled and her pale blue silk gown layered with flounces spread around her feet like an ocean wave. The pearl-trimmed bodice sparkled gently in the sunlight falling through the back parlor windows. She came to a giddy stop before the standing mirror in the corner and couldn't help but smile.

Reflected in the mirror, Loraine could see her mama reclining on the chaise. Smiling, Floris stretched out her arms. She looked posed for a portrait. Her baby-fine honey-colored hair was drawn up in perfect coils on either side of her face. Her dark eyes sparkled like a night sky though they were set deeper now and surrounded with tiny lines. Time had softened her once firm jaw and supple body.

"Mama, thank you!" Loraine said turning. Plucking at the cool folds, she tripped lightly to her mother's side and kissed her cheek. "I'll change now, and you can have your nap. Thank you, Madame Joneaux," she added smiling at the dressmaker waiting near the door with the dignity of a dress form. "You've outdone yourself. I have the loveliest gown in the world."

"And so you should," Floris said. Her words were always softened with a southern accent hinting at her French heritage. "Your coming out ball should be second only to your wedding. I've waited for this so long. Careful now that you don't tear the hem. Rest an hour yourself."

"I want to go to the beach today, Mama. It's warm enough."

"Not again, Loraine. It's not safe."

"But it's so good to get out, Mama! I've been standing here all morning. Please?"

When her mother looked away with a tired sigh, Loraine kissed her again. "I won't stay long."

Filled with happiness, Loraine hurried up to her room. Mama was such a dear! She burst into her bedchamber calling to her maid. Her window overlooking her mama's huge garden stood open to the salt breeze. Before shedding her gown, Loraine leaned out over the crumbly stone sill and drew the sweet spring air deep into her lungs. Then she closed her eyes and sighed.

Beau Mercedes!

She adored the beauty and strength of his name. She hadn't slept all night for thinking about him. Would he come to the beach again?

Her heart ached with hope. What a man! He was no boy like her chum Willy Peltin. Neither was he a dandy like that Roebling fellow Conrad she'd met once at a tea.

Beau Mercedes was more than a man. He was a sun-bronzed, blue-eyed sea god, the very essence of her dreams!

"You'll spoil that silk, Miss!" Teresa said coming into the sunny bedchamber with an armload of newly sewn gowns. "Don't lean so far out!"

Her secret was bursting to be told. Loraine spun around, yet she couldn't tell, not even her maid Teresa, her closest friend.

Loraine was a well-brought-up young lady, schooled ever so patiently at her mother's frail knee. One of her most important lessons had been on strangers. Until she "met" Beau Mercedes properly at her coming out, she could not *know* him.

Teresa unfastened the hooks down Loraine's back. While she carried the dress away for safekeeping, Loraine put on a plain brown muslin. She wiggled impatiently as her curly-haired Irish maid came back and did up the hooks.

Teresa was such a somber thing sometimes, like now, Loraine thought. The whole household was in an uproar over the impending ball—the first party in years—and all Teresa could do was creep about wearing her cow's eyes and her lips bent into a worried line.

She was the only Catholic servant to be found for miles and a godsend to Mama, but sometimes her gloom wore Loraine's love very thin. Loraine would never act like such a cowering ninny. She'd always walk with her head up and do just as she liked!

Tumbling down the servants' stairs moments later, she heard a familiar voice in the front hall. "Uncle Thomas!" she called turning from her escape out the kitchen door. She clapped her hands over her mouth, giggling. Papa didn't approve of old Dr. Baines, but Papa was at work.

"Where are you off to in such a hurry?" Thomas chuckled standing hat in hand, tall and thin like an oak. His head was free of hair except around the tops of his ears and at the nape where it hung long and white.

Loraine rushed to kiss him. "Isn't it a pretty day? I'm going to the beach. I always do when Papa's working."

Cupping the back of her head, Thomas kissed her forehead. "Take care you don't fall from that path."

"So near my ball? Never, Uncle! Why are you here? Did the fitting tire Mama that much?"

"It's the excitement of your coming out, I'm sure," he smiled. "Nothing to bother your pretty head about. Since your Mama's last attack I like to keep a close eye on her." He winked. "While your papa's out, that is."

Their eyes met in a thieves' smile. "She really is getting better, isn't she?"

"Let me worry about her. Go before the sun gets too hot. Don't be gone long though. Your papa may not be in much of a humor when he comes home this evening. On my way here I heard another bank closed."

Loraine tossed her long curls. She knew nothing of banking. "I'll hurry."

Once out in the garden, Loraine slowed. It was the loveliest garden in Union Harbor. Her friends' mothers had always been jealous.

She plucked a fallen leaf left over from last autumn from the water in the small stone pool. Sometimes, as beautiful as this place was, she felt haunted. She looked around, at the tall oaks and birches, and the tender yellow-green lotus tree near the gate. There was sadness here as well as comfort.

She darted down the path. The morning quiet was broken only by birds singing and the moist whisper of new leaves.

When she was small she'd played many a game of tag among these hedges. Her mother had given teas then and the guests' children had run through the green labyrinth like young goats. Loraine and her friend Nicolette Longford had spent hours on the lawns with their bisque dolls and china tea services. Now Nicolette, who was two years older than Loraine, was engaged to Loraine's big brother Byron.

Such folly! Maybe Nicolette *was* a bit homely. And maybe she *had* been compromised by that awful rogue, Conrad Roebling, who wouldn't marry her. (Nicolette wouldn't admit to a thing, and that made it all the worse.) But she didn't have to settle for Byron!

Loraine skirted a part of the garden that always left her uneasy and slipped through a bank of heady lilacs to the tiny back gate where the gardener dumped refuse. Years before she and Bryon had discovered it and could win any game of hide and seek.

Emerging from the thicket on the far side, she saw Beau sitting far below on a rock.

He had come! She covered her mouth to keep back a scream of joy. Gulls soared over his head. Waves lapped at his boots. He looked coarse and solid like the rocks and sand. Her heart leaped as if she'd just snuck a drop of her papa's best rum.

She rubbed her palms against her skirts and adjusted the scooped neckline of her bodice. Lifting her face, she crept along the path hoping to surprise him.

When Beau turned, she knew he couldn't see her. The morning sun had blinded him. Staring back toward her house, his handsome face was tight, and his eyes narrow. Loraine tried to swallow her heart.

She rounded the base of the path, gathered up her skirts and ran toward him. When he saw her his teeth flashed in a smile.

"Good morning!" she called. She cleared her throat and giggled.

Beau leaned back as if the rocks were soft as cushions. When he didn't say anything, she ventured a few steps closer.

"How fair he is." Loraine waved her hand like he had the day before. "Is he a vision?"

He laughed.

Loraine whirled around so he couldn't see her burning cheeks. He aroused in her such a delicious terror! Taking a deep breath, she lifted one arm and with the other embraced the air. She twirled and danced as close to Beau as she dared. "I'm coming out on Saturday," she said beginning to pant. Teresa had laced her to accommodate the new gown with its tiny waist. Loraine paused to catch her breath. "Will you come?"

Beau's smile faded. "I can't."

"Why? I want you there. I don't care if anyone else comes!"

"If I could I would be honored for sure, but I don't have a good coat. Or dancing pumps."

"Oh, that!"

Beau climbed down from the rock perch. His sturdy thighs rippled under his snug breeches. "Let's dance right here." He put out his hand to take her in his arms. "Sing something for me."

Shaking her head, Loraine shrank from him. "I can't sing."

"I thought such ladies as you had tutors and went off to expensive finishing schools." He caught her hand and swept her close in an awkward, silent waltz.

After only a few steps Loraine slipped free and moved away. "Not me. I know a little French—not as much as Mama—and she forgot much of what she knew. I can play the piano and I embroider very well, but Mama wouldn't let me go *away* to school."

"Is that why you're afraid of me?"

"I'm not! You're too forward." She pouted and took a few dancing steps away.

"We haven't much time to get to know each other. I'll sail soon."

"But you can't! I won't allow it. You *must* come to my ball. I want you to meet my mother."

As his face hardened, her heart pinched with pain.

"My sister may have moved into society," he said, "but I haven't. I'm nothing but a sailor. I don't belong at your ball. You wouldn't want your mother to meet me."

Loraine stopped waltzing. "Your sister? You're from Union Harbor? Why haven't I heard of your family?"

"You, my sweet, grew in a different garden." He came toward her with a heavy seductive smile.

Her face grew warm under his gaze. "You talk as if I was a child."

"You are, one far too innocent for your own good." Abruptly he turned from her and went over the rocks in a few cat-like leaps.

When he disappeared on the far side, Loraine followed. Twice she nearly slipped and twisted her ankle. With an awkward tumble she joined Beau in the secluded cove she'd never seen before.

Standing before him, she felt as if she'd crossed more than rocks. She'd crossed from safety to danger, from giggles to passion. That amused twist of Beau's mouth wrenched her heart. Suddenly, impulsively, she grabbed his face and kissed him. His lips were cool and hard and immediately opened to take control of her mouth.

She wrenched free. "You see? I'm not innocent!" But her heart threatened to burst from her chest. She wanted to *run!*

Beau's eyes darkened to the color of the ocean far from shore. When his arms went around her she knew she'd gone too far. She was lost to an undertow.

"My sweet," Beau crooned. He pulled her so tight her breasts squeezed against his chest. "I want you."

Loraine's body turned to liquid fire. Heat rushed through her like lightning. As Beau's mouth closed over hers again, warmer and softer now, she melted with sweet terror. Like a helpless puppy she began to shake. She tried to stop her knees from buckling and nearly fell down.

"Am I frightening you?" He looked curiously tender.

She shook her head. Then she darted away pretending she hadn't kissed him and he hadn't kissed her. She ran to the waves licking the sand dark. She felt nearly sick with desire and fear.

What had she done? Had he compromised her? Was she mad? She looked around at the beach no one else had seen before. Surely no one had ever been so wicked and bold.

She played tag with the waves until her heart slowed. Then she turned.

Beau had gone!

Dear God, no! She scrambled back over the rocks scuffing her ankles and bruising her hands. "Wait for me!"

On the other side Beau was nowhere to be seen.

Where had he gone? She was such a fool! She sank to a rock and buried her face in her hands. She didn't care about her ball anymore. Or her gown. Or anything! The only man in the world for her was Beau Mercedes!

She was so stupid. She scrubbed her eyes and her fists still trembled.

Looking up, she saw her house so solid and dignified there on the edge of the bluff. She hated it! Other houses were pretty and warm, like Uncle Thomas'. Papa wouldn't let her visit there anymore after Mrs. Baines died. Papa was *always* spoiling her happiness.

She wished she was someone else, a wench who knew kisses so well a man like Beau wouldn't frighten her. Then she'd show Papa who she would or would not marry!

Papa was horrible. He drank so much people talked. *Why* did he have to be ugly and smoke those awful cigars? And he always looked at her as if she was a horse—or maybe even a slave—he was considering buying!

She pummeled her knees. She knew what her coming out was really for.

Mama promised it would be glittering and fun. Mama said she'd be invited to teas and picnics on the village green with the best young men in Union Harbor—such as they were.

But would people who talked about them really invite her to parties? Already Byron was known for his visits to taverns. People even talked about Mama!

Loraine burst into tears. Papa was going to marry her off to the highest bidder and not even the finest silk gown in the world could make her forget.

Anyone might ask for her. She had a magnificent dowry, or so Mama said. When Loraine was a baby, Floris had inherited a third of her birthplace, Gautier Plantation in Louisiana.

"One day it'll all be yours," Mama had often said. And it had sounded wonderful—then.

Now it was like a death sentence.

Mama and Papa would never let her marry a poor hardworking man like Beau. If only Mama could *see* him, Loraine thought, her hope suddenly rising. Once she saw how handsome he was Mama would *insist* she follow her heart!

"I never had a coming out," Mama had always said. "I was betrothed to your father at twelve. There was no need for balls."

Her mother's face always grew pale when she talked of those days. Twelve! Loraine shuddered. The only thing *she* had known since she was twelve was that she'd someday have the grandest coming out in Union Harbor.

She didn't want to hurt Mama. She'd never shame her, but after two meetings and one terrible-wonderful kiss, she *knew* Beau Mercedes was the man for her!

Loraine dashed the tears from her cheeks. She hopped up and ran across the beach toward home. Tomorrow, she thought, *tomorrow* she would *not* be afraid!

King's Horse Tavern hadn't changed. Beau sat in a far corner watching all who entered. His encounter with the little DeMarsett miss that morning had left him aching.

How he did want her! And how he did want her papa's money. The promise of a ship was all that stood between Loraine DeMarsett and her virginity.

Beau gulped his ale. The old fart would have to pay handsomely to keep him off that sweet girl. No sane man could resist such begging eyes and pouting lips! And certainly not a sailor just in port.

A fleshy young man sitting nearby with a buxom doxy on his knee caught Beau's eye. That was none other than Byron DeMarsett, Beau thought. At twenty-six, he was the dead spit of his old man.

His hair was his father's, his face and figure, too. His eyes must be his mother's, dark and heavily lashed, a surprising feature for an otherwise laughable dandy in a sky-blue frockcoat and fawn breeches.

Loraine and that goose weren't of the same pod, that was sure. Loraine's eyes and hair came from her mother, but her face was leaner, her features more finely drawn and with more life, more spirit.

With longing Beau watched the doxy. Such a long while since the bevy of Polynesian beauties he'd enjoyed on the Sandwich Islands off Mexican California...Too long.

He wished he could have Loraine. There was something special about the trembling wonder of a virgin. And she was such a bold one!

That put him in mind of his first tumble. Maddie Horn had been just such a sweetmeat when he met her there at the tavern when he was still clumsy with a razor.

Rising, Beau went to the girl sprawled on Byron. "Do you know Maddie Horn? She used to work here." Since morning Beau's voice had lost some of its power.

"No, laddie," said the pink painted face with interest. "I don't. Sit with me, and I might remember."

Beau dropped a quarter eagle down the generous valley between the maid's breasts showing milky beneath the neckline of her bodice.

She squealed and clutched the cold coin where it had fallen deep in the folds. "Maddie wouldn't see the likes of you. She's always been on the straight. Come to my place later. I'll make you welcome."

"Hey, my girl! You're on *my* knee right now," Byron said grabbing her cheeks and twisting her face for a kiss.

"That I am, but you don't pay five gold dollars just for talk. Leave us go up to my room for a bit."

Beau watched the two weave up the stairs. The doxy's laughter followed him into the sunset. What *had* become of his first love?

Love she had been, too, when Beau was nineteen and unschooled in life's ways. He'd just come back from three years at sea when he met Maddie. His mother had still been struggling to hold onto the tavern. She'd taken up with some lout just to keep body and soul alive. Yolanda was at her finishing school. Beau still wondered if his sister realized all their mother had given up so she could look and sound like a lady.

Maddie had worked washing tankards and serving. At fourteen she'd been a solid girl, a bit broad in the beam even then. And how she had worshipped him!

Maybe that was why Loraine charmed him, Beau thought beginning to walk up the road. Maddie had once looked at him with that same intense need.

Beau had stayed in Union Harbor almost a year helping his mother at the tavern before going before the mast again. It took the better part of that year to persuade little Maddie to lift her skirts. Ah, but when she finally did...

Beau grinned. He lifted his head, gazing inland at the town instead of out to sea. He'd look her up, that's what he'd do. She'd be glad to see him. He'd certainly be glad to ease the pain Loraine DeMarsett had kindled.

Until he slipped into Yolanda's dim kitchen just past midnight that night, Beau's quest proved fruitless.

"Maddie Horn?" Yolanda's nursemaid replied. She'd overheard him ask Yolanda about her. The shapeless woman was warming milk for Yolanda's colicky two-year-old daughter. Beau still was surprised Yolanda had actually borne James a child. She wasn't an idle lass, in bed or out!

"Maddie's a laundress," the nanny said wiping her hands on her limp apron. "My sister lived by her when she still kept a room on Luggin's Wharf Road."

"Why cluck your tongue, old mother?" Beau asked wondering which turnip patch Yolanda had found this nursemaid in.

The nanny looked at him sharply and lifted her brows. "It ain't my place to say. Excuse me, sir. I must see to the babe. Miranda don't sleep well."

"She never has," Yolanda grumbled from her warming place by the low-burning hearth.

Yolanda had greeted Beau as she had the night before. Now she jerked her wrapper across her compact bosom. "You said just one night."

Beau grinned and lifted his shoulder. "Does that old turnip close her eyes to all your nighttime visitors? No, no, forget I asked. Let's not battle. What of Maddie? What became of her after I hired on the *Lightning Star*?"

"It wasn't my habit to keep track of your conquests." Yolanda smiled like a cat. "I was at the academy. Later, when Ma talked about her, she'd throw a sound curse your way. Did you soil the girl?"

Beau chuckled. "Don't black the kettle."

"Then be off with you. I can't dally in the pantry with you to all hours."

"That's a nasty turn of phrase. Tell me where Maddie lives, and I'll be off to darken her halls and shorten her sleep."

"North, near the river. Where else would one find clean water? Not in the harbor. Could be she's married. Some jealous husband might finish you."

"Not bloody likely."

• • •

Beau found Maddie's shack the next day. Well-placed questions and generous handfuls of DeMarsett banknotes led him to the Pomoset River. From a thicket he watched Maddie washing dirty shirts for her daily fare. The land thereabouts was thickly wooded, the only sounds birds and the rhythmic slap of linen against washboard. He was about to call out when a boy darted from the shack.

The boy was lean but Maddie was broader than ever. Her black hair still hung glossy down her back. She wore a plain cotton shirt overhanging a water-spotted skirt. Pushing hair from her forehead, she turned.

Thanks to the carpet of leaves, his approach had been soundless. Her sudden pallor warmed Beau's heart. She remembered!

The boy came to a halt and eyed Beau. "The water's hot, Ma," he said.

Instead of looking hang-back as Beau might have expected of so young a lad, the child squared sharp shoulders and faced Beau with a ferocious frown.

Maddie pressed at her back until she stood straight. The lines around her eyes eased. "So, you're back." Her broad sweating face showed no emotion. "I heard you was in port a few years back."

"I didn't stay long," Beau said. He remembered only too well that sour day he'd gone in search of a ship. He'd thought old John Roebling would give him one. After all, Yolanda had just wed James.

As he looked from Maddie to the boy standing before her, Beau could still hear the old man's dying laugh.

A saucy lad, that one, Beau thought. He rubbed his mouth. The last time he was in Union Harbor he should have looked Maddie up. She was a handsome piece.

"Don't come any closer," she said. "You charmed me once. 'Twas enough. There's only one reason you'd come to me now. I'm not your warmer any more. I speak to you now only because of my boy here."

A whispering breeze through the woods touched cold fingers to Beau's back.

Maddie laid her chapped hand on her son's shoulder and gathered up an angry handful of his flax shirt. "You've heard me speak of your father only once, Kane. That was because you asked after him. You deserved an answer. I've told you before, you were conceived in love. I bore you with love, but you have a stranger's eyes and a stranger's face. Look now at that man."

A cold spark went off in Beau's stomach. For a boy so small, that one looked fearless. His eyes were a clear blue and might have held

Beau's charm had they not been so full of hate. The boy's features were uncommonly pure. Beau knew he was a well-formed man, but that boy would have the world. The lad cocked his fine head as if he would take on Beau or an army. Beau couldn't boast a proud stance, only an arrogant one.

"Look well, Kane," Maddie said, her round face toughened by years. "It's the last time you'll ever see your father, I'll wager."

Beau turned away. She was right. He squared his own shoulders and strode back into the woods as if Maddie and the lad meant nothing to him. He made good time to the nearest inn where it took the rest of the afternoon to drink himself senseless.

Loraine stopped to empty her slippers of sand. She'd paced the beach into a froth. For the hundredth time she looked across the dunes *willing* Beau to come. She'd waited all the afternoon before—and had cried all the way home.

Now her stomach rumbled, yet she could not eat. Her eyes burned— she hadn't slept in days. Her heart and mind were possessed by Beau Mercedes. She could not forget his kiss.

She sank to a low boulder in exhaustion. Instantly she sprang up again.

There he was!

He strolled along the waves as if he had all the time in the world!

She ran and called until his head snapped up. He waved. Oh, she would go mad! She meant so little to him! "Beau! Where were you yesterday?" She gasped for air as she staggered before him.

He looked tired and withdrawn, maybe even angry! "I had business, my sweet. I should never have talked to you."

She struck his chest with her fists. Gasping, she drew back. "You're toying with my affections!"

His laugh exploded, erasing the line between his brows. "You read too many romantic novels. Let's climb over the rocks to the cove. I wouldn't want your papa to shoot me." He glanced up at the stone house glowering down at them. He ducked his head and hurried her along.

"Do you care for me, Beau?" she said once on the other side. "Or have you someone else?"

"You move too fast, my little temptress."

His eyes played over her face. She met them squarely though she was shaking again.

Abruptly he turned, scanned the bluff and found a sheltered place to sit. He looped his arms around his knees and stared at the horizon. His eyes blazed like blue suns in a way that quickened her.

"Go away, Loraine."

She shook her head. His words said one thing, his voice another. She crept closer. "If you could just come to my ball…"

"I have no use for dancing!" he snapped. "Or children."

She wished he had slapped her. She ran to him and stood over him. She would not be afraid! She fell to her knees, grabbed his shoulders and kissed him. Just as quickly he enveloped her with his arms and his fire. He rolled her back against the soft giving sand. His breath was warm and quick on her face.

"Are you sure you won't go away from me?"

"Never. I love you."

He chuckled.

For a second Loraine saw into his eyes, deep and dangerous, and fear welled up in her belly as quickly as desire. "You must come for me after my ball," she panted.

A warm rough palm closed over her breast! She sucked in her breath and held it. How had he done that? She was ruined! And yet she couldn't, wouldn't, stop him.

"We'll go away," she gasped.

Now those rough hands found a path among her skirts! He knew the way so well. Oh! He was so bold. She mustn't let him do such things, and yet with every touch she longed for more.

As the sensuous sea air caressed her legs, Loraine could see herself riding away with Beau on a great gray horse to a place where rules or manners didn't exist. The sound of her heart filled her ears. Her body quaked under Beau's hands—she loved him. Oh! how she loved him.

Then as quickly as he found his way about her, he set her free. He rolled away from her leaving her wet and cold. She came crashing back to earth with icy dread. If this was what Nicolette had done, no wonder she wouldn't speak of it!

The roll of waves and the call of gulls were the only sounds. Was this all? Why did she still hunger for him and at the same time feel such regret?

She pushed her skirts down and clutched at her bodice. Her breasts felt cold. Her hands were cold, too, and yet the sun was so warm.

He laid his arm across his moist brow and heaved a sigh. "Shouldn't you be off to your dressmaker now?"

Loraine's heart plunged deeper still. He sounded so distant.

Before she could burst into tears, she jumped up. She would throw herself into the sea!

Beau rose, too, and put his trousers to rights.

She couldn't believe she'd let him do what he had done! Her stomach curled into a knot of terror and sorrow. She would not cry! She held herself very straight and stiff. Every muscle in her body tore with the strain to remain still.

Beau took a few steps from her. When he looked back she thought his eyes looked as bitter as a winter morning.

He sighed then and held out his hand.

She ran to him and fell against his chest. He did love her! Just as soon as dawn broke the morning after her coming out ball, they would run away!

"Go home," Beau whispered. "I'll come again tomorrow." He lifted her chin and smiled a little. "What a wicked little lady you are."

Her heart ached, but as he kissed her and then launched her away toward the rocks, she *knew* he loved her. He must, for she had nothing more to give.

"Tomorrow," she whispered.

# Fifteen

Did trees have eyes? The way Loraine's back crawled she thought they must. Brushing at the wrinkles in her bodice, she crept along the stone path stopping now and again to shake the last grain of sand from her skirt. If Mama ever guessed what she had just done she would have another attack!

Loraine's own heart gave a sharp twist. She tiptoed around the back of the house to the leafy kitchen yard. From one of the open kitchen windows, she could hear the cook and Martha talking.

The cook lived with her husband, the gardener, and their thirteen-year-old son, her papa's groom, in a set of rooms back of the carriage house. Loraine heard the groom whistling in the stable as he unhitched the horse from her papa's new buggy. Loraine's stomach dropped. Papa was home early! She couldn't go in now! Surely her sin was plain on her face.

She rounded the house to her papa's private entrance and stood several moments listening. Her heart beat so wildly she feared she might faint.

Then she heard Papa's angry voice coming from one of the upstairs rooms—and *those* windows were closed. Perhaps her brother had gotten into more mischief. If Papa was in one of his tempers…

Perhaps if she hurried she could slip inside through his study. It was dangerous but could lead her quickly upstairs with no one the wiser.

His door was so heavy she could hardly open it. She wrinkled her nose at the odor of cigar smoke and sweat as she stepped from the bright sunlight to gloom.

Book closets loomed on all the walls. His cluttered desk stood in the middle of the chamber like a crag in a stormy sea. Loraine hurried to the heavily draped window where a crack of sunlight split the shadows. Part of its golden shaft fell across an open blood-colored velvet-lined case lying on the table under the window.

Inside the case lay two inlaid gold duelling pistols. They were the best of his collection. She'd heard Byron boast that their papa had as many as a dozen sets! Loraine fingered the burnished handles and cold muzzles with a shudder. They looked to be the only clean items in the study.

With her back twitching, Loraine dashed to the door. Quiet filled the outer hall. Taking the stairs two at a time, she was safely within her bedchamber in less than a minute.

Thankfully Teresa wasn't there. Loraine ran to the window. The gray-blue ocean stretched beyond the garden trees and melted with the soft blue of the sky. She dropped to her knees and hid her face in her hands.

"Forgive me, Lord. I was bewitched!" She'd never do such a thing again, she promised, but rising unbidden was the tingling fresh memory of Beau's kisses and hands and body. Mercy, how he had set her afire! And still she burned.

When Teresa came in later, Loraine had undressed and languished on her bed with an old copy of "Emma." She looked as if she'd been there most of the day.

"Did your walk tire you today, Miss?"

Loraine's cheeks flamed. With her voice light and casual she told Teresa about how pretty the beach had looked that day.

That night she scarcely slept for remembering. Again and again she promised herself she wouldn't go to the beach again, but when the sun grew high the next morning she forgot her vows. She went again to the beach and climbed over the rocks. Beau was there.

She crept home wearing the same wild flush upon her tender cheeks. By the third afternoon she came home with the warmth of Beau's possession still aching in her innermost being. Loraine dared mount the back stairs knowing the servants might see her now and not guess. She felt confident and cool. Only one more day and she'd be gone!

The kitchen was strangely silent that third day. Looking about with only a twinge of concern, Loraine took the back stairs somewhat reluctantly. She must tell Mama she had fallen in love. Mama would understand, and then the guilt haunting Loraine's sleep would finally go away.

Loraine nearly screamed when she surprised the cook and the housemaid eavesdropping at the closed second floor door. "What are you doing?" she demanded, her confidence shaken.

"Excuse us, Miss!" they whispered.

The cook sidled back down the stairs. The housemaid stood aside as Loraine opened the door and went into the hall. She looked back but the maid wouldn't meet her eyes.

She heard the voices then.

Mama and Papa were having another argument. She patted the moisture on her forehead not knowing if she was sorry or glad she couldn't talk to Mama after all.

Her mother's door stood opposite her papa's. For as long as Loraine remembered, they had never shared a bedchamber.

The hushed rumble of Papa's voice and the barely audible replies of her mother started her heart racing. She pressed her ear to the door. Hollow echoes through the oak made the conversation within sound dreamlike.

"...but we'll come through this panic if you get your wits about you." Papa's voice was higher and more raspy than usual. He was pacing. Loraine could feel the floor trembling. "I need that settlement! Will you just *listen?*"

Loraine couldn't hear Mama's answer.

"Your precious little wench is the key. Ah! Now I have your attention. You're not as mindless as you pretend."

Loraine jerked away from the door. She folded her arms and turned away. She wanted to burst in and defend Mama, but she was afraid.

When the silence grew long, Loraine leaned her ear and cheek back against the cool panels.

"Come, come. Aren't you even a little curious? His wife died of childbed fever. That's stroke of luck for us, don't you think?" Papa's voice grew silky with malice.

Loraine shuddered. What *were* they talking about?

"Look at me, Floris. I mean for her to marry that widower. It's our only chance."

Loraine's hands flew to cover her mouth. No! No! She felt molten, ready to explode. Marry some old widower? Dear Lord; Papa had promised her before she'd even danced a step!

"...our Loraine is ripe. Think of it, Florie. That house and Roebling himself. I hear he looks just like..."

This was a nightmare! Yet Loraine couldn't move away from the door. She was too paralyzed with fear to open it. What would she do?

"Haven't you dreamed of such a man for your precious girl?" Papa was chuckling.

Tell him no, Mama, Loraine prayed outside the door. Tell him no!

"Yes," came her mother's hiss.

As if all the demons in hell were after her, Loraine fled to her room.

It couldn't be! Mama wouldn't agree to such a thing!

She went from her window to the door and back again. She wanted to get out of the house, but she found herself unable to touch the door handle. Coward! Did she even have the courage to run away with Beau after the ball?

She sank to her bed and stared at the lovely white furnishings in her bedchamber. This wasn't real! None of the happenings of the past week were real. She had lived too long in protection and idle comfort to comprehend all the changes.

Mama had just been humoring Papa. Yes, that was it. Mama often did that.

She would talk to Mama later. For now she lay back and looked through the crocheted canopy over her bed. She was afraid now, but on Saturday, after the ball—and she'd endure that only for Mama's sake— she would *not* be afraid. With Beau at her side she'd escape Papa and his cold-blooded plans.

The following day was a riot of confusion. Loraine couldn't find a single moment to talk to Mama, and she certainly had no time to go to the beach! The impending ball made Loraine ill. Unshed tears filled her throat and kept her from enjoying even a moment of the frenzied preparations.

The young groom, the gardener and a rented butler cleared away the furniture in the front and back parlors. Then they opened the doors to the drawing room so that the whole of the lower floor, save the study, was open to the guests.

Floris supervised Martha, Teresa, the cook and her two rented maids, plus the housemaid in the cleaning and the arrangement of greenery and apple blossoms in every room. The house reeked of cleaning wax and sweating excitement.

Floris looked pale most of the day but her eyes sparkled. She'd waited eighteen years for this ball. Longer really. Loraine dared not spoil it. She helped as best she could, and all the while plotted her escape.

That night Loraine fell into bed aching for privacy. She dreamed of a dark locked room full of champagne goblets and apple blossoms. She awoke to the day of her coming out with a crushing headache.

All Saturday afternoon Loraine was bathed and powdered, primped and petted. Teresa wound each curl with extra care. Floris came in once during the exhausting preparations with her carved rosewood jewel case.

"These were my mother's pearls," she said, her eyes vague and misty. "I got them after my papa died. They'll look lovely in your hair tonight."

Though her heart wasn't in it, Loraine took them and thanked her mother. Over and over words raced through her head. "I can't marry any widower, Mama. I'm in love," she wanted to say, but her tongue stayed still. Her heart ached. She couldn't breathe a word for if she did she'd have to admit her sin. Mama thought she was so good, and she had so few things to make her happy. How could Loraine have been so selfish and careless?

The day grew long, and Loraine's temper grew short.

"Stop pacing!" Teresa told her for the dozenth time. The bedchamber glowed pink from the sunset. Loraine couldn't sit, couldn't eat, couldn't bear the way Teresa watched her.

"Don't you have something to do?" Loraine cried at last.

Teresa slipped out. Loraine went to the window. Would she really go away with him?

At last carriages began rattling up the cobbled drive. Resplendent guests alighted beneath the portico. Their talk and laughter filled the house. It was no longer her house nor her life. Tonight she belonged to Mama and the town. And tomorrow people would say, did you hear what that little DeMarsett girl did after her ball?

Her thoughts turned to Beau, to his smile and his lips, and the promise of freedom from this house and Papa's determination to marry her to the Roebling widower.

Why hadn't she realized it before? Suddenly Loraine smiled. The Roeblings married only high-born Boston girls. All she had to do was disenchant that old widower!

"What is it, Miss?" Teresa asked watching Loraine with a sharp frown. She'd come in while Loraine was thinking.

Loraine met her maid's dark eyes with equal sharpness. Teresa was a small woman of twenty-five. She'd come to work for the DeMarsetts three years before after a terrible Atlantic voyage in steerage.

Loraine had liked and trusted her from the first. Never had she known a more devoted servant. Though it wasn't proper to count a maid as friend, Loraine did.

"Because you're my one true friend, I want to tell you something," Loraine said smiling. She felt as if she'd aged years in the past few days.

Teresa edged closer.

"Promise you won't tell Mama until later?"

"Whatever you say, Miss."

Loraine began to untie the little knots of linen around her coiled gold curls. "Papa means to marry me off to some widower," she whispered.

"Oh, Miss," Teresa groaned. Her already pale cheeks went bloodless. "He's a hard-willed man to be sure."

"I won't bear it, Teresa, so I'm going away. Tonight."

Teresa blinked. Then a little smile pulled at her mouth.

"I am! You mustn't tell Mama, only later after I'm away, so she won't worry. I'll come back after I'm married and settled, so it won't be like she'll never see me again." The longer Teresa let her talk the more confident Loraine felt. It was all so simple!

"Married, Miss?"

"I've fallen in love," Loraine said, her heart growing lighter. "We mean to be together, Beau and I. No one can stop us."

Teresa swayed and then caught herself.

Loraine hugged her suddenly. "You mustn't worry. He loves me very much, I'm sure of it. We won't be rich, but I've had that and it hasn't meant a thing." Then Loraine hugged herself. "His name is Beau Mercedes. Isn't that just the most wonderful name you ever heard?"

"You'd best get dressed now, Miss," Teresa said, her eyes evasive.

"I'll be gone before dawn. Will you lay out my cloak?" Only the slightest twinge of fear nibbled at Loraine's determination.

Teresa nodded.

Loraine hugged her again. "I knew I could count on you to understand."

"I, understand, Miss?" Teresa shook her curls. "I have no use for…" She pressed her lips together. Pushing her ruffled cap back in place, she picked up Loraine's first petticoat.

In moments Loraine was laden with one padded and two starched muslin petticoats. Then Teresa lifted the cloud of blue silk over her head. Surely it was an omen, Loraine thought watching Teresa arrange the six lacy flounces at the hem. The first time she'd fitted her gown she'd met Beau. They were destined for each other!

The ruffles matched Loraine's off-the-shoulder neckline and those flounces just above the elbows where the sleeves met narrow cuffs. The bodice clung to her like a lover's embrace. A wide satin band a shade darker than her gown cinched her waist and matched her slippers.

When Loraine looked in the looking glass, her breath caught. Teresa untied her curls and smoothed them with loving care over Loraine's alabaster shoulders. For a moment her eyes lingered on the cleft of Loraine's bosom. Loraine realized with a bolt of terror that she had a hint of the sun's rosy eye on that supposedly never exposed skin!

She swallowed over the nervous lump in her throat. She could hear the violins now. The voices were rising. Teresa twined Mama's precious pearls in her hair. A loop danced cool against her back.

If only Beau could see her like this!

A hush fell over the guests gathered in the parlor. Floris stood beside her husband in the entrance hall watching Loraine descend the staircase into a sea of false curls and flapping fans. Floris put a shaky hand to her eyes. Everything was just as she'd always dreamed. Loraine was utterly beautiful, innocent, and wonderstruck by the joy of a *real* coming out ball.

The guests were admiring, the house warm and inviting. Floris dabbed at happy tears hoping no one would see her foolishness. Wendell led Loraine in the first waltz and every eye followed them. Clearly, Loraine was the prettiest girl in Union Harbor. Her face had a delicious natural glow. Her eyes shone warm like brown quartz. As one young man after another swirled her around the parlor she moved with an airy grace. The young ladies in attendance had good reason to be jealous.

Floris seated herself with the matrons and shook out her fan. She had hoped Thomas would come, and he had promised to try, but only an hour ago he had sent his regrets. He didn't often disappoint her.

She was just beginning to relax when she noticed Teresa waving frantically from the pantry door.

Excusing herself, Floris hurried to the kitchen. "What is it?" she whispered, her chest growing tight.

"You've always been good to me, M'lady. You gave me work when no one else would. I owe you."

"Now isn't the time for gratitude!" Floris cried.

"Oh, M'lady! I just don't know if I should tell you. I love the Miss. I'd never betray her but I think she's lost her head! She's planning something foolish."

Floris steadied herself. "Tell me what's happened."

"She's going to run away tonight, M'lady. To get married!"

Teresa caught Floris' arm and helped her to a stool. "Are you well, M'lady? Should I tell the master instead?"

"Say *nothing* to him!" Floris flapped her fan until her curls danced at her temples. "She knows no young man!"

"She just told me, M'lady. His name is Beau. Beau Mercedes."

Floris' pulse leaped. A loud ringing began in her ears.

Mercedes!

From some darkened chamber of her mind a terrible panic erupted. Floris came to her feet with a cry. "Stop her!" She felt herself falling through a black mist. Teresa held her up as she fought for strength. "In the name of God, stop her!"

The pantry gradually returned to focus. Music still lilted down the hall. Guests still laughed. Floris thought the world had stopped.

She shook herself. Her hands felt clammy. Forgetting her daughter's wide-eyed maid, Floris went back to the parlor.

From the nearest credenza Floris filled a goblet with champagne and swallowed it down with an urgent thirst.

Mercedes. Mercedes!

A queer rushing sound blotted out the violins. Floris looked at the window to see if a storm had come up. The night seemed perfectly still, a warm wonderful night for Loraine's coming out.

Floris shivered. There was no time to waste! Yet when she looked around the parlor filled with guests and dancing couples nothing seemed amiss. She must be going mad.

A mew of terror lingered in her throat. Loraine, my precious, what have you done?

Floris poured a second goblet. Teresa was wrong. Mercedes was...

She blinked.

She drank thoughtfully. The bubbling wine coursed through her veins. She knew no man by that name. The burning knot in her stomach didn't ease.

A cool hand touched hers. Floris started. "Oh, it's only you," she sighed at Nicolette's mother.

The powdery matron smiled. "You needn't worry, dear. They haven't been gone too long. Besides what more could anyone think of to gossip about at this late date?"

People were talking? Floris wanted to run.

Then she saw the objects of Abby Longford's attention: her buck-toothed daughter Nicolette and Byron. They strolled back into the parlor from the kitchen hall. They'd gone off to steal a kiss.

Floris laughed high and silly. Dear Lord, she couldn't worry about a wenching son. Her only concern was Loraine's future.

"Really, Floris! If Wendell would just free Byron those two could marry and we could dispense with this shame. Haven't I been through enough? Floris? You look unwell."

With care, Floris set her empty goblet on the credenza. Care! Take care. Think of a plan.

Another carriage arrived just then. The butler opened the front door.

Like a sensuous wind curling through each parlor, a second hush spread over the guests. Heads turned. The quartet missed a beat and went on slightly off key. Flushed and bewildered, Loraine spun past in the arms of a goosenecked boy. She was trying to see what everyone was staring at. Floris looked, too, and her heart trembled to a stop.

Reaching to pull her red wool mantle tighter she discovered with some consternation that she was wearing her burgundy silk. She hadn't worn red in years.

A man entered the glittering candlelit chamber. He towered over every head. His curly black hair tickled his high-back collar. He wore a stylish morning frockcoat, full-shouldered with broad sleeves and tailored in at the waist. It hung full-skirted over snugly cut black trousers strapped at the instep.

His ivory cravat was knotted above a ruffled shirt exposed beneath a brocade waistcoat.

The butler took his cape and bowed. The guests gave a gentle sigh. No other man in Union Harbor cut such a figure as Adam Roebling.

His younger brother Conrad called hello across the awed silence. His hair was a mixture of auburn and gold and he wore it in waves over his ears and nape. His green tailcoat and tight gray trousers made him the picture of fashion. He smiled like a varlet and gave his oldest brother a wink.

James, the middle Roebling brother, appeared among the guests. He was watching his ravishing wife Yolanda dance with one of the eligibles as if *she* were the debutante.

James' well-worn brown coat was out of date. His doe-brown curls were a mess as if he'd dressed for the ball in a hurry.

There the three Roebling sons stood like stately oaks above the fare. Floris had to sit down. She felt drunk.

With a brutal longing she looked at Adam Roebling. A cry in her heart faded like a sigh. Most of Wendell's ideas bordered on madness, but in this Wendell had been dead right. Loraine must marry Adam Roebling. She had been born for him!

Floris' eyes shot to her daughter. My precious, you can't know the happiness I've planned for you! You can't throw it away on...

A wall still appeared in her mind, a wall as solid as the brick surrounding her garden.

Mercedes? No. Loraine would have the Roebling name, the grand white house and boundless love.

A flurry of soft gasps momentarily distracted those staring at Adam Roebling. Floris had swooned in her chair. The electrified atmosphere in the parlor intensified, for it was well known the DeMarsetts lusted after the Roebling Line.

Far too many gentlemen present knew the fear clutching Wendell's mercenary heart. Union Harbor still quaked from the financial blows of the past week.

Banking houses were barred, having failed from overspeculation. Though the guests wore festive smiles, they were full of envy. At that moment, any man there would have traded places with Wendell and his bankrupt accounts. *He* had a daughter just come of marriageable age. And Roebling wanted an heir.

The ladies had paid little heed that week to the cries coming from the smoke-filled board rooms. Now their thoughts moved to young Loraine staring at the widower. The matrons remembered Adam's father. They remembered the two wives John had buried at Roebling Estate thirty years ago.

Now Adam's young Prudence, a fair-headed, milk-faced Boston debutante had followed suit. She had lasted longer than the other two Roebling wives. She'd borne three sons in such close succession she'd amazed the gossips. But a harsh hand still cast a shadow over Roebling Estate. Adam's sons died, each without a single breath.

To be sure, the Roebling men were magnificent, but their seed was formidable. Prudence Roebling tried to provide an heir a fourth and final time. That chilly December she died within hours of birthing a girl child she named Hope.

Everyone knew Wendell saw a match between his daughter and the iron-backed Roebling heir. But what fate awaited Loraine or her children? Pitying eyes turned toward the girl who would turn only eighteen in September.

A shiver of wonder went over everyone. Loraine had turned away from Adam! She smiled into Willy Peltin's pimply face and danced away as if the heir to Union Harbor's proudest industry meant nothing to her!

Loraine felt the eyes following her. She couldn't bear it! Without regard to the music she stopped dancing and headed straight for the credenza. She took a goblet of wine from the stone-faced rented servant and downed it.

From the corner of her eye she could see him. Adam Roebling moved with a measured step that made him appear…military. She expected him to stare at her; everyone else was. When he didn't, she felt vaguely uneasy.

She'd never seen such eyes, a deep, deep blue-black radiating a mysterious force. When it touched her it seared her with a penetrating quiver of intimacy!

Adam turned and greeted her father. A vile taste spread across Loraine's tongue. They were in league with each other. She'd have none of it! But how had he touched her with one brief look, and across the distance of the parlor? She loved another.

When he looked back his eyes were unreachable. She looked at her empty goblet with irritation. She mustn't drink too much, but then she reached for another. As she swallowed, she began to feel miserably hot.

Look at me, damn you, she thought, flashing her eyes at Adam. Dear God, look away again! She put the goblet down and watched it fall over. The servant righted it.

She looked back. Adam Roebling was coming toward her.

She wouldn't dance with any man Papa chose! She'd rather die than marry him. She loved only…only…

Like leaves in a storm, her thoughts scattered.

A surging, whirling force took possession of those within DeMarsett House's glittering chambers. Adam neared Loraine, and nothing else mattered.

She looked up, up, into eyes as bottomless and dark as the sea on a moonless night. His features were clean and sharp, chiseled of confidence, weathered by care. A deep crease along his cheek might have marred the quality of a lesser man, but on him showed like a fine crack in the armor, a crack perhaps only Loraine could see.

Those eyes, that haunting smile…They were like a greeting of long-forgotten tenderness. His silence spoke to her of intrigue, curiosity and wonder.

"Good evening, Miss DeMarsett." His voice was deep and warm. His long narrow hand slid around her waist. He arched the other for her to take in the next dance. Gingerly she touched her fingers to his palm. Her first step was a stumble.

He led her to the center of the parlor. When the quartet began to play, Loraine didn't hear. Though they danced three waltzes, he seemed to have no intention of letting her go! No man stepped forward to rescue her.

For a time there was no future and no past. She was a blue silk flower twirling in candlelight. As long as she didn't think, her feet followed the waltz perfectly.

When she did let herself admit she had never felt so…She knew of no words to describe this special waltzing heaven. Her heart twisted with shame. She loved another. Didn't she?

This arrogant widower wouldn't have her. She belonged to…

Her lover's name eluded her. She stared up at Adam's well-shaped jaw and that crack in his facade—or was it merely the mark of his iron will—and her neck tired. She stared then at the onyx stone nestled like a dark eye in the cloud of his white cravat.

Marry this man? She almost giggled. A tremor of terror started in her hand and spread quickly through her body. She flashed hot and cold and felt ill in an aching unmentionable way. Dear God, she didn't understand herself!

He was observing her! If he thought she was going to fall over in awe of him he was going to be surprised!

"Tired?" he asked.

With his head cocked like that he looked almost appealing. His voice was like Uncle Thomas', inquiring, not demanding.

"I'm quite well," she lied. She felt like a pool of warm tallow.

If only everyone would just disappear. If only she could think!

Again she craned her neck for a glimpse of that regal head. He looked everywhere but at her.

She shivered. "Excuse me, Mr. Roebling." She cleared her throat and wetted her lips. "I think I've torn my hem. Will you allow me to retire?" Her excuse sounded false.

His eyes reached her face slowly as if he was reluctant to look at such a mindless child.

She couldn't bear for him to think of her like that and began to tug free. In a petulant voice she said, "My dressmaker deserves much less than we paid her."

Such betrayal to Madame Joneaux's expertise! A pang of shame pierced her heart. She was true to no one!

"Are you aware of finances?" Adam asked, eyes sparkling with curiosity.

The music swelled discordant and loud. "I hate money," she hissed. She snatched her smarting hand from his grasp.

"Would you best suit a hard-working man then? Not an idle rich one?"

"I certainly wouldn't suit you!" Her hand flew to her mouth.

A smile cracked Adam Roebling's face.

Loraine laughed then, a laugh born of terror. And his hand tightened across her back.

"Please, Mr. Roebling! My brother will have to call you out."

"What a pity," Adam whispered. "I should hate to kill your brother. He's a bootless sop, unworthy of my time. What have you done to make him look at you as he does?"

"I hardly think you're proper!"

"I seldom am. What do you look for in a man then, if not riches?"

Loraine's mind seized upon the memory of warm sand on her back and desire freeing her from all confusion. She had known what she wanted then. Without caution, she said, "I want a man who wants me."

The waltz ended. Adam spun Loraine to a halt before her mother. Floris wore a look of strained hope so poignant Loraine forgot what she'd said.

From a graceful bow, Adam raised himself before the row of matrons seated along the wall like crows. His voice was just above a whisper. "I don't think you realized what you just said, Miss DeMarsett."

Loraine's cheeks flamed. At his words she felt a jolt so deep, so erotic her legs ached. What had she said? Did it matter? She belonged to...

Mama stared at her with dark blazing eyes. Loraine watched Adam Roebling stride directly toward her papa. What had she done?

Around four the guests began departing. Adam was among the last to leave. Feeling much the same as when he arrived, he emerged from Wendell's study. He certainly didn't feel as if he'd just bargained for a bride!

Adam extended his hand. "Thank you again, Mr. DeMarsett."

"I dare say Loraine will be pleased when she hears," Wendell said shaking hands.

Adam saw that Loraine was still dancing, now with Conrad. Her face looked pinched and weary. He was glad to see she disliked his youngest brother. "I hope so," he said.

"Her mother will see to it." Wendell smiled with his cheeks.

"No undue force, please," Adam said. "I had one arranged marriage. I didn't enjoy a reluctant bride. If you will, sir, arrange for us to meet in a few weeks. I'll speak of my intentions then and see how she feels. I mean to give her full rein."

Adam turned away then. He wished he could carry her home right then. The sight of her in another man's arms, especially Conrad's, a known rogue and despoiler, made Adam writhe.

DeMarsett continued his chatter but Adam paid little attention. He had come to the ball only out of curiosity. Was the DeMarsett girl as pretty as he'd heard? Would her father make some absurd proposal that they merge his Line with paltry DeMarsett Shipping?

Adam donned his cape and bid the fat man good night. She didn't even like him! That in itself was a wonder. He couldn't remember a time when some female wasn't fawning at his feet—even after he married Prue. This Loraine was a rare flower.

DeMarsett wouldn't get a merger, of course. Adam wanted Loraine, not her father. Adam merged with no man, not even a brother. The Line was his alone to pass on to a son as his father had done with him. He pushed away the memory of the three tiny graves in the family plot. And the white marble one set only last week over Prudence.

He lifted his head and tightened his lips. John had raised him to fierce independence. By the time he was twenty-five he had gone to college and captained his own schooner. He asked favors or advice from no one. He had always assumed he'd choose his own wife as well. That tart who had finishing school manners (and was now his sister-in-law) had almost trapped him. He gritted his teeth. Yolanda. He wished he'd never laid eyes on her. He paused at the portico while his carriage was brought round. He should go back and renege.

He didn't want another marriage, more difficult pregnancies, more icy heartbreak at the still small babies...

Adam rubbed his forehead. His head ached from too much champagne. What had he done? It was the champagne surely. Like his father, he was a killer of wives. He dared not marry again!

Perhaps, though, because he'd chosen Loraine himself, things would be different this time. Loraine had danced all night without stopping. The color in her cheeks was natural. And she spoke her mind.

He turned once to look back. DeMarsett still filled the doorway with his horrid little smile. Adam had changed his mind before. He could do so now. Wendell DeMarsett *had* laid this pretty trap to snare him.

He clapped his tall hat in place and gave a little wave. He climbed aboard his carriage and rode home in silence. Watching the dark woods joggle by, he thought of the day he'd bring Loraine home as his bride to his father's estate.

She'd be willing, or he wouldn't have her. He'd have an heir, but also a wife. An unwilling woman made a chilly bed, and above all Adam desired warmth. Could a girl with such hot eyes be anything but a breathing flame of love?

DeMarsett would get his settlement, a generous one; Adam wouldn't have his fiancée's family on the streets. The poor fellow was desperate, otherwise he wouldn't have given up his dream of a merger so quickly.

As the carriage slipped through the gate to the estate, Adam smiled. *His* wealth lay in land, and the mills in Marion and Saxwell. He had investments and corporations so numerous he didn't remember them all. A few failing banking houses couldn't cripple him, couldn't even concern him. He felt a sudden pity for the men who now grieved for lost fortunes. Money could be made by the bankful, but where was a man to find a wife to love him and survive the inevitable?

Once inside his house, a somber place since Prue's death, Adam heard the far-off wail of his infant daughter. Prue had named her Hope. *He* had had her christened Janine, after his Boston grandmother, God rest her soul.

Adam's scalp prickled. He'd have no more graves beyond the rose arbor. Loraine would give him a strong lusty heir and Roebling Estate would know spring again.

The last of the quartet closed the case on his violin and went off to Wendell's study to be paid. The hired servants moved through the lower chambers clearing away the debris left by the guests. Loraine was just heading for the stairs when Floris, visibly weaving from too much champagne, stopped her.

"Come up to my room for a toddy before you go to bed," Floris said. Her cocoa eyes burned so bright Loraine felt frightened.

"My feet hurt, Mama. I only want to go to bed. It was a wonderful ball—everything you ever promised. Thank you." Loraine watched for her mother to look pleased, but those dark eyes just flamed all the more.

"What did you think of him?"

"Who, Mama?"

"Adam, the widower." Floris clutched at Loraine's arm.

"I...I don't know," Loraine said after searching her thoughts. She couldn't say she disliked him. Her head still spun with confusion. "He seemed so much...above me."

"You made a handsome couple. Loraine. Loraine! He's such a..."

"I didn't mean height, Mama! He's a shipbuilder. I'm a child!"

There, she'd said it, and it was true! She didn't even know her own mind. Loraine stooped to take off her dancing slippers. Her toes ached and her arches burned.

"I'm so tired, Mama." She pushed her way up a few stairs. She heard her mother sigh.

At the top of the stairs, Teresa startled her. Loraine ducked past her and her veiled eyes.

"Loraine!" Floris called out.

"It's all right, M 'lady," Teresa said softly. "I'll see to the miss."

Loraine paused at her door. Her thoughts and plans, hopes and fears whirled in her head. Go. Stay. Go...

She must belong to herself, she thought at last. Papa was forcing his hand and Mama hers. Even from Teresa Loraine got the impression of control.

She would not be molded! She slipped inside her bedchamber and closed the door with her back. Moments later Mama's chamber door closed. Martha came up to help her dress for bed. Papa would stay below and drink himself to sleep with Byron—if he wasn't snoring into his chest already.

Like a midnight flower, Loraine's cloak lay open across her bed. She went to it and ran her hand over the silky cool velvet. Teresa wouldn't come to her now, she was sure. It was time to go. Beau was waiting.

Throwing the cloak around her shoulders, she went to her window. Outside the sky was a rich predawn blue. The last carriage had gone, and now the silence was moist and sleepy. Even the surf was quiet.

The hypnotic eyes of Adam Roebling appeared in her mind. The rumble of his voice warmed her. She put her fingers to her lips as she mouthed his name and found them icy.

Then she squared her shoulders. She went to her door and listened. The house seemed ominously still, as if waiting. "Mama, please understand," she whispered as she reluctantly took hold of the door handle.

Whisper-soft footsteps came down the hall. Loraine flattened herself against the wall, her heart drumming.

The footsteps stopped. Her door gave a slight rattle. Then the footsteps went away.

Loraine let out her breath. She looked down at the handle, at the polished brass plate and empty keyhole. Her fingers began to shake as she reached to turn the handle. It moved but the door didn't. She twisted harder, but it stood fast!

Baffled, she twisted the handle again, harder, until her wrist hurt. Then she covered her mouth.

She ran to the window. The sky had lightened to lavender. Birds sang their morning song of spring. The day promised to be lovely and warm.

The garden hung with mossy green shadows. Loraine wanted to call out but her lips wouldn't move. Her breaths came in short gasps, shallow and dizzying. She couldn't get out! There was no escape!

She ran to the door again and pulled at it. Then she laid her head against the hard wood, and the tears came.

Teresa found her mistress asleep by the bedchamber floor, the salty tracks of her tears still white on her cheeks. She bent and cupped Loraine's cheek. Loraine stirred and whimpered.

"Drink this, Miss," Teresa whispered.

Half asleep, Loraine obeyed.

Teresa drew the drapes against the pale morning sun and then dragged Loraine to bed. She pulled away the cloak, unfastened the gown and drew off all the petticoats until Loraine was naked beneath the quilts. Loraine opened her bloodshot eyes once and then they rolled back in her head.

"Is she all right?" Floris asked standing in the doorway.

"She'll sleep most of the day, M'lady. I gave her quite a bit." Teresa helped Martha guide Floris back to her bedchamber.

"Someday she'll thank me," Floris whimpered, and then she collapsed.

"I'll get the doctor," Teresa said.

Martha's square face looked unusually grim. She arranged the counterpane high under Floris' chin and grabbed Teresa before she could go out. "He can't help with this."

# Sixteen

Byron's head was splitting as he paced behind his father's desk in the warehouse office. It would probably be a rotten hot day. He'd had too much champagne at the ball the night before and then too many rums in his father's study.

Shifting on thick legs, he wiped his brow. Damnable business, this. He wasn't even sure he understood it.

"Adam Roebling's accepted," his father had said the night before. "He's agreed to pay enough to save my business. Get your wits about you, boy. Your neck's been on the block, too."

Bewildered, Byron had accepted a rum. "Roebling asked for Loraine? So soon?"

"She's finally going to be of some use to us. I have a task for you. If you succeed I'll let you marry that female, Nicolette. You still want her, I trust."

"Yes, sir. I do!"

"I once did business with a lout named Miles Mercedes," Papa had said. "He disappeared long ago. I thought I was safe from anyone learning of our dealings." He fixed his muddy eye on Byron. "It seems he had a son, a sailor who is in port just now." Wendell drew Byron into a shadow. "He came to me last week. I had to pay for his silence. I'll be damned if I'll give him more. I want you to close his mouth for good."

At those words Byron had gone cold. He liked to play the bully well enough, but to silence a man…

"The *Mercer Star* sails on the morrow," Wendell said. "I've arranged for young Mercedes to be lost at sea. Paid too well for that, too. All you have to do is get him aboard."

Nodding, Byron had shaken his father's wet palm. But could he do it? What kind of dealings had his father had that they should be permanently covered? For the first time in his life Byron was afraid of his father.

Now he waited in the office. Beau Mercedes was coming and expected another payment. Byron had a packet of blank papers prepared for him. Wendell had said he expected a ship, too! Even Byron couldn't expect such a thing, and he was of his father's blood, as close to Wendell as a brother!

Byron swallowed around a cottony tongue. Just get Mercedes aboard the *Mercer Star*. Only just.

He wasn't sure it'd be at all easy. Did Wendell know how Adam Roebling's father had died? Surely everyone remembered that—the Roeblings, for all their wealth, had scandals aplenty.

Through the office window he saw a figure slinking from one long morning shadow to the next. Still trying to swallow, he sank to the chair behind the desk. He shook out cold fists and then spied his father's best cigars. He was still lighting one when Beau slipped in.

"What're you doing here?" Beau's voice was low and menacing.

"My father's not well this morning. Up too late, you know. Have a cigar."

Beau shook his head. "How's your lovely sister? Did her ball go well?"

Byron tapped the packet of paper lying on the desk. "We'll see her at Roebling Estate very soon."

"You DeMarsetts move fast." Beau's eyes twinkled in a way that sent chills across Byron's back. He looked about the office with a yawn, and then slipped the packet inside his coat. "What of my ship?"

Byron rose, gathered up his cloak heaped across the corner of the desk, and spread his other hand to indicate the door. "Shall we go take a look at it?"

Though he looked faintly amazed, Beau's smile grew.

Two DeMarsett brigs lay at anchor in the harbor. Beside them rocked the loaded *Mercer Star* preparing to shove off for the China seas. As the two men neared the moorings, Byron looked up at the *Mercer*, smiling.

Beau did, too. "There's a beauty," Beau said under his breath. "Worth the wait. Tell your father he drives a hard bargain. For this I gave up…"

Sweat sprang to Byron's brow. He curled his fingers around the stout end of a club hidden within the folds of his cloak. Before Beau could turn and ask how a ship not of the DeMarsett packet could be his, Byron gritted his teeth and swung.

With a low thump, the club sank into Beau's neck and recoiled bloody and quivering. Beau collapsed without a sound.

Byron jumped back and shivered. That had been easy!

Two hands from the *Mercer Star* scurried down the gangplank and carted Beau's body away to the deepest holds, their pockets already jangling with the last of the DeMarsett fortune. Byron watched and closed his mouth. He swallowed at the metallic juices and then realized he'd bitten his tongue.

No one else hung about in the shadows. The ships groaned and creaked mournfully. Byron hastened away. His hands trembled and his stomach knotted. Damnable chore, he thought, but as he moved through the spring green morning, a smile spread across his pallid face. He could think of others he'd be glad to be rid of, and many who might pay for such a service as this! Already his pockets felt heavy with gold!

Now he could marry Nicolette. Rain or shine, coin or no, he'd have a warm bed. She'd not laugh or make bawdy remarks. She'd be silent and obedient.

A half hour later he strolled into his house and tapped at the study door. He found his father nodding over a manifest. The old captain raised reddened eyes and then sank back into his wing chair with relief.

Byron had finally done something that pleased him.

# Seventeen

Three weeks later Loraine emerged from her bedchamber. She had aged a lifetime since Teresa first locked her door.

Raising her head, she pressed her hand to the disquiet in her stomach. Adam Roebling waited in the drawing room.

"Miss?" Teresa whispered as she had so often in the past weeks, pleadingly.

Loraine shrugged away her maid's hesitant hand. It hurt to spurn her friend, but it had hurt far worse to be betrayed. She wanted to turn and forgive her. A comforting pair of arms would have felt so good, but she just couldn't. She was among enemies now. They had kept her from Beau. For the past weeks she'd been so miserable and ill she didn't even know if he had tried to see her.

At the top of the stairs she stood clutching the newel post listening to the voices coming from below. The stairs looked wavy and steep. She wondered if she had the strength to get down them.

Byron was just coming from his bedchamber. "Loraine!" he called.

She whirled. Her back struck the rail and sent smarting bolts of pain to her shoulders. She shook her head to keep from crying.

Her brother looked so like Wendell she wanted to spit on him. Under his vermilion waistcoat his belly quivered. He buttoned his straining frockcoat over it and scowled down at her. "You looked like you were going to fall."

"Perhaps I should."

"Ah!" he scoffed. "Roebling's not so bad. I'll wager you'll grow to like him. He has a smoldering temper, just like you. He holds his grudges to his heart, just like you, and bows to no one."

"Like me."

"You see? You were meant for each other!" he grinned and his little teeth flashed.

"I won't marry anyone but..." Loraine bit back her words. Her face grew painfully hot. She'd been alone so long now she'd forgotten how careful she must be.

"But whom?" Byron drew out the last sound like a hum.

"Get out of my way." She pushed her hands into his soft belly and thought of going back to her room. "I hate you. I hate everybody in this house."

"Even dear Mama? Poor little Loraine. It's about time she gave you a firm hand. It does my heart good to see you put in your proper place at last."

Did no one love her? Did no one care that she was held prisoner and that her heart was breaking? She slapped her brother and wished she had the strength to go on hitting him.

Byron grabbed her arm. "I've tried to help you," he hissed, giving it a twist. "You're just too stupid to know it."

She laughed with disbelief. "You wouldn't help a living soul. You're no better than Papa. Let go of me! I'm going back to bed. I don't feel well. If Adam Roebling wants me, well, he can go to hell."

Byron jerked her down the hall where no one would hear. "You better do what Papa wants," he hissed. "If you don't…"

"If I don't I'll be locked in my room. Next, I suppose he'll beat me. I don't care! I love Beau Mercedes. I won't marry anyone else!"

Suddenly Byron was shaking her so hard her neck felt like snapping. "How do you know him?"

"Would I tell you?" She jerked free and rubbed her aching wrist.

Byron looked very odd. "Beau Mercedes is dead," he said. "He drowned."

"You're lying!"

He clamped his hand over her mouth.

"Liar! Liar!" she screamed into his clammy soft palm. Then she couldn't breathe and twisted her head back and forth.

"Stop!" Byron hissed. He withdrew his hand and slapped her gently. "Have you gone mad?"

"He was coming for me!" Loraine gasped. "We were going away."

Byron laughed through his teeth. "Well, he went to sea instead. I saw him off myself. His ship…met with a storm. He drowned."

Loraine slapped away his hands. "You ugly rat. You're lying! You're just trying to hurt me."

"So help me," Byron said, his eyes glittering.

"But I've been waiting all these weeks…"

Her throat closed over a clot of tears. She sagged against the wall.

What was she going to do now? She had been so sure Beau would come. Even as the days slipped by and she was too sick to drag herself to the window, she was sure he'd come.

She looked up at her brother. That wild light in his eyes told her he spoke the truth. Beau *was* dead!

She covered her own mouth with icy hands. She wanted to be dead, too! She couldn't go on alone!

She pushed Byron away. They wouldn't defeat her, she thought. She lifted her face and took a deep breath.

"That's my sister," Byron said smiling. "I'll keep your secret safe. I'm sorry, really. If I'd known…" He licked his lips and looked around as if afraid someone might be listening.

Loraine steadied herself. She wiped her cheeks and swallowed. They wouldn't defeat her. They wouldn't!

The voices from below sounded louder more impatient. Adam Roebling waited. No one had said anything to her, but she knew why he had come. "Where's Mama?" she whispered.

"You *have* been in a muddle," Byron said. "She's been ill."

Loraine closed her eyes and fought to keep from screaming. "If she was really ill, Uncle Thomas would have come. She's just angry with me."

"There's 'Uncle' right now," Byron said pointing.

The good doctor was just coming in the front door. He pushed his hat and cape into the housemaid's indolent hands and rushed up.

Loraine flung herself into his arms.

"Now, now," Thomas said patting her back.

He smelled so good, Loraine thought of burying her face in his coat. Hold me. Hold me!

"I'm sure it's nothing," he said. "She'll be able to come down to dinner. You'll see. You don't look well yourself, child." He stood her away from him and scowled at her with loving eyes. "Roebling's a formidable beau, but you listen to your old uncle. Just be your charming self and nature will take its course."

"Oh, Uncle!" she wept. She felt like a leaf on the wind, pushed hither and yon as if she had no will of her own. Looking into Uncle Thomas' face made tears smart her sore eyes again. He thought she was just afraid to *meet* Adam Roebling.

Thomas turned to Byron then. "Off with you, my boy. I must talk to this child and then see to your mother." When Byron lumbered down the stairs grumbling under his breath, Thomas took Loraine's shoulders. "What is it?"

"Papa wants me to *marry* that man!" she cried. "I heard him tell Mama, and she agreed! What am I to do?" She began to sag but he held her up.

"He just doesn't realize how young and sensitive you are," he said sighing. "You're so lovely. Don't cry like that. You'll break an old man's heart. I love you like my own daughter. With my sons grown and gone to Vienna..." He looked away suddenly. "If it'll do any good," he said looking back, "I'll speak to Wendell. I can't bear that anguish in your eyes."

She nodded. Yes, that would work! Uncle Thomas would save her!

"But I think you're really upset because of your mother. I'm sure she's fine. She's strong, like you. You mustn't worry so much."

All he could think about was Mama! Didn't he know the terrible mess she was in? Loraine veiled her eyes. "If I was to marry, how would I know...when...when..." She couldn't bring herself to say the words! Oh, just to be dead!

Thomas sucked in his breath. Her eyes leaped to his face. He was smiling. Smiling!

"No wonder you're terrified of Adam. You've been listening to rumors about the Roebling wives. There's no truth to the stories."

Dear God, and that, too! Loraine thought in a panic.

"If you marry him, only if, Loraine, *I'll* care for you. No young upstart physick like James for *my* girl! As soon as you're with child I'll hover over you like a mother hen."

Loraine clutched Thomas' coat front. "How will I *know*...when there is a child?"

Thomas cleared his throat and his lean cheeks grew pink. "Ah... well, I'm sure you've heard the talk of feeling bloated and ill, but it's all muchly exaggerated. Your womanly time ceases, of course, and then you swell too big for your pretty gowns..." Thomas' cheeks grew redder. "This really isn't the proper time to discuss this. And I'm certainly not the one to tell you of such things. You'll simply know in your heart, and you'll be very happy."

Martha came out of Floris' bedchamber then and hurried down the hall. "I thought I heard your voice, sir! Please, hurry. My lady seems very ill. We should have called for you sooner."

Forgetting Loraine, Thomas flew to Floris' door. He was gone before Loraine could draw a breath. She really was ill! She wanted to follow him, but Mama didn't want her. She'd abandoned her. Teresa had betrayed her. Wendell had sold her like so much cargo...and Beau... Dear God, Beau was dead! There was no time to waste!

She took the stairs with care, down to the entrance hall that had been so carefully polished to impress Mr. Roebling. On rigid legs she walked into the drawing room. There he was.

Adam rose from the divan and smiled. "We meet again," he said. He wore a fire-blue tailcoat over a gold waistcoat and gray trousers. He looked taller than she remembered.

She drew a ragged breath. "How do you do, Mr. Roebling?"

"I'll leave you two alone," Wendell said from a shadow near the door.

Loraine jumped. She watched him go and wished he could take the odor of his cigar too. She looked about at her mother's carefully chosen furniture, the porcelain figurines on the whatnot, the thick Persian carpet under her feet...Her stomach rolled and threatened. She began to tremble, but no matter how hard she tried, her eyes always found the way back to Adam's face.

"Has your father spoken to you of me?" Adam asked, his voice mellow and gentle as if she was a skittish horse.

"He hasn't said a word to me in three weeks." She closed her mouth. She mustn't say that. She couldn't say a single word she'd planned. Everything had changed, and suddenly, maddeningly, she was almost glad!

Clasping his hands behind his back, Adam rocked on his heels. "Very well then, Miss DeMarsett. May I call you Loraine?"

His face went out of focus. Mustn't faint. Mustn't faint!

Over her silence he cleared his throat. "I've come to ask for your hand. Your father has given his consent." After a pause, he went on. "I'm honored by the offer of your dowry, the third of Gautier Plantation near New Orleans, but you should retain it for yourself. It means so much to your mother. If you'd like, we could go there for a wedding trip. I haven't been south in years."

Chills ran up and down Loraine's spine. He stood so tall, so grand. She felt dizzy, almost giddy. *Married*...to the Roebling heir, and his curse...

"If we were to enjoy good sailing weather we would be wise to leave for the Gulf before summer."

He kept waiting for her replies. She couldn't think of a thing to say.

The Roebling curse wouldn't affect her, she thought watching Adam grow anxious. Her heart twisted as she wished there was some other way to end this mess. He looked to be too good a man to deceive, but she had no choice. The heir she'd bear him wouldn't be a blood Roebling. The seed in her womb was Mercedes. That she knew as simply and surely as Uncle Thomas had said she would. The only thing missing was the happiness.

To keep from falling, she hugged herself. "I'd like a trip to New Orleans," she whispered. "I've always wanted to see the plantation. I'd be honored to marry you as soon as you'd like. Thank you."

Adam's brows went up, and then down. The crease by his mouth deepened. He came toward her and the force of him enveloped her. She couldn't move away. She could only look up, up into those deep blue-black eyes holding her spellbound. His hands closed over her arms and a current shot from his fingers to her heart. She could hear him breathing.

"May I kiss you, Loraine?" His voice had grown husky.

When she didn't answer, his face came closer. She seemed to fall into his gaze, tumbling helplessly toward the warmth of his lips.

His arms went around her, surrounding her in a column of pulsating heat. She closed her eyes and was carried away by the tide in her heart. His kiss took her beyond any sensation she'd ever known with Beau.

When he released her, she stumbled. Even though his kiss had been like the touch of the sun, hot and soft and gentle, her lips stung. She swallowed back a moan and bit her lip. She wanted him to kiss her again and never stop!

# Eighteen

Union Harbor buzzed with the news that Loraine DeMarsett was to wed Adam Roebling on the last day of May.

As soon as Father Michael of the Catholic parish in Boston received word of his invitation he started for Union Harbor. Floris was ready for him; she had improved since Loraine went to her the night of her betrothal to show her the heavy gold ring mounted with a black pearl which Adam had given her.

"I've accepted, Mama," Loraine had said with a look on her pale face that tore Floris' heart.

In the following week so much was done Loraine's head spun. She fitted for a wedding gown that took a dozen seamstresses to complete in time. The house was transformed into a showplace. Debts mounted. Wendell drank and Byron watched with wonder. Dr. Baines could only marvel at Loraine's grace in handling the whirlwind courtship.

Then on Wednesday Loraine rose with the dawn to be wed. Again Teresa tied her hair into perfect curls. She laced Loraine into a new whalebone corset trimmed in pink ribbons and imported lace. Loraine then vomited her morning's tea and biscuits, and fainted.

By two that afternoon she was ready as she would ever be. Teresa hooked the ivory satin bodice, hand embroidered from the cap sleeves to the cuffs. She spread the bell skirt over six petticoats. Loraine pulled on white kid gloves studded with pearls and Teresa twisted pink and white rosebuds in her hair. She arranged an embroidered band of net down Loraine's back and then stood back to admire her creation.

"Beautiful!" Floris cried when she came in. "You're going to be very happy."

Though Loraine looked especially pale, she nodded and smiled. Her eyes were huge and dark, almost too large to be pretty. She moved past the looking glass as if made of wood. Floris kissed her and then, holding a kerchief to her lips, hurried out to greet the guests.

The upper rooms buzzed as noisily as the lower parlors. The sounds came to Loraine as a soft din. She dared not think. A primitive instinct guided her now.

As the music began below, her bedchamber filled with chattering girls. Nicolette, in yellow silk, was her maid of honor. Yolanda, her matron of honor, was dressed in blue and looked like an aquamarine. The bridesmaids exclaimed over Loraine's gown, but she hardly knew they were there.

When the procession began Loraine stiffened. Praying her stomach would permit her to finish the day, she followed everyone to the stairs. Garlands of white and lavender iris twined with ivy graced the banister. Candles filled the air with the smell of wax and smoke.

In the parlor she saw not a single face. She was aware only of her heartbeat, loud and insistent, and the charging of terror like lightning in her soul. She walked down the aisle between rows of chairs nearly lost under colorful skirts and saw one man at the far end of the room. One face. One smile. Adam Roebling.

Soon she'd be at sea and could be sick without alarming anyone. What a relief it would be to be free of all these eyes. Her feet felt heavy as stone. The words of the ceremony droned in her ears. Another ring appeared on her finger and suddenly it was all over. She looked up into Adam's shining eyes and whispered in her mind, forgive me.

"Did you hear me, Miss?"

Loraine shook herself. Though her head spun from too much champagne, she finally focused on Teresa's drawn face. "Is it time to go? I'm so tired." She rubbed her forehead and kneaded her throbbing temples. Her gown was so tight she felt as if she might explode.

The evening cast Loraine's white bedchamber into soft blue-gray shadows. She longed to lay down and sleep. Just sleep.

"You've heard not a word, Miss! He says I can't go to the estate. Not tonight. Here's your cloak, Miss. Your trunks left this afternoon. Who will unpack them? I heard he sent all his servants away! How will you manage?"

"Of course you'll go with me. How else will I hide my morning illness?" Loraine stood on quivering legs and accepted the weight of the new rose wool cloak lined with white satin.

"But he said…"

172

"Don't bother me with this now, Teresa! I can't take any more. Come to the estate on foot if you must. Adam's household is mine now, too. I'll have some say in things." She closed her mouth against hysteria. She had gone and married him! Now what?

She shivered violently. What a monster she was. What had Adam done to deserve her treachery? She tightened the cloak around her shoulders and went out. The house stood hushed and waiting. Adam stood by the open front door. Outside his carriage glistened black in the glow of the portico lanterns. Four matched bays pranced in harness and beyond were the warm shadows of the night.

Sated from the grand feast, the guests gathered around to bid Adam and Loraine farewell. In two days the Roebling clipper *Phantom Queen* would carry them away to the Gulf.

Mama looked so small next to Papa, Loraine thought, her heart hurting. How she longed to be rid of all these lies—but the lies were only beginning. She had sinned her way into a lifetime of them. At least Mama's eyes glowed with joy. And Papa looked relieved. Loraine couldn't hope for more.

Adam donned his seal gray manteau, tall hat and worsted gloves and nodded toward his carriage. He looked frighteningly dignified as he smiled and said good night to everyone.

He helped Loraine into the carriage warmed by grates full of coals hidden beneath the seats and it rolled away amid a chorus of cheers.

Loraine wanted to get out and run!

How she longed for peace, a warm, lazy afternoon on the beach… She tried to remember how Beau had kissed her and her cheeks ached with her shame. She couldn't believe she'd ever been so wicked. Or stupid. And she couldn't seem to stop. She felt carried away by some invisible force. She understood at last the meaning of a hurricane sweep, a wind of incredible power that rose from the pit of storms and flattened everything in its path. That was her life.

A warm solid arm stole around her rigid shoulder. That mysterious warmth she'd felt when Adam first kissed her the week before began to melt her terror. At least if she was to be storm-tossed she had been thrown into the arms of a man she feared could conquer her woman's heart.

She glanced at Adam. The planes of his face were sharp and proud. His dark eyes glittered with some inner fire. When his lips curved into a smile the force of it sent relaxing radiant heat through her body. She eased back against him and the pain of her fears eased.

"You've hardly spoken all day," he whispered.

She nodded. She'd never felt so quickly comforted, so safe and secure. She tipped her face toward his, and without thinking, kissed him lightly as if she'd done it a thousand times.

Delicious heat flowed through her trembling limbs. New strength filled her. She turned to enjoy the full pleasure of his lips closing over hers. He made a sound soft in his throat, like a mingling of surprise and approval. It kindled a fire in her, a fire deep and urgent, more demanding than anything she'd known with...

That other name evaporated from her memory like a morning mist under the searing rays of a conquering sun. Her girlhood dreams and her little girl's heart disappeared leaving her open to the victory of the sweep's power.

By the time the carriage stopped in front of the broad steps of Roebling Estate, Loraine was tangled in Adam's arms. The almost playful nibbling of their kisses had given way to passion. She couldn't get enough of his arms and his lips. She had no thoughts except for the nearness of him, the soft press of his cheek on hers and the gentle rasp of his chin across her throat. She was overtaken by his magnetism, his inner fire, hardly aware of being lifted and carried up the steps to the pillared doorway, or through the candlelit entrance hall to the curved staircase.

His house smelled of polishing wax and hearth fires. Paneled walls glowed with the yellow gleam of candles set in brass sconces. Upstairs a crackling fire greeted them. One flickering candle stood on a black walnut table.

Smiling, Adam set Loraine upon her unsteady feet in the grand master bedchamber. Green brocade drapes covered twin windows on either side of the chimneypiece. Two wing chairs banked the broad stone hearth. The floor was covered with several carpets in blacks, greens and browns.

But for Loraine only the bed caught her attention.

She'd never seen a tester draped in gold velvet. Satin cord held back the drapes revealing posts carved in a double serpentine as thick as her leg. A coverlet couched with gleaming thread lay across the broad expanse. The pillows were white as clouds, the linens smooth as silk. It was a bed made for passion.

Adam removed the cloak from her shoulders and made her jump. Their eyes met a moment and Adam slid his arms around her again. He'd taken off his manteau and frockcoat. His silk shirt felt cool and slippery as she ran her hands over it in wonder. Such fabric on a man!

He turned her and kissed her. "Welcome home, Bride," he whispered, his voice husky, his face a mirror to his thoughts. No mystery cloaked his eyes now. She saw the very bottom, to the naked core where he lay open to her, wanting her.

She turned her face up to be kissed and her neck fairly snapped as the force of his will bent her back into the hard circle of his arms. She clutched at his back for support and caught only handfuls of silk. His lips were so soft and yet demanding, his hands warm and yet hard. The hooks down the back of her bodice began to come loose. Panic swelled in her breast. Wait! she thought. I need more time. Just a little more time.

"I should call for my maid," she said clearing her throat.

"Let me assure you," Adam chuckled against her throat, "it's entirely proper for me to help you undress."

Her bodice came away in his hands then. He pulled the shoulders down exposing the dainty rows of white lace on her corset cover. Her nipples began to hurt with desire.

"Besides," he said, his eyes growing wide and dark. "There's no one here but my manservant."

She couldn't breathe! Every time she turned she wound herself tighter wanting him, not wanting him. As she stepped from the voluminous going away skirt and watched Adam toss it over one of the wing chairs she wondered if she'd ever grow used to being near this man. He set her blood afire!

Now he just looked at her. Her corset cover was a work of art in lace and silk embroidery. One by one she untied her six starched, padded and boned petticoats until they fell one by one to a heap on the carpet.

Clumsily, Adam's long tanned fingers worked the tiny mother of pearl buttons down the front of her corset cover. It fell back leaving her shoulders bare. Her knees trembled beneath the lace-trimmed drawers. And her stockings began to slip.

He pulled off his shirt and for Loraine the room whirled. His chest was broad and firm, rounded with rippling muscles like some statuesque beast. He sat to yank off his boots. Even his bared feet aroused her.

It felt like an intimate dance between them, layers of carefully sewn beauty now coming away in their eager hands to reveal their naked beauty.

When he came to her again and took her in his arms, all she could think was that in moments he'd free her of the corset and then she'd be able to breathe. He would lay her upon the bed and fill the aching need in her heart.

The laces opened. They both tossed the corset away. And his hands closed over her breasts. She arched against him and found his lips. Her drawers joined the lacy heap. She stood a moment in electrified silence as he looked at her. She hadn't known she could want something so much. She hadn't known she could think such bawdy thoughts and silently beg to be taken with all the power that was in him.

But she did.

She lay back on her marriage bed relishing every ragged breath she drew. She relished every quivering kiss, every warm caress, every new sensuous discovery.

They didn't hear an exchange of sharp voices just outside their door. When it opened, Adam raised his drugged head. A pinched white face peeked in, a worried face turned suddenly to horror. Loraine was too lost to know or care what was happening. Adam had found a place of intensity so delicious Loraine didn't dare lose the momentum.

Clutching his trousers together at the middle of his waist, Adam climbed off the bed. He crossed the bedchamber in three furious strides and found his manservant, the bewhiskered Silvers, just outside holding a curly-haired maid under his massive arm.

"Forgive me, sir! I couldn't stop her. She bit me! She insisted she must help her mistress."

"Who *are* you?" Adam demanded casting a fevered eye on the cowering girl. Instantly he hated her.

She stared at his fist holding his trousers; there was no disguising his desire. A scream erupted from her throat. She tore free of Silvers and tried to push her way past Adam into the bridal chamber. "Animal!" she croaked, leaving a sore trail up his arm where her nails raked.

Adam seized her and cut off her breath with a forearm across her throat. Silvers rushed ahead to the servants' stairs at the far end of the hall and opened the narrow door. Adam smacked the girl alongside her head and dazed her. Then he dragged her squirming slight body to the door.

"Get yourself gone from my house or I'll kill you," he hissed giving the girl a shove. He expected her to run down the stairs in terror.

With desperate strength she held Adam's arm even though it seemed she hated to touch him. Though her body was being propelled toward the stairs, she tried to run back down the hall. The result was a gasp, a quick flash of her widened eyes, then a sickening tumble and muffled scream as she fell backwards into the darkness of the stairwell.

Silvers hurried down and bent over her with a lantern. The light fell across her body. "It's all right, sir," Silvers called.

Adam closed the door.

Loraine lay as he had left her, a writhing mass of golden curls and milky skin so perfect and warm he forgot everything.

She accepted him without reserve, and though he was out of control now and cared nought for her innocence, she seemed to accept him as wholly as if his wild passion was her uttermost desire.

Loraine pulled him to her young breasts with a cry of ecstasy. She filled the bedchamber with a soft high moan Adam hadn't known could pierce him so. He hadn't known a woman could reach a release so like his it could bring tears and laughter to them both.

When he joined her on that laughing plateau, he realized he'd wed much more than a beautiful girl. He'd wed a woman, one who needed him. With a helplessness he hadn't known since childhood, he knew he had fallen in love.

# PART TWO

## Nineteen

The July heat rose in waves above the cane fields. Gautier Plantation hummed with sounds—frogs, birds, mosquitoes, like a constant pulsing chorus as cloying as the air.

Loraine opened her eyes and sighed. Sweat rolled down her neck. She and Adam peeled apart and lay panting. For a time they had put the plantation and its rotting smells from their minds. Now, as their hearts slowed and their bodies cooled, the guest room and its draped bed came back to them.

"I can't say much for this house," Adam said wiping his forehead with the frayed corner of the bed linen. "It's clean enough, but…"

"I hate it," Loraine said. She lay flat and exposed, never tiring of her husband's eyes. "No wonder Mama seldom spoke of it. Can you imagine a lifetime with that spider?"

Adam chuckled. "Your aunt couldn't have always been a spider. I suspect she was once quite pretty."

"I think you're blind," Loraine said smiling and kissing his cheek. "She sounded nice enough at dinner last night, but now and then…Did you hear her that time she called me by Mama's name?"

"She's old, Loraine." He folded his hands behind his head and watched the mosquitoes trying to get through the mended holes in the netting.

"And the way she talks to her houseslaves…Let's leave today. Please?

I had a terrible dream last night."

Adam rolled to his side and stroked her from belly to breast. "About what?"

Loraine shuddered. "I can't tell you."

He chuckled again and then got up closing the netting with care.

She watched him cross to his clothes and shake them out one by one, looking for she dared not think what—spiders, snakes, lizards…

"She offered a tour of the fields today," he said of their conversation with Fabrienne at dinner the night before. "I would like to see them. This plantation is partly yours, and I should look after it for you."

"I'd rather be back at our hotel in New Orleans. I never slept in a softer bed."

As he buttoned his shirt, Adam turned to her. He usually wore linen so soft and supple it fell across his shoulders and chest like her kisses. He looked misty through the netting, his dark eyes veiled like when they'd first set eyes on each other. He seemed dreamlike, and still she marveled that she was his wife.

"We can leave tomorrow if you want," he said reaching for his boots. "Will she be insulted?"

"I really don't care. I don't like her. And now that I think about it, I don't think Mama wanted me to come."

He came back and opened the netting. His eyes traveled over her body admiringly. "You'll feel less superstitious on a full stomach. Come see what the maid left."

"I thought I heard someone come in earlier. All night I felt watched."

"Even in your dream?"

"Then especially."

Loraine shuddered at the memory of the laughter, the pain, the sensation of spiders crawling on her, of suffocation. She'd awoken with a cry and then clung to Adam's back until she fell asleep again.

It seemed odd to feel ill at ease now. Since leaving Union Harbor she'd felt so well! While aboard the *Phantom Queen* she had dared hope she had been wrong to think she was pregnant. Only the absence of her menses proved the truth. Surely the dream was a warning that this unbelievable happiness, this perfect marriage with Adam couldn't last. She didn't deserve it, but oh, how she did enjoy it.

"Can we go home soon?" she asked as she pulled on the yellow silk wrapper he had bought her in New Orleans. "It was so nice on the ship. I loved the sound of the sea."

"Whatever you want." He kissed her forehead and brushed his hand across her breasts. "I'll probably be gone by the time you're dressed."

She watched him go and then turned away to hide her face. There was something very wrong about this place. It was like an abscess, a hollow throbbing to be filled. If only she knew with what. She didn't want to be alone there.

It was a lovely old plantation house of red brick set in the middle of a broad emerald lawn banked by oaks and so close to the river she could hear the muddy water lapping along the broad pier.

At least from a distance the house looked lovely. Inside the evidence of age was carefully hidden with paint and furnishings, but even Aunt Fabrienne's diligent houseslaves couldn't erase the smell of years rising in each room like morning mist over the river.

Aunt Fabrienne kept a perfectly ordered household. Her houseslaves were mannerly and quiet though they spoke only if addressed and did their duties like zombies.

Loraine was still buttoning her pretty white cotton dress, the one printed with little flowers and birds, when she heard Adam ride away with Mr. Pace, the steely-eyed Cajun overseer. She'd seen the man the afternoon before shortly after they arrived by flatboat. He had ridden up on a magnificent red horse—and behind he had been leading a runaway slave by a rope around his neck. He wore a scraggly beard to cover a birch-white scar from his left ear lobe to the corner of his mouth. Loraine had seen him in her dream, too, and shuddered remembering.

"Mr. Pace has worked for us since before Papa Gautier died," Aunt Fabrienne had said as they adjourned to the vast south parlor that afternoon before. Through the bank of windows overlooking the garden Loraine could see the Spanish moss hanging from the twisted live oaks like hair flowing on the thick breeze.

"He's very loyal, considering he's white trash. And after Papa thrashed him, too."

Loraine still wondered about that.

When she went down for tea—she couldn't stomach the breakfast the maid had left—she found her aunt seated on the same straight-back chair in the south parlor. Her grayed honey-colored hair was pulled back into a perfect knot. She wore a black morning frock as preserved as her face.

"Morning, Aunt," she said. "May I put flowers on Lusey's grave today?" Loraine sat opposite her aunt and accepted a tea cup. "Mama often talked of her old Mammy."

The old woman looked as if she never smiled or frowned for fear it might mark her narrow cheeks. She turned cold amber eyes on Loraine. "Your mother always did have an unnatural feeling for darkies. I told you last night, Loraine, Lusey's son takes care of that."

"But Mama would want me to…"

"Willful child!" Fabrienne's lips turned to a tight line. She quickly stopped herself and shook off unpleasant thoughts. "Your mother's wedding was in that garden right over there." Her speech lilted in a southern singsong heavier than Loraine's mama's. "I should have married first, but…" The wrinkle-free face remained smooth and unperturbed. Her knuckles grew white as she held the arms of her chair. Though she didn't move, the air around her seemed to tremble.

Loraine put down her cup.

"We might visit the family tomb later," Fabrienne said. "Mother, Lalange, and of course, Papa, are buried there. But not today. I'm not up to it today. Let's go up and say good morning to Dulcine before we retire for the afternoon."

"Is she up to another visit so soon?"

"Nonsense," Fabrienne said rising. "Come along."

Loraine rose from the musty sofa and followed her aunt up the twisting staircase. Her stomach felt uneasy for the first time in weeks. The furnishings inside the plantation house were even more beautiful than in Adam's house, though the humidity had warped the wainscotting and darkened some corners with mildew.

With regal dignity Fabrienne walked to the last door in the upper hall and tapped. "Dulcine, dear sister, are you awake?"

Loraine shuddered. She got the sudden eerie feeling she'd been in that hall before listening to that same syrupy voice. She had met her other aunt the day before. The sight of that pinched face nested in the pillow had so terrified her she had nearly screamed.

Dulcine bore her fifty odd years in all the ways Fabrienne did not. She lay in a feather bed that cupped her like a hand. The smell of her room turned Loraine's stomach.

"I care for my sister myself," Fabrienne had said with her head held high.

"Does she ever get up?" Loraine had asked.

"I wouldn't allow it! She's much too old and weak. We Gautier women are extremely delicate."

Aunt Dulcine had said a few raspy words Loraine couldn't understand and then fell asleep. Her face was so feathered with wrinkles she could have been seventy or eighty.

Now the thought of entering that chamber again made Loraine roil with disgust. Fabrienne opened the door and stood aside. "She gets lonely, dear little niece. Mind your manners now, and speak softly."

Loraine couldn't help but sink to the nearest chair and pull her fan from her pocket. "I feel unwell. Please express my regrets."

The old woman leveled brimstone eyes on Loraine. Creeping close, she bent to look into Loraine's eyes. "You may think you're special, my little miss, but you'll soon learn you're nothing but a slut." Her eyes glowed like a wildcat's.

"What?" Loraine stumbled to her feet.

The woman's decaying teeth showed in a smile so dark it brought Loraine's stomach up. The tea she had drunk erupted and splashed on Fabrienne's hem.

"No!" Fabrienne cried drawing back. She raised her claw-like fist.

One of the houseslaves responded to Loraine's screams.

"You did that on purpose!" Fabrienne cried.

Loraine kept her hands clamped over her mouth. Her stomach felt like it was trying to escape her body.

"Don't worry, Old Miss," the girl slave said. "It only tea. I clean it quick. It leave no spot. You see. I make it good as new."

"Papa tolerated no stains," Fabrienne said, her eyes averted from the puddle. "Get it up. Get it up!"

Loraine looked to the slave for help. She saw plainly a look to go away down the hall. She took one step and had to grab for the chair.

Fabrienne watched, the fire in her eyes fading. Suddenly she swirled into her sister's bedchamber as graceful as a dancer.

"You look poorly, young Missus," the pretty slave in brown calico said. "Best you be out of sight 'fore Miz Fabrienne come out of there. She got a temper, she does. Wants her house jes' perfect. Wears us out if we don't keep it jes' so. Thinks her papa, Old Mister's, coming back to cane her if she don't do things right. I remember that old gentleman. No heart. No sir. No heart. Done lost it when the old mistress died. Many years ago. My mama tol' me. Now that one..." she said nodding toward the open door. "She buried her heart with her papa. These folks is Frenchy, you know. Got a heap o' passion, but not a lick a sense. I'm glad I's a plain girl and ain't got such worries."

"When will my husband be back from the fields?"

"Menfolk hereabouts generally gone all day. Cain't nobody stomach Old Miss for long."

Fabrienne appeared in the doorway. The slave jerked away as if she had been slapped. Loraine edged back, her hand tight over her mouth. Her aunt's face looked almost blue. When Fabrienne spoke, Loraine felt a sudden draft swirl down the hall. "My sister's dead."

An hour later Adam rode in from the fields alongside Mr. Pace. He swung down from the blooded horse and let the overseer lead her away to the stables.

"This is a mighty fine walking horse, Mr. Roebling. You be glad to get him."

"Send him upriver right away. I want him in my stable before fall."

Adam turned, pleased with his purchase, and the lay of the plantation in general. Old Gautier had been dead fifteen years but the fields went on producing. He'd have to see the factor when they got back to New Orleans. He'd learn the worth of the land and then...

Loraine was sitting under an oak in the yard looking like a lost child. When she heard his boots on the gravel lane, she whirled, her face tear-streaked. She gave a hysterical cry and flew into his arms. "I can't stand... me a slut...lying there cold...made me...held my head down..." She threw herself back to the grass, clutching her stomach and heaving.

"Loraine!" he shouted yanking her to her feet. "What's the matter?" Then he had to slap her.

She screamed and fell against his chest sobbing. "She's a witch! I can't stay here another minute."

She pulled at his coat. The look in her eyes filled him with terror. He tried to lead her toward the house. She needed a brandy.

"No! No!" she screamed, her face drenched with sweat. "I won't go back in. We must leave! Now! Please, Adam! I'm afraid!"

He could feel the seams of his coat beginning to give.

"Aunt Dulcine died in the night. She was cold..." The blood drained from Loraine's face so suddenly Adam feared *she* was dying.

"I had to kiss her. She held me down...and I wouldn't. I...Aunt Fabrienne slapped me. Adam, take me away!"

She sagged in his arms and her eyes rolled back.

"Loraine!"

She hung limp in his arms. Her head lolled back, throat stretched, pulsing. He eased her to the grass.

His mouth dry, he looked back at the red brick mansion. A peculiar chill shivered across his back. He wasn't superstitious, but he recognized evil when he felt it crawling in his gut.

He called to one of the black faces peering from a window. Then he lifted Loraine and carried her toward the carriage house. Before sunset he was driving a small carriage along the muddy road toward New Orleans.

Every mile eased his panic. He hadn't even stopped to gather their belongings or say goodbye. A pox on Gautier Plantation. If ever there was a place cursed, it was that old house. He shuddered to think what must fill that crone's head. He'd had to leave quickly to avoid killing her for terrifying Loraine so. Instead he lashed her best horses until his teeth ached.

He should never have taken Loraine there. At the first decent dwelling he'd call for a doctor. Please God, he thought, glancing at her unconscious face wobbling with the rhythm of the ruts and potholes. I was too proud to pray before. I'm praying now. He swallowed hard and laid on the whip.

Autumn came to Union Harbor slow and cool, turning the oaks copper red and the maples yellow. Loraine couldn't remember when she'd seen the trees prettier. She was so glad to be home and safe with Adam's eyes following her every move that everything seemed to have a special bittersweet beauty.

She moved now as if walking on glass. The visit with her Aunt Fabrienne still unnerved her and sometimes disturbed her sleep, but she was learning fast to put unpleasant thoughts from her mind. Since returning from their wedding trip, she found even pleasant thoughts had a haunting effect.

Within a few days she was rested enough to visit her mother. She expected to feel uncomfortable in her old house, but when her carriage pulled up in front of the door she felt awash with sadness.

"Let me look at you!" Floris cried, hugging her and showing her inside. "You've become a beautiful young woman!"

"You're looking well, too, Mama." She followed her mother into the parlor and sat in her best chair.

They talked of the sea voyage, of New Orleans and the ever-changing fashions. When it was time to speak of the plantation they were both uneasy.

"I have sad news, Mama. The day we left, Dulcine passed away."

Floris looked out the window and crossed herself. Loraine couldn't guess her mother's thoughts.

Then they spoke of Byron's upcoming marriage to Nicolette in the spring. "He's changed, too," Floris said. "He's working long hours, and the business is holding—thanks to Adam's help. We were very nearly on the street."

"You were right about Adam, Mama. He *has* made me happy."

Loraine put the unbidden thoughts of her secret from her mind. She didn't want to think about that. Everything was going too well to spoil, but like the plantation house, unfriendly memories lurked here as well.

She thought of the old doctor who had examined her when she and Adam reached the neighboring Ricebourgh plantation.

"Nothing ails this little Yankee bride," Dr. Edgers had boomed without so much as laying a hand on her. "She's only pregnant."

Adam had been fretting near the door of the fine bedchamber— the Ricebourghs were an old family of formidable means. Adam had straightened his back and looked at her. His face softened as he crossed the room and sank to his knees by her bed. "Why didn't you tell me?"

She burst into tears.

Dr. Edgers decreed she'd deliver in February when the moon grew full. Adam delighted Loraine with his concern. Should they hurry home, or would that be dangerous? Should they stay, or would that be far worse?

In the end they decided on the safety of Union Harbor and Roebling Estate. The trip home was quick and pleasant. Loraine forced herself to be happy, and all at once her burden ceased to be a shameful sin and transformed into the vision of a little child. Until then she hadn't realized a new life was living inside her. The only heartbreak came when her baby quickened. She spent that night in silent tears.

So much treachery…Loraine shook herself. Perhaps it was enough to repent. Clinging to that hope, she forced a smile. One more lie in the clumsy web—Mama, Adam and I are proud to announce…

Looking at her Mother, Loraine thought those days before her ball seemed ages past. Beau's name sometimes came to her in the small hours of the morning, but his face?

It grew dim. His mocking voice was only a murmur. She could recall the sight of the gulls or surging waves, but not Beau. He was part of a dream, and how Loraine wished she could wake from it.

"You look so thoughtful," Floris said reaching for Loraine's hand. "Is Teresa better?"

Another shaft of guilt cut Loraine's heart.

"All those weeks on my wedding trip…I never even thought of her!

And if it hadn't been for her…" Loraine licked her lips and blinked. "I spoke to Adam's brother James yesterday. He said she's mending. He assured me the break was simple and will leave her with only a slight limp." Loraine sighed again. "I wish someone had told me she fell. She would hardly speak to me."

Floris shushed her. "No one wanted to worry you. Teresa told me the stairway was dark. She didn't know the way—I don't know why she went in the first place. It was good of Adam to let her stay. Now tell me the rest. Do you…*like* your husband?"

"Adam's so good to me, Mama! He treats me with such care. I more than like him. I think…I think…" Her throat closed. How could she go on pretending…"I'm afraid I can't know what love is because…" She raised her eyes to her mother's face. "Oh, Mama!" She got up and sprawled at Floris' feet and buried her face in the muslin folds of her skirt. "I love him! But how can I be sure! I'm so stupid."

Floris laughed. "Trust your heart!"

"I can't. I thought…Dear Mother of God, I'm ashamed to tell you. I love you so, Mama. I never knew how much until now. I'm so sorry I worried you after my ball."

"I understand better than you know." Floris' cheeks glistened with tears. "I once yearned for freedom, too. Now that you've seen the plantation, you can see why. And we all do insane things in the name of love."

Longing for absolution, Loraine wept until her mother's skirt grew dark with tears. "I'm going to have a baby."

Her mother's hand tightened on her arm. "You'll be all right. Thomas will see to it."

Loraine raised her face. An overwhelming weariness washed over her. She hadn't intended to confess. Now she could see there was no other way. "My baby will come in January, Mama."

Floris didn't move. Her eyes grew as dark as chestnuts, but the light that told Loraine her mother could see and hear her dimmed.

"Mama?"

Her mother's face softened as if her muscles were melting. The grip on her arm relaxed. Floris sank back into the pillows on her chaise.

"I'd feel better, I suppose, if I told Adam. I owe him that."

The hand on her arm tightened again. Loraine whimpered and tried to pull away.

"You're hurting me, Mama!"

Floris' eyes focused on her as hard as wet stones. "You were running away."

Loraine nodded. Ribbons of pain ran up her arm. "I thought I *loved* Beau. I thought I knew my own heart. I didn't know what could happen."

A tremor passed from Floris' hand into Loraine's aching arm. Floris' lips quivered and curled. "Mercedes."

The way she said the name sent chills down Loraine's back. "I had to marry Adam because Beau died, Mama. I didn't know what else to... Don't look at me like that!" Her mother's fingers felt like they had sunk to the bone!

Floris snatched her hand away as if burned. "Mercedes!"

Loraine drew her stinging forearm against her breast.

"You laid with him?"

Penance, Loraine thought. "Yes, Mama," she said to the floor.

"And you carry his...child? You've no doubt?"

Loraine wept. "Tell me what to do!"

For several minutes the only sound was Loraine's sobs.

"Do nothing. Go home."

"But Mama..."

"Mercedes blood stains all. Go home!" Floris whispered. "Take what happiness is left. That's all I can give you."

Floris rose from her chaise and went to the door with more strength and speed than Loraine had ever seen.

"Hold tight to love, Loraine. Fight for it. Fight to the death."

# Twenty

Thomas tore through the gate to DeMarsett House. He scarcely felt his feet touch the cobbled drive as he leapt from his buggy and plunged toward the door.

Before he could knock, it opened and there stood Martha, broad and comforting, her aging face calm. "Thank God you're here so quickly! She's taken a bad turn."

He took the stairs two at a time. "Away from the door!" he puffed. He pushed his way through the servants hovering anxiously outside Floris' bedchamber.

He hated this old room, he thought. "Ready the back parlor, Martha. I want her out of here once and for all."

Wendell was standing near the window. He pulled at his jowls with shaking hands and then rubbed his balding head. "She's been like this since this afternoon."

"What happened?" Thomas bent over Floris' still form on the bed.

"Loraine was here, Doctor," Martha said. "After she left my lady came upstairs and collapsed."

Thomas took Florie's wrist. Her pulse was fluttering and erratic. She was looking at the ceiling and the whites showed around her eyes.

Thomas turned away. He covered his dimming eyes and sank into a nearby chair so hard his bones cracked. Then he reached into his bag for his spectacles.

Martha laid her hand on his shoulder. He looked into her eyes. Her smile was the only light in the room.

"Send for Loraine," he said. "And...ask Dr. Roebling to come, too."

Martha's smile faltered.

"Ask them to hurry."

The bedchamber emptied and suddenly Thomas was alone with Florie. He dragged his chair closer to her bed. The room was dim and overly warm, so like those summer nights long ago when Florie was lost inside herself.

Four long years he'd tended her shell. He'd done everything he could think of to help her then. He'd studied every medical text. He'd even prayed.

She had lain like this so still and quiet, her young face placid as snow. When Mrs. Worley sickened and died from a dislodged clot in her leg that traveled to her heart, he had been afraid to leave Florie alone. Mrs. Worley had sat with her every night.

He asked Martha to sit with her, but she had grieved so for her aunt, Thomas had feared she'd do Florie more harm. And so, despite his concern that it wasn't proper he himself stayed with her during the night. In this very chair he'd sat, chin on chest, thinking, watching, hoping. He even let Wendell send for that sister who, when she arrived, reminded Thomas of a walking corpse!

Now he pulled Florie's hand to his lips. "My love," he whispered. "Don't leave me again."

He remembered how the temptation crept upon him in a dream, how in that dream Florie called to him from her soft warm bed and begged him to comfort her.

Each night he sat watching her. Sometimes she'd breathe heavily, sighing provocatively. Even unconscious she could seduce him, and in the end he found himself wanting to lie beside her.

Who would ever know, he had asked himself. How could it hurt? He lay with her body cradled in his arms. He had stroked her and kissed her hand. Some terrible pain had driven her away. Only love could bring her back. Even after all these years he was convinced he had, indeed, prodded Florie from that mysterious cave in her mind.

He had known his dear wife missed him those long nights, but she had always been capable and strong, a cheery, robust woman suited to wifing a physician gone all hours. She was rosy and smiling even as the cholera took her in '32.

Now Thomas forced himself to pull instruments from his bag. He listened to Floris' faint heart, felt the clamminess of shock spreading through her body. His own heart shivered. This was not one of her spells. He felt suddenly stupid and weak, just as he had after that first time he touched her as a woman.

"Floris?"

He felt a flutter of movement in her hand. Her eyes opened and, after a moment, covered the distance from whatever shore she saw to his face.

"Thomas!" she whispered. "My good, good Thomas."

A sob caught in his throat.

"Tell her."

Thomas tore himself from his own anguish. "What?"

"Tell Loraine...all." Florie rolled her eyes around the room. She seemed to be looking over her bedchamber as if she hadn't seen it in a long while.

"I don't understand," Thomas whispered uneasily. He had pretended so long he couldn't imagine allowing even himself to admit the 'truth' as he knew it.

Florie met his eyes again. He felt afraid, fascinated. He pulled her hand to his lips. Her fingers were cold, but her eyes glowed.

"Do you remember?" he asked and held his breath.

She nodded.

"Everything?" he asked probing the pain in his heart. "You remember John...and me, too?"

Blinking slowly, she nodded, her eyes still glowing. Her hand slipped from his grasp and touched his cheek like a kiss.

Thomas yearned to hold her as he had those few precious nights nearly twenty years before. In spite of herself and her exile, she had responded. He had penetrated her dream world and rescued her. He had given her Loraine who filled her years with love and purpose. He had given her back her life.

"Thomas," she whispered. "Have you always loved me?"

He couldn't trust his voice, but at last he croaked, "Yes," and felt his face go wet. "Yes!"

She seemed to be trying to explain something. He was afraid to listen, but he wanted to make things easier for her. He strained to understand, and suddenly he saw her eyes spark with some hurtful thought.

"Is your mind clear now? Do you remember everything? Even the hurricane?"

She nodded, her eyes swelling, her breathing rapid. "Mercedes," she whispered.

Thomas frowned. "What?"

"In the mud."

She looked so agitated Thomas felt frightened. "Whatever it is, it doesn't matter."

Her fingers hurt his arm. "Wendell sent a man. In the storm." She drew a deep breath and seemed to relax a bit. "To kill John. To kill me." She closed her eyes and sagged.

Thomas shook her. "What do you mean? What really happened that night?"

Floris rested, breathing with effort. "I...killed...the...man. In the garden." Her grip loosened. "His name was...Mercedes."

"You must be dreaming!"

"In the mud. You're the only one who knows."

He wanted to run out right then and choke the truth from Wendell's fat mouth. He should have killed him long ago—that day he punched him, any time after that—but he'd been a coward.

Always a coward. He'd stood by while Florie wasted her heart on John Roebling. He'd stood by while Wendell abused her. He'd even forsaken his own daughter.

"I'll tell Loraine I'm her true father," Thomas said shaking. "I'll protect her. You do remember she's mine?"

The strain faded from Floris' lips. "Yes! I tried to shelter her. I tried...so hard. But I've driven her to..." Floris rose up stiffly, swiftly, as if pulled by invisible strings. "Help her!"

Thomas grabbed Florie's shoulders and forced her to lie back. She'd be all right, he told himself. Now that she remembered, they could have a life together.

Thomas leaned over her and kissed her. The response in her lips made him want to laugh and cry for joy. He slipped his arms under her and pulled her against his chest. Burying his face in her wispy graying hair, he rocked her. "My precious," he whispered. "I love you."

Her head tipped back. She smiled, a small light in her eyes erasing all cares. "Dear Thomas. I've looked everywhere for love, and here I had it all along in you." She raised her hand again, but it moved as if weighted in stone.

He kissed her and heard the words he'd waited for since that first day he was called to attend her. "Thomas, I love you. God bless you."

Once again Thomas lay down beside Florie, holding and stroking and kissing her, but this time he couldn't bring her back.

It was already dawn when Loraine came out of her mother's bedchamber. She could smell the hearth fires but she felt no warmth. She held her arms folded tightly across her chest. She didn't dare look at anyone.

At once Uncle Thomas was at her side. He helped her downstairs. She could feel his hand trembling.

Adam waited in the parlor.

"I must talk to Loraine privately," Thomas said to him. "Then I want you to take Loraine home and put her to bed. A rum might warm her."

The October winds moaned softly in the eaves. Martha brought a cup of tea and Loraine sat stiffly looking at the steam rising from it.

Mama was gone.

What on earth was she going to do now? How could she go on without her? This could *not* be real! She couldn't bear it!

Smelling heavily of rum, her father came in looking bewildered. His shirt hung out and his trousers were soiled and creased. James came in just behind him and urged him to sit.

"She was fine this morning," Wendell said in a little voice. "I didn't think she was really sick."

James laid a comforting hand on Wendell's round shoulder. "Death comes as a surprise to us all." Then he flushed as if realizing how useless his words were.

Thomas pushed them both out and slammed the parlor door. "Loraine," he said. "Are you all right?"

She looked up. Uncle Thomas looked odd.

"I must tell you something. You'll find it hard to believe, but believe you must."

Nodding, she tightened her arms and couldn't stop shaking.

Thomas sat before her and, without waiting, plunged into his story. "I met your mother when she was a bride…" He carried his tale through to the day Loraine came into the world.

For several moments Loraine sat in silence trying to absorb his words. He had said Mama never loved Papa, that Papa was a bad man and used to beat Mama. Uncle Thomas said she fell in love with another man and tried to leave Papa, but a hurricane upset her plans and for years afterwards Mama was sick.

The most amazing part was that Mama had fallen in love with John Roebling! She had even gotten pregnant, but lost the baby during the storm.

"Mama never told me," she whispered.

"Of course she didn't. She didn't remember until tonight. Something happened to make her remember."

"She *never* loved Papa? Why then did she marry him?"

"That's another story, Loraine," Thomas said growing impatient. "Do you know what happened today to make her remember? Was your…father here?"

"He was out, I think. I told her about my visit to the plantation, about Aunt Dulcine's death. I didn't tell her how mean Aunt Fabrienne was to me. I didn't want to upset her."

Loraine suddenly felt an explosion of fear chill her belly.

"What is it? Do you remember something?" Thomas grabbed her hand. "Tell me!"

"I *did* upset her. I told her…" Loraine looked into Thomas' eyes and felt terrified. She couldn't tell him the truth. Not after what it had just done to Mama! "I told her I'm pregnant."

Thomas' face showed a mixture of emotions. "She was worried about that damned Roebling curse." He covered his eyes and sighed. "Don't *you* worry, dear. I'll look after you. You'll do just fine. I won't trouble you any more tonight. You've had enough. But there is one more thing I must tell you. I mean to expose Wendell for the vulture he is, and I want you to understand why."

Loraine watched his face harden with hate.

"You must vow never to tell anyone what your mother told me before she died. Are you listening?"

He looked almost wild with his hair jutting all over his collar and his eyes glinting. "Wendell sent a man to stop your mother and John from running away. It was just before that hurricane. John couldn't get to her and Wendell had left your mother alone in the house. She told me tonight she had to kill that man. I can't imagine how, but she did it. She killed Mercedes to save herself. She couldn't face what she'd done, so she retreated into a fantasy world for four years. When she realized she was carrying you, she was able to take up her life again. Do you understand what I'm telling you, Loraine? Wendell drove your mother to murder."

Thomas' words faded.

Mercedes!

She could feel Thomas' hands holding her up. She wished she could retreat into her own dream world as her mother had, but nothing happened. She could still feel herself sitting on the chaise. She opened her eyes and could see Thomas peering at her. Outside the door she could hear Martha weeping, and the wind, and her heart beating.

Mercedes!

"Wendell couldn't have fathered you, Loraine. He's had a disease…"

Loraine shook her head. She didn't want to know these things! She put her face in her hands. "No more!"

Thomas shook her. "Look at me!"

"One other man has loved your mother all these years. One man has loved *you* and has feared to claim you. But I claim you now."

Loraine laughed. She covered her mouth and laughed and cried as though she'd gone mad after all. *"You're my father?"*

Thomas crushed her to his chest and Loraine's crying laughter filled the house.

"I'm not alone!" she wept. "I'm not alone."

# Twenty-One

"What am I to do with you?" Thomas called from the terrace doors. "Come in out of that wind!"

Loraine turned from the view of the sea beyond the trees. She shielded her eyes against the slanting afternoon sun falling from behind the rooftop. "Uncle Thomas!" she laughed as she waddled inside and hugged him. "What brings you here today? You're not due until Friday."

He put his cold hands against her cheeks. "Lonesome for my girl," he whispered. His eyes twinkled. From his pocket he withdrew a small wooden figure. "I finished it last night. I'm too much of a fool to wait. I had to give it to you now."

"You carved this yourself? When did you find the time?" Loraine turned the whittled sailor boy over and over in her hand. The cuts were crudely done and yet there was precision to them. The small face and cap, the little coat, trousers and boots, every detail was there in beautiful simplicity.

"That's the advantage of age. Time. Do you think your baby will enjoy it?"

Loraine's words caught in her throat. "Yes! Thank you. Come have tea with me. I did get a little chilly standing out there."

"You're not taking care of yourself, young missus," Uncle Thomas scolded following her into the parlor.

"But I am! I'm eating enough for seven, sleeping until all hours. The servants think I'm a slug-a-bed. But sometimes..."

Thomas took his chair and leaned forward, his shining pate mottled with age. His hands he held gently folded like instruments waiting to administer care.

"Don't look so concerned! I'm fine, really." She arranged her bulk on the lounge. "You old hen! I love you. I am tired, of course. This baby is so heavy. It's not that. The dreams about Mama stopped weeks ago. I told you that, too." She smiled as she wrapped her thin fingers around the warm fragile cup. The maid had set the tea cart close to her lounge.

"Something drives you to stand in December wind," Thomas said.

"If you must know, it's this house. Too many people! All day, questions! Where does this go? What's to be done about that? I think Isa sends all the maids just to plague me."

"She's deferring to the mistress of the estate, as she should," Thomas said nodding firmly.

"Not Isa. She's run this house since Adam was a boy. She even rules old Silvers, and he's a fellow I wouldn't tangle with. Let's not talk of them. They weary me." She looked thoughtfully at the carved figure and then lifted her head with a smile.

Yolanda swirled in then. She'd covered her broad crimson skirts with one of Isa's severe aprons. "Oh, I didn't know you had a visitor. Are you all right, sister-in-law?" Yolanda's mask of concern had unnerved Loraine at first. Now Loraine understood it for what it was, Yolanda's way of scaring her, or trying to.

"Yolanda is organizing a Christmas party to celebrate Hope Janine's first birthday on the twenty-seventh," Loraine said.

"We haven't had a party here in years!" Yolanda said, seating herself and helping herself to tea and cakes. She sounded as if she'd ruled the house long before Loraine came.

"A good idea," Thomas said. "As long as you don't overdo."

"That's just what I said," Yolanda interrupted. "That's why I'm doing everything for her. I'm making all the arrangements. I've invited…"

Loraine stopped listening. She wasn't up to a party, not in her condition and certainly not one where everyone would be celebrating the coming birth as well. She felt as if her baby were ready to be born any moment, that she couldn't carry the burden another day.

"Loraine, are you well? Look at her, Dr. Baines! She gets like that so often these days. James swears she's going to have twins by the looks of her. *I* never got that big with Miranda—and she was a large baby. Shouldn't Loraine be in bed from now on?" Yolanda got to her feet, her mask of concern quite convincing. "I told Isa to ready the birthing room, but…"

"No!" Loraine cried, standing. "I've told you every day this week I won't have my baby in that room. Tell her, Uncle Thomas! Tell her."

Thomas rose quickly and took Loraine's shoulders. "You'll have this baby anywhere you like. Why don't you go on about your preparations, Mrs. Roebling. And no more of your speculations. Loraine is carrying her baby in a normal fashion. Her welfare needn't concern you."

Yolanda's eyes flashed.

When Yolanda first began her visits shortly after Loraine's mother died, Adam had said, "We've had nothing but trouble from her since she got her hooks into James. But what can you expect from a Mercedes? She's little more than a strumpet. If I could, I'd wipe the name Mercedes from the face of the earth."

"What did she do?" Loraine had asked with a faint heart.

"Not her. Her brother. He murdered my father."

Loraine heard Uncle Thomas calling to her. "What?" she said with distraction.

"*Are* you all right? You're *not* letting that girl worry you, are you?"

Yolanda had disappeared.

"She wearies me. Uncle. Everyone wearies me. Mama never had to contend with a housekeeper and droves of in-laws. Why don't you look in on little Hope Janine as long as you're here? She's been cranky, and honestly, I don't think anyone cares what becomes of the poor mite."

Thomas regarded her with skepticism. "Surely Adam dotes on her. And this party…"

"Adam can't bear the sight of her. Oh, I don't mean he doesn't love her. I know he does. But you know how he expects so much of everyone? He expects the most from himself. Somehow…"

"Does he love you?" Thomas demanded.

"I think so. Yes, I'm sure of it. At the same time I know he hasn't completely gotten over his first wife. This birthday only puts him in mind of her death, and Yolanda refuses to see that. Sometimes I think she's doing it to aggravate him. And me. Certainly she's doing it for her own glory."

"Where do you get all these notions?"

Loraine smiled just a little. "I do sound peevish, don't I? Well, I have little else here to occupy my thoughts. I sit with my teapot and watch all the little dramas about me. I think of Mama, and…Wendell. And you. And everyone. Life is like ripples on the water, intersecting and widening…"

"My, you *are* thoughtful," he teased. "I think this party of Yolanda's may do you some good after all."

"I don't think it'll do anyone any good, Uncle."

The housekeeper swung the parlor door open. "A messenger for you, Doctor."

Thomas let his arms drop. "An old friend of mine has the lung fever," he said reaching for his coat and hat. "I made him promise to send for me if he got worse. I'll be back on Friday."

"And you'll come for Christmas dinner?" Loraine said following him to the front door.

"Have you forgotten? My boys are due back any day from Vienna. I'm joining them in Boston. They mean to look for a practice…"

"Then you'll not be here for the party!"

"I'm afraid not. Don't scowl, child. I'll be back in a week or so. There's plenty of time!"

Loraine watched him go and her heart twisted. Time.

Isa glided out of sight leaving Loraine in the echoing entrance hall. The floor tiles gleamed in the sunlight falling through the fanlight over the massive white door. She could hear the maids scurrying to and fro in the parlors and dining room readying for Yolanda's party.

She hurried back to the parlor and took up her cloak. Slipping through the terrace doors, she found her way through the garden to the knoll that overlooked the waves on the rocks below. Under the shelter of an oak she hid from the wind and let the tension flow from her body.

Loraine wondered at herself. She wasn't really unhappy in Adam's house. She didn't mind so many servants so much. Not even Isa. She minded Yolanda, but only because Yolanda was a constant reminder of Beau and his eyes.

Yolanda was like a shoe that pinched, or a sore finger, bothersome but easily ignored. She was poised and quick while Loraine felt out of place and clumsy. Too much had happened since spring for Loraine to live each day with grace. Even her baby didn't seem like such a worry anymore. Loraine was secure in Adam's care—to herself she dared call it love. And she had Uncle Thomas' blood running in her veins, not a drop of DeMarsett.

The truth about…about Wendell, hadn't even shocked her, though his death had been one more blow in a long series. Knowing he wasn't her true father surely helped. When the scandal of his slave trading burst upon Union Harbor only weeks after her mother's death, Loraine could only thank God Floris hadn't lived to see it.

Just before landing in Cuba, one of Wendell's ships had been boarded. The condition of the slave cargo had been deplorable. An abolitionist town like Union Harbor had seized upon the news, firing sermons, fueling freedom groups. One would have thought the name Wendell DeMarsett synonymous with the devil.

To Loraine it almost was.

She wished she could call Thomas her papa, but the word papa had been tainted, and besides, she'd insisted they keep this secret their own. "Think of Mama," Loraine had said at the funeral. "Let her name rest, at least for now. It's enough for us to know."

And Thomas had reluctantly agreed.

Loraine knew she was being selfish. She'd had enough of notoriety. She was thinking of Thomas, too, though, of his reputation and that of his sons.

Later when Wendell was found dead in his study…three days after his business collapsed…

The wind moaned through the branches. Breakers crashed against the shore. Uncle Thomas had known about Wendell's trade. He'd set the authorities on him. With Floris dead there had been nothing to stop him. In a way, Thomas had killed Wendell DeMarsett.

Through it all Loraine and her baby survived. Though Adam was constantly busy readying for winter, looking after the mills, waiting for his "son," Loraine dared admit she was getting along well. She had a feeling the storm tearing at her life was over. Unless she admitted her baby was a Mercedes, and she didn't even think of that anymore, how would anyone ever find out?

Now only her brother lived in the great stone house on Atlantic Avenue. Martha had retired to a grandniece's house near the Marion mills. Teresa, though she was still recovering her broken leg, served Loraine as a part-time lady's maid. The rest of her time she spent helping the nursemaid with Hope Janine. She was good at that. Loraine supposed Byron had hired a housekeeper or some such to manage the house, though how he afforded it she didn't know or care.

"Ah, there you are!" her brother-in-law James called striding through the barren hedgerows, smiling as always. His boyish face had a winsome look Loraine often found disconcerting. "Yolanda told me I'd find you with Thomas in the parlor."

"He was called away," Loraine said. She was grateful when James moved close, blocking the last bit of wind.

"You could catch a fine chill out here," James said.

"I need a little quiet now and then."

James nodded. "Yolanda is vigorous these days. I don't know what possesses her. I'd come to think of her as rather lazy, if you want to know."

Loraine didn't, exactly.

"What am I to do about this place?" she asked. "Will I ever be a true mistress?"

"Let Isa handle everything."

"I wish Adam would send her away." The thought of the housekeeper's face made Loraine feel colder than the penetrating wind.

"She's like a mother to him, to all of us, I suppose," James said. He patted her hand.

Loraine felt a bit uneasy. He had familiar ways about him.

"Be patient, Loraine. Isa's old."

She cast James an embarrassed look.

"Come back inside now," he said. He reached for her hand. She took it. Was there something in *his* touch, too? She pulled free and busied herself adjusting the folds of her cloak over the bulge in her belly.

Just before they reached the terrace, Loraine paused. She saw that Adam was back from the yards. He was just passing a door visible through the terrace doors. Yolanda was close behind, reaching out to him.

Loraine turned away, angry and afraid. "Tell me how your father died," she said. "Adam won't."

James' face rose to a ruddy hue. "Adam can't. It's odd you should ask."

"I need to know."

"Adam was closer to Father than either Conrad or me. Father was a silent man given to dark moods. Sometimes he'd go to the knoll and stare at the sea like you were doing."

Loraine looked up at James. He seemed too sensitive for physicking, yet his eyes were deep and wise like Thomas'. He was calm and comforting, and sometimes Loraine forgot he had a life apart from caring for patients.

James leaned against the low wall surrounding the terrace. "I had been back from medical school only a month or so and was trying for a place in Union Hospital when Father took Adam to Boston. Do you know that story?"

"Pieces," Loraine said. The back of her neck prickled.

James folded his long fingers and stared at them as if reading. "Adam had been seeing Yolanda." He looked up for her reaction and reddened. "Oh, you didn't know that. Forgive me for telling you then. Adam doesn't care for the memory. Yolanda was very young, fresh from an academy in New York. Her mother worked at a tavern, I'm told, and sent Yolanda away so she'd catch a good husband. Yolanda set her cap for Adam, the best to be had that year. You were probably still in short skirts." James stretched, keeping his voice light. "Father would have none of her. No tavern wench for *his* heir. Prudence's family were distant cousins of Adam's mother...And so it was arranged. Quickly.

"Adam came home married. I heard no more of Yolanda until she called for me one night. I realized too late it was a trick, a trap. She's expert, you know. And beautiful." He cleared his throat. "I compromised her. Does that shock you?" He looked puzzled when Loraine just went on staring at him. "I wanted to do the honorable thing. If I didn't, my appointment at Union Hospital would have been lost. And I have a rather bothersome conscience. Besides, I wanted her. Father would have packed me off to Boston, too, but I managed to marry Yolanda before he found out about us."

James dusted the top of the wall. "He built us a rather nice little house near here. Then came the epidemic. I'm sure you remember that. Yolanda's mother died. It was a hard time for her, the only time we were close, really. My first months at the hospital were grueling. We were only just recovering when Yolanda's brother returned from sea. Beau never went to school. As a boy he was constantly nipping at the heels of the local authorities. He liked everything easy, Yolanda told me. And he wanted everything he saw, the easy way, like her, I think.

"He came here one day and asked for—demanded—a ship from Father."

"Why?" Loraine asked.

"By virtue of his connection with our family. Yolanda. Father laughed in his face.

"For years Father had kept a pistol in his desk. Adam claimed it was there after that hurricane—you weren't even born yet. Father must have taken it out and threatened Beau. Somehow it went off. He died of a chest wound before word even reached me at the hospital. It was hard on Adam. Then Prudence began delivering stillborn sons..." James fell silent.

"When my time comes..." Loraine said putting her hand on his sleeve, "please let me have my baby in my own bed."

"Haven't you all those heavenly saints to protect you?"

"Don't laugh!"

James' face softened perhaps more than it should have. "I'm sorry. Forgive me. Of course, you shall have whatever you want."

"Promise?"

He patted her hand. "Stop your fretting. Pregnant women love to count their fears. You should know better."

• • •

The next afternoon Yolanda ordered her driver and carriage to ride along the Pomoset River instead of going to the main house as she had for the past week. She had borne all the slights and insults she cared to. Before long the carriage reached a small clearing and a shack nearly invisible in the trees.

The driver knocked for Yolanda and a rather tall buxom woman came to the door.

"Yolanda! What brings you this far?" Maddie Horn asked peering from the doorway.

The weather was wretched, neither rain nor snow, a nasty combination keeping sensible people indoors. The late afternoon sun was lost behind a deep blanket of gray clouds. The wind was harsh, crying in the tree tops.

Yolanda leaned out her carriage door but didn't step into the mud. "I'm looking for my brother."

"It's been months since I saw Beau."

Maddie looked older than twenty-two, Yolanda thought, older than she'd expected after only seven years. Feeling rather smug, she opened the door a little wider so Maddie could see the rich brown velvet of her fur-lined cape.

"Did he say where he was off to? Or when he'd be back?" She decided against offering Maddie the coins in her hand. Why pay for what might come free?

A small boy appeared from inside the shack. He looked across the muddy yard at Yolanda with curiosity. What a cute little pecker, Yolanda thought.

"Go back inside," Maddie said sharply. She pulled her door closed and stood in the sleet. "He came for only a few minutes. I sent him away."

Yolanda yanked the carriage door closed. She sat a moment fuming. "No idea where he is then?" she called through the window.

"I didn't care all these years. I still don't. If you find him, ask him to stay away from here." She cast her eyes toward the door of the shack. "I have my boy to protect."

Of course! Yolanda thought. She opened the door and stepped out. The rain soaked through her hood. "Beau's boy?"

Maddie's face grew hard. "We're not ashamed."

"Why didn't you ever..." It was pointless to question Maddie. She was no talker. "Take this, will you? Let me do something for you both."

"You're kind to offer, but no." Maddie's tired young face softened somewhat. "I'm sorry I can't help. I assumed Beau went to sea again."

Yolanda shook her head. "I don't know. I've had a feeling... something happened."

"Like last time? I didn't see him that time, but I heard. Maybe you'd like to come inside. I'll cook tea and we can talk. Forgive my manners. I don't get many visitors."

"Some other time, Maddie." Yolanda tried to force the coins into Maddie's hand.

Maddie only shook her head. Feeling disgusted, Yolanda went back to her carriage. If she was a poor laundress she'd take perfectly good gold eagles.

Her driver helped her back inside. She pulled off her muddied slippers and threw them down. Now she was shivering and the cape was ruined.

"If you don't mind my asking, why are you looking for him?" Maddie asked. Her hair stuck to her head now, and the rain had turned definitely to snow.

Yolanda fingered her own limp blonde curls. "I'm giving a party for my niece's first birthday. I thought it might be amusing to have Beau show up. And I have been wondering..." But not so very much, Yolanda thought. Only a little. "I've looked everywhere...I thought perhaps he had taken up with you again. How is it you're not married, Maddie?"

"Good luck in your search, Yolanda." Maddie shook the rain and snow from her skirts and slipped inside her shack.

The rain drummed gently against the carriage top. Yolanda threw off her soggy cape and sighed in disgust. Amusing indeed. She was lonely for her own kind. If ever there was a lonely place, it was her own dismal house and that dismal estate.

"Home," she called up to her driver.

The carriage wheeled in the mud. She huddled close to the grate and cursed her brother. She'd been glad to see him last spring. She'd forgotten how good it was to have him near. For all her callous words, she had enjoyed having him back. She'd just forgotten how to show it. It got her precious little.

Now she had Loraine and that damnable pregnancy to contend with. The family was in an uproar—such annoying preparations, such fussing over the pale-faced creature who endured such heartache...Damn the bitch. She was not better than she should be.

Yolanda had lost a mother. No one fretted over her health. Admittedly the death of Loraine's father had shocked everyone—a suicide, some called it. Yolanda shivered and warmed her hands over the coals in the grate. She knew the loss of a father, too. No one clucked at her in pity.

What had Loraine ever done to better herself? Yolanda had struggled every step of the way—and had to settle for James in the end. *Poor* little Loraine had everything thrust upon her...The whole marriage made Yolanda ill.

It was just plain foolish to keep hoping to snare Adam's heart after all this time. Yet Yolanda did. If there could ever be any hope of making a decent living with James the doctor, she might be satisfied. But Yolanda suspected as long as a simpering little idiot like Loraine lived in the grand house, and she lived in a little brick cottage off in a corner of the wood, she'd never get any of the things she dreamed of.

The carriage paused at the estate's gate.

"Well? Go on. I'm chilled to the bone."

"If you don't mind my saying, Ma'am. I couldn't help overhear you asking after that young sailor."

"Your ears are getting too sharp for your own good, Lewis."

"For finding folks, and such like, the fellow to see is young DeMarsett. I'm told he hangs about taverns and keeps his fingers in all manner of pies. If anyone would know where your brother is, he would."

Yolanda almost laughed. Of course! Conrad had told Beau to see Loraine's own miserable father about a ship. "Drive me to the wharf then. And remind me to give you something extra this week."

"Yes, Ma'am."

Quickly the snow collected on the wet fields and tree branches. By the time the carriage reached Luggins Wharf Road the damp had penetrated to Yolanda's skin.

The driver stopped first at King's Horse.

"See if DeMarsett is here," Yolanda called up. "Ask him to come out, if he will. And bring me an ale. I'm freezing."

Lewis ducked into the misty doorway. It wasn't long before he was back with a foaming tankard and a broad young man wearing long side whiskers.

"My pleasure, Mrs. Roebling!" Byron DeMarsett said lurching inside the carriage, throwing it off-center. "What can I do for you?" He pulled the door shut and looked her over with small slippery brown eyes.

Yolanda drew back from the odor of alcohol on his breath. "I hear you perform a number of services for those who can pay, Mr. DeMarsett." She drank deeply of the ale.

"That I do." Byron watched Yolanda reach for her reticule.

She drained the tankard and counted out all the coin she had at the moment. Then she smiled for the florid young fat man across from her. "Could you tell me where someone is?"

"For that I'd bring him on a silver platter." Bryon put his hand on Yolanda's knee.

A peculiar shiver went over her. It had been a good while since she'd felt that particular desire. Conrad had grown tiresome with all his talk of love. What resources had he? James, of course, had never stirred her. More the opposite. Adam was another matter, but he had that plump pregnant little wife...

Yolanda gnashed her teeth. What did that ninny have that she didn't?

"Do you always do business with the personal touch, Mr. DeMarsett?" she asked pushing Byron's thick fingers off her leg.

"I don't let a single opportunity pass by."

She liked his suggestive eyes on her. He thought her a beauty.

Snake-quick, his hand darted to the hem of her skirts and traveled deep within the layers of petticoats. "You've been in the rain, Mrs. Roebling. Your thighs are cold."

"I suppose you think you could warm them?"

His hand found a deeper target—a warm one.

Yolanda gasped. The touch of that hand, none too gentle or gentlemanly, aroused her. She hadn't thought it possible!

"Who do you want me to find?" he whispered. "Can he do better than this?"

Yolanda made a little cry and slapped Bryon. He withdrew his hand with a little shrug and a smile. She put the coins into it. "I'm looking for my brother."

Now his eyes were even sharper. She saw sweat spring to his brow. "You do know where he is!"

Byron pocketed the coins and rubbed himself. "At the bottom of the sea. He's dead. Since May, I think. Did no one tell you?"

Yolanda sagged back against the seat. She couldn't speak. Then she sighed. Somehow she had suspected as much. She had been expecting it a long time. To hear it as fact shouldn't come as such a surprise.

Byron looked amazingly relieved by her reaction. "Isn't there something more I can do for you?" His hand found its way back to her knee. "Comfort you, perhaps?"

"Your touch brings me no comfort," Yolanda snapped, squirming. "There's nothing anybody can do to bring me what I really want, not so long as your sister lives in the house that should have been mine."

"She did do well, didn't she?"

"Better than she deserves."

"It's interesting you should mention my little sister and just when we were talking about Beau. What I could tell you about those two would be well worth a little more of your Roebling cash."

"I have no more with me," Yolanda said.

Byron's eyes lingered on her bosom. She toyed with her straggling curls. "I'm only the wife of a rather unambitious physick. Could we strike a bargain?"

"I'm sure."

"Then tell me what you know."

"Let's settle the payment first," he said, hands going for her bodice.

She let him find his way inside and watched those large hands cover her high rounded breasts. He was a skillful man and aroused her curiosity as well as her desire. Was he good at other things?

"Meet me tonight," she whispered. "I'll leave my kitchen door unlocked."

He said nothing, but it was apparent he meant to be paid there where the carriage stood. The idea threw Yolanda into a frenzy. In moments she straddled his lap. His face disappeared between her breasts, leaving only the top of his head and his thinning curls visible.

For a few heated moments Yolanda didn't care if all of Union Harbor saw the rocking carriage. Then as quickly she moaned in surprised satisfaction, she dug her fingers into his shoulders and pushed him away.

Byron chuckled as he righted his trousers. "Loraine wanted to marry Beau. Did you know that? She actually thought she was going to. How they met I'll never know, but…"

"They *knew* each other? That's *all?*"

Byron stopped her hand before it could strike his cheek. "She swore she'd marry no one else. When I told her he drowned, she accepted Roebling's offer quick enough. She's a minx, my little sister is. Knows what side her jam's on."

"Pig!" Yolanda hissed adjusting her bodice. Her cheeks burned.

Byron grabbed her hot cheeks with cruel fingertips. "But you paid, and eagerly. Next time you have need of me, bring your Roebling gold and I'll do you proper. You best bring a heavy purse, my girl, because I like my whores a bit plumper than you."

Through her bodice he tweaked her nipple sharply and launched himself out of the carriage before she could get her breath.

"Home, Lewis!" she cried slamming the carriage door. She threw the tankard out the window and drew down the leather curtain.

Lewis mounted his high seat and cracked the whip. The ride home was long and cold. Yolanda couldn't decide which surviving DeMarsett she hated more.

James strode into Loraine's parlor smelling crisp as snow. "It's a blizzard out," he said kissing the vicinity of Yolanda's forehead. "Is Adam back?"

"He's gone to Saxwell," Loraine said. "One of the company houses burned down. He's helping the family."

James raised his eyebrows. "Such Christmas spirit."

Wearing green watered silk, Yolanda sipped at her heavily laced tea. "I didn't know Adam's heart was so soft. Isn't it marvelous what a good wife can do for a man?"

James looked away. "Yes." Then he brightened. "I see the house is ready for the holiday guests. We'll have a pretty Christmas. Where are the babies?"

Yolanda waved her hand toward the ceiling. "Out of sight, out of mind."

She'd come in from a long carriage ride only an hour before. Loraine had dared hope she'd decided to stay away a day. Now she sat with a calculating stare that was truly unnerving.

Isa appeared in the doorway. "Will you be staying for dinner, Miz Yolanda?"

Loraine stiffened. Isa didn't even bother asking *her* if Yolanda, James and Miranda were welcome to dinner. She asked Yolanda.

"Have you bothered with her at all today?" James was saying as he removed his snowy coat and handed it to Isa.

"She likes this nursery better," Yolanda snapped.

"If we had more children…"

Yolanda shushed him. Then her voice slithered back to Loraine's reluctant ears. "But James darling, pregnancy is so tiresome and brings on such dreadful pain and crippling complications. Would you have me look like…" She let her voice trail off.

Loraine looked down at her bulging rose kerseymere gown and shivered. Feeling old and ugly, she pulled her wooly shawl tighter. Yolanda was so beautiful and once Adam had wanted her.

She blinked and banished the foolish thoughts.

While James and Yolanda continued their sniping in the next room,

Loraine dragged herself upstairs. She was about to turn into the master bedchamber when she heard little Hope crying in the nursery above.

She mounted the second flight of steps. The third floor was drafty. At the nursery door she paused to catch her breath. Her eyes stole to the nearby door, the birthing room.

No need to worry, she assured herself. She slipped into the nursery and found Maude Dyer, a reliable old nanny from Adam's Boston stock, on her knees among broken miniature teacups.

Miranda stood sniffling in a corner. Turning back reddened eyes as pretty and naughty as her mother's, she tossed her yellow ringlets. "I hate you," the pretty ruffled four-year-old snapped. "I'll tell Mommy."

"Tell you shall, little missy," the nurse said, her starched brown muslin uniform crackling as she crawled about the carpet gathering pieces. "You're a devil of a girlie. If you were my charge I'd cane your fat fanny."

Loraine laughed as the little girl's pink tongue darted out.

"Oh, Missus! I didn't hear you come up. Forgive me. The child vexes me."

"And her mother vexes me." Loraine went to Hope's canopy-draped cradle and gathered her up. "Afternoon, little treasure," she said.

Hope Janine was a solid pink lass with her papa's dark curls and her mama's finely bred features. Loraine nestled her face against the babe's head and suddenly her heart hurt.

When her own baby was born, would she—could she—love it?

A violent bolt of fear weakened her. She sank to a chair.

"You look pale, Missus. Best lie down a bit. You wouldn't want to…" The nurse shut her mouth. She dumped the broken china into a basket near her sewing box. "I've gone through the trunk you had sent up. You've some lovely gowns here, Missus. Have you looked at them yet?"

Loraine joined Maude by a small leather trunk banded in wood and cornered brass. It had been her mother's. Inside were lawn and cambric baby dresses that had been handed down for years. Some were hers and some were so old they could scarcely bear touching.

Maude held up intricately laced and embroidered pieces, petting the tucks, cooing over the sheer beauty, but Loraine saw only the books. Her mother's favorites lay on top of a pile of tissue almost as if she had packed the trunk just for Loraine. And there was the faded diary, the red leather worn on all the corners almost like a Bible. Loraine could almost hear it calling to her to be opened and read.

"Look at this," Maude said lifting the christening gown from the tissue. Its tiny bodice was covered with vines and flowers of the finest silk thread. The three-foot-long skirt swirled with every imaginable design. Maude spread the back of the skirt and pointed to the space near the bottom. Names had been embroidered near the hem, and by the faint yellowing of some of the stitches, it was evident that years separated the work.

Florette Toule.

Floris de Joi Gautier.

Loraine Gautier DeMarsett.

Where were her aunts' names? Where was Byron's?

Handing Hope Janine to the nurse, Loraine took the feather-soft fabric and drew a shaky breath. She really was going to have a baby, one who could fit into these tiny gowns. She pressed the fabric to her lips and shivered. She loved it. She loved her baby! Thank God! Even if she lost everything else, she'd still have her baby! She'd have a girl, she decided. She'd know how to protect a girl. No mistakes. No lies. No unhappiness whatsoever.

But she would not put thread to this lovely old gown. The name Mercedes didn't belong on it. She put it down quickly and turned away.

Going out of the nursery, Loraine looked down the narrow hall, dim in the late afternoon light. After a moment she put her hand to the handle of the birthing room. It felt strangely warm. Her heart began pounding.

It was only a room, she told herself. It contained one high narrow brass bed, one oak bureau, two cane chairs. The chimneypiece had lovely cherubs and roses painted on the tiles. Rose garlands cut deeply into the woodwork.

She looked back at the bed. Its posts were tarnished, its coverlet a coarse homespun, and dusty.

"What are you doing in here?" Yolanda cried, sounding pleased with her discovery.

Loraine spun around. For a moment she looked at Yolanda as if she was a ghost. Saying nothing, she hurried from the naked birthing room and headed for the stairs.

Yolanda was right beside her. "Let me help you. Careful!" she said as Loraine stumbled and nearly fell from the first step.

The lower landing yawned up at Loraine as if trying to drag her down. She grabbed the banister and yanked free of Yolanda's fingers.

"You're far too fat to be rushing about like this. You should try to take better care of yourself. At least Prue didn't let herself go like this. If Adam was my husband I'd be very careful." Yolanda's smile flashed.

Loraine turned hot, tired eyes on Yolanda. "I'm tired of you."

Yolanda drew back. Taking hold of her skirts, she swirled down the stairs like the north wind.

Loraine went to her room then and laid down. Her head was pounding. She pulled the little carved sailor boy from under her pillow and looked at it. Then she turned on her side and closed her eyes.

Adam dismounted and gave a deep sigh. The ride from Saxwell had been overlong. His bones ached with the cold. A stable boy led his Kentucky thoroughbred away leaving Adam standing in the snow.

Through one of the parlor windows he could see greenery draped on the mantel. He supposed Yolanda was still hanging about then. Going in, he lifted his head and smiled. He had a special surprise for Loraine. He'd purchased a small house outside Saxwell. After the new year he meant to take her there. She needn't fear the Roebling "curse."

If the house hadn't been built by his father he would have gladly sold it. And the thought made his heart ache somewhat. He loved it, its white sprawling beauty, the black oaks twisting into a swirling white sky and the sea shining silvery and cold beyond.

Inside, the house was warm, but unusually quiet. He decided on a drink before going in search of Loraine. He wanted his hands warm.

A welcoming fire crackled in his library hearth. Adam closed his door and then turned, startled. In the chair opposite his desk Yolanda sat looking like a ruby nestled in black velvet.

She was still dangerously beautiful, he thought. He glanced up at the portrait hanging over the fireplace. It seemed his father's eyes snapped in disapproval from the old canvas.

"I've been waiting for you," Yolanda said, her voice warm as brandy.

Adam poured and drank more brandy than he'd intended.

Her skirts swished as she rose and glided toward him. She smelled musky and warm, unlike Loraine who always smelled of sunshine.

Yolanda touched his arm. He grew cold. He looked down at her and watched the glow in her eyes fade. "We once meant so much to each other," she whispered, sulking, her lips fascinating to watch. "Do you remember how much you wanted me then?"

"I remember more than you'd like me to."

Her lips pouted pink and wet. "I married James just to be near you."

"I think you're drunk."

"I come here just to be near you. Is it as hard for you as it is for me?" Her eyes went over him suggestively. "Your pretty bride doesn't like me. She just told me to leave. I look at her and pity you, Adam. She moves like a cow." Her hand slid up his arm. Her skirts pressed around his legs, whispering and soft. "I've waited a long time, Adam. Now that Loraine's too big to give you pleasure..." Yolanda raised her cold blue eyes and smiled.

Adam felt a flicker of response, but it quickly died. Anger flooded his face. "I'll have none of you, now or ever," he whispered. "I value loyalty. You're nothing but a harlot."

Yolanda snatched away her hand. And her skirts...

Adam saw he had wounded her, and well...

"Loyalty," she spat. "*Do* you value it? I wonder. Have you *looked* at your wife these past weeks? She's so sweet. And you look calf-eyed at her. Take off your blinders, Adam, and *really* look at her. Then ask James if I'm not right. Either you rushed up her petticoats before you wed her, or someone else did."

# Twenty-Two

Bits of snow kissed the windowpane. The soft crackle of the fire faded and even the wind stopped. No murmur of servants' voices came from the hall. A hush had fallen over the house.

Loraine sat up from her marriage bed feeling a cold dread steal across her like a snow drift. Outside her door she heard that measured step she remembered from the first time she saw Adam at her coming out ball. Each footfall was more ominous than the last.

What was wrong with her? She couldn't breathe. It was only Adam home after a long day. She stood and straightened her skirts over her bulging abdomen.

The door crashed against the wall. Like a shadowy monster Adam stood with his fists rigid by his sides. Then his shoulders sagged. He closed the door and struck her with his open stare.

"We have something to discuss."

Was he ill, or drunk? His cheeks were red. His eyes glazed. Something terrible must have happened. She wanted to rush to him and give comfort, but felt rooted by the bed.

"You look tired," he said. "I should ask James, or 'Uncle' Thomas if you're carrying twins. I don't want twins. Two can't run a business. One always courts deceit and the other falls into a fatal trust. Perhaps marriage is like that."

Why was he angry? If it was anger. He looked almost pained. Each time his eyes darted over her and then away she felt the pain. He seemed to be prodding a sore place and then flinching.

"My father once said, 'Trust a man and die at his hand. Trust a woman and lose your soul.'" Adam shook off the memory. He met her eyes. "Until now I never understood what he meant. And I never understood why you so intrigued me. Now I think I do. See how you stand, how you face me? You never waver. There are times when you fall into my arms soft and demure. My ardor rises like the sun. But you have always had a unique strength."

"I'm not strong," Loraine whispered. She curled her cold fingers into fists to warm them.

"Oh, yes. I forgot to include modesty in your list of virtues. Innocence, charm, sensuality...Make this creature your own, I told myself. She'll bear sons. She'll make a warm wife. You were good at that from the first."

Loraine grabbed the velvet drape for support. He knew!

"Do I frighten you, Loraine? Should I be concerned for your health?" He held his fists behind his back as he came nearer. "You're small and encumbered, but you don't cringe from me. I think you're too strong."

He looked into her eyes a long time. To Loraine his eyes looked like black stones. The burning light of love in them had dimmed. He turned away toward the door. With his back to her he asked, "Have you deceived me?"

She reeled. Oh, God! Let this not be happening.

"Is that my child you carry?"

Her hands went over her belly. She could go on lying, she thought. She could spare him this, but she was so tired. The weight of her lies felt like an anchor holding her fast to the shame of her childish spoiled past. She could tell the truth and free herself and Adam. She looked back with a soft regretful sigh.

Let it be over. She'd had his love and trust for a while and that must be enough. But even as she watched the last of the color drain from Adam's face, she held out hope that he might yet understand. After all, he had said he loved her!

Adam opened the door. He was breathing heavy and slow. "Who?"

She buried her face in the drapes. She had never dreamed he'd ask that.

"Who?" His voice cracked.

"He was only a sailor. You wouldn't know who he was." God, she was still lying! Must she tell him?

"*Who?*"

"His name was Beau."

Adam whirled, his eyes wide. "Mercedes?"

"I'm sorry!" she cried. "I was a fool...I was afraid...Forgive me. I love you. I really do."

For a moment she feared he'd rush across the room and strangle her. She half wished he would. Instead he thundered out and slammed the door. After a reverberating pause, a key rattled in the lock.

"Not that!" she cried running and hitting the door with her fists. "Send me away, but don't lock me in!"

She waited for an angry reply, a curse, anything, but he didn't return. No one came.

The next day James came. And a week after Christmas Thomas came, but Adam sent them away. The family celebrated a somber Christmas, and Yolanda had her party at her own little cottage. It was a disaster.

All the while Adam stayed in the great white house overlooking the winter sea, drinking. And Loraine stayed in their locked bedchamber, weeping.

The second time Thomas was turned away he took himself to James' cottage. "What was their quarrel?" he asked as James welcomed him from the cold.

"I can't imagine!" James said. "Will you have a toddy before you go back to town?"

Thomas knocked the snow from his boots. "I don't like this a bit," he puffed. "Everything was fine when I left."

"How was your reunion with your sons?"

"Gratifying," Thomas said smiling a little. "They're full of modern new ideas. I feel rather backward in the face of their knowledge. Oh, thank you," he said warming himself over the hot buttered rum. "What could possibly make Adam behave this way? Have I done something to anger him?"

James went on shaking his head. "It's not you. He won't let me in to see Loraine either. Yolanda knows something, but she's not talking. In the past week she's turned into a perfect shrew. I have half a mind to see a lawyer and be free of her."

Thomas raised his brows. "That bad?"

"You have no idea, Thomas, how ugly a beautiful face can be."

"Have you *seen* Loraine since I left?"

"Yes, she was fine. I did think at the time that her baby was very high, possibly dangerously large. I haven't pressed Adam thinking maybe all this would bring on an early delivery."

Thomas shook his head. "Loraine's strong like her mother was. She'll go to term." He thought of that morning they found Florie in the muddy garden. Suddenly he could hardly swallow. "I thought I liked Adam."

James made a bitter laugh. "He's the image of Father."

"If that's so, it's not good. John was a man of passion, but one who could, under certain circumstances, be defeated."

"My father passionate? Not hardly, Thomas. And defeat? Never! This *spat* between Loraine and Adam can't be anything serious. What could possibly come between them?"

Thomas shrugged. "I wish I was equal to such passions."


After another week Thomas grew angry. He'd ridden to the estate every day and been turned away every day. He gave up patience and forced his way passed Silvers.

"She has no need of you," Adam said barring the way up the stairs.

Shivering in his snow-caked coat, Thomas looked up into the shadowy second floor. "What have you done to her?" Memories of Florie's secret bruises made him wild with fear for his daughter.

Adam laughed. "Nothing. Go away. We don't need you. James will attend Loraine from now on."

Thomas grabbed Adam's lapels and gave him a smart shake. He would have struck his face if Adam hadn't so quickly recovered his surprise. Like a common criminal Thomas found himself propelled out the front door by the collar and seat of his pants.

As he tried to regain his footing, he slipped on the icy veranda. He had to grab a pillar to keep from falling. "If you've laid a hand on her..." Thomas shouted, shaking his fist.

Adam closed the door.

Thomas was left in the wind. It certainly didn't do to anger Roebling. He tried to go around to the back but found he had twisted his ankle. Surely Adam, who had shown nothing but adoration for Loraine up until now, would not have harmed her.

Thomas hobbled back to his buggy, and with reluctance, headed for home. He would have to think of some other way to see that Loraine was safe.

By nightfall he was abed nursing a full sprain and a magnificent pain in his head. The next day he sent messages to Adam. Then James. Two days later a note arrived from Loraine.

"Dearest Thomas, Please don't worry. I'm well. Forgive my husband his unforgivable behavior. It's justified. Your loving daughter, Loraine."

After reading that, Thomas suffered a severe attack of indigestion.

He sent for James and soon the young physick was at his bedside. "Adam let me in to see Loraine this morning," James said pressing his thumb into the soft fat flesh of Thomas' ankle. "She's just fine. Really she is. But this rift between them is..." James shook his head. Then he sat down. "If I didn't care so much for Loraine and if I didn't pity her and Adam, I'd be shocked by this. But who am I to judge? I've lived with my own folly nearly five years. Don't look so concerned, old sir. You can't cure us all. We're fools, every one. Lie back and don't fret. Loraine explained everything to me."

Enraged by his incapacity, Thomas sank back. "What is it, then?"

James rubbed the back of his neck. "She carries another man's child."

"That's absurd!"

"I thought so, too, Thomas. But it's plain she's due for delivery any day, not next month as we both thought all along."

Thomas remembered with a cold shudder the day Loraine asked him about the signs of pregnancy. Suddenly he felt very old. What a terrified little child she must have been. And that was what Florie must have meant by help. Loraine needed his help. He groaned.

"I've moved into the house temporarily. Life with Yolanda has become hell, and honestly I can't stand the sight of her. She told Adam about Loraine's deception. God, if I only knew how she knew..."

"I want Loraine to come here," Thomas said. "I'll see to her."

"If only Adam would let her go! I believe he has a brain of stone. He keeps her locked in that bedchamber as if..." James sighed. "I'll tell Loraine you're improving, though I'd say by the colorations, your ankle is not good. She's worried about you. And Adam. And me, of all people. She's concerned for everyone but herself. She's taking this as if...as if she welcomes it. It must have been a terrible burden."

Two days after James moved into his old room in the main house, Yolanda and Miranda arrived. "I won't be left behind while you hover over that strumpet's bed," she snapped, throwing down her carpetbag.

James looked at her with a feeling of hopelessness.

From that moment on the house hung in breathless suspension. Every morning Yolanda joined Isa in the pantry. Over tea they would discuss Adam's problems. "We've got to help him," Yolanda would say and take comfort in Isa's complete agreement. At last she was accepted in the family, for whoever Isa accepted, held a special place in the house.

On the morning of the eleventh, Yolanda said that again and watched Isa look up, her eyes sharp, her mouth a tight pucker.

"I haven't liked that bit of baggage since I first laid eyes on her. She's nothing but a whore," Isa said.

"It's my own brother's child, too," Yolanda said shaking her head as if she couldn't excuse him anymore.

Isa's mouth grew tighter. She looked as if she'd forgotten Yolanda was a Mercedes.

"We'd all be better off if that baby died," Yolanda whispered.

Isa nodded slowly. Yolanda leaned forward and whispered. She watched Isa's eyes grow wide, then narrow.

Isa made a small smile. "But will he agree to it?"

"If we handle him right, he won't be able to resist. And I'll take care of James."

Just after midnight the pains started. The small cramps quickly grew to nagging squeezes that kept Loraine pacing by the big cold bed in the locked bedchamber. At dawn she rang for Teresa to build up her fire.

She huddled in her wrapper trying to remain calm. Teresa knocked. "Isa doesn't answer my knocks. Miss. She has the key."

"Wake James then."

Nearly two hours later Isa admitted James. "Is it time?" he asked bustling in with a forced smile.

Loraine looked up from her cocoon of quilts. "What kept you?"

"It's *cold* in here!" he said putting his hands on her belly and then smiling. "Just go on sleeping as much as you can."

He called for a fresh hearth fire and Loraine drifted off to sleep listening to him berating Isa for her neglect.

When James came in after lunch he gave Loraine a potion to help her sleep. By dusk her labor had improved to the point where James brought in his bag and took his place in the chair by her bed. After a time she grew confused and tired. James watched her struggle, and waited. At the slightest sign of danger he intended to call for Thomas; Adam be damned.

No complications arose.

The room grew dim as Loraine worked feverishly to expel her burden. Teresa brought tea once and then hurried away, her face a mirror to her panic. James was tying stout rag ropes to the bedposts when Isa came in just past eight.

"Where's Adam?" James asked pushing the velvet drapes aside so he could position the ropes.

Isa looked down at her writhing mistress, her belly so full, her face red and drenched with sweat. Her face registered no emotion. "He is in the library."

"Still drinking? The coward."

Isa's look left him shivering. "It's time she went upstairs." She went to draw back the covers.

A particularly sharp pain gripped Loraine suddenly. James and Isa watched her arch up to meet it. She held her breath and then let out a long deep grunt.

"She's having her baby right here," James said pushing Isa aside. "Loraine needs her friends near, not her enemies. Tell Adam I want him to come up. Now."

"He wants you to take her upstairs," Isa said as if he hadn't spoken.

James got an ugly chill. "We can't move her now! She's about to deliver."

James felt small and helpless still before his old nanny. Then he saw Yolanda lurking near the doorway. She sauntered in dressed as if going to a ball. She came to James and kissed his stubbled cheek.

"Why are you here?" he demanded.

"We've all agreed it'd be so much better if Loraine's baby died," she smiled looking down at Loraine with icy victory.

James felt as if she'd punched him. He shook a trembling fist at her. "You couldn't." Then he began to feel sick. "You don't really mean…By God, I think you're capable of anything."

Yolanda's face grew hard. "This is my brother's child, James. I'm not entirely without feeling for him. But even you have to admit a Mercedes baby has no future here."

"I won't let you kill it! You'll have to kill me first."

Loraine was weeping now, fighting her contractions, suffering. James should be helping her. He pushed his wife away and went to Loraine to take her hand.

Then he turned back to Yolanda. "We'll just see what Adam says when he sees her like this. Maybe you've forgotten he's already watched three of his own babies die. I don't believe anything would convince him to let you…"

"Adam is unconscious," Yolanda said, a twinkle lurking in her arctic eyes. "While you were up here I was working on him and finally he agreed. I have his blessing, James. I suggest you do as I say or we'll simply lock the door on you. Then Adam will probably lose them both. Again."

She slipped her hand into James' and whispered her plan as she and Isa had told it to Adam all day, incessantly, persuasively, with all the brandy he could hold.

After a few moments James pulled free of Yolanda. He wanted to cry. He went to the lovely bride on the bed and lifted her. She twisted in his arms like a dying fish torn from the sea and followed Yolanda and Isa upstairs to the birthing room.

A single candle burned.

Loraine couldn't stop shivering. Every inch of her hurt, but she climbed from the pit of pain ripping open the secret places of her body and saw shadowy figures standing over her. They were washing her legs.

With a scream, she knew she no longer lay in her own bed! She couldn't move her arms to push the shadows away! When she twisted to be free, the pain returned, deeper, spreading red and hot and relentless. She was engulfed in its tide. She forgot everything but the inescapable task of expelling the mass from that bulging tender spot between her legs.

Mama! she thought. Uncle Thomas! Help me! Mother of God, let it be over!

At the final moment when the red curtain of unconsciousness threatened, Loraine screamed, "You left me to this!" but she couldn't say Beau's name. Her body was wrenched as if she'd been dropped from a cliff. She heard—sensed—a flurry of activity, a hushed silence full of shushing and scuffling feet. Then a delicious surrender settled over her. The pain ceased. She listened, waiting…waiting for that first cry…

A door closed.

On her knees in the shadows near the servants' stairs, Teresa listened and waited, too. After the last scream, she crossed herself. They were killing her mistress! Then the silence swelled her terror. She rose to her feet.

Some beast of a man had raped her mistress and now these servants of the devil were killing her!

Teresa knew rape. In the steerage section of that ship where her mother had breathed her last listening to her muffled cries, Teresa had learned about men. Men were vile. Loraine never would have soiled herself on a man, not willingly.

Teresa wiped tears from her cheeks. Poor Miss! Teresa had been remote and angry with her since the wedding, but now her love and pity returned. She must help!

The door to the birthing room burst open. Teresa fell back into the shadows of the hall. A splash of yellow candlelight fell across the narrow carpet and then disappeared. Two women, Yolanda in her velvet skirts and Isa in her black muslin, hurried down the staircase. Their footsteps sounded like soft thunder.

Ignoring the sharp ache in her leg, Teresa hurried after them. By the time she found a vantage point between the balusters, Yolanda and Isa were already to the first floor.

Silvers held out Yolanda's cloak. Then Isa handed her a small bundle. Yolanda tucked it beneath her cloak and slipped outside into the winter wind. All the lamps flickered as the cold swept in. Teresa was sure she heard a faint cry, almost like a mew.

She must follow Yolanda! She crept around to the first step, every nerve tensed, her fear gone. Then a shadow fell across her path. She whirled, and looked up into James' haggard face.

Isa and Silvers were coming up the stairs now like a pair of haunts, dangerous and unpredictable. Teresa ran back toward the servants' stairwell hearing their footsteps rush up behind her.

Isa caught her arm and whipped her around. "How did you get down here?" She gnashed her teeth as she looked back at Silvers. "I thought you locked her door." She gave Teresa's arm a jerk. "You saw nothing," she hissed. "Swear! Swear you saw nothing. On your life."

Teresa nodded so hard her teeth chattered.

A tortured scream ripped through the house, echoing, rippling with pain. Teresa broke free of Isa's bruising hold and hobbled back toward the birthing room where James leaned against the doorframe. His lips were drawn back in a grimace as he wept.

"What did you do to her?" Teresa grabbed his lapel.

As Isa and Silvers began dragging Teresa back toward the servants' stairs, James said, "I told Loraine her baby was born dead."

# Twenty-Three

In September Loraine wasn't sure if summer had ever arrived. She laid a single rose on the little white stone in the family plot and then turned away. This would be the last time.

At first she'd visited her baby's grave every day. From the foot of that tiny mound she watched spring come long and cool to the woods.

Then she came less often.

Summer if she could call it that, was late and rainy. Even on the warmest days she wore black wool. Whether the sun shone or not those long summer days of 1838, Loraine didn't notice.

The time had come for her to put away her mourning gowns. She must think of something else. What, she wasn't sure, but she had shed all her tears. The place she'd readied in her heart for that Mercedes child remained empty, but she had mourned him and now laid him to rest with all the other hopes lost from her girlhood.

She walked away from the family plot with her head high. She straightened her shoulders feeling younger than perhaps since Mama died. Sometimes she wished she'd been strong enough to see that little white coffin put in the ground, because at times that small life so wrought with troubles seemed never to have existed. Perhaps, as James had said so often, it was better this way.

There on the back terrace, that lovely curve of stone with a low wall banked with flowering shrubs, sat Teresa and Maude with Hope Janine. What a comfort that little girl was.

Loraine was about to join them for afternoon tea when she saw through the far line of copper tinged oaks Adam's carriage coming up the drive. The horses scattered fallen leaves like confetti.

She missed Adam. Since December he'd slept in the dressing room adjoining their bedchamber. After her baby's death he left her door unlocked but seldom if ever looked at her. And he never asked after her.

In February they were taking meals together again and by March he spoke to her. She couldn't hope for things to ever be right between them again, yet he hadn't divorced her. She took comfort in that.

She longed for those early months of their marriage when his eyes followed her with longing and when their nights were filled with passion and delight. She started down the side path hoping to happen on him as he alighted from his carriage out front. Perhaps today he'd smile.

From the bushes by the farthest column she watched Adam step down to the drive. His gray tall hat made him look long and lean. The cut of his coat was good. She still marveled that once such a man had loved her. As he gave his driver the command to go on, Loraine stepped forward to call hello. Then she saw a delicate hand edged by yellow lace wave from inside.

Yolanda!

Loraine turned away, her heart aching. She hurried back around the house. The lovely shadows across the lawn and the comforting curve of leafy oaks overhead didn't calm her. She couldn't appreciate the banks of late summer flowers. Yolanda was there. Always Yolanda.

She must stop being a fool. She would never get Adam back. The pain in her heart surprised her. Shaking off tears, she stepped up to the terrace. Always she felt as if she was moving in a dream. Her life had no purpose now. Byron and Nicolette had married. Thomas had to stay home because of his inflamed ankle. James visited more often than was necessary, and Loraine enjoyed that. She always noticed a kind of illusive admiration in James' eyes. Sometimes she even entertained fantasies about him, but felt safe in that because nothing would ever come of it.

James was far too proper, even with his familiar ways. Loraine wished she trusted herself that well. She suspected if a man, any man, so much as laid a hand on her she'd melt into his arms and fancy herself in love. She was true to no one, not Beau, nor Mama, nor herself. She had even wearied of mourning.

"There you are, Miss," Teresa said from the terrace. Like always her curly hair was escaping her starched cap. "We were worried. Maude took the little miss up to nap. You look cold." Teresa pulled off her own shawl and laid it across Loraine's shoulders. Making a hesitant smile, she looked up with her head cocked, as if fearful. As grateful as Loraine was for Teresa's renewed friendship, her demeanor was irritating and tiresome.

They turned at the sound of hoofbeats coming from the garden path. Conrad reined in and swung down from his roan mare. His smile was a flash of teeth in a rather pale face; his amusements kept him out of the sun.

"My dear Loraine," he said without even seeing Teresa. "Good afternoon."

Teresa faded back into the house.

"I thought perhaps I'd find Yolanda with you," he said. Conrad looked less his usual self, Loraine thought. There was a tightness to his otherwise careless mouth. Some of his youthful spark had disappeared over the summer.

"I saw her go by…in Adam's carriage," she said lowering her eyes.

Conrad pulled off his gloves and sat down on one of the iron benches. He let his hands fall between his bony knees. "Outclassed again." He looked up at Loraine with a smirk. "You've caused me a lot of heartache, do you know that, my sweet beauty?"

Loraine's heart gave a little leap as she edged toward the double doors.

"At your coming out you were as uncharming to me as any young lady has ever been. Then you went and married my brother as if someone had lit a fire under your petticoats. Bearing an heir such as you did, and under such questionable circumstances, hasn't done me any good either. Yolanda and Adam are bound by it, you know. She's convinced she'll take your place any day now. That leaves me precisely nowhere."

Loraine found his speech incomprehensible.

"Ah, Pretty, I see you're in the dark." He got up and came to her. "I harbor an attraction for lovely yellow-haired females. For quite some time I found favor with Yolanda." His eyes went over Loraine's face with flickering interest as he fingered her curls. "You may find it hard to believe I could be hurt by so heartless a lady as the other Mrs. Roebling, but it seems I am. As long as you and Adam play at your tiresome game of wills, I hold no hope of getting Yolanda back."

Conrad pushed aside the edge of Loraine's shawl. His smooth cool fingers fondled her shoulder.

"What does James think of all this?" Loraine whispered appalled that such a gentle man as James could be saddled with a woman openly unfaithful.

Then a sharp pang of guilt and understanding made her see that Adam looked to be in the same sad spot.

"I see many thoughts behind those mysterious eyes of yours, Mrs. Adam Roebling. Of James, I don't know his thoughts. He seems not to care what Yolanda does. He has his dedication to the putrid work of physicking. By choice *I* am idle. Might I find solace here?"

Loraine felt mesmerized. Conrad's voice was smooth and his eyes suggestive. He kindled fires in her, but not of desire, of longing for

Adam, of reassurance that she was still attractive to even such as he, and yet unmoved.

Loraine stepped back. "You're lucky to be free of Yolanda. She's a Mercedes and Mercedes blood stains all." A shiver went up Loraine's back as she repeated her mother's words.

Conrad laughed. "How your eyes do burn when you say that name."

"I'll have no truck with a Mercedes, nor anyone else who does," she said aware that even as she spoke there was one tiny spot in her heart for a Mercedes. She'd have liked for her baby to have lived. How she ached to fill that cavity.

Shaking his head, Conrad turned away. "You may have a point. We haven't been a family since she slipped her claws into us. Ah!" he said looking across the terrace at a tall figure watching from inside the door. "Adam! Your wife's been entertaining me."

Adam glowered as Conrad glided through the doors, but there seemed to be a twinkle of approval in those hooded eyes.

At last, she thought. She'd done something right! And she *didn't* melt at the touch of any man. Conrad left her utterly cold!

After dinner Loraine crept into Adam's library for a sip of his brandy. Teresa often brought her a small glass in the evening. Now she was upstairs readying a late bath.

A bath had become a frequent pleasure of late, the steaming water, the perfumed bubbles, a warm candlelit room afterward where Teresa would brush out her long golden hair. Then Loraine would fall into bed with her fantasies and the sound of Adam readying for bed in the next room.

She poured herself a generous drink and swallowed some. She liked the library. It was an intimate room, dark and musty with all the old books. The broad desk stood under the Palladian windows. She could imagine him doing his work there. Because it was September there was no hearth fire but the first time she'd stolen into the library for a drink a blaze had sent leaping orange dancers across the deep dark carpet and paneled walls.

She poured a little more brandy. Her eyes traveled the book closets mysteriously lined with gold stamped leather volumes. So much to know about Adam and the Roeblings, yet the only thing she knew for sure was that John Roebling, her mother's lover, had died lying across that very desk.

A little giggle escaped her lips. Married to the son of her mother's lover. Pregnant by the man who killed him. She couldn't have hurt Adam more if she had tried.

She found her glass empty again and refilled it. She might have been a harlot but she hadn't succumbed to Conrad. And he had been blatant. She'd show them, especially Adam. She'd put passion aside.

"And here I thought Silvers had taken to pilfering my liquor stores," Adam said coming in the other door.

She nearly dropped her glass. Just to know he was in the same room set her veins on fire. His voice could touch the deepest part of her. If only it were the voice she'd come to cherish on the *Phantom Queen* and in Louisiana.

"Do you want something?" he asked moving into the light.

"I didn't realize I was taking so much. I'm sorry. I should've asked."

He was close now. Her mouth went dry. "Why should you ask?" he said softly. "You're my wife."

She kept her eyes averted. To look at him would be her undoing. Was he drunk, or sober, friendly or not? She couldn't tell.

"But how could you ask?" he said touching her shoulder with one rigid finger. "We're like strangers. You look well, Loraine."

"Thank you."

"Look at me."

She shook her head.

"I was surprised to see you with Conrad. Did you know I was watching?"

She looked then and gasped. She tried to shake her head. He must hate her! His eyes were shadows. If he hadn't stopped her, she would have run out. His fingers burned her arm. She wanted him to shout at her or slap her, anything to end the deadlock.

"Do you still love...Beau?"

Shaking her head violently, Loraine tried to push past him. He wouldn't let her go.

"*Do* you still love him?"

"No!" She pushed at his hand. "I thought I did once, but..."

"Are you sorry the baby died?"

"How can you ask that? Of course I am. I don't know to this day why Beau compromised me. I thought he loved me, but now I know the kind of man he was. I hate him. Losing a baby that lived inside me to the last was punishment enough. I believe God is satisfied. Stop looking at me like that. I truly can't go on like this. Either we're husband and wife, or we're not."

"Would you have me as husband again?" he asked, his voice husky.

She made a small moan in her throat. Her head swam. She couldn't give in! She carried a legacy of unwise love and must overcome it. She must prove to Adam that she was stronger than this.

Pulling free, she ran out of the library to the staircase. When she reached it, she turned. He stood in the doorway, watching. And still she couldn't read his face.

She felt a little better after her bath. She sat before her dressing table watching Teresa through the looking glass. Teresa brushed her hair with loving strokes. The silver-handled brush looked heavy in that small white hand.

As the lamp beside the bed grew low Loraine closed her eyes. All her cares flowed away as Teresa stroked and lifted her hair. The bath had made Loraine feel warm and slippery. Her dressing gown, a rather transparent lawn with deep ruffles at the neck and sleeves stuck to her damp skin. Soon she'd lie in the broad bed and the friendly crackle of the hearth fire would talk her to sleep.

It had once been so good with Adam, and those days seemed to belong to another age. She'd harbored her secret then. If nothing else, she was free now. Perhaps in time he'd come to her again and put his hands on her.

She could almost imagine the feel of it, the delicious touch of his warm lips on her breasts, the gentle fire of his hands stealing over her.

She felt dizzy and could scarcely open her eyes. She looked at the scene in the looking glass dark and sultry. Her own face was flushed and slack from the brandy. Too, too much brandy. And there stood Teresa behind her, her cap off now and her dark curls loose. Loraine had always thought Teresa kept her hair tied up under the cap but it was cut short.

Teresa's eyes glowed with devotion. Always there was that yearning on her face and that ever-present cringing.

Loraine felt so good, so relaxed and pleasant. Her breasts tingled with desire. Her nipples were tight just as if...as if Adam were kissing her.

She realized Teresa had stopped brushing her hair. Teresa had one hand on her shoulder. Her sheer dressing gown had slipped, or been eased back. Teresa's other hand...it seemed to be hidden...inside the neckline of Loraine's gown. Teresa was caressing her.

Teresa's eyes indeed glowed with love and devotion. Unwittingly Loraine flinched and Teresa snatched her hand away leaving Loraine's shoulders and breast uncovered.

In the picture framed in the looking glass Adam appeared. "This is amusing," he said.

Teresa screamed.

Clutching her dressing gown closed, Loraine turned. Before she could speak, she watched in amazed horror as Teresa flung herself at Adam and clawed at his astounded face.

"Stop!" Loraine cried, jumping up, stumbling in circles. Adam yanked Teresa around so that her hands could do no more damage to his cheeks. In one quick motion he lifted her up by the back of her bodice. The seams gave way. As he dragged her toward the door, Teresa's bodice came away in his hands exposing her corset cover.

"I told you once to get out of my house. I let you stay only out of guilt, but now I'm done with guilt, and I'm done with you!" He gave the bell pull a vicious jerk.

Teresa went on screaming and struggling. When she realized her underclothes were showing, her screams rose so high and hoarse they ceased to produce sound.

Adam flung open the door. Silvers, in an old red velvet dressing gown and striped blue and white nightcap, hurried from the servants' stairs.

"Get her out of here," Adam snarled, throwing Teresa into the old man's arms. Teresa looked mad with terror.

Adam slammed the door. "Is *she* my rival as well?"

Loraine backed herself against the wall and began to sink. Adam thundered across the room and yanked her up by her shoulders. He tore one ruffled shoulder of her dressing gown aside and sneered when she tried to cover herself. With teeth clenched, he took the back of her head and bent her back. "By God," he hissed. "I'll not be the cuckold of a damned crazy serving girl. Are you my wife or aren't you?"

Loraine struggled against her own desire to surrender. She tried to tear free and yet at the same she strained upward for a kiss. When her lips touched his she closed her eyes and let Adam's bruising kiss demolish every shred of her will. She submitted to his fury, to her dressing gown being torn from her back and hands violent with desire taking possession of her body aching for love.

Adam carried her to the bed and threw her on it. Never taking his eyes from her, he stripped off his shirt and trousers. It was a turbulent reunion. They were sore when it was done.

Then they lay quietly. They had no more need for talk or explanations or even vows. They had each found their way back through the storm.

# Twenty-Four

"Am I right? Am I going to have another baby?"

James smiled. "In the summer." He helped Loraine from her bed. "This time we'll be successful."

Loraine covered her mouth with a trembling hand. "Adam will be pleased. Nothing must go wrong this time. Nothing."

James gave her a peck on the cheek. "I'm happy for you. When will you tell him? Now?"

"It should be a special time—wait! Must you go so soon? Won't you stay for tea?"

James looked reluctant to speak. "I'm off to see Teresa."

Loraine held James back. "Is she ill?" Then she looked down, ashamed. "She's not mad. I'll never believe that."

James shook his head. "I wish I could agree. I see her every week and, to be honest, she's not better. Byron and Nicolette can't take her much longer. I don't know what else to do but…"

"Not an asylum!" Loraine's heart shivered with horror. "I won't stand for it! Teresa was my friend! I feel as if I've deserted her. Couldn't Uncle Thomas take her? She'd work hard."

"You know how feeble the old doctor is, and she's given to fits of screaming. I might as well tell you plain, there's not much hope for her."

"Then I must go to her! She feels abandoned. James, please!" Loraine looked into his sorrowful brown eyes. "Why can't I?"

"It would endanger your pregnancy." He put out his hand and touched her arm. Then he withdrew it self-consciously. "You know how you feel after visiting Thomas."

Loraine struck her fists to her sides. "I've done many things wrong, James. It was heartless and selfish of me to let Adam send her back to DeMarsett house. I wanted my husband again and *she* paid the price. I've been avoiding her and now see what else I've done? I've driven her mad. If I comfort her, you'll see. She'll behave."

"Adam won't let you."

Loraine turned away. "Why must I always be torn?"

James was out the door and halfway down the staircase when Loraine caught up to him. "I'm going with you," she said, her heart beginning to drum. "I wouldn't do anything to jeopardize what Adam and I have found since September but I won't hide from my duty. This is my chance to make up for a lot of things."

"I'll wait for you in my buggy then," he sighed. "Wear a heavy wrap. It's getting cold."

In the library Loraine found Adam bent over a roll of drafting paper. On it was still another design for a clipper—the fastest yet. Before he could ask her about James' visit, she kissed him and said, "James is off now. I'm going with him to see Teresa. I *need* to see her, Adam." She explained what James had said.

Every word darkened Adam's eyes. "You have an unnatural affection for that witch," he said pressing his fist into the paper.

"Witch!" Loraine laughed. "She's just a poor sick child. I won't bring her back. I promise."

Adam looked hard at her for a moment. She had forgotten how frighteningly dark his eyes could get. Was Teresa worth angering him? Then he turned to his plans, his mouth tight.

It would be all right, Loraine told herself, running out to fetch her cloak from the maid. She hurried into the late afternoon sun certain she would be able to bring Teresa to her senses. Perhaps it was selfishness driving her again, she thought pausing by the buggy. If Teresa was well again, Loraine could sleep.

She'd tell Adam about the new baby as soon as she returned. He'd be so surprised and pleased he'd forget all about Teresa. This baby would live and be the true heir to the Roebling Line. Adam would forgive her anything for that.

"Make up your mind, Loraine," James said gently. He lifted the lap robe and she climbed aboard the buggy.

Everything was going to be just fine from that moment on! she thought.

The road into Union Harbor was whisper quiet through the wood. Only the call of an occasional barn owl broke the steady rhythm of James' bay kicking up dust. The forest floor was a deep carpet of brown oak and maple leaves patterned in lines of sunlight and shade, golds and blacks. Big gray boulders were all but lost among them. Past the wood along the bluff the sea lay like a sparkling sunlit blanket. Loraine missed seeing it from the beach. A year and a half had passed since she spent her spring days on the sand. It seemed more like a lifetime.

At that late hour the town was quiet. A lumbering hay wagon passed them and turned onto Atlantic Avenue. Loraine felt a queer dread at seeing the old house again. She hadn't been home since Wendell's funeral. Byron and Nicolette had been married in the white-steepled Presbyterian church and, though they invited Loraine and Adam to supper many times, Loraine had always declined. Her excuses had been genuine, but the truth was she couldn't bear the sight of her brother or the rooms she had once called home.

Now the house appeared in the blaze of an orange sunset. The gray stone and ivy looked afire against a pink cloud-swept sky. James reined in and they both stared. It was beautiful and yet frightening. The light faded quickly then and the house sank lifelessly into a dusky shadow.

Loraine thought of her mother then, of the brief bright moment that had been her life and her love. Loraine carried on for her now, and suddenly she thought she must go back to Adam. He was all that mattered.

As if propelled by an unseen force Loraine found herself standing on the cobbled drive. "Aren't you coming in?" she asked looking back at James watching her.

James was long in answering. "I'll wait."

The wind sent a shiver through her woolen cloak. Then she turned foolish thoughts aside. She owed Teresa one visit.

Her rap sounded hollow. Presently an old woman in a cottage cap and apron answered. Loraine didn't recognize her but supposed her to be Byron's servant.

"Is my brother in? I've come to see Teresa."

The old woman made a sinister sound in her teeth. "That one's mad, she is. Belongs in a cell."

"You mustn't say that!" Loraine said sharply. "Teresa has had a hard life."

"Ain't we all. Master's in his study."

Master, Loraine thought watching the old servant disappear into the shadows at the end of the hall. She could hardly envision Byron as master of anything.

Loraine closed the front door herself and the full impact of being home again assailed her. The house was dirty. Here and there the walls sported bare rectangles where Floris' prized paintings had once hung. Even some of her furniture was missing.

Loraine knocked at the study door. When she got no answer she crept in, fear rising in her throat. She almost expected to find Wendell waiting behind the desk ready to scold her as he had when she was little. One oil lamp lit the chamber. A sour collection of smoke and alcohol odors assaulted her nose. Byron was sprawled in the wing chair behind the desk, looking like a croissant. He was polishing one of Wendell's duelling pistols with the tail of his shirt. Seeing Loraine, he leveled it at her face. The dark muzzle made an ugly sight.

"Put that down! You could kill someone! I want to see Teresa. How could you let James talk of putting her away?"

"I told him he'd better, or I'd do it myself. The damn girl's a nuisance. Nicolette's afraid of her, and I've no desire for a moody bride. Take Teresa back with you. You're the one who unhinged her. From what I've been able to gather of her ravings you live in a den of sexual horrors." He chuckled as his eyes played over her.

"You're disgusting!" She couldn't stand the sight of her brother, her half brother she reminded herself. "Where is she?"

"Locked in the attic. You'll find the key on a peg outside the door. Mind, don't let her out. She's a raving maniac."

Loraine flounced out of the study and attacked the stairs. By the time she reached the attic she fought for breath. The corridor was dark and wind moaned in the eaves. As Loraine fumbled at each door a chill crawled down her back.

At last she came to a locked one. She patted the wall and discovered the key. When the door swung open to a small crude chamber lit by one small gable window, she could see a narrow cot by the far wall. Teresa was crouched on it. She made a guttural noise that raised the hair on Loraine's arms.

Maybe James was right.

"No…" Teresa whispered as if her throat was raw. "Not again. Not again. Not again!" Her voice rose to a hoarse screech.

"Keep her quiet," bellowed Byron from the distance of the first floor.

"It's me," Loraine said softly, gently, poised to yank the door shut if necessary. "Don't you know me, Teresa? I've come to visit. How are you feeling?"

Ghosts seemed to be hovering in the shadows. Must be mice, Loraine told herself. Her skin crawled. She wanted to run.

"Miss?" came a pitiful gasp. Then she heard soft weeping. "Oh, Miss."

Loraine rushed to her, sat on the edge of the cot and took Teresa in her aims. "It's all right," Loraine said just as she did if Hope Janine woke from a bad dream. Teresa wept into her cloak.

"Forgive me, Miss. I was wicked. Take me back. *Please* take me back! I won't say a word about it. I promise not to tell. Just don't let them get me. I won't tell. I won't be wicked. Just make him stop."

"Hush," Loraine said, her heart quivering with remorse. The poor girl was jabbering nonsense. "You'll be all right. I'll see to it. Why, look at you! Your hair's all a-tangle, and…where's your dress? You're wearing only a chemise. Have you no blanket? When did you eat last?"

"Take me back. *Please!*" Teresa tore at Loraine's arms until they ached.

"I don't think I can tonight," Loraine said as sweetly as she could. "Adam wouldn't…"

"Beware, Miss! He's a *bad* man. He tried to kill me."

"Now, now. I know how awful it must have been. I'm so sorry you've had to stay here. If you can just hang on a little longer…"

"No! I won't stay. He's a beast. He's cold. I won't do it. I won't do it."

"Be quiet now," Loraine snapped. "If you're not…"

"I know. I know," Teresa panted, her eyes darting to the corners and back to the open door. "I'll be quiet. Then he won't come. I'll be quiet. I don't want to do it."

"Do what?" Loraine whispered. "What are you talking about? Who are you talking about? Has Byron hurt you?"

"All men hurt me. On the ship by my mother…All of them…All of them."

Teresa's body quaked in Loraine's arms.

"And *him!*" She turned fevered eyes on Loraine. "Does he hurt you, too? How did you get out? Locked doors! Locks and keys. They hurt me. I hate them. I hate them!" Teresa screamed.

"Sh-h-h! You mustn't worry about *me*. I'm happy now."

"Yes, happy now. I'm happy, too, now that you've come. I was afraid you wouldn't, but I knew you were a prisoner. I knew you'd try. Men are bad, Miss. Very bad. Very evil. Don't let them touch you. I should have told you before. It's bad. Very bad. He hurt you. I knew he did, but I couldn't stop him. I tried, but I fell down the stairs. He pushed me. He did! He *did!* On your wedding night. He's a beast, Miss. All men are beasts. They rape and laugh…"

Teresa snuggled into Loraine's bosom. Loraine was too stunned to speak.

"But we'll be all right. Help me get out, Miss." Teresa pulled up the soiled hem of her chemise exposing her ankle. It was tied to the cot's frame and was so clawed and chewed it couldn't be undone.

Loraine felt as if her stomach were full of stones. Swallowing at something hard and sour, she got up. Teresa pulled at her. "Wait! Let me think." She put a shaky hand to her forehead. Her fingers were like ice. "You hurt your leg on my wedding night? You were at the estate that night?"

Teresa nodded. "I went to help you. I knew you'd be alone with him and I knew he'd want to hurt you. I *saw* him hurting you!"

"No, Teresa! He didn't hurt me. You say he pushed...It couldn't be. He was with me!" Loraine shook off Teresa's hand and made a half-hearted attempt at the knot. Teresa's ankle was chaffed raw. Who would've done such a thing to her?

"All men hurt," Teresa said with perfect certainty. "They have the weapon."

"Stop it!" Loraine cried with a hysterical little giggle. "You're mixed up. You've had a bad time here. You're hungry and cold and afraid. Be patient, and I'll untie you. Did James see this? Has Doctor James really been here?"

Teresa looked bewildered.

"Maybe I'll have to get a knife," Loraine said in exasperation as she bent back one of her nails trying to get at the knot.

"Don't leave me!" Teresa shrieked. She threw herself off the cot, landed on her hands and knees with a cry, and crawled after Loraine, dragging the cot a few inches. "Don't leave me!"

"I'll be right back! Stop that now, and get up. You must show everyone you're well and sound, or I'll be helpless. You mustn't worry about me, Teresa. I'm happy again. Truly I am. Adam loves me, and I love him. We're going to have another baby."

Loraine waited for her happy news to calm her old maid. Instead, Teresa's eyes nearly bulged from their sockets. Her mouth opened to show all her teeth. She made that hideous guttural noise again. "Another baby! Lord have mercy. He'll take it, too, and throw it in the sea."

"Don't *say* such things! I think James was..."

"*He* knows. Ask him. Ask that whore, Yolanda. Ask *her*. She carried it off! Ask the housekeeper. Ask the manservant. They all know. I promised I wouldn't tell. They said they'd kill me. It was a bad thing to have that baby. Bad for you, and I wanted you to be happy again, so I said I wouldn't tell. Ask them!"

"I can't believe what you're saying!"

"Believe! Ask *him*. *He* did it. I heard it. It didn't die. I heard it cry!"

Loraine steadied herself on the doorframe. She couldn't remember that time clearly. After the baby died she had nightmares. She'd wanted to die, too. James had given her sleeping potions.

Teresa's hand strained toward Loraine, her fingers spread and trembling. "I swear it was alive. I saw them take your baby!"

Loraine rolled around the doorframe and yanked the door shut. She scarcely heard the screaming from within. Shut up! She couldn't think, and she *must* think.

She heard thundering footsteps. She raced down the narrow attic stairs to meet Byron on the way up. She hardly saw him as she flew passed, her feet taking the steps in perfect rhythm.

In seconds she was outside. She grabbed the rim of James' buggy wheel and held herself up, panting, almost retching. James leapt down, rounded the back of the buggy and put his arm around her waist. She flung it away.

"Tell me the truth."

In the light of the street lamp glowing nearby, James' face looked waxen. Someone slammed the front door. Teresa had stopped screaming. The air trembled.

"Did my baby die?"

James' mouth stretched open as if he was going to shout. She held his horrified stare and watched his cheek twitch. He swallowed then. "No."

She collapsed.

It was something like a faint, only Loraine could still see and hear and think. She let James lift her into the buggy. She sat limp and dazed as he climbed in and whipped his horse. The buggy jolted into the street back up Atlantic Avenue and through town. By the time they reached the estate's gate, Loraine could move again. She laid her hand on his arm and whispered for him to stop.

James looked startled. He jerked the reins so hard his horse reared.

"I'm not ill," Loraine said impatiently. She grabbed the seat until the buggy steadied. She was weary of being sickly. She straightened and shook off her stupor. "Tell me all."

James opened his mouth but no sound came. The woods closed in on them as if listening. The swaying lantern sent arcs of yellow light back and forth across the road. The leaves rustled like voices.

After a long wait, he cleared his throat. "The morning you went into labor Yolanda started in on Adam. She got him drinking and never stopped hammering at him until he would've done whatever she wanted just to quiet her. And she was very convincing besides. When they told me the plan I had no choice. They would have locked me away from you, and you might have died. I'm sorry, Loraine, but I couldn't let you die.

I had to agree to their plan. I thought it might really be better for you in the long run. I knew Adam eventually would take you back. He never stopped loving you, and I was right. See how he…"

"All this time you let me mourn a dead baby who was not dead? It nearly broke my heart!" Her cry was swallowed up by the woods.

James nodded. "You have your deceptions. We have ours. If Adam hadn't taken you back, I…" His hand stole across the gulf between them and touched hers. Then he leaned against her, his face too close, his eyes too naked. "I was watching out for you. Yolanda wanted Adam and still does. Loraine, we…"

She turned cold eyes on him. James faded back, abashed. Her lips trembled as she asked, "Is my baby alive still?"

James shrank into his manteau, dejected and ashamed. "Yes. But I don't know where. Yolanda said she'd take your baby to a foundling home where he would be adopted and live a good life. I agreed and haven't asked her about it since. There was no reason to."

"Foundling!" Loraine gasped. She felt weak again and that fueled her anger. "*My* baby."

"It was the only way. That baby was a Mercedes. His father killed my father. Can you forget that?"

"Yes!"

"Well, we can't."

"An innocent baby! You both are fine cowards," Loraine snapped. "Take me home now. I want to see how Adam fares when *his* deceptions are exposed. Righteous bastards, the lot of you!"

Her feet touched the drive before James had fully stopped the buggy. She stormed up the steps and into the hall brushing aside all waiting hands. Even Silvers, tall and gaunt in his livery, shrank from her glare.

She threw her mantle to the floor and watched Isa come in and stoop stiffly to retrieve it. Loraine gave her a withering look. "Get out of my sight. All of you. You had your victory. You thought you had me beat. Well, hear me now. I know what you've done and you sicken me!"

Adam appeared in the library doorway, his face a mirror to his amazement. "What's going on, Loraine?"

"So threatened by a baby, were you, Adam?" Loraine advanced. "No wonder you didn't want me to see Teresa. She just told me what you did. I didn't want to believe it. I didn't want to believe you could be so cold-blooded. But now I have proof. You thought you could take my bastard baby and break my heart. Did that appease you? And to think I worshipped you. I prayed you'd forgive me someday and take me back. I make *myself* sick. We're even now, Adam. A lie for a lie."

"Get hold of yourself."

She walked up to him and slapped him. "I want my baby back. I mean to have him, too. I don't care if the devil fathered him. *He* is innocent. I sinned. Not him. I suffered, but he shouldn't have to, not an innocent. Bring him back, Adam, or you'll never lay a hand on your true heir." She clasped her hands over her belly. "Yes! In the summer. To think…" Her voice broke. "Oh, God. To think all these months I thought…"

She spun around with a choked cry. The room winked into darkness.

# Twenty-Five

Spring came early. The rain and high March wind kept the temperature cool, but soon a blanket of green covered the town promising a beautiful year.

By May the oaks on the estate had leafed out lush and heavy, but that afternoon Loraine saw little of the beauty. She sat beside James in the buggy, longing to be home and in bed. Since early morning they had ridden nearly twenty miles. Her back cried for relief.

James was about to turn down the road toward his own house. "We'll talk to Yolanda again," he said to Loraine's questioning look.

She shook her head. "I'm too tired. She's lied to us again. I doubt anything we say will ever change her mind." She held tight to the little carved sailor boy Uncle Thomas had made for her so many months before.

James reined. He looked tired, too. "I'm so sorry. I wish we'd found him today. This is an awful strain on you."

She patted his hand.

"I know of a few more foundling homes, but I'll go alone from now on." He stopped her protest. "In a week or two you'll have a healthy new baby to care for."

She nodded, waiting for James to drive on. When he didn't, and instead raised his eyes to peer at her, she felt uneasy.

James swallowed. "I don't think we're going to find him."

"Don't!"

"I hate to say that, especially now, but I've thought about this a long while. How far could Yolanda have taken a newborn in the night? She may have left him on any doorstep. I think the longer we look, the less chance we have of finding him."

Loraine's threatening tears came quickly. She leaned against James' shoulder. He was too good at putting her fears into words.

"Turn your thoughts to your new baby. Let's give up, now, before you harm yourself with more false hope. You've grieved long enough."

"I hate Yolanda!" Loraine whispered. "I shouldn't want that baby, not a Mercedes, but if I had him, if he was raised with love, don't you think that would make a difference?"

"Of course," he whispered stroking her hair.

"Bad can be turned into good with love, can't it?" Loraine asked.

James' eyes swelled dark and heavy. He kissed her cheek. "You could do it, but I'm afraid in this case it's hopeless." He searched her face. "Sometimes I think about going away. Illinois needs doctors."

Loraine looked away, startled, and afraid to look at James. In her secret fantasies she'd thought of going away, too. Always when there was trouble she wanted to run. She put her face into James' shoulder.

"I can't let myself even think such a thing," she said weeping for all the lost hopes and wasted hours. She rubbed her thumb across the surface of the whittled figure in her pocket. She had worn the edges smooth.

A few hours later she sat sipping tea. The sitting room was quiet. It was a comforting room, one she'd redecorated and moved into since that horrid day last November. She couldn't share the master suite with Adam anymore.

The happy sounds of little Hope Janine's chatter came from the new nursery next door. Loraine had had that room done over, too. No more babies relegated to the cold third floor.

Putting aside the thin china cup, she turned from staring out the dark square of the window. Soon there would be a new heir for Adam, or perhaps the daughter she longed for. She should be looking forward to the coming birth, but instead she endangered her health riding all over the countryside torturing herself over the forlorn faces in foundling asylums. She could only think of that stolen babe of Mercedes blood. She yearned to hold him in her arms. All she had was a bit of wood.

When she looked up, she was startled to see Adam watching her from the doorway.

"I heard you crying."

"It's nothing. Leave me alone."

"Are you well?"

"*Make* Yolanda tell what she did with my baby!" Loraine said jumping up. "Please? I can't go on like this."

"Loraine, I've tried."

"Try harder! If you cared for me you'd do everything in your power. Look at us. After all this time, this impossible deadlock. If only we could get away."

Loraine paused. Her back began to ache.

With a strange light in his eye, Adam stepped into the sitting room. His hair was tousled and gray. The crease beside his mouth had grown deeper, the planes of his face more pronounced.

"I never had a chance to tell you," Adam said, "but some time ago I bought a small house in Saxwell. I was going to take you there. Would you like to go now?"

"Now?" She took a breath and held it. The pain in her back eased.

"It would be quiet and safe. We'd find a midwife..." He ran his fingers through his hair and looked touchingly vulnerable with his curls jutting back. "You still don't trust me, do you? I wish you would. I thought I'd never forgive you. You knew another man and you tricked me. I couldn't abide that, but I still wanted you. Finally I put it from my mind. All of it, Loraine, Beau Mercedes and my father's murder—the lot of it. I wanted you for my wife. You carry living proof that for a while we were happy again."

A cool sweat broke out on Loraine's brow. Her back tightened. The pain crept around to her belly. It was a deep ache not so different from the ache of love, love come to fruit.

"Don't stare at me like that," he snapped. He crossed the room quickly and put his hands on her shoulders.

A thousand thoughts battled in Loraine's mind. James, the dismal common room of the foundling home they'd visited that day, the morning she woke to the realization that Beau's baby had died...She remembered nights she and Adam spent together when they were first married, and then last fall after Teresa went away.

Loraine looked up into Adam's eyes. She was afraid. Just the nearness of him sent her heart racing. Oh, how she wanted everything to be right again!

Still the memories held her back. All the betrayals, hers, his, the horror of the birthing room...Her back felt as if someone was twisting a dull knife in it. She needed to sit, but Adam held her.

Had he pushed Teresa? Was his desire for her so strong he could do such a thing? *Did* he love her, or was it an uncontrollable need, like hers, that made him want her in spite of everything?

Would she wake later to find herself tied to that bed in the birthing room?

As her belly tightened, Loraine stiffened. She needed James now. Her fear was more real than any desire.

Adam let her go. He squared his shoulders and went back out. "You'll take me back, I suppose, when we return your Mercedes bastard?"

We? She twisted away so he couldn't see her face. A rush of warm wetness ran down her legs.

"Too bad Beau died," Adam said darkly. "I wish he hadn't. I wish you had run off with him as you planned. I wish I'd never laid eyes on you."

"I wish *you* had been merciful and smothered my baby. I wish you had killed Teresa, too! You're a clumsy criminal, Adam. Union Harbor is littered with them."

"I'll not crawl to you again."

She whirled. His face looked molded in marble. "Was that crawling? Mother of God, you're proud."

"Like you."

"Maybe I *should* go away!" she cried wishing she could throw Adam out. She wished to slam the door in his face. Instead she struggled to sit.

"Not while you carry my son."

She laughed, her face wet with tears. "Get out!"

The door trembled after it slammed. The great silence of the house swallowed the echo. Loraine dashed away her tears and got unsteadily to her feet. The pains were quick and hard, different from before. She went to the door, one hand on her belly, the other on her mouth. She jerked the bell pull.

She expected to hear eager footsteps come up the hall. When no one came she stifled a hysterical giggle. Maybe Adam had dismissed all the servants the way her papa—the way Wendell used to when he was angered.

She opened the door. Maybe she could get to James in time. Isa appeared at the end of the hall. Since November she'd been forbidden to set foot on the second floor. The very sight of her brought up Loraine's quivering hatred. The old woman's face was like Satan's own angel. There *were* evil forces loose in the world, Loraine thought with a shudder. She wished God would have pity on her.

"Yes, M'lady? You rang?" Isa rasped, her eyes devoid of any feeling.

"Send for James," Loraine said, her voice too high and weak.

Isa inclined her head.

Loraine pushed her door closed. Then she locked it and took the key with her to the nightstand. She locked the door to the nursery, too.

Safe, she thought, working her way back to the bed. She was shivering from her wet skirts.

After a time she gave up trying to unfasten all the hooks down the back of her bodice. She tore it off. Her skirt's ties annoyed her, too, but at last she threw the heavy linen to the floor.

She put on a fresh nightdress and lay down to wait for James. Maybe she would go west with him. They'd take Hope and maybe even Miranda...

The lamp grew dim, but Loraine couldn't move to turn up the wick. Frighteningly fast her pains gathered momentum. She arched up, grabbing her knees. The urge to push felt oddly satisfying. "Tell James to hurry!" she called out.

With the third push she let out a loud cry, not a scream, just a call of immense effort. Surely God was a man, for no woman would have designed a birth passage so narrow!

She gathered all her strength. There was no escape. She gave a mighty push, and with a throat-tearing grunt delivered herself! For a moment she fell back panting. Her legs trembled as if from ague. She wanted to cry. She wanted to laugh.

Then she heard a sputtering sound. She rolled to a sitting position and saw a red wiggling boy child with a face as indignant as Adam's! And wet dark curly hair, and fists.

"Dear God."

Someone began beating upon the door.

Loraine didn't hear. She petted the slippery arms of her newborn son. He was alive! She was alive. The Roebling curse was broken!

The paneled door exploded from the frame and crashed to the carpet. As Adam bolted in the baby began crying in earnest. Adam rocked as his feet froze in mid-stride.

James stumbled around him. He stopped, too. He hadn't even taken his coat off yet. Loraine had never realized how much the two of them looked alike. She laughed. She wiped away her tears and laughed.

Creeping forward, Adam's and James' faces were comic studies in surprise. Adam stopped near the bed, but James came to her and kissed her forehead. "Well done!" he smiled. "You shouldn't have waited so long to send for me."

Loraine turned her eyes on Adam. He stepped closer, his eyes fixed on his son. When he reached out to touch him, Loraine drew back gathering the baby into the wet circle of her exposed legs, back to the nest from which he sprang.

"Bring me my first born," she said.

Shock traveled from Adam's hand to his eye.

"*Make* her tell you where he is."

Without a thought for her audience, she opened the throat of her nightdress and pulled her baby to her breast. The ripe swell popped out. She stroked his tiny angry face clean as he rooted and began to suck. For a long time she thought of nothing else.

# Twenty-Six

Yolanda led them a merry chase.

Through the remainder of the summer and far into autumn James neglected his practice to ride far and wide in search of a child he didn't expect to find.

Loraine spent her days in the nursery absorbed with her new son, Garner, a robust healthy Roebling son. She ordered a new cradle for him, having had the old nursery stripped and locked. The birthing room was locked, too. If Adam hadn't refused, she would have called in a priest to exorcize the ghosts lingering there.

Soon the autumn storms passed into winter. James gave up his treks to Boston and Salem and took up his medical practice again. He returned to Union Hospital and buried himself in his work. He was doing well of it until December when Loraine invited the family for a long Christmas stay. Hope Janine was going to be three years old and they would celebrate.

As soon as Yolanda heard of it she ran to Isa, her only friend and confidante on the estate. In the pantry of the main house she took tea and gathered all the family gossip. It had been far too long since she'd visited. She had been content to wait, certain her lies were keeping Adam and Loraine miles apart.

"How is it with them?" she asked Isa trying not to show how alarmed she was. Surely if Adam and Loraine were inviting everyone back, everyone must be forgiven. Things must be going far too well.

The old woman couldn't smile, but her gray eyes snapped. "They are civil." Her tone said more.

"And at night?"

"I keep watch. He still sleeps in his bed, and she in hers."

Yolanda sagged with relief, but it was short-lived. Isa implied the impasse wouldn't last much longer. Yolanda made a point to visit Isa every day, and even so she grew more and more uneasy.

She and James and Miranda arrived on the nineteenth, taking up their usual suite down the hall. Conrad left his boarding house in town, deserted his fellows and rollicking fests to come home for this first holiday with the young heir. The house was warm and comfortable. With each passing hour Yolanda grew more desperate.

On the twenty-first Isa succumbed to a sick throat. That, at least, occupied James, who otherwise was off visiting ailing patients or receiving gifts of wine and cakes at the homes of those he'd cured.

Yolanda stayed underfoot of the servants in the pantry, drinking brandy-laced tea and listening to Loraine bustle about her house preparing for the happy reunion of the Roebling clan on Christmas Eve. That Loraine wouldn't look at Yolanda or even acknowledge her presence only set Yolanda's nerves more on edge.

If Loraine and Adam could overcome the disappearance of that dratted baby, where did that leave Yolanda? James bored her to the point of madness. Conrad had grown so tiresome since she told him to be off—that was when she was sure Loraine would soon be gone. What was the use of finishing school airs if she always had to settle for second best?

"Go ahead, Hope," Loraine said. "You can play with Cousin Miranda. I'll make sure she doesn't pinch you."

Little Hope Janine was a spindly child. That evening she wore a red and white gown Yolanda had insisted upon. It was a color far too gaudy for her. She toddled across the grand parlor toward the pine nestled in the corner. Miranda sat under the tree picking at the doll Loraine had ordered from New York. She seemed to like it.

Seeing Hope approach, Miranda jumped to her feet and growled. "It's mine!" Her long yellow curls hung in a tangle over her round shoulders. She had dirtied her stockings, crawling on the hearth, and the pink satin sash on her organdy gown had slipped below her tummy making her look a lot like a puppy.

Sighing, Loraine handed Garner to Maude. "Take him up to nap. I'll be up for his midnight feeding." She was about to prevent Miranda from attacking Hope when Conrad strolled in. All these guests, Loraine thought. Adam's reunion was growing wearisome.

"My sweeting," Conrad crooned, holding still another goblet of wassail in his long thin hand. "You're in your element here. Screaming, squawking babies. What a delight, and how they become you."

"I hoped you'd gone out for a while," she said unperturbed. Conrad came to her and pulled her away from Hope's hiccupping sobs and the toothy snarls of her fat cousin.

"A Christmas kiss?" Conrad grinned.

"You never get enough, do you? You're an obnoxious rutting beast, Conrad Roebling." Her words were harsh but held a teasing note Loraine couldn't disguise. For all his conceit, Conrad wasn't all bad. Sometimes his was the only smile in the house. And he visited frequently.

Conrad pursed his lips and shook his head. "So cold a heart you have. Do you run with the minx, Yolanda?"

"Don't you have some wench waiting?"

"*You,* perchance?" he grinned. "I must do the rutting, as you so delicately put it, for us all. James' bed is cold. So is Adam's, I trust. Why does gold on the finger harden the heart and freeze the breast?" He pressed his palm to the front of Loraine's red velvet bodice.

She didn't flinch. Neither did she slap away his hand. Her response was one of surprise and mild anger. She put on a mask of boredom and hoped he'd just go away. It was impossible not to feel *something* when a man like Conrad flirted so brashly.

"Oh, dear," Conrad sighed, clucking his tongue and drawing away. "You *are* of the north. Your breath blows cold, and your skin is as pretty as ice. I wouldn't have you if you lay naked in the hearth."

He laughed, but his face was red.

Loraine reddened, too. She *did* feel cold.

From the hall, Adam watched the interplay. He'd come when he heard Janine's and Miranda's screams. They were quiet now, stuffing their faces with the Christmas sweets which had been tied to the pine branches with narrow red ribbons.

Would he never come upon his wife that she wasn't in the arms of some other man? She looked unmoved, but could he be sure?

Adam turned back to his library and its dark safety. There he could sit under his father's portrait and gather strength from it. No woman had ever weakened John Roebling. He had married and raised his sons and built an empire from nothing.

Closing the door Adam went to the decanters on the library table. Loraine hadn't stolen in for a toddy in months; and he'd waited every night. Damn stubborn woman, he thought, swallowing the smooth brandy. Such nasty pride.

He heard his door opening. A small hand curled around the edge. His heart leapt.

Yolanda pressed the door closed and leaned against it. She looked especially beautiful in midnight blue taffeta. The froth of white lace at the neckline was so low Adam had little left to imagine. She made a pretty smile. He was surprised at how thin she was. Her collar bones cut across her chest.

"I hoped I'd catch you alone, Adam," she whispered, crossing to him.

He wished she was Loraine.

"Adam," Yolanda whispered. "I have a present for you." He turned, curious. She put her hand on his arm. He couldn't feel it. Maybe he was dreaming. Sometimes he did dream of Yolanda, purring and naked, in spite of himself.

She pressed herself to his chest, her breasts hard lumps, and kissed him. He felt a small stirring of interest. He wasn't meant to be celibate. No Roebling was. And she was so willing.

"Lock the door," she whispered.

He made a move to obey her.

That's how he thought of his step toward the door, obedience. He stopped, blinking. He put his drink down. His brain felt muddled. He felt just as he had that night Yolanda convinced him to let her steal away Loraine's child.

His cheeks tightened.

Yolanda was so beautiful. She pressed herself against his arm. Her bodice dipped lower and lower. "For just a little while," she whispered.

Adam turned away. She was a witch!

"Don't," Yolanda purred. She began to tug at the shoulders of her gown. "Don't think of her. She doesn't love you. Not like I do. She loves James. They're going to run away. She's a harlot, Adam. Can't you see that? First it was Beau. Now…"

He put his hand on the corner of his desk for support.

"Look, Adam," Yolanda was saying. "Look at me. You want me. I know you do. Let yourself forget. Take me. I need you, Adam. I always have."

He looked. Somehow she'd gotten her bodice unhooked and had pulled it down. Her breasts were small and nicely rounded with pink swollen nipples.

He pulled his eyes away.

"Look, Adam! You're lonely. You need me. Let yourself go. It'll be good for us."

A groan came from his throat. Yes, he ached, but the ache was for Loraine. Only Loraine. He whirled. Yolanda was cupping her breasts and smiling.

"You're no better than your murdering brother. I wouldn't dirty my hands on you."

He marveled at the change in her face. Yolanda's smile was replaced with a cry of pain. She came at him with nails flying. They tore across the side of his neck before he twisted her wrists behind her back. It was a pretty sight and suited her.

"You're not a man," she hissed, spittle bubbling on her lips. "You can't escape me. I own you. I can keep you from your child bride as long as I want. *I know* where the brat is, you know. And I'll never tell. Break my arms. I won't tell!"

Adam flung her and sent her sprawling across his carpet. He rounded his desk and sat. His knees were weak. His chest ached. He was afraid he might actually cry.

Yolanda picked herself up and marched on him. "I have you in my hand, Adam Roebling." She held out one of her little hands curling the fingers like the jaws of a trap. "You'll never be free of me because I can make you do whatever I want. You're my puppet. I say, let's steal away the baby, and you nod your wooden head. Look at me, Adam. Aren't I right? Aren't I?"

Adam raised his head. Yolanda smiled. She was right. He was no stronger than James, no better than Conrad. He'd bent to her will, a tavern wench.

He pulled open the center desk drawer. There lay his father's pistol, the one Beau Mercedes had taken from him and fired. Adam reached for it. He put the charge in the pan, drew back the hammer and aimed at Yolanda.

She screamed with laughter. "You haven't the courage to do it!" And she lunged with both hands.

She caught the long barrel pushing it up and back. The pistol exploded, wrenching both their hands. Yolanda fell against Adam, and they toppled backwards as the chair fell over.

Blood welled on Adam's temple. Yolanda screamed.

In seconds James came running from upstairs. Conrad followed, still holding his wassail, still smiling. They glanced at Yolanda, her bodice still lowered and her breasts bouncing with her hysterical cries. Then they saw Adam sprawled behind the desk beyond the overturned chair, his arms flung out, palms up.

"Good God," Conrad whispered, his smile gone.

Loraine ran through the door and stumbled to a stop. Her eyes swept around the library, taking in Yolanda, her breasts, the lingering pall from the pistol charge and its acrid smell. She saw James and Conrad stooped behind the desk.

"Get my bag!" James whispered. "I can't tell how bad it is."

Conrad darted out.

James looked up and wiped his forehead leaving behind a smear of blood.

Loraine screamed. She stepped closer, saw Adam on his back, eyes closed by a curtain of very red blood, and she screamed again.

Haltingly she went even closer, her hands before her, fingers spread as if afraid to reach out. She stopped screaming though her face remained frozen in the same open-mouthed grimace. In the background was Yolanda's hysterical laughter as she fell back against one of the book closets, clutching her stomach and throwing back her head.

Loraine fell to her knees beside Adam's unconscious body. She took his bloody head into her lap. She looked at James and he flinched. "Is he dead?"

"I don't think so."

With a groan she fell across his face and kissed him until her lips were wet with his blood.


The house was still. Loraine slept in a chair by the master suite door. When it opened she jerked awake. James stepped out and passed a hand over his eyes.

"He'll have a smart new part in his hair after this," he said laughing weakly. "But he'll live."

Loraine began to laugh. She ran to his arms. "Thank God! Thank God!"

"Did Yolanda say what happened? Adam just mumbled something about wooden toys."

Loraine shook her head. "She went home. I never want her here again. Are you sure Adam will be all right?"

"We have only fever to fear now."

"Thank you," she whispered squeezing his hands.

"I'm sending for Thomas," James said then. "Don't look alarmed. I just hope the old fellow is up to it. I don't intend to be here much longer. I've decided to take Yolanda and Miranda west."

Loraine looked at James as if he was deserting her. As quickly as that thought came, Loraine realized she'd been counting on James to take care of her if, after all, she and Adam never reconciled.

Already James looked as if he'd arrived in some distant territory. She watched him go down the stairs as if he'd just lost a patient, not saved one.

Then she sank to the chair again. Just where *did* her heart lie? She had once thought herself in love with Beau. He turned out to be a worthless rake. She had thought she'd grown to love Adam, yet she could still entertain fantasies about James and his gentle kindness and his soft brown eyes. She could even enjoy the banter with Conrad, and his roving hands.

Did she love no one with all her heart and soul?

She looked at the door and beyond to what she could see of the velvet draped tester. She knew suddenly with a deep down sorrow that she had *never* given her heart completely to anyone save her mother. And Mama had died.

She had loved her baby, Beau's baby. He was gone. Her eyes darted to the nursery door and a bolt of fear went through her. When she gave her heart she opened herself to pain and loss. She was afraid to lose anyone more.

Her little son Garner lay next to Maude in the nursery. Now Hope was tucked in, too, the both of them snug and safe. Yet at any moment they might fall sick and die.

Somewhere her first born son lay—alive and well, or dead and cold. Loraine doubled over the pain in her heart. To love meant to feel a crushing, burning fear, a dread of what might happen.

Adam moaned. She jumped to her feet.

Beau had been a tease, Conrad a tease, even James with his hints and hesitations, a tease. James didn't really love her anymore than she really loved him. No one loved her as she wanted to be loved, wholly, passionately, unfailingly, except...

She went into the bedchamber and looked down at Adam's ashen face in the marriage bed, his head wrapped in white, a red spot over one temple.

Adam loved her and hated her. He needed her and spurned her, kissed her and pushed her away. She saw pain etched in the lines around his eyes. The corner of his mouth turned down now. She had done that. He was living, breathing proof that someone had opened his heart to her, and known the pain of betrayal. Day by day she stood aside as he tried to close his heart once again, close it as surely as John before him had had to close his heart in order to survive.

Could she stand by and let that happen?

Loraine wasn't so sure she had the courage to love. She'd never really tried, and maybe now it was too late.

She sank to her knees beside the bed and pulled Adam's cool hand to her lips. To love Adam meant she must give up hope on the baby she had lost, because to love Adam meant to forgive him.

So, if she must…

She looked at Adam's sleeping face and let the floodgates in her heart open. What she felt then didn't hurt. She felt suddenly filled with peace. She lay her head on his arm and for the first time in more than two years, perhaps even longer, she could live with what she was.

# Twenty-Seven

## Spring 1840

Beau Mercedes pushed his way through the door and sneered at Byron DeMarsett cowering behind the desk. "Since your father's dead, I'll give *you* what I lived three long years to return and give him."

Before Byron could believe his eyes—Beau Mercedes returned from the dead—Beau's left hand shot out dragging him up and over the desk by the throat. Byron let out a terrified squawk just as Beau's right fist sank into his face.

With Byron sprawled unconscious and bloody across the desktop, the oil lamp still tottering, Beau turned to survey the dark chamber.

Dismal place, he thought. Then his gaze fell on the only items worthy of note in the chamber, a pair of magnificent duelling pistols nestled in a velvet-lined case. He went to them, smiling and jerking at the tight cravat wrapped about his neck.

Just what he needed, inlaid gold to seize the dream of a lifetime.

He should have waylaid a brawnier traveler, he thought shrugging in the tight tail coat. He could feel the seams straining as he shook raindrops from the shoulders. But sometimes he had to settle for what he could get. No more. The fine coat and breeches made him appear prosperous. He had no coin, but that he'd soon remedy.

He heard a soft rustling sound behind him. He whirled, dipping in a graceful motion, hand to boot, and instantly stood poised, knife at the ready. He stared at a scrawny buck-toothed woman standing in the dark doorway in her nightdress.

She clapped her reddened hands over her mouth, her eyes rolling. As he replaced his dagger she steadied herself on the nearest table. "Have you killed him?" she whispered.

"Not yet," Beau smiled.

That wasn't the beautiful Loraine he remembered. Beau took a step forward. This one sure wasn't much to look at. "And who might you be?"

She waggled a finger at Byron's body. "His wife, Nicolette."

"Ah," Beau said with some surprise. "You have my heartfelt sympathy."

A few minutes earlier an old shrew had given Beau entry at the front door. She'd told him the old captain was long dead, exposed, as she had put it, as a filthy slaving pig.

"So who lives here now?" he had asked peering in the door.

"The pig's own shoat."

"Why work for such as that?" he'd asked.

"He pays."

And so Beau had gone into Byron's study and vented his long-held revenge.

Now for the young wife Beau moved his face to charming lines. She went to her husband and stared at him seemingly more distressed by the blood on his cuff than that coming from his nose.

"I can assume, then, the fair Loraine wed Adam Roebling?"

Nicolette's eyes snapped to his face, hardened eyes, he thought. Unhappy eyes.

"If you've come to rob us, sir," she said surveying Beau with doubt, "you can see we have nothing. These are hard times."

"You have these," he said lifting one of the pistols from the case with due respect. "I'll have one for a start."

"Who *are* you?"

"Beau Mercedes. I once captured Loraine's heart, and I mean to have it back. And more. Where is she?"

Forgetting her unconscious husband, Nicolette moved into a pool of lamplight. The shadow of a bruise accounted for her woeful appearance.

Beau sucked at his sour tongue. "I want to talk to Loraine."

"She's at Roebling Estate, of course. Sound asleep, as I was, I'm sure. Are you sure he's not dead?"

"I'll kill him when it suits my purpose. Be a good woman and fetch Loraine for me. And while you're galloping about, take a message to the other Roebling men, Conrad and James. You know them, I trust."

Nicolette nodded.

Beau wondered if she had the wits to carry out his plan. "Tell them to meet me at the main house no later than dawn. I have business with them all." He took a few steps toward Nicolette. "Can you do that?"

"Yes."

"Will you? I'll make you glad you did. Tell Loraine to come here. Alone. Tonight. Can you convince her to come?"

"She has no use for her brother or…Oh, I know a way!" She

almost smiled.

Beau grinned. "Hurry on then. What have you to eat?" Nicolette waved her hand. "Take what you can find. I think the housewoman just ran off. She thought you were going to murder us in our beds."

Beau listened then as Nicolette grabbed a cloak and clattered out into the rain.

He tested the weight of the pistol and smiled. With luck he'd get all three Roeblings this night. In short order he'd marry Loraine and be the richest man in Union Harbor. The son of a thief, was he? He'd show the whole town his sum and substance.

After loading the fine old weapon, he leveled it and swept it around the room in a deadly arc. Momentarily he pointed the glittering gray and gold muzzle at Byron. Then he moved on. He might have uses for such a man.

He jammed the pistol in his belt and filled his coat pockets with balls and powder. In the kitchen he found a bare ham bone and some cold gravy. As he pushed the bowl to the floor in disgust, Nicolette rode off. He'd expected such a frail-looking bird to go by carriage. That meant Loraine would be there soon. He'd have to hurry.

Gnawing on the joint, Beau Mercedes mounted the stairs. He went from dark chamber to dark chamber finding nothing of value. Many of the upper rooms were bare. One held only a bed and wardrobe.

He happened on the attic stairs and ventured up. Those damp cubicles were as empty as the ones below save for a few chests, two spilling over with finery many years old; linens, china and some figurines in French porcelain.

He couldn't carry any of that. Beau shrugged and moved on. Then he came to a locked door and unceremoniously kicked it open. He expected to find the true cache of valuables missing from the rest of the house. Or, possibly, valuables Byron himself had yet to discover. Surely there was *something* left of the DeMarsett fortune.

He saw only a black chamber lit by one gable window. The echoes of the increasing storm shook the rafters. As he snorted in disgust, a sudden scream cut through the wind chilling his bones.


Nicolette stood shivering in the doorway of the last tavern she cared to try. "If you see Conrad tonight," she shouted over the thunder, "tell him to go to Roebling Estate. Tell him it's a matter of life and death."

The tavern keeper grinned with tobacco-dark teeth. "You ain't his cup of tea, M'lady. He likes a bit more spice."

"Tell him Beau Mercedes is back."

Nicolette slogged back to Byron's old horse. He'd long since sold their carriage. She supposed she should have been glad she didn't have to *walk* to the estate.

She scrambled astride the sway-backed beast and galloped into the sheeting rain. Drops pelted her face. The wind yanked back her soggy hood and the rain soaked her hair and ran down her neck. She nearly missed the road curving north skirting the bluffs to Roebling Estate.

She didn't wonder why she obeyed a man who had just stormed her house and laid out her husband cold. She just obeyed, same as she obeyed her own parents when they said she'd best settle for Byron and be glad there was a man who'd have her.

That ale-tender thought she wasn't Conrad's type, but it hadn't been so many years ago he'd courted her. She wished she really had been compromised. To be talked about and shunned for a few hasty kisses was a cruel joke.

Perhaps that was why she obeyed this Beau Mercedes. She hadn't seen Conrad since her wedding. Maybe now...She must find something or someone to make her life worth living. As it was, she was going mad in that gloomy stone house. Byron had once been reasonably kind to her. Now he was just a stupid drunkard.

And Teresa? What of that poor creature locked in the attic? Why did Byron go up there so often? The housewoman fed Teresa and carried up the wood for her grate. Nicolette shivered. She knew. She knew too well and just didn't want to think of it.

She passed the gate of the estate at a full gallop. After convincing James to meet Beau and delivering the message to Loraine, perhaps Nicolette should just keep going until one or the other, she or the horse, dropped dead. That certainly was worth considering.

The wind blew colder as she reined before Dr. James Roebling's dark house. Her knuckles were raw by the time a sleepy-eyed maid answered. Nicolette shivered so hard she couldn't speak.

"Do you need the doctor?" the maid asked. "We've about come to the end of it, you know. We're going west. Even me, so he's not taking patients. I'll wake him, but I don't know."

"Who is it?" a shrill voice called from the upper landing.

Nicolette looked up into the shadows as she stood dripping just inside the door. Yolanda was prettier than ever. Some women had all the luck. Like Loraine.

Jerking the sash of her dressing gown, Yolanda hurried down. "What are you doing here at this hour?"

"Give your husband a message," Nicolette panted replacing her hood and turning. "Beau Mercedes is back. The doctor is to…"

"Beau?" Yolanda gasped.

"James is to meet Adam at the main house," Nicolette said going back out into the howling wind.

"Wait!" Yolanda called. "Stay and get warm. Where…"

"I've got to fetch Loraine. Beau wants her. And then…" Nicolette paused before dragging herself atop the horse again. "I don't know what he means to do. He just wants to see all the Roeblings."

Then Nicolette was high on the horse pounding down the road in the murky rain. Yolanda called again but Nicolette DeMarsett disappeared into the darkness.

Beau! Beau wasn't dead! Yolanda clapped her hands together and laughed. It was the miracle she'd been waiting for!

James stumbled down the stairs and accepted his great coat and bag from the bewildered maid. Half asleep, he asked, "Where am I needed?"

Yolanda put her hand on his arm. "My brother's back. He's *not* dead! The beggar's cheated death, too! He wants you to go to Adam. I suppose he means to claim Loraine."

James' brow drew together in a puzzled frown. He set his bag on the seat of the hall tree. "I'll not go. They don't need me. Wake me for breakfast."

"Wake yourself," Yolanda said going to the closet and pulling on James' mackintosh. "I have an errand."

From the stairway James watched her go out and his frown deepened. At the door, Yolanda turned and laughed. "I have Adam now!"

"Loraine never loved your brother," James shouted.

"Maybe not, but if she wants her child she'll do whatever Beau wants. I'll see to it. Why do you think I saved the brat? It would have been easier to wring its neck."


"I'm sorry to wake you, M'lady, but there's a lady to see you. Says she has an urgent message. She come all this way in the rain, M'lady. Says her name's Nicolette Demars, or something like that."

Loraine came instantly awake.

What could Nicolette possibly want in the middle of the night? Loraine climbed from the bed. As she tore on her wrapper and hurried downstairs, the tall clock chimed quarter of four.

Nicolette sat huddled before a fire in the grand parlor. Wearing a quilted morning coat, Silver stoked the coals.

"What's happened?"

Nicolette looked up, her skin white with cold. Rivulets of water ran down her cheeks from her hair. She accepted a cup of tea from the maidservant and held it close to her lips. "It's Teresa," Nicolette said. Her teeth began to chatter. "She's sick."

Loraine turned away. "You came all this way for nothing. I can't go. She doesn't need me."

"Please," Nicolette said looking alarmed. "It could be the end to..." She looked as if she meant to say more and stopped herself.

Could Teresa really be sick? Loraine turned to Silvers who was just slipping out the door. "Will you wake Adam?"

"He's still in the library, M'lady. With the good doctor."

"Uncle Thomas is still here?"

"The storm, M'lady. It's bad. If you mean to go out you'd best wait until morning."

Nicolette leaped from her seat. "Teresa may not last that long! Take my horse..."

"You rode here by horse?" Loraine gasped. "All right." She put a shaky hand to her brow. "Sit and drink your tea. I'll go. Silvers, wake the groom and send my carriage around." She glanced at the windows running wet from the gale and shivered. "Did you send for James?"

With sly eyes, Nicolette nodded and gulped her tea. While waiting for the carriage, Loraine went to the library. The chamber hung with smoke. "You're up past your bedtime, Uncle," she said kissing his bewhiskered cheek. "What do you two find to talk about to such an hour?"

She looked at Adam seated in the other wing chair before the low fire. By the look of his squint and the tight lines across his forehead he had another of his headaches. Since the accident he'd developed megrims. And double vision as well.

Thomas patted Loraine's hand. "We have our subjects. What are *you* doing up? Storm bothering you? Your mama didn't like them either. I could prescribe something."

"My sister-in-law Nicolette just brought a message. About Teresa." She looked quickly at Adam and saw no response. Nervously she held her uncle's bony shoulder. How glad she was that he had started coming to the estate to attend Adam. He was happier up and about, and Adam needed his company. "Nicolette says Teresa won't last the night!"

"What makes her think that?" he asked trying to rise. "I'd better go."

"Please, Uncle. If you go anywhere, go up to bed. Teresa's probably just...confused again. I'll go. It's been so long and...I really feel I should."

The old doctor shook his head. "Stay clear of that girl now. Her mind's gone. Unhealthy atmosphere, that house. Always was. Up to bed with you. You, too, Adam. Take an extra drop of laudanum for the pain." His voice softened when he instructed Adam.

Adam went on glowering into the flames nibbling along the lower edge of the logs.

Loraine couldn't bear the sight and ran out. Thomas joined her in the hall. "I won't be gone long," she said wishing she didn't have to go.

Thomas pulled the library door closed. "There's not a thing anybody can do for Teresa. And this is no time to be traipsing about town. Don't go. It's not worth the risk. Whatever ails Teresa will keep."

He stopped at the foot of the staircase and shook his head. "These big old houses. I get strange fancies whenever I'm in them."

"You came here many times before I was born, didn't you, Uncle?"

He nodded. "Births and deaths take me many places. I leave it to young James gladly, and here he'll soon leave us. This old warhorse is too old to go back into battle."

"Mama came here, too," Loraine said.

Thomas looked surprised. "How did you guess?"

"I've read Mama's diary at last. There are many hours to fill since..."

"By all logic you should have been John Roebling's child," Thomas sighed.

"I am, now, in a way, Uncle."

Thoughtful, she and Thomas went upstairs in silence. At the door of the guest chamber Thomas smiled wistfully. "As your...father in heart as well as body," he said kissing her, "let me presume to advise you. Forget Teresa. *Adam* needs your help."

"But it's because of me she's..."

"If you choose to hold yourself responsible for someone's well-being, look at Adam. Yolanda stole his manhood. A man cannot be so wounded. Not a man such as he. All men, in their strength, carry the seeds for great weakness. *We* are the delicate creatures of this earth, Daughter, not you females. If you love Adam, tell him. If you don't, set him free."

"I've tried! He doesn't even look at me. He hasn't for months. I was at his side the morning after the accident. When he opened his eyes I kissed him and begged him to forget everything. I promised to start over, to forget my Mercedes baby. Even that he didn't hear."

"You mustn't give up! The Roebling men fall hard. Only your own strength can mend the damage." Thomas rubbed his eyes. "Did I tell you I'm going to Philadelphia for the summer? My oldest son has found himself a wife."

"I'm glad for him, Uncle. Send my best. All summer? I'll miss you! I feel so alone sometimes."

"And whose fault is that?" He went into his chamber and closed the door.

He didn't understand! Loraine was trying, crying and dying inside in hopes of sharing her newfound love with Adam. He only rejected her— again and again. He was like a shell.

And what if Teresa was dying?

What if, indeed?

She hurried downstairs. Adam still sat before the library fire. She wanted to rush to him and fall at his feet.

The line beside his mouth cut so deep now. Get up, damn you, she thought. Don't drink away your life!

All the things she wanted to say rang in her ears and stuck in her throat. She needed a sign, something to show her his heart hadn't hardened beyond recall.

"Adam? I won't go if you'd rather I didn't."

He said nothing. Nothing!

It *was* too late. From the very first it had been hopelessly too late!

She turned, choked with sorrow. And she was angry, too. She'd opened her heart…

There *was* still something Loraine could do—for Teresa. By going where she was needed Loraine could try once again to undo the harm she had wrought. She took her cloak from the waiting maid and hurried out.

The rain had slowed to a gentle patter. The thunderheads moved out to sea. Lightning flickered through the oaks in the distant darkness. A timid moon peeked from behind a bank of heavy clouds and lit low flying wisps of gray racing to the north. The wind was still sharp and penetrated Loraine's cloak. Her wrapper and nightdress were poor protection beneath it. Goosebumps rose on her bare legs.

At last the groggy groom brought the carriage. Loraine jumped into it, laced the reins between her fingers, and urged the horse down the muddy lane between dripping, whispering black branches.

The wind shivered through the treetops. The glowing night eyes of deer and other creatures watched from the thickets. DeMarsett House had never seemed so far.

After a miserable half hour ride, Loraine reined beneath the portico. A magnificent black thoroughbred stood tethered at the garden gate. Everything seemed like a dream, the whinnying horse, dripping branches, moonlit clouds fleeing overhead.

She slipped across the puddled cobblestones and knocked. She blew on her reddened fingers. No one answered. She twisted the cold handle and crept in. The house was silent and dark save for one low lamp burning in the study. The house smelled like a cave.

Surely if Teresa was sick, Byron would be there to meet James at the door.

She peeked around the corner of the study door and saw Byron laying face down across the desk. Before she could cry out, a man stepped from the shadows near the draped window. She saw the glint of a long duelling pistol muzzle, sleek and gray with curlicues of gold.

Her heart stopped. She made a small cry and clutched her throat.

"Aren't you pleased to see me?"

Her throat opened and closed. She couldn't breathe.

"I'm a bit late, but I'm here at last. You're even more beautiful than before. What's this? She does not speak! Perhaps she is..."

"No!" she croaked. "You're dead!"

"Not bloody likely, and no thanks to your father or brother, the black-hearted pigs. Welcome me home with one of your sweet kisses, my love. The memory of them kept me alive three long years."

"Byron told me you drowned!" Blackness began to close over Loraine's eyes, blotting out the patter of the rain on the glass.

"That may have been the plan," Beau smiled, "but I don't die so easily. Come here, Sweet. You once begged me to marry you. Now I shall."

He was still sun-bronzed, still solid and strong with hair burnt to a particular shade of gold, almost like brass. He was still a sea god with crystal blue eyes and a bewitching smile. But Loraine's eyes saw more now, three years more, the sharp angle of his brows over his nose, the tight little smile, and the faint curl of his upper lip.

Shaking her head, she edged around the doorframe and made a dash for the door and her carriage. She had been tricked into coming here. Adam would think...She had to get back!

In a flash Beau joined her. A rippling arm in straining rain-spotted tan wool barred her way. "Has your love faded?"

"You killed John Roebling!"

"And your father almost killed me!" Beau shouted. "Luckily we had fever and I was worth more to the captain of the *Mercer Star* alive and working than floating on the foam. Did you know your brother opened my skull with a club? I woke in a black ship's hold to the eyes of a hundred starving rats."

"You compromised me and then deserted me!"

"And spent the last year fighting my way back from Canton to you. I'm lucky to be alive. As for John Roebling, he was old and needed killing. Tonight I mean to finish the job. You're going to help. First Adam. Then James. Conrad, too, if he's forgotten his friendship. You forgot me easily enough, I see. But then you were effortless prey to begin with. I can't expect better. Do you like Roebling Estate? Did you bear an heir yet?"

*"How* could I forget you? I bore you a son! Yes! I *had* to marry Adam, and I wish I'd…"

Beau looked surprised. Then he made an amused sympathetic smile. "You'll be glad to rid of him then."

"If you're in a killing mood, add Yolanda to your list," Loraine screamed. "The night your son was born she stole him away. They told me he was stillborn."

Beau looked rather bewildered. "Stole him away? Why?"

"To torture me. Because no one wanted a Mercedes baby. I've never seen him."

Beau brightened. "I have other bastards."

With a horrified cry, Loraine wrenched passed Beau and ran out. Beau caught her and spun her around. He jerked her against his chest so hard his coat buttons cut into her breasts. "I care nothing for a lost baby. I want what I've always wanted, and you, my precious girl, will give it to me." He pushed her toward his horse. "Hike up your skirts, and I'll give you a boost."

Loraine broke free and ran for the garden gate. When she pushed, it fell in. She ran into the garden across muddy flowerbeds and through raking hedges, hoping to reach the far gate to the beach. A high voice from the house stopped her.

· On the sill of Loraine's old bedroom window, Teresa stood poised. She looked across the garden pointing with terror as if she saw ghosts. The wind pulled at her thin chemise, white and eerie in the moonlight. Her narrow legs were silhouetted underneath.

Astride his horse, Beau moved up beside Loraine and scooped her up with one arm. She hung gasping until she grabbed his waist and pulled herself up.

The horse reared. Loraine clutched Beau's chest pressing her face into his wet coat. God help me, she cried. Then the horse sprang away at a full gallop. Loraine heard a long haunting scream behind her that ended just as if it had been cut with a knife.

Every light blazed in the main house of Roebling Estate. In the pale mist rising from the grasses, the house shimmered like a diamond. Beyond lay a receding bank of clouds huddled on the horizon. Faint flickers of lightning danced along the sea.

Loraine tried to pull the pistol from Beau's belt but he struck her hand as if he meant to crush it. She yanked it to her mouth and sucked at the pain. What was she to do?

Beau guided his black horse along the narrow path leading to the back of the house. In the growing lavender dawn the terrace slowly became visible. Beau pushed Loraine to the ground and swung down beside her.

"It looks like everyone's here." He brushed at his coat sleeves and adjusted the angle of the pistol handle in his belt.

Loraine couldn't believe her visits to the beach had come to this. "I won't let you kill them," she said.

Beau leveled his bitter eyes at her. "Won't you?"

"You can't make me marry you."

He considered that without much concern.

Then a faint chuckle came from the double doors. Adam stood in the dark watching them, weaving slightly. His pistol hung in his hand catching the light from the softening night sky. He still cut a fine figure, but Loraine knew he hadn't slept. And he'd been drinking. He may have taken some laudanum, too. Dear God, he was already a dead man!

"Beau, don't!" she wept. "I'll go away with you. Come away now."

With a sneer, he turned to her. "What good are you without *his* wealth? You're lovely to look at, my sweet, but you'll look lovelier in black. When you believed me dead did you wear black for me? I doubt it. Dry your tears, now." He moved work-hardened hands from her gold curls to her wet cheeks. From a distance it must have appeared that she and Beau still cared for each other.

She jerked away. "Go back inside!" she screamed at Adam. "He's got one of Papa's pistols."

Nodding and raising the muzzle of his pistol slightly to indicate the knoll beyond the garden, Adam said, "Do me the honor, Mercedes."

Beau advanced through a line of hedges. Keeping each other in sight, he and Adam walked to the knoll. They looked as if they were enjoying themselves.

Loraine ran to the house. "Someone help me!" Her voice echoed throughout the lighted silent chambers. No one came.

She ran back outside. Through the garden paths to the farthest reach of the garden she ran. Beau and Adam were standing in the sparkling rain-wet grass beside a low stone bench priming their pistols. Their faces were etched with humorless smiles. Their eyes glinted with hate.

Then they began pacing. One long stride. Two. Three…

Loraine wanted to call out, but her words froze in her throat. If she called to Adam, he might turn and lose his aim. If she called to Beau, Adam would think…

Mother of God, she couldn't look away! Soft footsteps came up behind her. Too late! No one could stop them now!

Eight paces. Nine.

"My God," James whispered, still panting from his long ride. "It's true."

Loraine raised her hand for silence.

In a slow-motion ritualistic dance of death, Beau and Adam turned to face each other. Each held his pistol muzzle up to keep the charge in the pan. Beau leveled his pistol, cocked the hammer and took aim. Adam didn't move. He didn't lower his pistol. He waited.

Beau seemed a little unnerved. He hesitated before firing.

His shot rang out clear as the night sky faded from lavender to morning yellow and soft blue. The eye of the sun crept up over the horizon white and gentle, shafting through the last of the thunderheads like fingers of light reaching up from the sea.

Loraine watched a puff of pistol smoke drift across the knoll. Neither man moved now. Loraine held her mouth. Beau had missed! She took a step forward. James stopped her.

"Look," he whispered.

Adam's shoulder and shirtsleeve drew dark in a downward stain.

James had to grab both Loraine's arms to hold her back. "You can't! Adam hasn't taken his shot."

By honor, Beau was bound to stand and wait for Adam's shot. He aimed and waited. Beau's face mirrored the torment.

Adam closed his eyes. The pistol dipped ever so slightly.

"He's dead!" Beau called out, smiling as he turned toward Loraine. He began to walk toward her and, as he did, he reloaded, making ready another charge. He glanced up at James with a smirk as if to say, you're next.

"Mercedes?" Adam called.

Beau's brows angled in sharply. He took several more steps before turning. He was out of range, but in a direct line with Loraine and James. If Adam took his shot now...

Loraine watched Adam's pistol inch back up. A scream rose in her throat as she met the eye of the muzzle.

Beau waved his pistol as if about to say something to Adam, but fire exploded from Adam's pistol. The smoke obscured his clenched teeth.

Loraine covered her ears and screamed. James staggered back.

Half turned, arm out and pistol poised, Beau hung motionless in the air. Time stopped. The wind stopped. The sun dimmed momentarily and then flared. Like a heavy oak, Beau fell onto his back, arms outstretched.

James rushed forward. A stain spread across Beau's chest. "He's dead."

Adam sank to his knees. He leaned on his pistol struggling to breathe. His left arm hung limp. Blood dripped from his rolled-up cuff.

Loraine began running. The closer she got the lower Adam sank. "Adam!" she called, throwing out her arms. "Adam!"

He looked up. Intense weariness ravaged his face. As she fell to her knees beside him, he let go of the still smoking pistol and caught her in his arm. Their lips met and held.

"I love you," she wept.

He buried his face in her neck. "And I love you."

A few eternally precious moments later, Loraine and Adam struggled to their feet. They heard voices. Across the garden bathed in gentle morning sunlight Thomas Baines and James stood over the body of Beau Mercedes. Thomas pulled off his morning jacket and covered the handsome features frozen in disbelief.

Loraine looked away. It was over! Finally, absolutely over!

From the terrace doors Yolanda called. James began walking toward her. He stopped abruptly.

"Can you walk?" Loraine asked Adam, thinking only of him now.

"It's a simple wound," Adam said masking his discomfort. "But let me lean on you."

Smiling for joy, Loraine accepted the burden. They walked unsteadily toward the sunlit terrace. The stones were turning a brilliant yellow. Loraine felt blinded.

Adam stopped. His hand tightened on Loraine's shoulder.

Yolanda stood in the doorway clutching a little boy in front of her skirts. She was crying, her eyes fastened on the lump under Thomas Baines' jacket out in the grass.

"Here's Loraine's bastard!" Yolanda shrieked. "Come with me now, Adam, or I'll kill this boy."

She held a tiny pistol to the child's head. She nudged his yellow hair with it. He was so frightened he simply stood sucking his thumb, his clear blue eyes round and red.

He wore a shirt and trousers of homespun and couldn't be any older than two and a half.

Loraine moaned. Adam held her up. She moaned again. She looked up into Adam's face but didn't know what he was thinking or feeling. When he took an unsteady step forward, his mouth set in a grim line, Loraine let her arms fall away from him. She looked from him to the dear, dear little child and began to weep.

"Put away your pistol," Adam said to Yolanda as if she posed no threat. His voice was calm hinting at resignation. Just as he had with Beau, he moved with precision. Yolanda dared to smile.

Clutching at his wounded arm, he went to her looking as if he meant to encircle Yolanda's shoulder.

Loraine let out a whimper of disbelief.

Yolanda tucked her tiny pistol behind her back, and, smiling up at Adam with a self-satisfied simper, nudged the bewildered toddler out of her way. Tears welled in his eyes as he looked from one tight-faced stranger to the next. The sun glared in his eyes. He rubbed them and began to wail.

"Let's go," Adam said artfully ushering her inside.

James stood agape.

Loraine wanted to scream. "Do something!" she said to Thomas. He just frowned.

Inside, suddenly Yolanda squawked. She and Adam struggled quick and fierce like predator and prey. Adam wrenched the pistol from her hand and snarled, "Don't come back." He pushed her headlong down the hall.

Yolanda slipped and fell. Howling like a wildcat, she picked herself up. "You'll be sorry!" she screamed.

Adam pursued her. Loraine heard a slap. Another and another.

James ran through the doors. He stumbled to a stop as Adam returned emptying her pistol of ball and powder.

Out front the sound of a carriage racing away echoed across the morning calm.

Adam turned to Loraine, tall, dark and monstrous as he had that long-ago night when they first did battle. "From this day forward," he said in a loud clear voice, "that boy and Garner are both my sons."

Loraine was almost too stunned to move. Then with a little laugh, she ran to the sobbing child and fell to her knees before him. She drew him gently to her breast. "I'm your mama," she whispered. "You're home at last."

Adam sank into a nearby chair. In moments James was tearing open the bloodied sleeve inspecting the hole in the fleshly part of Adam's shoulder. Adam winced but kept his eyes on Loraine and the boy in her arms. His face was as soft as the morning.

Loraine slid to the floor. She had everything now. Everything! The Mercedes name would never be heard again. This child would be a Roebling and know only happiness. When she turned to Adam she knew nothing would ever again come between them.

# PART THREE

## 1842

## Twenty-Eight

In the spring of 1842 Loraine Roebling was delivered a daughter.

Loraine named her girl child after her mother's middle name, Jolie, meaning pretty, a name that could be traced back in the Gautier family tree as far as the mid-1750s and the grand Parisian courts.

The name was particularly appropriate, for those past two years and the ones to follow were the most beautiful Loraine had ever known. Hard times were over. Union Harbor recovered from the financial turmoil created that terrible spring of 1837 when the banks fell. The shipbuilding industry sprang to life with such vigor even Adam Roebling scrambled to keep up.

Yet keep up he did. As little Jolie grew, the Roebling Line sent forth a formidable fleet. Before James took Yolanda and his daughter west, he explained the first Roebling infant Loraine bore, Clayton, had not died at birth, as everyone had been led to believe. He'd been sent away to a healthier climate in the hopes of strengthening his weak heart. He hadn't been expected to survive the Massachusetts winter. Now he was well and back to claim his rightful place as heir beside his brother Garner.

Perhaps some thought the frail boy a love child. The Roebling men were certainly creatures of passion and capable of infidelities. Conrad wouldn't say for sure where the boy came from. Soon he was too busy with the Roebling mills in Saxwell to worry about one tot. He only came home for holidays and never did take a wife.

Old Isa could no longer feed the wagging gossips' tongues. In January of 1840 she had lost her battle to lung fever. Silvers hung on until 1853 when he died in his sleep.

The DeMarsetts fueled Union Harbor's whisperers a long while. The son of the slaver, Byron DeMarsett was accused of murdering a mad serving girl. She had been found dead below an open window in the house garden the very morning Adam Roebling felled a rather obscure sailor in a duel.

At the inquest it was proved Byron had been in no condition to murder anyone. He'd been himself beaten, and it was decided an intruder had driven the unstable Irish girl to jump.

Following his acquittal, Byron disappeared. His relieved wife Nicolette returned to her parents for a time. Soon she took up a household of her own and gave piano and voice lessons until she began working at Union Hospital.

Some of Byron's unsavory acquaintances thought he may have gone to New York. As it was, he left the stone house unattended. For years local school boys claimed it was haunted. Everyone agreed it was an eyesore. So, in the summer of her thirty-fifth year, Loraine sold the land and had the pleasure of seeing those cold gray stones pulled down to the rotting foundation. A small church was built there. Only Floris' prize garden remained. Soon Atlantic Avenue was paved all the way around the oaks to Boston Path.

Stately homes sprang up all over town. Still, none was lovelier than the Roebling mansion. Its white wings and fluted columns grew more beautiful with the years. Under Loraine's loving care, the gardens there became a showplace. If anyone recalled that once the house and grounds had been thought cursed, they were too old to be believed.

Thomas Baines spent his last years traveling between Union Harbor and Philadelphia. He died there in 1849 when both his sons and their families moved to the California frontier.

And so it was four Roebling children, Hope Janine, Clayton, Garner, and Jolie, grew up on an estate of quiet prosperous dignity. They knew every comfort and enjoyed every privilege. Their parents were openly in love. It was a happy family. Nothing marred the perfection Loraine and Adam built, save one small detail.

Young Clay Roebling, heir to the Line, was really a Mercedes. As much as they tried, Adam and Loraine never quite forgot. And so they watched...and waited.

# BOOK THREE

## Jolie

# PART ONE

## 1860

## Twenty-Nine

"Wait right there," Jolie called, splashing in the surf some twenty-five feet from the sand. "Leave my clothes be!"

Clay shielded his eyes and watched his little sister swim toward him with a sure reach. Those slender young arms cleaved the waves like the prow of a newly launched clipper ship. Even from that distance he could see her smile and that quality of goodness in her face that made her special to everyone.

He settled himself on a piece of sun-bleached driftwood rooted there on the beach and looked south to the bay at its teeming shore. He was mindful of his tan cloth coat for he was due at the docks to watch *Phantom of the Seas* set out on her maiden voyage. The new clipper was his father's proudest achievement, sixteen tons burthen, a figurehead of a painted mermaid...

A flash of pink skin and dancing dark hair caught the corner of Clay's eye. Jolie darted for the shelter of the brush and donned her petticoats.

Ever since she was a tot she'd loved the water. Clay thought of the picnics they used to have on the sand. His mother might take down her stockings and get her toes wet, but from the first Jolie had always doffed every stitch and plunged in. She was like a beautiful smiling fish.

"What are you doing here?" Jolie asked breathlessly as she emerged from the bushes, hooking her pink checked bodice. Her full skirts edged with a deep flounce lifted with the breeze. "I thought I'd have the beach to myself today."

"Mother just got a message a while ago," Clay said. He watched his sister's cinnamon brown eyes brighten with interest. "She wouldn't say what it was about and went straight up to her room. I have to go down for the launch now. I'll ask Father if he knows what it's about. But maybe you should be nearby in case Mother needs someone."

Jolie ran her fingers through her hair. It dripped down her back staining the cotton pleats in her skirt. "It can't be anything serious, can it? Do you suppose something's happened to Uncle Conrad?"

"That wouldn't upset her like that," Clay said.

"Well, even if she never really liked Uncle Conrad, she'd still care. I'll just *ask* her what the message was. You wait for me. I want to go to the launch with you."

"With wet hair?" Clay asked grinning.

"It'll dry. You should have reminded me about it this morning. Then my hair wouldn't *be* wet. Oh, I wish I could be *on* that ship, but Mama says no voyages this summer. I think she must be getting old."

"Just careful," Clay said. Their mother was that, all right, he thought. Careful to a fault. "You're much too pretty to take to Paris or London this season," he said throwing his arm about her shoulder. "Mama will have your ears when she finds out you've been swimming again. In your altogether no less. What would you have done if some pirate came along?"

Jolie made an impatient face. "I think I'd like to be carried off. I'd love an adventure! Being a girl is dull!"

Laughing, they both turned at the sound of thundering hooves coming up the beach from the south. The galloping horse and rider tore up a rain of sand. In seconds the tall young man in a loose white shirt and tight tan trousers reined before Clay and Jolie. His dark curls were frozen in a backward tangle that made him look as if he was still riding into the wind.

"Garner!" Jolie cried running up and grabbing the horse's bridle. "Let me ride Thunder. Just for a moment."

Her second oldest brother looked down with a grin. "Mama wouldn't like it."

"Please!"

"Have you been home yet?" Clay asked coming up behind Jolie. The top of her wet head was just below his eyes. For a girl so tall she was as graceful as a doe.

Garner's sea-dark eyes flashed as he looked toward the house, one white corner of the north wing just visible beyond the trees atop the bluff. Then he brightened for Jolie. "I've been out all morning."

"Mother got a mysterious message," Jolie said tugging on Garner's dusty boot. "It can't be another notice of your terrible grades." She turned and gave Clay a wink.

"Not this time of year," Clay said and was relieved to see Garner was for once in a decent mood.

Garner swung down. Before either young man could assist her, Jolie hoisted herself onto the back of the great red horse and vaulted away at a full gallop. The sand blasted in all directions under the attack of Thunder's driving hooves.

Clay and Garner watched Jolie disappear. A moment later she came riding back hugging the horse as if she'd become a part of him. Her hair streamed into the wind, and they could hear her laughing.

"Is Mother all right?" Garner asked never turning to look at Clay.

"I don't know. I came to get Jolie in case..."

"Isn't Hope up there?" Garner asked. "She can look after Mother as well as any of us. Aren't you supposed to be at the dock?"

Clay nodded. "Are you coming?"

"Why should I?"

"*Phantom of the Seas* incorporated some of your designs," Clay said, his impatience fueling his temper.

"But it should have *been* my design, not just part of it. You go. I'd just gall Father and frankly, I'm tired of his wrath."

"You could try to..."

"I'm tired of trying!" Garner snapped, his long dark face beginning to move to lines very much like those of his grandfather John's portrait in the library. When he looked like that Clay hated him and didn't know why.

"Let's not argue in front of Jolie."

"We're not arguing," Garner said, his voice sullen.

"She won't know that."

"I think if it wasn't for that girl our family would argue itself to death."

Clay wondered at that. The Roeblings were tightly knit, perhaps too much so. Set apart from normal village life by their wealth and the overpowering size of their estate, and a heritage of stone-faced men and beautiful fragile women, the Roebling clan led a somewhat exclusive daily life.

Garner's face was carved of stone, Clay thought. His own face was more open, quick to grin, quick to frown. Clay was easy to read, and consequently his parents, his mother in particular, fretted over him.

Even the Roebling girls, Hope and Jolie, had their small problems. Jolie longed for adventure. Her hours at the piano, embroidery frame and with the French tutor were torturous. She was happiest wet and sweating like a lithe young beast. And as for Hope...

Clay's darling dumpling of a sister, who was only a year older than he, kept herself buried in her garret. Father wouldn't let her go to any woman's academy, wouldn't let her sail, wouldn't let her look at books on design or business or even join in a conversation remotely touching on shipping. Her place was in the parlor with Mother and the French porcelain. Poor Hope, about as fragile looking as a tender-eyed whale.

Clay shook his head. He recognized his sister's inner beauty, even if everyone else whispered that with her great girth she'd surely be an old maid. At twenty-three, Hope had never even entertained a beau. She'd foregone the offer of a coming out ball—much to Mama's anguish. Hope seemed not to care. She was happiest with her nose in a novel.

For that matter, pretty Jolie, who shared the Roebling height with Hope but not the excess tonnage, cared nothing for callers. And for her there were offers aplenty. It looked as if she would turn down a coming out, too!

Full of such thoughts, Clay and Garner had fallen silent. Now Jolie pounded back and reined before them. Her face shined. Her hair had been braided by the wind and framed her face with twisted tendrils of deep burnished gold. Her cheeks were marred by a few faint freckles Clay thought rather handsome, but how their mother did fret over them.

"Come down from there," Clay said unable to mask his smile.

"You have no sense of adventure!" Jolie said throwing her legs over the horse's back and coming to a bouncing stop before her brothers. "The rebel and the rake you both are and not a drop of the devil in either of you. You content yourself to smolder under Papa's iron thumb and worry Mama to no end. You should break free! You're both old enough!"

"Listen to her," Garner said. "You'd no more break Mama's heart than we would."

Her smile dimmed. She'd been teasing, they knew, but there was truth behind all their words. Their mother had set her heart on something for each of the Roeblings, Hope and Adam included. Out of love they dared not reveal that each chaffed in her mold.

"You're both somber today," Jolie said shaking out her mass of snarls. "Which of you is Papa after now?"

"He says I must go to Boston," Clay said. "He wants me working at the Wilton shipyards—since I don't want to work here. Start at the bottom, he always says."

"And you'd rather go before the mast."

Clay's eyes turned to the sea like a compass pointing ever north. His father had said one day he *could* go, but every time Clay even mentioned a ship or a voyage, his father turned blue-black eyes on him and made Clay feel as if he'd just asked to rape the nearest virgin.

After waiting so long Clay wasn't even sure himself if sailing was what he wanted anymore. He just knew he didn't want to spend blistering and freezing days clambering over a ship's cradle in the shipyards of Union Harbor.

"Why can't you just *tell* Papa you don't want to go to Boston?"

Clay laughed a little and gave Jolie a playful chuck under her chin. "Everything is so simple to you, Jolie." He caught Garner's dark eyes as they skirted the deep grasses and headed for the path leading up to the garden.

"I think you *need* to get away. Both of you. *I'd* go if I could. Just for a while."

"Listen to her," Garner said, pulling his horse behind him.

"Well, if you really want to know, I think what you both need are sweethearts."

"Bewitching mermaidens like you? No, thank you, my pretty little sister. Hurry on now, before you get yourself in a peck of trouble. And mind you, don't go swimming like that again. Our town's overrun, and it's not safe."

"Our own stretch of beach is."

Clay shook his head. "You truly don't realize how pretty you are, do you?"

"Tell him to stop, Garner!"

Garner nodded as if to say it was the unavoidable truth.

Jolie blushed. "What do either of you know of pretty girls? All you want to do is go to sea and get scurvy."

Clay threw back his head and laughed.

"And I don't even *know* what *you* want," she said turning on Garner.

"You wouldn't like it if I told you."

The three of them topped the bluff and stood a moment looking back at the sea. It was a clear deep blue, as dark and mysterious as their father's eyes—and Garner's, and the smoldering ones in the library portrait. To the north the horizon swept around and met the pale line of the beach teeming with gulls. The woods met there, too, a blackish green as primitive as what their forefathers must have seen at Plymouth.

To the south was the great harbor so filled with barques and schooners, and magnificent Roebling clippers, they couldn't see the water.

The breeze pulled at Jolie's hair. With a slim hand she gathered it and pulled it over her shoulder, a deep shining mass reaching to her waist. She began twisting it into a knot.

"This whole town belongs to us," Jolie said, not as a spoiled child might, but as if the weight of responsibility rested on her shoulders alone. "Yet I don't think any of us is truly happy anymore. We once were. Last spring. Last year. What happened?"

"I, for one," Clay said rather darkly, "am of voting age now. I'll cast my ballot for Mr. Lincoln. Our whole country lacks the contentment of a year ago. Wealth won't spare us that."

"I won't believe there will be a war. Not over something as small as an election."

Garner's eyes flashed. "Believe what pleases you." Then he mounted his horse and rode off, away from the stables, toward the north and the woods.

Jolie frowned as she and Clay wound their way through the gardens to the back terrace. Voices came to them from the double doors leading into the morning room.

"Who are those people?" Jolie whispered pointing toward the house.

The late summer sun glinted off the windows. Clay shielded his eyes. He didn't care who was there. "I'm off to the yards now," he said feeling a sudden panic. That house was big enough to swallow a man.

Jumping across the shallow terrace steps, he took the stable path at a run. The house was fearsome in that light. Though it was beautiful, when he was younger he'd had nightmares filled with blinding sunlight, and distant voices. He preferred a kinder light, filtered green and the sound of running water.

In the stable yard Clay's chestnut mare, Bessy, was waiting. Maybe he wouldn't go to the yards after all. Why couldn't he just tell his mother and father he didn't want to inherit? Then he shook himself, mounted and rode between the avenue of twisted oaks toward the road. He felt as if someone was watching him and urged Bessy to a sudden gallop.

• • •

Jolie watched Clay disappear beyond the hedges, his pure straw-colored hair shimmering in the sun like silk. Jolie's oldest brother was muscular and stocky, about as different from Papa and Garner as fresh water and salt. He took after Mama, as she did, she thought. That lighter hair and smaller build was the mark of the Gautier line.

Dismissing both Clay and Garner as incomprehensible young stallions beyond her ken, Jolie waltzed into the morning room. She knew Mama wouldn't scold her for swimming. She and Mama were comrades. Despite the fashion of milky white skin and enough petticoats to clothe six women, they shared a love of freedom, sea and sun. If Mama were twenty years younger she would know the pure pleasure of the sea water on her skin, too.

Jolie plucked at the folds of her pink skirts—she'd left her crinoline in her room and now looked and probably smelled just like a drowned rat. A pretty one, Clay would say. Jolie hoped so. She had her vanity though she hid it as best she could. She knew all too well she was too lean and tall to be thought ladylike.

She saw her mother talking to two women in the entrance hall—or rather, the women were exclaiming and looking about, and Mama was... just standing there, rigidly, as if she had hurt herself. Jolie quickened her step.

One of the women was pushing a peculiar looking cane mesh chair on wheels. Both women had pure yellow hair just like Clay's! Both kept that bright hair contained in harsh black net chignons trimmed in peacock blue tassels and ribbons. Jolie cringed.

Their gowns were that same flashing blue-green, blinding amid the whites, browns and golds of the entry.

During her growing up years on the estate, Jolie had enjoyed the company of many a dignitary. Occasionally Mama gave parties and teas for some of the best known merchant captains in the world. When California erupted in gold ten years before, Jolie had met in these spotless halls the very captains who broke records for days around the Horn.

Jolie therefore recognized wealth and power at a glance. The two visitors weren't that. The ring of their sharp voices told Jolie as much.

Jolie was just about to call out hello when her mother heard the swish of her skirts. Jolie froze, and made a little smile hoping to hide her sandy bare feet. Her hand went involuntarily to her ravaged hair. Then she saw her mother's expression.

Loraine's gold curls were tamed into a knot at her nape. Only a few wispy white tendrils around her face betrayed the careful order of her life. She wore gray silk trimmed with dark blue cord and buttons. She moved with the dignity befitting the wife of the famed shipbuilder Adam Roebling. At forty she was considered one of the handsomest women in Union Harbor.

Her usually genial face had gone white and taut, however. A fine network of lines at the corners of her eyes betrayed a terrible inner turmoil.

"Mama?" Jolie whispered. Forgetting her disarray, she ventured closer.

The two visitors turned. They were uncommonly handsome though their gowns were dated and the handiwork plainly clumsy.

The older woman's face had a harshness to the contours, a coldness in the eyes Jolie at once disliked. The younger woman didn't smile at first and looked ill at ease.

Suddenly Jolie realized a man sat in the wheeled chair. As the women turned him around, Jolie could see he was hollow-faced and gray-skinned. His hands rested on the arms of the peculiar chair limp and trembling, yet his eyes shone with warmth.

"Don't tell me! Let me guess! Uncle James? Aunt Yolanda?" Jolie clapped her hands in excitement. "And Cousin Miranda! Aren't I right?"

As if made of wood, Loraine nodded.

"All the way from St. Louis! Are you staying with us?" Jolie cried. She rushed forward and kissed her uncle's feather-soft cheek. "You've been ill. Then you *must* stay!"

Loraine made a small sound in her throat.

"You can be none other than Jolie," James said, his voice as feeble as his appearance. "I've been battling the lung fever. My ladies brought me home to..."

"Then you've come to the right place! We'll take good care of you!" Jolie wouldn't let him say what he'd intended.

She saw her mother's strained face and went to her, looping her hand in her mother's crooked elbow. Where was Mama's usual hospitality? What Jolie had heard over the years must be true then. Years ago there had been a falling out among the Roebling brothers. Jolie had surmised as much listening to the letters that arrived every year at Christmastide. Before a crackling fire they had been read without emotion, a cold wind among otherwise warm and happy holidays.

Jolie watched her mother's eyes go over the two women as if she was looking at an open wound. "Show them the guest suite," she croaked. "I'll tell the cook to set three more places for dinner." And she edged away down the hall.

Jolie moved eagerly to her task. "The guest suite was once your bedchamber," she said smiling at her uncle. "Mother told me that much, but...I feel as if I hardly know any of you. Why didn't you visit before now?" She took her uncle's arm and helped him rise from the chair. The manservant appeared from his station by the cloakroom and took up the chair. "Leave it down here, thank you," James said to the half Chinese. "I'll manage upstairs just fine."

"Are you sure?" Yolanda snapped.

James appeared as if he didn't hear her. He turned his warm brown eyes to Jolie and seemed to draw strength from her. "You're as pretty as your mother."

"Don't you start! You'll turn my head. Tell me about St. Louis and the frontier. Are there many Indians? Did you enjoy the travel?" Out of politeness she turned her attention to her aunt and cousin though their hostile stares unnerved her. "I imagine you hated to leave your home."

"We had the finest house in Wellsboro Ferry. That's north of St. Louis on the river, you know," Miranda said tossing her lump of black-netted yellow hair.

"It was a morbid life," Yolanda said pushing her way past Jolie. She opened the doors to James' old rooms. "I'm *glad* to be back."

Jolie's stomach tightened.

"We'll take a house in town as soon as possible," James said. "Has anyone ever gone over to our old house? I missed it."

"Not in years," Jolie said throwing open the windows and running a tentative finger over the dustless dresser. She smiled proudly. "I imagine your stay with us will be a nice long one. There's not a house to be had in all of Union Harbor these days. A lot of people are banking on a war, you know. Isn't that awful? The Union at war with itself, the very idea drives me mad. Papa and my brothers argue like statesmen about..."

"How *are* your brothers?" Yolanda interrupted, her eyes flashing like little knives.

Jolie blinked. "Why...fine, really. Garner's going back to the university in a week or so. This will be his third year...But, of course, you know that from our letters. Clay may go to Boston."

"Clay," Yolanda said as if tasting the name.

"And how is Hope Janine?" Uncle James said sinking gratefully to the nearest chair, his breathing labored.

"She's upstairs in her...We call it her lair. All she does is read. She's terribly smart."

"No husband?" Miranda inquired, her heavy brows lifted.

"She's too busy filling her mind with words," Jolie laughed.

"She must be an old maid then."

Jolie bit her tongue and forced herself not to reply, "Like you, Cousin Miranda?" Already Miranda Roebling was twenty-five.

"Charlie will bring up your trunks," Jolie said instead. "Can I bring you anything? Tea? Sandwiches?"

Yolanda paused from her frowning inspection of the suite. "I'd like to speak with your mother."

"Yolanda! No," James said, his eyes marked by pain.

"Will we see everyone at dinner?" Miranda squawked. "All these years I've only heard names and had this faded likeness." She held up a box-framed daguerreotype. "I want to see everyone in person."

"Uncle Conrad lives in Saxwell, as you know. We'll send him a message and he'll be here in a day or so. Everyone else will be here, I'm sure."

Jolie went on chattering and then, as quickly as she made them welcome, she bid them a good rest and escaped to wash her hair.

Something very odd was afoot.

# Thirty

Jolie paused at the top of the stairs. The house trembled with silence. Suddenly Jolie tumbled down to the entrance hall bursting to ask her mother a thousand questions. She turned toward the servants' hall expecting to find her mother directing preparations for dinner when their half Chinese manservant called her from the front door.

"Missy Jorrie!" He motioned toward the door, his black almond eyes glistening. "This lowly servant not want to go back to Canton! Have very proud ancestors. House of Ching. This one not of house of Mercy-days."

"What are you talking about, Charlie?" Jolie asked impatiently. "Where's Mama?"

The tall Chinese boy gestured toward the door in unhurried yet unmistakable panic. "Don't want to go back. Much happy here."

"Of course you are. Who said you should?"

"Madame Lo!" he said becoming more agitated. He couldn't say certain English sounds and therefore called Jolie's Mother "Madame Lo."

"Nonsense! Take up my aunt and uncle's trunks now. I'll speak to Mama." -

Going out the door, Jolie found her mother leaning against a pillar. A stab of alarm made Jolie stumble. "Mama! What is it?"

Her mother met her eyes slowly. "I won't have them in my house, or that half Cantonese either. *He* could be a Mercedes! Any man could!"

"What are you talking about?"

Loraine shook herself. A shred of reason returned to her eyes. "I'm going…out." She looked up at the house as if repulsed. "Get your cape and come with me."

Jolie grabbed her mother's arm. "What was the message you received this morning? Clay said it upset you."

Her mother's eyes showed white all around. "It said they were coming! Then they were here! Twenty years…"

"Is that what's upsetting you?"

Her mother looked around in terror. "Where's Clay?"

"Come inside and have a little drink. I've never seen you like this! I'll get your shawl. Your arms are like ice!"

"*Where's Clay?*"

Jolie drew back. "He's gone...to the yard, I think. Mama, you're frightening me. What is it about Uncle James and Aunt..."

"Don't say that name! Dear God, what can I do? I can't stand the sight of that woman!"

Jolie took her mother's shoulders and shook her. "What are you afraid of?"

Loraine began to shake her head. Her eyes grew dull. "I'll never be rid of Yolanda and the Mercedes blood."

"Mercy-days?" Jolie almost laughed. "Is *that* what Charlie meant? Mercedes? Is that someone's name?"

Loraine's eyes bulged. Then, abruptly, she sagged. Squawking in surprise, Jolie helped her mother inside, back to her father's library. She seated her mother beside the unlit hearth and poured her a brimming brandy.

"Will you *please* tell me what all this is about? Until a little while ago I thought my biggest problem was my wet hair and sandy feet."

Jolie sank to her knees beside her mother and looked deeply into her face, more deeply than she had ever looked before. Jolie was eighteen years old and suddenly felt like an ignorant sheltered child.

Her mother drank the brandy so fast her eyes grew wet. After a moment she relaxed a little. "I'm too old for this."

"You're not old!"

"I won't have them stay in my home, Jolie," Loraine said as if she hadn't heard.

Jolie sighed. "But they *are* here, and Uncle James is plainly very weak. I'll tell Aunt Yolanda you can't possibly see her right now. Do you want me to go after Papa? Or shall I send Charlie? We can find them a house tomorrow, Mama. Surely one night..."

"I sent Charlie away."

"What has *he* to do with this?" Jolie cried.

"He's from Canton!"

"Have you lost all your senses?"

Loraine buried her face in her hands. "You're right. You're right. Charlie's done nothing. Apologize for me." Then she held out the empty glass to be refilled.

Somewhat reluctantly, Jolie obeyed. The tall clock chimed three of the afternoon. Papa and Clay wouldn't be home for a while.

With growing amazement, Jolie watched her mother down the second glass of brandy.

"She wants to speak to me?" her mother whispered.

Jolie could only nod. She wanted to help and felt utterly useless.

Her mother winced. "Mother of God."

Then Loraine pushed Jolie's comforting pat away and pulled herself to her feet. She poured a third glass to the brim and drank as if parched. Jolie wasn't sure even her father could drink that much so quickly and remain standing!

As if coming about in a stiff wind, Loraine turned from the rows of crystal decanters in the great dark library. She looked for a moment at the portrait over the mantel, then at the massive desk. Her eyes grew heavy-lidded as the brandy took its toll. She lifted her chin as if it weighed like marble. Then she looked at Jolie.

"Tell her I will see her in my drawing room."

Loraine turned toward the door. Step by step she moved down the hall to the stairs. Jolie watched her mother pause and look up as if gathering her strength for a battle. She was a rather small warrior in gray silk.

Jolie put her hands over her mouth. Only an unexpected undertow could make her this afraid.

Loraine's drawing room was still across from the master suite. She stationed herself beside the sunlit window hoping to put Yolanda at an uncomfortable disadvantage.

"Let's not bother being polite," Yolanda said only moments later. She seated herself on the rose velvet divan and helped herself to tea and honeycakes. With a full mouth she gazed at Loraine, her amber eyes squinting into the glare of the sun. "I hated the frontier," she said. "Dirty, cold, lonely. We were hungry most of the time. It's been a long, long twenty years. I trust you know what I want to talk about." As abruptly as she began eating, she stopped.

Loraine marveled at how little time had changed Yolanda. She still had her willowy figure, but the years of hardship had removed all trace of softness from her cheeks, and the blue-green taffeta surely didn't become her.

All the words that rose in Loraine's throat turned to bile. She watched Yolanda's false smile turn to ice.

"My brother's son…" Yolanda shook her head just a little as if she still couldn't believe it after all these years. "The Roebling heir." Then she laughed. "How jealous Beau would be!"

Loraine couldn't move. Her lungs emptied until they felt flat.

"He can't be happy as a Roebling. *I* haven't been." Yolanda looked as if she hadn't enjoyed herself so much in years. "Doesn't it bother Adam to disinherit his own *true* son? Or *is* Garner Adam's true son?"

Loraine couldn't help curling her fingers into fists. She drove them deep into her skirts to hide them. "What do you want?"

Chuckling, Yolanda rose and dusted her bell skirt. "I want what I've always wanted. Adam and all the power and wealth his name provides. For a while I thought I'd lost it forever. You probably thought you were finally rid of me. Well, you should know better than anyone that the Mercedeses always come back."

"And Beau died," Loraine snapped. "Give it up, Yolanda. You don't frighten me anymore."

"Don't I? Do you always tremble like that? Have you a palsy? All right, maybe I have no hope whatsoever of getting Adam away from you. I grew tired of him years ago anyway. But I have never given up my dream of power and wealth. You and Adam can still give me that. I had a good long while to think and plan as I grew old in the West. I knew of only one way to get what I wanted. That meant patience. Years of patience. When, I asked myself, would be the perfect time to come back and open this festering kettle of fish? When Clay was a tender boy of ten, a bristling lad of sixteen, or now, a young man of twenty-one? I admit I might have come sooner. I think Clay would have found our Mercedes saga interesting listening when he was sixteen. But James wouldn't come, and we have had nothing since we left here. Nothing!"

Yolanda took a few steps closer.

"All these years I've waited for this day. I've planned it down to the last word. You're going to give me everything, Loraine, everything because one word from me and Clay will hate you until his dying breath." She puffed with pleasure. "Wouldn't Clay find it interesting to hear how you *sent* him away the night he was born?"

Loraine toppled back into the nearest chair. Her heart shivered.

Yolanda shook with laughter. She went to the door and paused. "I could tell Clay how *I* searched and searched for him in the asylums. You didn't want him but…" She chuckled some more. "Don't have an attack. There's no need for me to say a word. Yet. All I ask is you find us a *very* nice house. As soon as possible. I'll be speaking to Adam on the subject as soon as he returns from the yards. I just wanted to make sure I'd have *your* help. Enjoy your tea."

Several minutes passed before Loraine stopped staring at the place where Yolanda had stood. She felt numb.

Soon Yolanda would tell Clay the truth, a very twisted truth. No matter what Loraine might give her, as soon as she could, Yolanda would tell Clay anything she pleased. Just as Loraine had lived in fear of this day, Yolanda had lived *for* it.

Loraine got up. The drawing room reeled before her eyes. As if her feet hurt, she walked to the window. She stood staring at the buds on the oak just outside. The budded branches moved in the sunlight like dancing arms. For the last twenty years Loraine had been happy, content. She'd dared believe the turmoil over.

What if she killed Yolanda? What if she simply took Adam's pistol from the desk drawer and ended everything? Then Loraine laid her head on the cool glass. What a coward she was! There was only one thing left to her.

The tall oaks that had been young and slender in his father's day stood looming and black now. Adam slowed his horse to a walk and looked across the lawns of his estate. Spring had spread her gentle hand across the land, and now late summer lay heavy upon the grass, hot and yellow like the sun burning his neck.

Clay, who had ridden ahead, slowed, too. He looked back at Adam with a question in his bright blue eyes.

Sometimes in the back of his mind Adam wished Clay was tall and dark-haired like young Garner. It would've made Adam's life so much easier. That shine to Clay's straight yellow hair had once been a painful reminder but Adam could look at it now and smile. For a son not of his blood, Clay was truly the one to carry on the line.

Clay was steady. He shouldered responsibility. He did his duty, unlike Garner who was wild and liked innovative, sometimes foolhardy ideas.

Adam watched Clay in the saddle. Neither he nor Clay had ever felt easy with the other, yet there was a certain kinship between them only Adam could appreciate. That stocky blond young man was the apple of Loraine's eye, her special love and her special burden. For that alone Adam had found the boy occupying a tender place in his otherwise cynical heart.

Too quickly for Adam's liking, they reached the house. Adam felt dwarfed by the massive pillars, the towering white walls and gleaming windows. A groom came and led away their horses. Clay liked a little mare he called Bessy, a riding horse much like Adam's own roan. Garner preferred his thoroughbreds, red-eyed, nostril-flaring beasts that carried him across the turf and gained him a true title of a Roebling son. What might he have been if he'd had his true place as firstborn?

"Where is everyone?" Clay said dusting his coat sleeves as they started inside. "I thought Jolie and Hope would be here to greet us."

As Adam followed Clay inside he felt the urge to give his "son" a stout clap on his shoulder. The boy was too strongly tied to the family. He needed to get out in the world and that was why...

Like always, however, Adam couldn't quite bring himself to embrace Clay. Some invisible barrier had always held him back, not the mere fact that the blood was not the same, and not the hair color. The resistance ran too deep for Adam to understand. Perhaps he didn't want to admit even to himself that this young lad, who was a lad no more, was closer to his heart than Garner. A true Roebling was a hard man to court. Adam found that in himself, and Garner. It had been especially true of John.

A distraught maid appeared to take their hats and coats. Both Clay and Adam turned to the sound of running footsteps on the staircase.

Jolie tumbled halfway down and then stopped. She clutched the banister panting. Half her dark gold hair was done up in curling rags. She looked touchingly silly.

"Papa! Clay..." She glanced back upstairs and then down over the banister into the long afternoon shadows in the back hall.

"Did you ever find out what the mysterious message was that Clay told me about?" Adam called, startled by the echo of his overly cheerful voice.

Jolie looked so like Loraine with her hair falling across her shoulders like a fall of silken sunlit water. Jolie was his treasure. Adam had always delighted in her for no other reason than she was a girl child and born with no clouds over her head.

Before she could speak, however, Adam had a brief glimpse of another face. He saw white skin and dark haunting eyes. Though Jolie's eyes were much lighter and warmer than her grandmother's had been, in that soft fading light she looked startlingly like Florie DeMarsett.

Adam had been feeling warm and complacent with the success of the launch behind him, and his pleasant ride home with Clay. Now a flicker of alarm made the warmth drain from his face. He felt the pull of years heavy down his spine, and his shoulder ached suddenly where a puckered scar indented deeply into his aging flesh.

Jolie, his precious, the echo of two former generations of beautiful, heart-strong women, took another step down, closer to him, with a look of pleading he couldn't ignore. "Papa!" she said as if ready to beg.

Then his library door opened. The patch of darkness at the far end of the hall filled with a surprising gown of iridescent blue-green. He heard the harsh whisper of the taffeta. His scar flared with pain just like it had when he accidentally fell from his horse a few years earlier while racing with Garner. He had thought then the scar would never hurt as much again. Now the old wound so long healed throbbed with the depth of his shock.

Adam took a step toward young Clay, almost as if to protect him, but even as he did he felt the contentment and security of the past twenty years crashing down around his heart.

Wearing a smile ever more embittered by time, Yolanda walked toward Adam. She seemed thinner, sharper, like an old knife honed to the very last keen edge.

"Be a gentleman, Adam, and welcome us back."

Clay turned to Adam, his face round with curiosity and confusion. Adam knew his heir had never heard *anyone* speak to him like that before. Or perhaps somewhere in Clay's memory lived Yolanda's deadly voice.

"Is James with you?" he asked.

Yolanda made a face as if to say, unfortunately, yes. "He's been ill a good while. He wanted to come home to die."

Yolanda was holding a photographic likeness of the family which Adam had had made several years before and sent west. She held up the ornate brass box-frame and peered at it with a rancorous smile.

Then she looked at Clay. Her smile widened. "So this is your oldest boy," she said smooth as maple syrup. "The last time I saw him…"

All the while and without a word of his own, Clay watched the unspoken battle between Adam and Yolanda's eyes. From her place on the stairs, Jolie watched, too, a look of dread in her eyes. When Adam realized her look, he started toward her. Something must have happened already. He must go to Loraine at once.

"He doesn't look at all like a Roebling," Yolanda said with mock surprise. "Why, I'd say he looks much more like me!"

Adam turned. His chest grew tight. Yolanda shrank from him, but only a little. A wicked light made her eyes like flames.

"Why are you here? You know you're not welcome."

She looked as if she hadn't expected him to speak to her like that in front of Clay or Jolie.

"Uncle James has the lung fever," Jolie whispered.

"Have you spoken to Loraine?" Adam asked. Good Lord, how long had she been there? What damage had she already done?

"We just had the nicest chat. She's promised us a fine new house." Yolanda advanced on Adam and tried to take his arm. When he pulled away, his lip curled in disgust, she darkened but went on in the same gay tone. "Let's have a drink and discuss this in your library, unless of course, you'd prefer to talk over old times in front of your dear children."

Adam looked up at Jolie. She expected him to go to Loraine, surely, and yet hoped he'd rid them all of this viper.

Clay's face was a masterwork in disbelief. Not only was twenty years of patience and love crumbling before Adam's eyes, his son's respect was, too.

Adam marched to his library and listened to Yolanda follow. He prayed he'd think of a way to get rid of her. Yolanda swirled through the door as he paused and looked back. Then with a tight swallow he closed himself in with her.

"*What* is going on in this house?" Clay asked, joining Jolie on the stairs.

She shuddered. "I don't *like* her! There's something awful about her."

"That's not like you," Clay said remembering with a pang her happy face of only a few hours ago.

"I know, and I don't like to admit it, but…Did you *hear* how she *talked* to Papa? Mama didn't even want to stay in the house after Aunt Yolanda arrived! I've never seen her act as she has today. I feel like…like everything I've ever known in the world to be real and…understandable has just changed forever! Do you know Mama was gulping down brandy like water before…I'd better see how she is now. Rouse Hope from her lair, will you? And where's Garner? Did he go to the launch?"

"If I know Garner, he's halfway to Saxwell."

"At a time like this he should be *home* where he belongs!"

"And just how were any of us to know this was going to hit? Aunt Yolanda waltzes into our lives and flattens us all like a hurricane sweep."

"Aren't you at all upset?"

Clay paused outside their mother's drawing room. He took his little sister's face in his hands and kissed her forehead. "You'll make a dozen little babies a fine mother someday, do you know that? You worry every bit as good as our own dear mama. I dare say *anyone* would need a drink to match tongues with that frontier shrew. Mother's no stranger to drink, and neither am I. You ought to try a bit yourself. Then you wouldn't get little lines across your pretty forehead over a simple bad-mannered visitor."

"Stop treating me like a child! Something's about to happen, and I'm afraid!"

"I'll fetch Hope then, and we'll have a council of war."

"Mama?" Jolie whispered, appearing in Loraine's doorway. "Clay and Papa just got back."

Loraine opened her eyes with effort. Her daughter looked like a tot with her hair tied up. Loraine's heart ached.

She straightened in her chair by the window and tried to get a deep breath. "I must speak to Clay," she said beginning to feel ill from the brandy she'd drunk. "I don't want you to talk to Yolanda. Or Miranda. You must hear everything from me."

"You mean about Grandpapa DeMarsett being a slaver? If that's what's upsetting you, I've known that for years."

Loraine got up but her legs would hardly support her. "There's more."

Jolie crossed the cold chamber and threw her arms about her mother's shoulders. She felt so solid and strong. For a moment Loraine clung to her, drawing strength from the clear young heart.

"Everything's going to be all right," Loraine found herself saying. With a Mercedes in the house again she could say such a thing! "Go on now and send Clay to me. Remember. Listen only to what *I* tell you."

With an eager nod, Jolie darted out. Loraine was alone. She lifted her face and drew the breath she needed. A great cold wind swept down from the north, a wind promising to tear open her life's secrets and lay them bare for those she loved most to see.

"Still reading?"

Hope looked up from her wing chair. "Clay!" She pushed herself from the broad leather seat and threw out her arms.

Clay strode in and grabbed her into his arms kissing her cheek. For a moment Hope Janine felt light and lovely. Clay's eyes glowed as he gazed down at her.

"How was the launch?" she asked.

*Phantom of the Seas* took to the water just as you said, heavy but proud. You should have come."

Hope shook her head. "You know how I felt about that. Sit and have some cakes with me. I just stole them from the kitchen myself. They're for dinner. Are we having guests? I heard a carriage arrive a while ago."

"Lots of excitement downstairs. Jolie wants you to come down and help."

Hope shook her head again.

"You stay up here too much," Clay scolded.

"You would, too," Hope said patting her bulk under the soft folds of an overblouse fit only for an old nanny. She sat and tucked her legs back under herself, retrieving the book she'd been reading.

"Have you poked your nose outside your door all day?" Clay demanded crossing the room and sampling one of her cakes.

"No one's missed me."

"You look pale." His eyes were kind as he smiled down at her. "It's so nice out."

"Maybe I'll go out tomorrow," she said. "I want to finish this."

Clay slapped his thigh. "You try my patience, my girl!"

"Do I now?"

"Up here all day, reading, eating. You should be out swimming and riding like Jolie. Life is for living!"

"Jolie and I are cut of different cloth, my boy. If you've come just to plague me, go back down again. I'm perfectly content as I am. Unlike you and the rest, I do exactly as I please, and I'm the only one happy amongst us."

"Who arrived from Illinois today? Why is the house silent as a tomb? Aren't you curious?"

"You know enough for both of us. You'll tell me in due time anyway."

"You drive me mad!"

"So you've told me many times."

"Get up! Get some color in your cheeks!" He tugged at Hope's hands and tried to pull her to her feet again. Though he was a number of inches taller than she, he was no match for her bulk.

"Leave me be, Clay! Can't you see I'm happy here as I am? I don't have to see anyone, and no one has to see me."

He let go of her hands and stared at her. "I'll admit you've done a fine job of masking your beauty, but *I* know it's there. Some young swain is crying for your warmth and love."

Hope bellowed an unladylike laugh. "You dear fool of a brother. Sit down and pour out your heart. Papa's after you again, isn't he? Why can't you just accept the fact that you were born for greatness? The yards are yours. Papa is growing tired. He longs to turn everything over to you. You can handle it! I know you can!"

Clay dragged a chair directly in front of Hope and planted his stocky body before her. His face burned with intensity. "How can I manage such a business if I don't know what it feels like to captain a ship...to..."

"To wield the tar brush and hoist the main sail...Clay, stop tormenting yourself. You can *do* it!"

"Could I bear it if I wasn't the best? Could he?"

"And you have the gall to hound me because I stay in my little chamber and read. We *all* hide. I can do it so much more easily than you. I'm a woman and nothing in Papa's eyes. No, don't protest. You know it's true. What you need is a diversion." She popped the last tea cake in her mouth. "Why don't you take up eating? We could grow fat and old together."

Clay let his hands drop. His head hung between his shoulders.

Hope put her hand on his warm cheek and felt a rush of love for the "little" brother she'd always protected. "All right. Let's both try to please Papa. I'll forego my cakes and you go to Boston. I would go in your place if I could! I'd love it. You don't know how lucky you are."

Clay smiled and warmed her.

Then came a frantic little tap at Hope's door. Before being invited in, Jolie burst inside. "Clay! I've been looking everywhere! Mama wants to see you right away."

"Mother's little helper," Hope said in a gentle tease. "Come and sit, Jolie. Tell me everything. Who's here? I heard a carriage hours ago but no one came to insist I present myself to be frowned at and pitied. Is it some dignitary with a hawk-faced wife? A priest from Boston? None of these? Who then?"

"I'll see to Mama," Clay said going out and leaving Hope feeling abandoned. If only he knew how bored and lonely she really was in her small suite of third-floor chambers.

Jolie sank into the chair Clay had vacated. She stared at the door with rounded childlike eyes. Hope loved her for her sweetness and hated her for her natural beauty in the same rush of emotion. With a sigh, she closed her book.

Some days life just wouldn't let her alone. There were days the wind's cold breath made her room bitter days when her body ached and reminded her of her long suppressed womanhood and the burden of her aloneness and the secret memories of her childhood, days when those she loved, like Clay and Jolie and even hot-blooded Garner intruded upon her peace.

Tears suddenly rushed from Jolie's cinnamon brown eyes. Hope was startled, for she hadn't seen her little sister cry in ages. She was quick to laugh, to pout, to snarl like a little tiger, but tears? They had never been Jolie's weakness.

Jolie told Hope everything that had happened since Uncle James and Aunt Yolanda had arrived that afternoon. When it was all out, she demanded, "Do you remember any terrible secrets?"

"No," Hope said getting up with effort and shutting her door. She had been unprepared for real trouble.

*"Nothing* about Clay?"

Hope began to pace. "All I remember," Hope said stopping, holding pudgy fingers to her lips, "is that Clay was frail. After he was born he went to a special place to get stronger. Uncle James told me that, as you know. When I was small I thought he meant Clay had died. After all, he had told me my own mother had gone away."

Jolie nodded, dashing away tears and leaning forward.

"He didn't talk much as a boy. Nanny and the tutors always fussed at him." Hope resumed her pacing. Jolie expected her to find the solution and suddenly Hope felt angry. "I don't like this." She settled back in her chair, one long since discarded from Papa's library. She pulled a basket of corn muffins from the shelf beside her favorite books. Her hand took up the uneasy pacing from basket to mouth. "I'm glad Uncle James is back. I suppose, though, he'll be sorry to see me like this. He always said I'd grow up pretty."

"And you are."

"Don't flatter me. I know how I look."

They heard shouts.

Jolie reached the door first and flew down the hall. Looking down the stairs into the second-floor hall, she saw Clay disappearing into his room. His door was just beyond Papa's dressing room. Jolie's room was across the hall, Garner's next to it. She tumbled down the steps intending to follow Clay.

From her mother's drawing room she heard weeping.

Jolie stopped, wanting to go in both directions. The weeping grew louder, a kind of despairing sob that frightened Jolie.

She found her mother hunched on the edge of her chair, bent as if in pain. Jolie crept nearer and knelt. She put her hands on her mother's lap, more to comfort herself than her mother.

After a long wait, Loraine gathered her wits and looked toward an open leather and brass-trimmed trunk standing against the wall on the far side of the table.

Jolie went to it. Whisper-thin baby dresses had been thrown to the floor. A long loop of pearls lay on the table. Jolie remembered hearing how they had looked to Papa when Mama wore them at her coming out ball.

The family's prized christening gown and its nest of crisp tissue had been pushed aside. Grandmama's favorite novels lay in a heap. In growing irritation, Jolie looked about. Then she saw the red leather-bound diary. It lay with its spine partially broken on the floor near the trunk. It looked as if it had been thrown there.

"Is *this* the secret?" She held up the small volume that fit so snugly into her palm. It felt warm, almost alive.

"Read it," Loraine said, her voice raspy. "Then I'll tell you what I just told Clay."

Jolie shuddered. A mysterious cold wind penetrated the chamber and swirled around her. She slipped to the floor and opened the diary to the first page. "Florie de Joi Gautier DeMarsett, April fifteenth, 1811," had been written in a tiny precise hand on the fly leaf. Jolie began reading.

"Clay!" Hope lumbered out into the afternoon shadows following her yellow-haired brother as he marched across the terrace carrying a bundle under his arm. "Where are you going?"

Clay paused once to look back at the house, his face set and hard. His blue eyes swept across the garden to the barely visible knoll now hidden behind a bank of shivering birches. Then he moved on toward the stable. He didn't seem to see Hope.

She ran after him so fast her whole body crashed up and down. When she caught him he was shouting at the stable boys.

"Where are you going?" she panted pressing her fist to her bosom. "What did Mother say?" When he looked as if he wasn't going to answer, she seized his sleeve.

Clay looked changed.

"You're not going anywhere until you tell me what she said. Look at you, running off like a…"

Clay flung off her hand and began to march away without his horse.

"Damn you!" Hope cried chugging after him. "Have pity on me. I can't match your stride."

They moved out of the stable boys' hearing and, at last, Clay slowed. He kept his face turned away. Hope watched his adam's apple bobbing beneath his neckcloth.

"Aunt Yolanda said I looked more like her than a Roebling."

Hope swallowed over a dry tongue. "Well, you do. What of it?"

"Go back to the house. I'm off to seek my…destiny."

Hope took his arm with both her hands and jerked him to a stop. "Let me guess. Mother told you something you think is a terrible sin. I can tell you, Clay, that you don't know sin at all until you know mine. Whatever she told you, I love you still."

Clay's face softened. His eyes grew moist. Just as quickly they grew sharp again. "Sin."

Hope's cheeks grew hot. "You're a love child, are you not?" She tried to soften her words. "I've always suspected it, at least from the time I was old enough to conceive of such things. You were always different, like me. That's why we've always been so close."

"For a sister, you're too smart," Clay whispered.

"Not smart, Clay, just old enough to remember the day you came home to live. It's hard to believe Father would be unfaithful, but…"

"Father?" Clay laughed. "All my life I've tried to live up to his ideal, knowing, mind you, that I didn't have it in me, and all along…I'm really just a *Mercedes!*" Clay cried with laughter. "I'm not a Roebling at all. I'm not heir to the Line. The burden's not really mine! It's Garner's! I'm a bastard! I have nothing to live up to but that!"

Hope looked up at Clay, at the laughter and pain in his eyes and was sure she was hearing things. "You're Aunt Yolanda's son?" she whispered. "My God, no wonder…"

Clay moaned. He threw his arms around Hope and cried into her neck. "No, no, no," he mumbled, his tears feeling hot and wet on her skin. "Not Papa's bastard. Mama's! You and I don't share a drop of the same blood. Can you believe that?" He looked down at her suddenly, intensely. "I could kiss you…" He pressed salty lips to hers and then jerked back. "And it's not a sin!"

Hope tore away from him.

"Don't look so horrified," he laughed as he wiped his eyes. "At least now I know why I never felt I fit. I'm not crazy! I truly don't fit! My father was Beau Mercedes. Imagine, a stranger for a father. A total stranger. He was a sailor and...well, there's more but Mama will have to explain it to you. I doubt I could do her saga justice. Beau was Yolanda's older brother. He was killed right over there. On the knoll. Father killed him in a duel. Do you believe that? I'm going into town now, Hope. I'm going to...celebrate. How do you like that? No more burden. No more heir. No more...name." He paused and cleared his throat. Then he frowned at Hope.

"Mama's bastard?"

He nodded with a wry smile. "She says she was young and foolish... Well, I'm young and foolish, too. I mean to go away from here and find out just what sort of man I really am."

"You can't leave me now!" Hope cried.

"I can't stay!"

"But I need you!"

"You have Mama and Jolie and Garner and Papa. They'll always belong to you. There are no secrets about you."

"But there are! Don't leave me!" She pulled Clay to her bosom and just as quickly thrust him away. She clutched at her hair. She looked up at Clay. "With Uncle James and the rest here, Uncle Conrad will come from Saxwell!"

"What has he to do with all this?"

"I can't tell you. Go on then! Go away and leave me. I don't care. Dear God! I wish I was dead!"

Clay shook her. "What's the matter with you? Just because I'm going doesn't mean I don't love you anymore."

"Do you remember the Christmas I was eight? The Christmas I was nine? Every year Uncle Conrad came from Saxwell?"

"You were always ill."

Hope's heart began hammering with fearful force. The words bubbled to her lips, words that had bubbled dozens of times and had always been held back. Shaking her head, she felt tears smart her own eyes. "How I longed to tell you and couldn't. It was like a nightmare, but I began to believe I deserved it. After all, I always loved you." She covered her eyes as if she couldn't see him and he wouldn't be able to see her. "Uncle Conrad is not the kind to leave alone with a little girl." Peeking between her fingers, she watched understanding dawn dark on Clay's face.

She burst into a wild laugh. She had said it at last! She was free of it. She had shared it and now the burden was half as heavy.

"It's not so bad to not be a Roebling, Clay. Please, don't go. I need you too much. Don't you see? Now my sin is half as great, for I love you."

Clay took a step away. A thousand thoughts played across his face. He looked as if he wanted to stay and share with her the pain and freedom of the truth, but suddenly he was running across the dappled grass to the lane that led to the gate.

Hope called out, but he didn't stop. She watched him until he was out of sight. She hated and loved him for going.

She turned back to the great white house expecting to feel the same terrible need to hide. Surprisingly she felt light and free. She walked back without the usual constant gnawing in her belly. When she reached the path to the terrace she saw seated in the second-floor window, Loraine, her stepmother. Loraine looked so lonely.

Hope hurried inside and climbed the stairs to the drawing room. If Conrad did come, she'd be ready.

Hope was stronger than Clay, or any of them! When she went into the drawing room, she didn't even smell the honeycakes on the tea cart. She saw only Jolie sitting on the floor reading a small leather-bound diary, reading and chewing off her fingernails, her eyes wide, too stunned to cry.

In the face of so much anguish, Hope didn't understand why she felt so suddenly relieved. Maybe for the first time in her life she felt needed.

# Thirty-One

Adam unlocked the bottom drawer of his desk and searched among some papers for the cash he usually kept there. "How much will it take to be rid of you?"

Yolanda sashayed to the desk. "All you've got."

At the unexpected sound of running footsteps in the main hall, Adam looked up. He kept his eyes away from Yolanda. His clenched teeth ached enough. He didn't care to add the sight of Yolanda to his pain.

He heard someone call Clay's name.

Poor Loraine, he thought counting out a more than generous settlement for Yolanda. By now Loraine must be writhing in fear. Yolanda looked as if she'd tell the final Roebling secret at any moment, and enjoy doing it.

And poor Clay? He was a sensitive young man pressured by an over-expectant father, doted on by a guilt-ridden mother. He must never learn the truth. Years ago hadn't secrets and truths nearly ruined Adam's marriage?

Adam closed the drawer. He held out the stack of greenbacks. Yolanda's fingers brushed his as she took them, smiling.

He couldn't seem to avoid seeing that flash of teeth or those hard eyes. God, the woman was ugly!

He rose and went to the door. "You can have my best carriage," he said waiting for her to follow. "It'll get you around town until you find one of your own. Yes, yes. I'll pay. I can see I'll go on paying until I die. I recommend Union Hotel. It's new. Tell them, of course, that I sent you. I'm sure you'll get the Captain's suite."

"You don't know how I've waited for this day," Yolanda said beaming, cocking her head in an effort to look pretty.

"Does it ever bother you that everywhere you go, people suffer?" Adam's voice sounded too soft. A monstrous hate boiled in his chest like a knot of vomit.

Yolanda's eyes narrowed a fraction. "Does it ever bother *you* that even after all this time I still hold you in my hand?" She curled her fingers along his cheek. "Nod your noble head, wooden man."

Adam resisted the desire to throttle her. With surprising calm, he met her cold amber eyes and saw there, for the first time, the deeply rooted fear, the base insecurity of Yolanda's petty existence. "I've already looked myself in the eye, Yolanda. You forced me to do that. Since then I've known what I was. I've lived with my successes and my failings. Can you say the same for yourself?"

She laughed and tossed her head.

Together they went into the hall to the stairs and started up. "James will be pleased to see you," Yolanda said, no trace of weakness in her voice. "If he hasn't already coughed himself to death."

"How long has he been sick?"

"Not long enough," was Yolanda's winking reply.

God help him, Adam wished she was dead! He wished it so hard his head ached now. His whole being ached.

They found James on his back in the same suite and the same bed he'd occupied as a boy. He lay with his thin white hands folded on his chest.

Hearing the door, James opened his eyes. His smile came to his eyes first, then his lips. "Adam," he whispered. "I've missed you."

Staring down at his younger brother, Adam knew his shock was too plain on his face. "For God's sake, unfold your hands! You looked dead!" Then stiffly Adam bent over James as if he meant to kiss him, or shake him, he knew not which. James saved him by pushing up on one elbow. What resulted was an awkward embrace.

"You look remarkable," James said, plainly envious. "What are you now? Fifty?"

"Fifty-four," Adam said. "You could use a good physick, but then you always did neglect yourself."

James threw off his coverlet, laughing faintly. He felt for the teacup sitting on the bedside table and, finding it still warm, drank from it. "I knew once I got back I'd either get better or die peacefully. At the sight of you I feel better."

"You should have warned us you were on your way," Adam said wishing Yolanda would disappear. There was so much he wanted to say to James, so many questions, so much to fill in the years since James had gone off almost in exile.

"I know, and I'm sorry. I know it's not easy, but then I'd hoped…"

"Where's Miranda?" Yolanda interrupted.

"I heard some shouts a while ago and sent her to see what was wrong. I was worried our arrival upset everyone." James began to cough gently. After a moment he turned away, growing red-faced as the cough racked his chest and would not subside.

At that, Miranda burst in. She paused at the sight of Adam, who couldn't help look her over from her netted hair to her dusty blue slippers peeping from the hem of her gaudy gown. She flushed and looked to her mother. "You'd think someone had died the way the Roebling women in this house are carrying on."

James held his breath and stopped coughing. He looked sharply at his daughter. Between a few last dry rasps from his lungs, he asked, *"What is everyone upset about? Not us, I hope."* He looked back at Adam and then rose with renewed strength. "I told Yolanda we shouldn't come."

Yolanda waved the greenbacks. "Let's be off then. This house is still as dreary as ever."

At the sight of her mother's loot, Miranda's eyes lit like bonfires. She squealed and snatched at the money. "I want a new dress and bonnet! And stays, Mama! I look fat compared to Jolie. And I want..."

Yolanda's eyes blasted her daughter into silence. "Adam was kind enough to offer a little help in getting started again," she said so sweetly Adam looked at her in wonder.

*"You're* welcome to stay as long as you like," Adam said to his brother. "I knew Yolanda, however, would want to be in town near the shops."

"You're much nicer than Mama said!" Miranda laughed planting a wet kiss on Adam's cheek.

"I'll see what's going on with Loraine," Adam said making a quick retreat for the door. He longed to wipe his face.

"Let me go with you," James said. "I want to reassure Loraine we don't intend to intrude on your hospitality." He met Adam's eyes to say more.

Yolanda slipped up beside James and took his elbow. "We'll *all* go tell Loraine we're on our way out."

"Not until after dinner, Mama," Miranda called as she preened before the standing mirror in the corner.

Moments later a chill went up Adam's spine as he entered his wife's drawing room. Loraine sat in her favorite reading chair by the southern window where the sun shined in every day. Hope was beside her, one plump pink hand on her shoulder. He heard Yolanda gasp at the sight of her.

Jolie sat on the daybed. That dratted red-leather diary of Loraine's mother was in her hand. She stared at it, her cheeks still glistening with tears.

Adam felt suddenly cold, as if he'd just fallen into a winter sea. Loraine had sworn she'd never let *anyone* read her mother's diary! It contained the details of Loraine's birth, the strange fact that old Thomas Baines had fathered her, not Wendell.

Adam had never read the diary. He preferred to avoid any more complicated stories of mixed-up romance in his wife's French heritage.

Why would Loraine tell that story to Jolie now ten years after Thomas' death? Surely it could mean nothing to Jolie. And why did Hope look as if she'd just consumed a twelve course banquet?

He had no time to reflect. Three pairs of eyes converged on Yolanda as she stepped into the drawing room behind him. Loraine's brown eyes, Jolie's cinnamon and Hope's deep blue sparked with unmistakable wrath. Adam felt the heat of it and was glad, for an instant, they weren't looking at him.

Yolanda's smile withered. She drew up within herself looking haughty and self-righteous. "We needed the money."

"Did you give her something?" Loraine demanded, her voice high and wild. She tried to get up but Hope kept her in place.

More and more Adam was growing alarmed. Loraine looked as if she might break.

"Don't give her a penny," Loraine hissed. "There's nothing more she can do to us."

"Did you say something to Clay? Already?" James asked, turning on his wife.

"Of course not! I mean him no harm. I just…Stop looking at me like that! All of you. I didn't tell him a thing. I only saw him a moment. Have you all gone mad? I don't have to stay here and be treated like…"

"That's right, you don't!" Loraine said throwing Hope's hand away and rising. "You don't have to tell Clay the truth, not your truth or mine. I did it for you, just now, and I'm glad! I have nothing more to fear. Not you, Yolanda, or your lies. Clay knows everything."

"He'll be back, Mother," Hope said staying close behind, her round face serene.

Jolie looked from one face to the next and then covered her own and wept. "Clay never did a thing to hurt anyone," she said through her fingers. "And now he can't stand the sight of us. I don't believe any of this! It's all a nightmare!" She jumped up and ran to Adam. Her hands felt sharp through his coat sleeves. "Tell me it's all a terrible story someone made up."

Adam looked over Jolie's shining hair still tied with strips of white cloth into bouncing knots. "You told Clay? Everything?"

Loraine nodded, her eyes locked with his. "I had to. It was that or wait until Yolanda told him. Ask her what she would've said."

Still the impetuous little fool, Adam thought shaking his head. She could have waited! What would an hour or a day have mattered? He would have paid for Yolanda's silence. He would have...

He looked about, his own breathing labored now. He felt powerless again, just as he always had where Yolanda and her tricks were concerned. He'd thought he'd mastered it all, with time, with patience, with love for a boy not his son or heir.

"Clay left," Loraine said softly. "He swore he wasn't upset or angry, but he left."

"He'll be back!" Hope said again. "He needed time. Wouldn't you?"

"Where?" Adam asked.

Loraine shook her head. Hope did, too.

James had edged back toward the doorway searching for support. Yolanda still stood with her chin up and her arms folded. "I never said I'd tell him," she snipped. "Loraine has brought all this foolishness upon herself."

With one magnificent rounding sweep, James drew back his hand and slapped Yolanda so hard her head wrenched to the side. Instantly her lips and nose were bloodied, the perfect imprint of his fingers etched upon her pale cheek.

She made a thick moan over a quickly swelling tongue and staggered out clutching her jaw, her eyes rolled back in agony. Miranda had come to stand in the hall, and now she screamed.

Yolanda seized her daughter's shoulders to keep herself upright. "We're leaving!" she said in a pained mumble.

"But, Mama!"

"Then stay, you selfish whining bitch! I don't need you, or anyone!"

Yolanda found her way to the stairs. As she stumbled down, she kept patting her lips and looking at the blood on her fingers. By the time she reached the entrance hall and pushed her way through the clutch of wall-eyed servants gathered near the stairs, Adam and everyone could hear her crying. Miranda followed her out.

"Dear God, Adam, I'm sorry," James said after a long silence.

As if he hadn't heard, Adam went to Loraine and drew her to his chest. He watched Hope square her broad shoulders and push back her dark curls. "I'll go after Clay," she said.

He put out his hand to stop her. For a moment he wondered how long it had been since he'd touched any of his children. For so long now they had seemed too far into adulthood to approach. "Let him come back when he's ready. It is a lot to swallow in one dose."

Loraine drew away from him then. "I don't think he should have gone at all! I thought he took my story well, and then suddenly…Doesn't he realize what you and I did for him? Doesn't he know what I've been through? I begged him to stay, and he only laughed. He laughed, Adam! Do you think he hates me now?"

Adam clutched her to his chest and ached for her. He knew the fear of losing someone.

"He should come back when he knows what he wants to be," Loraine said into his coat. "He's the Roebling heir. We *gave* him that. You nearly died to give him that! But if he wants to be a Mercedes…" Loraine tipped back her head and looked into Adam's eyes. The whites looked sore, the brown flecked with terror. "He has our love, Adam, but he has Mercedes blood!"

# Thirty-Two

Clay staggered against a piling and clutched at it like a lover to keep from falling on his face. He stared down into the oily undulations of the harbor water, deep and black and quietly laughing.

Bastard. Bastard, the dark water said, tickling the mossy thick pilings. Clay reared back and lifted his face to the cool night air. He was free of his burden, free to do whatever pleased him. Thank you, Mama, he thought, sagging a little. Poor old dear, sobbing like that over so ancient a sin. He'd kissed her and told her it didn't matter. He'd shouted at her when she insisted he stay. He didn't have to anymore. He was free!

Freedom. He'd chafed against the mold all his life and now it was broken. All his fears that he might never measure up to the Roebling name were for nought. He had only to make sure he *didn't* live up to the name they had taken from him. Mercedes.

Chuckling, Clay staggered across a timber-strewn shipyard to the next cluster of lamplit taverns. The voices and laughter within were a comfort. Garner was no stranger to the wharves, but Clay had always stayed clear, setting, he had thought, an example for the Line.

Now he brought himself up in the nearest bright doorway. He'd lost track of how many he'd already been through. A pall of smoke hung near the beamed ceiling. The alehouse was old and nearly deserted. He made his way to a table in the rear on feet that could no longer tell the difference between boot-hardened earth and time-polished planks.

An old fellow, a fisherman most likely, sat hunched across from the spot Clay chose. Clay sat hard and nearly fell over. The old fisherfellow lifted tired wet eyes in disdain. His cheeks were mapped with years of toil, his brows like overgrown hedges.

"Let me buy you all the ale you can hold," Clay said reaching across to shake the stranger's hand. He was regarded with a fishy eye as blue as Clay's own.

"I thank you, lad. Be you the Roebling son? I seen the *Phantom* slide out this morning. Too broad a sow for my liking. I'll take me skiff any day."

Clay nodded. "Too broad. Too heavy. Too grand for me. No, old father, I'm not the Roebling heir. I'm a free man. Maybe you knew my father. Have you heard of the Mercedes name?"

A smile appeared on the creviced face. "You be no Mercedes whelp. Look at your hands, your eyes. Clean and bright as a babe's. I'd trust a lad like you."

"But not a Mercedes?"

The ale-tender brought two foaming tankards and Clay drank, looking over the rim at the fisherman.

"I know one Mercedes I'd trust with my own daughter, if I still had one. The lass died long long ago. The cholera, you know."

Clay nodded. "Where can I find this trustworthy Mercedes?"

The old fellow smiled. "If you're not the lad I saw at the Roebling yard this very morning standing beside old Adam Roebling himself, who might you be then?"

"My mother's secret."

The old man drank down his ale then and pushed himself to his foot and peg. "'Tis a sorry thing to bear no name, my son. Good night to ye."

Clay sat a good while drinking, thinking, plotting his next move which came to him as nothing more than dark undulations in his dimming mind.

What were they all doing now, his family? Were they comforting his mother in her hour of distress? Perhaps he should have stayed after all, but she hadn't believed how the whole fantastic plot had delighted him. To be free…To be himself, with no name…

He *should* go back, he told himself, attempting to rise. He found his legs mere jelly. He called for still more ale, missing the old fisherman who had momentarily welcomed him back to the real world. That was just it—his problem now. Clay felt as if he'd stepped off the ship of life and lay adrift watching everyone else hurry by.

He buried his face in his arms knowing he couldn't go back. Not yet, anyway. If he did he might spill Hope's terrible secret, and for that he could see no relief in telling. He must stay away until he could hold his tongue, or until he had pounded his Uncle Conrad into fishbait.

"More ale!" he called, longing to silence his mind. "More ale for Clay *Mercedes* and freedom!"

Then he settled his cheek against his folded arms again, closed his eyes and let himself cry. He had no more restraints to complain about, no more family demands. His future as a man was what he made of it, and that was a burden more fearsome than he had ever known.

Kane Mercedes threw open the door of his mother's shack to the face of his old friend Irish, a fisherman who'd lost one leg so long ago no one could remember him whole.

Irish tipped his cap. "Evening," he said smiling, his eyes twinkling in the lamplight shining from the table behind Kane.

"What brings you out so far?" Kane asked, his voice soft yet full enough to bounce off the nearby trees. Neither was he a tall man, though his shadow cast a black cloak across most of old Irish.

"I met a lad tonight. At King's Horse," Irish said. "He's probably soupy by now. Been drinking and asking after the Mercedes name. Claims he's a Mercedes. Thought you might like to take a look at him."

"A Mercedes? Not likely! Come in and have a drink with me."

The old man shook his head. "It's a long way back, and it's late. My bones are tired."

Kane bid the old man good night then and watched him limp away into the darkness. A stiff breeze had come up making Kane's neck hair creep.

"What do you think?" Maddie said coming up behind him. She put her hand on his shoulder.

Reaching back, he closed his hand over hers. "I thought you were asleep."

"The old fellow knocked loud enough to raise ghosts. Will you go?"

"Can't do any harm."

"You had a long day. Shouldn't you catch your sleep?"

"I'm not a babe, Ma! Nor an old codger. I could use an ale, and it would amuse me to see one who would claim to be a Mercedes." He turned and smiled down at his mother. The idea of finding a brother again pleased him.

"You haven't forgotten, have you? All these years…" Maddie shook her head. "I'll never forget the look on your face when your father's sister brought that baby to us. Um! So long ago."

Kane nodded. That time belonged to another age, when he was young and helpless—well, never so very helpless, really. With a name like Mercedes to defend, and bastardy as well, he had never been given to weakness. But it had hurt him far more then, to be alone and born to shame. Those two years with little Robin, as he had called the baby, had made Kane feel part of a real family. He'd been too small to care about much else.

"I'll never forget when she came and took him away again," he said remembering that black night. "Go back to bed, Ma. I won't be long."

"Don't get into another of your fights."

Kane laughed and kissed his mother's forehead where the once thick dark hair grew gray and thin now. "I'm no ruffian."

"But I sometimes wonder if I was wrong to teach you pride, even in a name like Mercedes," Maddie said.

"You had little else to give me." Kane reached for his dark blue jacket. "Don't fret now. I'm a man long since grown."

"And long overdue for a wife," Maddie added for the thousandth time.

Kane went out into the windy darkness shaking his head with a laugh. She never tired of reminding him, the old girl didn't.

Wife? He had no use for one, no use for some sweet wench who would sour like wine and grow sharp-tongued like all the women of the wharf. Though he wasn't without his brief loves—the women of the wharves had once been girls and he'd once been a lad of hearts—he took his pleasure rarely now. Now he was a man, with an aging mother, and no true name. What woman wanted that in a husband?

His long stride carried him quickly to the road that led to town. Every day he walked it to the shipyards. He knew the new clipper ships from keel to sky sail, and loved them. He dreamed sometimes of sailing one. The most he could ever hope for, even with all his reading by lamplight, was to build them. He might have liked working for the Roebling Line—he'd watched *Phantom of the Seas* rush away from the cradle that very morning. She'd looked like a dignified lady as she settled herself in the water amid the usual dockside cheers. Then she had glided away to her new Boston owner, and Kane's heart had ached to see her go.

At twenty-nine, however, Kane Mercedes couldn't afford ambition. The only dreams he allowed himself were to please his mother as best he could. Secretly he longed for more elegant things—elegant females being among his fancies. And because he was a Mercedes with that infamous heritage, he held back his desires to things he would have to defend the least. As bastard of a murderer and grandson of a known thief, he had plenty to fight for as it was.

As he turned down Wharf Road, the thought of meeting yet another Mercedes bastard bothered him only a little. He knew of only one other bastard son—the infant they'd taken in and cared for two years when

Kane was eight. He'd never realized until then how lonely he was. He didn't admit now how lonely he was still.

He'd often wondered if there were more bastards scattered to the far corners of the world. No doubt there were. He just never expected to find one shouting out the news in a crowded tavern so close to home. Memories lived long in such places.

King's Horse was rocking with laughter by the time Kane walked in. The shoremen and dock tarpots were gathered around one far table. Grinning faces turned when Kane approached. The men sobered and stepped aside.

"This here's your brother!" one of Kane's mates said slapping him on the back with a drunken snicker.

The old fellow who had brought word of this new Mercedes nudged Kane and pointed to a mug of steaming Java coffee set before the straw-haired man sprawled across the table.

Before Kane could speak, King's Horse's proprietor pushed his way through the crowd. "You're not busting up this place again," he shouted, waving a meaty arm. "Curse the day I ever took over this place. Your clan's been a thorn in my side from the first. Off with the both of you."

"Business ain't suffering," Kane said looking about. He'd never liked the man who'd taken over for his grandmother Ruby, though he'd generously kept her on until she died. "I'll have him out of here soon as I know what he's about."

"He's lost his senses," one of the onlookers said, pointing with a sloshing tankard. "That's no Mercedes. That's Clay Roebling."

A murmur of renewed interest shivered across the crowd. Suggestive comments niggled at the edge of Kane's hearing, but he was too occupied to take offense. Someone else's honor was at stake here. He'd take care.

He took hold of the tousled head and lifted it. Eyes as blue as his own rolled in the face of a very drunk lad. "I'm Kane Mercedes," Kane said just as he had many times in the past, loud, strong and proud. He had always let it be known he wasn't ashamed to be called bastard. He'd just better not hear it.

"My name's Clay Roe—Mercedes," Clay said over a thick tongue, and his eyes rolled back until only the whites showed.

Kane forced coffee on him but Clay was out cold. He was a handsome enough lad, young enough maybe to be that babe Kane had called Robin. A prickling of excitement sparked Kane's heart. He took the lad's arm and slung him easily onto his shoulder, and Clay was no slight fellow.

"We'll settle with you on the morrow," Kane said to the proprietor as he went out.

Laughter followed them well beyond the wharf. When Kane felt Clay coming to consciousness, he set the lad down just in time to watch a jet of ale erupt from his mouth and land in the gutter.

After a moment Clay wiped his mouth on his sleeve and stood weaving. At last his eyes met Kane's.

"You'll live, my boy, through no fault of your own." Kane grinned at the gray face.

"Who the hell are you?"

"I'm Kane Mercedes," Kane said again. He topped Clay by only an inch. Clay's hair was yellow, while Kane's was brown. They both wore it swept to the side, though just then Clay's was all over his head like straw in a basket.

Kane began to laugh.

Clay scowled and doubled his fists.

"Come home with me, Robin, my boy," Kane said looping his arm around the young man's shoulders. He felt fatherly though only nine years separated them. "I know someone who will be thunderstruck to see you." They went up a hill and into the wood. "The others will have a time figuring out your drunken raving. They think you're Adam Roebling's son, but I know who you really are. I fed you warm mush and changed your wet drawers myself. You were a scowling towhead then and a scowling towhead now. Do you ever smile? We never guessed you went to that estate. You *have* been lucky!"

Clay expressed his doubt with a grunt.

"I've seen you many times at the yard with your father. I never matched you, though, with that babe I loved."

"I was still Clay Roebling this morning," Clay said.

"This morning was long ago," Kane laughed slapping Clay's shoulder. "You don't remember me, but we're brothers. I wear homespun, you wear Saxwell linen. Was your mother the lady of the estate or just a serving maid?"

"She *is* the mistress," Clay said, his tone warning.

Kane said no more. They just walked. If the boy loved his mother still, then he was man enough for Kane and Maddie.

•••

Rain drummed steadily against the windows. Jolie watched the silver rivulets trickle down the glass, unable to think of a single word to comfort her mother. Since the trouble had erupted with Aunt Yolanda's arrival days before, Jolie's mother had been disconsolate.

Jolie turned to look around the grand parlor and the empty chairs. She felt a sharp pang in her heart. Mama had time to grieve over Clay. She took Hope's comfort with open gratitude, and had sent Garner back to his university with copious tears. Yet where in this ocean of storms did Jolie fit? "You're too young to understand," Mama would say. "Be happy. Go swimming and let me be."

Jolie felt shut out and unneeded. Where had the bond gone, the comradeship, the special mother-daughter link that had carried Jolie through a perfect childhood?

How could Mama forget her? And how could Jolie feel so utterly, hatefully selfish? Shouldn't Jolie stop thinking of herself and think of poor Clay, gone days now? Didn't Mama have the right to weep and worry?

Jolie turned back to the rainy windowpane with a sigh. She must not bother Mama with her own silly needs. She must stay out of the way, be cheerful and do whatever she could to ease the burden. But how she longed to scream out her own needs. "Don't forget *me*, Mama!"

"Miss," came a tentative voice from the doorway of the grand parlor. "A man's at the door. Your mother's sleeping and the master's gone out. What do I tell him? He walked all the way from town."

"Let me see his card," Jolie said.

"No card, Miss! He's just a shipwright, and soaked through."

"What does he want?" Jolie felt bewildered.

"He said, 'I want to speak to Clay's mother.' That's just what he said. 'Clay's mother,' I thought I'd best tell *someone* since the young master's run off for so long now."

Jolie silenced the maid with her finger to her lips. "Give him a towel and fetch tea. I'll receive him. Does he look decent, or should Louis be on hand?"

"Louis is down with the grippe again, Miss. That's why I answered the knocking. Didn't you hear it? He looks very nice for such as he is. I've took a fancy to him." The little maid dipped a curtsey and rushed away giggling.

Jolie tidied her hair wishing it knotted like Mama's, but her hair was long and heavy and always came loose. She tugged her bodice and arranged the folds of her dark blue bombazine. The skirt was monstrously heavy over the crinoline. She felt like a freight barque coming about as she heard heavy footsteps near the door and turned.

With a twinkling eye, the maid admitted the visitor. "In here, sir."

Jolie's breath went out. She couldn't get it back.

The man had combed his wet hair to the side. It lay sleek as hot chocolate across his forehead. On his collar it was longish and made wet circles across his shirt yoke. The loose boatman's shirt was carefully handstitched of a coarse weave Jolie had never seen. His trousers were rain-spotted, mended at the cuffs, and his boots ancient. He carried his dripping blue jacket over his arm.

"Miss Roebling?" he said in a deep voice meant for a wealthier man. His face was broad and friendly, already hinting at a grin. His eyes were bright and penetrating, sweeping about the parlor with interest.

Jolie tried to close her mouth.

"Is your mother very ill? I've come to set her mind at peace. Clay is with me, and he's well."

"He is?" Jolie squeaked. She sounded as if she hadn't been worried to distraction over him herself.

"Excuse me." He bowed awkwardly and grinned over his own lack of graces. "I'm Kane Mercedes. I know you've never heard of me, but I happen to be another son of Beau Mercedes. And..." He went on to explain how Clay came to be staying at his mother's shack by the river.

When Jolie continued to gape—only half hearing Kane's story, more fascinated by his voice—he went on to explain how he and his mother Maddie were asked to take Clay in more than twenty years before. "He was a scrawny red rat of a babe, and I loved him on sight," Kane said with a grin. "He reminded me of a baby robin I once tried to save."

"He lived with you those two years?" Jolie whispered.

She had never seen such blue eyes, dancing with amusement, full of mischief. His face was broader than Clay's, the planes softer and fuller. And he was several years older. They both held their mouths tightly, as if fighting ready. Jolie glanced at the hearth wondering why the fire blazed so hot. The coals merely glowed. She looked back at this Kane Mercedes and sighed.

"Will you tell your mother I came?"

Jolie nodded. The story really was true then, and still she hardly believed it. The puzzle went back more than forty years to the heavy green heat of Louisiana, to another mother and daughter who had been close and then torn apart.

Kane turned to go.

"Wait!" Jolie gasped. "You've come so far. Please, sit. I've sent for tea. Let me see if Mother will come down. She's been so worried. We've all been in a muddle since...Well, I'm sure Clay's told you everything." Her words trailed away. She fought a terrible heat creeping across her cheeks. "Are you sure Clay's well? Won't he be coming home?"

Kane worried his soggy cap in work-hardened hands. "He's sober and eating now. He's well in body again, but...He's swamped, Ma'am. To be truthful..."

"Please, call me Jolie. *Jolie,*" she said carefully with a soft 'J.' "That's French for..."

Kane's face hardened sharp and proud. His eyes became shaded under a defiant brow.

"Forgive me," she whispered. The heat from her cheeks flowed over her body. She'd never had trouble charming young men before. This one certainly didn't look charmed.

Her heart twisted.

"To be truthful, *Miss Roebling,*" he continued after an uncomfortable silence, "Clay doesn't want to come home."

"Then we'll just have to fetch him!"

"If you want my opinion..." He paused to see if she did want it, and softened again when Jolie eagerly waited. "His *father* should come for him. Clay's lucky to have had a father, true or not. I told him so. He ain't likely to get over this until he knows his father's feelings. If you will, tell Mr. Roebling he's welcome at my mother's house any time. We're humble folk, but clean."

Jolie nodded, hastening to reassure him as she might a servant, and then bit back her words. "Papa will be there as soon as he hears Clay's there. Will you please wait until I speak to Mama?"

Kane drew a breath. "If you think she'll see me. Remember, I'm a Mercedes."

Such a fuss, Jolie thought hurrying out. Mama would see *this* Mercedes was different!

Such a name. Since she had heard it a few days before she'd never known a word to be more heavy with mystery and loathing. Mercedes! She ran up the stairs, her corset pinching unmercifully. The house still trembled silent and waiting for the...end. Jolie shivered.

She burst into her mother's bedchamber and found her in her dressing gown before the looking glass. Well, Mr. Kane Mercedes would just have to wait until she dressed.

"Clay's all right!" Jolie cried rushing and putting her hands on her mother's frail shoulders. How glad she was to bear the news. Now Mama would be happy again. "He found a brother who has taken him in. That's where he was those years you lost him. He lived with this shipwright and his mother. The man's here right now and wants to see you. He's very nice, Mama. His name's Kane Mercedes, and he has the most brilliant blue eyes!"

Every word registered on Loraine's face as pain. She twisted away.

"Won't you come down? Please, Mama? For me? Come down and..."

"Mercedes blood stains all! I'll see no Mercedes. Ever!"

"But we must fetch Clay home," Jolie cried. "I want this to be over!"

"If Clay ever comes back, he comes as a Roebling. That's what Adam and I gave him!" Loraine turned, her face rigid. "We gave him the chance to be a man, not a monster. Is there another Mercedes? Mother of God, there's no end!" She acted as if the fault was all Jolie's. "Your own grandmother killed a Mercedes! Never forget that, Jolie Roebling. You read her diary, how Miles Mercedes tried to rape and kill her. That man's son raped me! Yes, Beau did. I know that now. I was innocent and he compromised me. My mother planned everything so carefully for me, just as I have for you and all my children. I was a fool and spoiled it for all time. If I had only listened to Mother and done as I was told... *You* listen, my girl. Get that monster out of my house. Never speak of him again. Never!"

"But Mama, you're wrong!"

"Not this time. You're too young to realize, just as I was too young. I didn't trust my mother, and look what it got me. A Mercedes son. A bastard son who has run away from me. I'll not beg Clay to come back! If he wants to be a Mercedes, he won't *be* my son anymore!" Loraine wiped her mouth. "Dear God, I see that look in your eye! You're bewitched already! Let Clay go! It's best for all of us. If he comes back...he *must* renounce the Mercedes name!"

Jolie backed toward the door. Mama was wrong, so terribly wrong! And yet...Mama had once been bewitched by the blue eyes of a handsome Mercedes. Was Jolie bewitched?

As if in a trance, Jolie went back down to the grand parlor. When she appeared in the doorway, Kane rose from the divan. His mouth was tight, those magic eyes shadowed again. "She won't see you," she said, her voice dull.

Kane put his cap on and walked out. His boot brushed the hem of her wide skirt as he went through the doorway. How could she look at that man with anything other than hate?

Kane paused at the front door. She had more to say to him, but couldn't say a word. Clay was to come home a Roebling or not at all. She couldn't say that! If Mama was truly abandoning him, giving him up for always, if she could do that, she could do that to any one of them!

Could Clay renounce his blood and come home? Could life ever be what it had been before? He had been a Mercedes from birth and all the years of his growing up. He hadn't changed. Had he?

Jolie looked into Kane Mercedes' eyes and felt an explosion of pain in her heart. Mama was wrong! Mercedes blood was no different from any other. It wasn't the blood that made a man, but the heart, the soul, the mind. She was wrong, for this Mercedes, and Clay, too, were different from the ones before. A person wasn't born to love or hate, good or evil. A person was what he was by his life, his acts, his dreams and desires.

Jolie watched Kane go out, closing the door carefully against the rain. Part of her went with him.

# Thirty-Three

Jolie stopped to empty her slippers of pebbles. With every mile the woods grew more dense and little was left of the afternoon sun. She hadn't thought Maddie Horn's shack would be so far.

Now she had matching blisters on both heels. Her skirts were gray with dust and she was growing cold. Here and there a maple had started to turn yellow. Already the wildflowers were fading. How she wished she was back in her room snug and content.

She trudged on, determined to find Clay, though, and fetch him home. Only then would her life get back to normal.

Clay had been gone nearly two weeks now. He'd sent no message, so if it hadn't been for that visit from the shipwright no one would have known what had become of him.

Didn't anyone care, Jolie wondered. Mama was better now, basking in Papa's close attention. Hope was up and about taking over duties that had been Clay's, and doing remarkably well. No reports of disreputable behavior had come from the university.

"I'm giving Clay all the time he needs," Papa had told her.

"I'm waiting for him to come back as a Roebling," Mama said whenever she sensed Jolie's patience had grown dangerously thin.

Their excuses infuriated Jolie. How could they sit back while Clay tried to piece his life back together among strangers?

Each day she had watched her family recover. Uncle James grew stronger with Yolanda and Miranda out of sight and mind. (Word had come from Uncle Conrad that they had arrived in Saxwell safely.) Each night Jolie stared through her white lace canopy wondering if Clay had recovered.

She could wonder no longer.

And something else kept her awake. Though it shamed and inflamed her, she couldn't be rid of it. Kane Mercedes' face.

Just as Mama and Papa, Hope and Garner took up their lives again, she, too, found new thoughts and dreams plaguing her. How could she think of a man at a time like this? She'd never been given to romantic fancies before. And if that wasn't bad enough, he was a…

Jerking her shawl more tightly around her shoulders, Jolie quickened her pace. Damn that name. What was a name but a word? Kane Mercedes had opened her heart and quickened her soul. If she found Clay, she might see Kane again, and that kept her moving through the whispering leafy shadows along the Pomoset River.

At long last she found the shack. It was a squat log house surrounded by a low wall of stones. As she approached, Jolie heard soft laughter inside. The clearing reminded her of a leafy room, damp and cool. The overhead branches made a soft canopy and the nearby river slipped away like a thief.

At her hollow knock the voices within the shack stopped. Moments later the door swung open. Broad and smiling, Kane Mercedes stood before her holding a Kentucky rifle. Jolie's heart jumped.

"Who is it?" came a woman's soft voice.

Beyond, in the cozy firelight, Jolie saw Clay seated at a trestle table, a spoon half raised to his mouth. At the sight of her he set it back in the wooden trencher and sighed.

"Afternoon, Miss Roebling," Kane said showing Jolie in.

Maddie rose from her stool at the end of the table and extended her hand. Kane's mother was much smaller than Jolie had imagined. She was a round little woman who looked like a wren. "Won't you sit?" Maddie said smiling. Kane's smile was hers.

Jolie dropped onto the bench opposite Clay. "Thank you," she said drinking of the cold river water Kane brought in a battered pewter mug. She felt like a princess taking tea with peasants. She looked up at Kane and felt her cheeks sting with excitement.

"What do you want?" Clay asked scowling at her. He took up his spoon again but didn't eat.

"You're so abrupt!" Maddie scolded, clucking her tongue. "It was good of you to come, dear. Clay misses his family."

Clay made a face.

"You do!" Maddie chuckled coming around and nudging him. "You have a pretty sister. Which are you, dear? Hope or Jolie?"

"Jolie," Kane said quickly, with a soft 'J.'

Jolie's heart thumped. He remembered! "I've come to ask Clay to come home," she said.

Clay dropped his spoon and got up. "Why should I?"

"Hear her out first," Maddie said.

"I'll go home later."

"Why not now?" Jolie twisted to watch him pace behind her. "I don't think any less of Mama for what happened so long ago. I know you don't. Papa feels…"

Clay turned. The firelight lit his hair to flame. "Father feels I let Mother down by leaving. He doesn't want me back, and I'll wager Mother doesn't really want me back either."

"No!"

"They felt they had to hide the fact that I was born a Mercedes. They thought they gave me something better, but to me it wasn't. They were thinking only of themselves. Father wanted his heir and Mother her virtue, so they stuck the name Roebling on me. That didn't change me. The only Roebling in me now is what Father taught me: to be like him. Would Father stay where he didn't fit? Would he do what everyone told him he must?" Clay's eyes were wild and he'd grown red-faced. The past weeks had weighed heavily upon his thoughts. She should have come much sooner.

Maddie put her hand on Clay's shoulder. "Finish your stew. Your temper's too hot."

"Should he stay?" Jolie asked, feeling that Maddie somehow possessed the answer eluding the rest of them.

"Have some supper with us," Maddie said reaching for another bowl.

Impatiently Jolie shook her head. She had no appetite.

"Clay should do what is in his heart," Maddie said. "He just doesn't know what that is. He's like a bird fallen from the nest. Which way to fly?"

Clay looked pained. "You talk like I'm a boy wet behind the ears."

"And who's been drying you this past week?" Then Maddie softened her eyes as she spooned stew into Jolie's bowl. "One dark night long ago we took you in. You were wet then. My heart broke at the sight of you. Kane called you brother from the first." Maddie turned back to Jolie. "Don't be hard on Clay. He's had a nasty shock, and he's ashamed."

Clay threw up his arms. "They're glad to be rid of me!"

"Oh, sit, you lubber. That hot temper used to get your father in plenty of trouble. I loved him once. Beau Mercedes was the handsomest seaman alive, but after a time my heart soured. Either you take hold of your life now and set your course true with your mind and heart, or your temper will rule you the rest of your days. I'll not be proud of you then."

She set the bowl before Jolie. "Eat," she said. "You need it."

"Will you be going back with your sister?" Maddie asked later after they'd eaten.

Clay had folded himself before the hearth and looked to Jolie as if he belonged there, not in a leather wing chair at Roebling Estate. Clay shook his head.

"Then, Kane, you'd best walk her back. The wood's no place for her. Tell your folks I may not be quality, but I gave Clay my wing once and do it again gladly. He's like my own lost boy. Your mama will understand that."

Maddie lent Jolie an extra shawl for the trek back.

"Thank you," Jolie said hugging her before going out. Even though Clay wasn't coming home she felt better than she had in days. "I'm glad Clay's here."

"Come back yourself sometime," Maddie said.

Jolie hugged Clay's stiff shoulders. "Come home soon. Please? We all need you."

Her gentle tone seemed to reach him and he smiled. "I like it here," he said. "I've never had so much time to think. Give my love to Hope."

Jolie grabbed Clay's face and kissed him. "Soon," she said again and then hurried out.

She was well beyond the lamplight's reach before Kane followed. She didn't want to think of them then. Clay was all right and that was all that mattered.

The way back seemed even longer in the dark. Kane's soft footsteps on the path behind Jolie nearly unnerved her. They went for miles without speaking. Gradually Jolie forgot the shack and Clay and all the events of the past weeks. She became aware only of Kane, of his tread, the faint sound of his breathing, the swish of branches as they wound their way toward the road.

"Won't you walk with me?" she said at last. "I can't see the way." Which was true enough.

Kane's shadow moved beside Jolie's. Now and then their arms brushed. His silence worried her.

"I'm glad Clay's with you and your mother," she said, hoping to break the quiet.

"Are you?"

"It couldn't have been easy for your mother raising..." No, no, that wasn't a proper subject!

"It wasn't. Mind those roots across the path."

As he spoke, Jolie stumbled. Kane's arm was around her instantly. A sudden bright light filled Jolie. She felt as if she glowed where Kane's hand touched her arm.

She looked up into the shadowy shape that was Kane's face. The faint light of a quarter moon dancing on the oil-dark water nearby reflected in Kane's eyes like a glitter of twin stars. Even though no words were said, she felt as if they were talking. His eyes spoke to her heart.

He gave off a solid warmth that made Jolie feel small and protected. She hoped they never reached the road, that they could go on walking forever.

What did those brilliant eyes see? He could look so solemn one instant and flash a smile the next. Did he like her? Was she too young to hope...

His fingers laced deeply into her hair suddenly, lifting her face and urging her upward. She felt his breath against her cheeks, then his lips on hers. The warmth was like no other. His mouth was so very soft and tender, and wet, speaking intimately of him.

A bit abruptly Kane drew back. "Now your trip won't have been a total loss." That disarming smile flashed, no trace of heat or desire in his eyes.

"If you think..."

"Miss Roebling, what I think doesn't matter. What does is my name, and *yours*. For a moment my curiosity got the better of me, but I want no part of the Roeblings. You're a dangerous breed."

Adam closed the ledgers and leaned back in his desk chair. The library was lonely without the voices of his sons. There had been a time when Clay's and Garner's disagreements had worried him. Now he longed for those times lost forever, thanks to Yolanda.

He stood and massaged the ache in his shoulder. The house was silent. Hope had gone to the yard—he couldn't stop her. She knew just what needed to be done, as Clay had once. Adam conceded to her with a certain relief. He didn't need to worry about her. She had found her niche, and to his amazement, reminded him that *she* was eldest and therefore heir!

He was just coming out of the library when Jolie arrived. He caught a glimpse of an average-sized man in the darkness as Jolie returned a shawl and said a curt goodbye.

That must be the young shipwright, Mercedes. Adam had made inquiries and learned Kane was trusted among all men at the docks. Though he kept mainly to himself, he was well liked and worked hard. Adam had sent an offer for Kane to work in the Roebling yards. A good shipwright was a valuable find, and Adam had hoped for some word, some new link that would bring Clay back. Kane Mercedes had refused. And no message arrived from Clay.

"Where have you been?" Adam asked when Jolie returned and saw him smiling faintly at her.

"I went to Clay." She sounded fiercely angry.

Adam drew a deep breath. "Is he well?"

"Yes, and he's…They're really very good people. I liked Kane's mother. She's taking good care of Clay. I only wish…" Suddenly her face was awash with tears. "You and Mama should have gone! Roeblings! We think we're so special." She waved her fists. "We're rich and proud, but we think only of ourselves."

She ran up the stairs, sobbing.

Adam was stunned.

Hadn't he made the right decision not to pressure Clay now? Or was he really just afraid to go, afraid to feel powerless again?

Adam went up the stairs feeling old and lonely. Loraine had retired early. At least to her he was still the most important person in her life.

He found her propped in bed reading that diary again. She had a morbid fascination for it. When he came in she casually closed it and laid it aside. "You look tired."

He lay beside her thinking of Clay. Over the years there were times he was short, times he was unjust, overcareful, sensitive, though in the long run he had thought he'd done well. "I think I know how to get Clay back," he said. He began telling Loraine how he proposed to mend the damage.

When he turned, she was crying. She waved her hand as if he shouldn't be concerned, yet his heart twisted. "Let me think," she said getting up and going out.

He supposed she was going for a brandy. She was growing frail, and he worried. He ran his hand over the place where she had been sitting, absorbing her warmth, longing for the easy times again. Weeks had passed since he'd made love to her.

On the table lay the diary. He hesitated before picking it up. Undoing the latch, he watched it fall open to a time-worn section. Florie DeMarsett's script was beautiful. She wrote of the beach and her desire to swim.

Adam had seen his mother-in-law only a few times before he married Loraine. Her intense eyes had always bothered him. Then with a spark of surprise, he remembered.

His stepmother's funeral, the grand parlor draped in black bunting, the crisp smell of pine…The memory came fresh and clear a red mantle, a young woman's hauntingly beautiful face, her tears. As Adam read the entries about that day and Florie's impression of him as a boy, he could see her.

He read on and on, skipping some parts until the whole tragic love story filled his drumming heart with bittersweet understanding. When Loraine came back into the bedchamber, her face flushed, Adam closed the diary.

Why hadn't he guessed? He laid his hand on the diary. Its life was gone. It had passed into him. It glowed on Loraine's face. It raced ahead in the determined young breast of his daughter Jolie.

Gingerly Loraine sat on the edge of their marriage bed, the place where they had been lovers and warriors. She slipped the diary into the nightstand drawer. Adam hoped she wouldn't have to take it out again.

He cupped her warm cheek with a trembling hand. How many times had he looked at her face and wanted her with no real idea of who she really was?

Had he ever known who *he* was? He felt like a posturing fool, a cock of the walk. His pride seemed laughable. He thought of his father, of that portrait over the desk in the library below. Those weren't the eyes of stoic strength and victory over the deaths of two wives. Those were the embittered eyes of defeat, of a man who had lost his love.

"Why do you look at me like that?" Loraine whispered.

Adam loosed her hair and let it flow across her shoulders like golden waves. "We never did swim like we planned."

Loraine's lips began to tremble. "Jolie does it for us."

Together they laid back. They needed no bolts of lightning now. They enjoyed a wonderful peace, a knowing so warm and clean, a love so gentle and enduring they had no need to speak of it. Adam drew Loraine to his chest. "I love you," he said.

She put her cheek on his chest and lay very still. Adam knew what to do. In giving his whole heart with no bargains, no gifts and no undying vows, he felt Loraine's love flow into him just as freely. This was marriage, he thought. This was a new beginning.

# Thirty-Four

The *Lady Loraine* rocked in her moorings. Deckhands ran about readying to sail. A brisk wind buffeted two awestruck men grinning at the rail. Clay and Kane Mercedes leaned over and waved at the group of people watching them from the dock.

"This will be so good for them both," Maddie Horn said, her hood tugging in the wind. "I never thought Kane would get a chance to sail, and now, to go with his brother…" She dabbed at her tears and waved back.

Loraine couldn't take her eyes from Clay, from his smile. He was going away, and that was all she knew. She was happy for him, of course. She waved like the rest, but her heart was breaking.

Adam squeezed her shoulders. "Best get back in the carriage now. You'll catch a chill."

"Just a moment more. He looks so much older, so small way up there."

Adam didn't comment. Clay *did* look different. That was what had first struck Adam when he walked into Maddie Horn's shack the week before. Clay had been hard to talk to, but he jumped at the chance to sail the New Orleans packet.

"You've always wanted to sail," Adam had told him. "To the Gulf and back under Captain Graves, and you'll be ready to captain your own ship—if that's what you decide you want."

Clay's eyes had shone like stars. He had turned to Kane. "Come with me!"

Kane had laughed—Adam had liked him from the first. "I'm no sailor," he'd said.

"Go," Maddie had said, the pain of love bright in her eyes, too.

And in the end Maddie convinced them.

Adam quickly arranged the voyage. They had family dinners at the estate complete with all the conflicting feelings. That very morning at a grand breakfast, they'd all toasted Clay's and Kane's voyage south, and

**321**

now Adam watched the last lines cast off. He was praying a lot these days, he thought. Godspeed, Clay. And you, too, Kane Mercedes.

Just before the gangplank was drawn up, Clay bolted down it and ran to them all standing shivering in the wind. He looked taller, thinner, his hair shining in the sun. For a terrible moment both Loraine and Maddie thought of Beau, and they said quick prayers, too.

With that wonderful smile, Clay kissed his mother and Maddie. He pecked Jolie's cool cheek and then lingered with Hope, clasping her hands in his. "You'll take care of things while I'm away," he said.

Gulping back tears, Hope Janine nodded. "*Learn* something," she said.

"Say goodbye to Garner for me," he said turning to Adam. Then quickly, awkwardly, the two embraced. Adam gave Clay one quick clap on the shoulder. Then Clay broke free and ran back to the *Lady*.

Now the *Lady Loraine* was cast off. She drifted into the open harbor. As her sails went up and caught the wind with resounding whacks, Jolie shivered.

She held her breath to keep from crying. There Clay went, a whole man again, off to adventure. He might never come back, and he'd merely pecked her cheek. *She* had brought Papa to his senses. *She* brought Clay back into the family, and he had hardly noticed her since!

She turned away, despising herself. She was plainly jealous. Of course she was overjoyed for Clay. She only wished *she* had found happiness with the rest.

There went Kane Mercedes with Clay. Kane was nothing to her, and everything. She hated him! She hoped she never saw his face again!

Her heart twisted. Oh, how terribly wrong she'd been about him. He wanted no business with Roeblings, did he? How quickly he took the offer of the trip to New Orleans with Clay. He was no better than his conniving father. He was after the Roebling power and wealth, and she *hated* him!

As full of malice as her heart was, it still bled to see Kane fade to a speck as the *Lady* cut farther and farther to sea. She wouldn't have hated him nearly so much if he hadn't hurt her so. Of a dangerous breed, was she? He only knew the half of it!

"They'll be back by summer," Maddie said. She'd been watching Jolie, and her smile made Jolie even more testy.

Jolie tightened her lips and started for the carriage. Summer, Jolie thought. By summer she would have completely forgotten Kane Mercedes!

# PART TWO

## 1861

## Thirty-Five

In November Union Harbor celebrated the election of Abraham Lincoln. By mid-winter most of the southern states had seceded, and the Union prepared for war.

No word came from Clay or Kane. No one knew if the Roebling clipper *Lady Loraine* arrived safely, or if it had even been able to dock in Confederate New Orleans.

By April, when war officially broke out, James was well enough to move into town. He took up work again at Union Hospital.

Shortly before the final quarter examinations, Garner Roebling left the university to join the navy. By July he was a captain of a man-of-war and wrote home that he'd soon be headed south to blockade a Confederate port.

With Hope's help, Adam kept up with the staggering demands for warships. Occasionally Loraine did volunteer nursing at the hospital, and there she met her old friend Nicolette again. She welcomed the renewed friendship and began inviting her for small dinner parties when James could come.

Jolie filled her days with thoughts of gowns and curls, and her nights with grand balls where she danced with soldiers from every Union state. She was the belle of Union Harbor, pretty, bright, intelligent and tireless.

When she wasn't dancing, she was riding Garner's thoroughbred or slipping off to the beach for a swim. She kept busy enough to avoid the discontent in her heart. Life at Roebling Estate had achieved a new contentment. Though she never recovered her intimacy with her mother, Jolie could truthfully say the family had healed, all except those residing in Saxwell.

Summer was especially hot that year. Jolie couldn't remember when she'd felt so uncomfortable. Most evenings the family retired to the terrace where on one side Adam and Hope, and perhaps James and architects or soldiers enthralled with the new Hope, work-slim and too smart for her own good, sat discussing war. On the other side, when Jolie wasn't at a party, Jolie sat with her mother, Nicolette or other women whom Loraine invited to keep her mind away from New Orleans.

The town was always in a turmoil. The mails were slow, newspapers garbled and always the flow of soldiers, equipment, camp followers and the like choked the streets. Adam found it necessary to hire a few hardies to guard the grounds after dark.

It was on such a hot summer night one of the guards brought a man he'd found at the gate to the door. A thunderstorm had passed by that afternoon. Everyone was on the terrace enjoying the cool fresh air.

"Don't get up," Adam said going inside with the guard. "You needn't worry."

With her forehead permanently creased by worry, Jolie's mother watched him go. In moments Adam was back and called to James.

"What is it?" Loraine said hurrying after them.

Jolie and Hope went inside, too.

"It's not Garner?" Loraine grabbed at Adam's coat sleeve. Her voice broke. "Not Clay?"

"Conrad is here," he said. "He lost his horse in the storm and had to walk the rest of the way. Wait here." He didn't notice how Hope stopped and turned deathly pale. "James, come with me."

"Has Conrad been hurt?" Loraine asked.

"There's been an…accident."

James followed Adam into the grand parlor. Adam closed the door. After a moment of bewilderment, Loraine wandered off for a brandy.

"What do you suppose happened?" Jolie asked, turning to find herself alone in the entrance hall. Hope had vanished.

She crept to the parlor door and inched it open.

"I know, I know," her uncle Conrad was saying into his hands. He was sitting on the divan. Adam and James stood over him. Their faces were an unbelievable mixture of emotions. "I was a fool, always a fool where Yolanda was concerned. I should never have taken her or Miranda in, but…"

He mumbled into his hands for a good while. Adam bent closer to make out his words. James didn't look as if he wanted to listen.

"Then I found she was seeing my friends. She had hurt me so many times. I was angry…Miranda was so willing and had no one else. At first it meant nothing to either of us. I wanted to get back at Yolanda. Miranda scared her beaus away—I was helping her."

He looked away suddenly. Jolie couldn't see his face or hear his words. She hadn't seen her uncle in over a year. His clothes were wet and disheveled, his hair thinning in back.

"Then Yolanda discovered us," he said, his voice lifeless. "I didn't think she cared. She had the others to amuse her. I didn't know how she felt until it was almost too late. Little by little she began poisoning me! I was half dead before I realized! We quarreled. She fell…" He fell silent. "I tried to get word to you in time, James. Her funeral was this morning. I left Miranda with my housekeeper. I want her to stay on, of course, but I suppose…"

Jolie left the door ajar and started for the stairs. Aunt Yolanda was dead.

Feeling ill, Jolie dragged herself up the stairs. Moments later she stood in the doorway of Hope's third-floor rooms. "I didn't listen long enough to find out just how it happened."

Hope sat in her old chair. On the floor around her were the plans and ledgers usually gracing Papa's desk. On the table beside her was a tray of biscuits left from dinner. "Good riddance," Hope said over a mouthful.

She stuffed another biscuit in her mouth and bent to push about some papers. A large crumb fell from her lips to the rug. She stared at it and stopped chewing. With a startled expression, she looked at the biscuits as if they'd appeared on her table by magic. Then she swallowed.

"Go away," Hope said, rising from her chair and unhooking her snug bodice. She had changed so from the year before she was like a new person. Though she could hardly be called slender yet, she was no more the plump Roebling dumpling. "I have work."

"Clay wouldn't recognize you," Jolie said, feeling ignored and useless as always. She wanted to stay and talk but no one had time for her now. She was beginning to understand how Clay had felt all his growing-up years, mismatched. She didn't fit either.

"I don't want to hear about Clay or Aunt Yolanda, or Mother

or anyone, least of all Uncle Conrad! I'm busy, Jolie. Go dancing or something. Go see those soldiers who were here. I have a lot of work! Important, necessary work!"

Jolie went out slamming Hope's door. She found her mother in the bedchamber below brushing out her hair.

"Did you hear the news?" her mother asked.

"Is it true? Are we finally rid of Aunt Yolanda? I know that's not nice but..."

Loraine dropped her hairpins on the dressing table. She sat suddenly and covered her mouth. Her dark eyes were pained. "I'm trying not to, but I want to laugh. She was trying to push Conrad down the stairs when she fell herself. She's gone. Really gone!" Loraine erupted with a giggle.

Jolie rushed to her and fell at her feet. "Oh, Mama!" She laid her head on her mother's knee. "She took so *much* from us."

Loraine stroked her hair. Then she laughed a little more. "Get up, dear. You're too old for this. Are you going to the Allendale ball on Saturday? You didn't forget to send your reply." Loraine broke off at the sight of Jolie's stricken face.

"I'm *not* too old, Mama! I need you! I've been so alone..."

Loraine moved a letter that had been lying in plain sight on her dressing table under her jewel box. She looked back at Jolie. "I hadn't realized you were unhappy."

"What was that?"

"Nothing. What's wrong, Jolie?"

From the way her mother was behaving, Jolie was suddenly sure the letter was important. She snatched it up and saw the return address: New Orleans. "It's from Clay!"

Loraine took it back. "It's addressed to me, and it's *not* from Clay. Jolie, I'm tired now. Why don't you go on to bed? There's nothing we can do for James now, or Conrad."

"Who is it from then?"

"My aunt, if you must know. Jolie, please! This is none of your business."

"You haven't even opened it!"

"Leave me now, Jolie!" Loraine snapped.

With a cry, Jolie stormed out.

• • •

Hours and hours passed before the house was completely quiet. Jolie's eyes never closed. She tried to think of all the upcoming parties, or the letters and invitations on her own dressing table from admirers and hopeful beaus. It all seemed so ridiculous suddenly, dancing and laughing in the midst of a war.

She ached to talk to someone. Hope was her only choice, but she was still furious with her. Where did Hope get her ideas that she was so suddenly important? Just because Papa wanted to send her to an academy now...

Jolie got up. Her back ached. She was restless and hungry, lonely and exhausted. Perhaps Hope had just been upset.

The hall was dim and silent. Jolie could hear the gentle murmur of her parents' voices within the bedchamber. Creeping up the stairs to the third floor again, she nearly screamed when she encountered Conrad standing near Hope's door.

"Are you lost, Uncle?" she whispered.

He whirled. She could smell the brandy on his breath. The bottle was in his hand.

"Come. I'll show you the way."

"Pretty little Jolie," he mumbled, taking her elbow and following her to the stairs. "All grown up and the toast of Union Harbor. Miranda hates you to her bones."

"I'm sorry," Jolie said shushing him. It couldn't be true, what she'd heard him say in the parlor. He had meant he was like a father to Miranda.

They stumbled down the stairs. Jolie tried to guide him quietly to his room. "Must be careful on stairs," he said. "I almost died, you know. Yolanda never loved anyone, not even herself. But I loved her." Then he chuckled and it sounded more like a sob. "No one has ever loved me until Miranda. Did you know that, pretty Jolie? I was raised by a hawk-faced old crone who carried a switch. I never knew my own mother. Not one kind word for me. I was always trouble. Always in the way."

Jolie's heart softened. "I know just how you feel. You need to sleep, Uncle. You've had a hard time and too much of Papa's brandy. Let me take that for you. Off to bed now before..."

"You have a kind heart," Conrad said smiling down at her as she opened the door. "Go in and light the lamp for me. If I do it I'll just break it and maybe burn down the place. Adam wouldn't like that."

Jolie slipped into the stuffy room and fumbled on the table for the lamp. When it flickered and sent up a smoky wavering flame, she went to throw open the windows. No one had even done that for him, and it was so hot! No wonder he turned to anyone he could find.

The door closed. Jolie turned and there was Conrad so close behind she could hear his breath rushing in and out. "Stay and talk to me," he said taking her arm and leading her toward the bed. "I don't have anyone to talk to, and I need to talk. Yolanda died in my house. I don't know now if Miranda will stay with me." He ran a trembling hand over his eyes.

He was still tall and lean but old now. The hollows in his cheeks caught the shadows. His hair stuck up like Garner's did when he ran his fingers through it—just like Uncle Conrad was doing now.

For a moment Jolie thought of Garner, far away somewhere on a warship. He might look like Conrad someday. "Have you ever done what you really wanted, Uncle?" she whispered. "Or have you always done what you must?"

Conrad blinked. "You *do* know how I feel. Do you know how much I hate Saxwell?"

"Why do you stay then? Do you hate running the mills, too?"

He shook his head. "What else am I good for? I threw away my youth waiting for Yolanda. All she ever wanted was Adam. Adam and the money, and the name. The name smells of scandal, you know that? Roebling! John Roebling was an orphan from an English workhouse. What does that make us?"

Feeling as if she'd found a friend, Jolie took her uncle's hand. "Go to sleep now. You'll feel better, and in the morning you'll know what to do."

"If you'll stay with me," Conrad said pulling free and slipping his hand into her dressing gown. "You're prettier than Hope, anyway."

He moved so quickly and easily Jolie could only gasp and stare at the hollows in his face. He looked harmless enough. He looked like he needed her help, her understanding.

Squirming free, Jolie edged toward the door. He got up and followed her, still looking hurt and lonely. His arms went around her. He pressed her back against the door. His mouth came down on hers.

"You're nicer than Miranda, too."

Jolie's skin crawled. "You can't do this! Please, stop!"

"They always say that at first. You'll grow used to it, my sweeting." His hands moved over her breasts.

Before she knew what she had done, her nails were cutting across his cheeks. She fell out the door. The hall was still dim and silent. She ran to her room and locked herself in. For several moments she stood listening unable to breathe for fear Conrad would follow.

She shuddered at the thought of him. Miranda! And Hope, too. Dear God, was she surrounded by monsters?

When she heard nothing, she sank to her knees and wept. She had to get away! Away from this house and its secrets.

In the morning Conrad had gone.

# Thirty-Six

Jolie could scarcely see for the sun reflecting on the water. She swam out as far as she dared and then let a wave throw her back toward the sand.

The sea grew colder every day. She felt it in her bones, in the growing ache of every muscle as she put off getting out and dressing.

Thunder waited patiently in the grasses. The proud thoroughbred lifted his head and looked north. Swimming in closer, Jolie looked, too. This part of the shore, though private, wasn't unknown to strangers any longer. Each time Jolie swam there she took a great risk of being seen.

Though no one was in sight, she swam to the sand and dashed for the protection of a clump of brush where she always left her clothes. This place was her only sanctuary now. Her house could be both lonely and stifling. She had nothing to do. Weeks had passed since she'd gone dancing.

Her petticoats felt heavy and bothersome though in the slight breeze the protection of the linen felt good on her legs. She tied the ribbons of her camisole and was about to lift her skirt over her head when she heard soft footfalls beyond the brush.

A man stood a few feet away. His dark brown hair hung ragged around the collar of his faded and torn blue jacket. From a sun-bronzed face masked by a wiry unkempt red beard blazed brilliant blue eyes.

"Kane!" She clutched her skirt to her throat. "Are you real or am I dreaming?"

He just stood, his arms limp at the sides of ragged trousers. He was barefoot. Then his teeth flashed behind the stretch of a rosy lower lip.

Without a word he joined her in the cover of the brush. In one deft motion he circled her waist with broad sun-darkened hands and lifted her high above his head!

Just as quickly he put her to her feet again. She hardly had time to protest before he covered her mouth with a kiss that heated her blood and blasted her heart.

"Where did you come from?" she gasped, wanting so very much to be furious.

"I thought I'd never see home again," Kane said turning. He looked up at the bluff, at oaks and maples tinged red and russet and gold.

Jolie grabbed his coat sleeve. "Where's Clay? He's not dead! What's happened to you?"

He staggered against her barrage of questions. Under his magnificent tan his skin seemed somehow fragile. Sunburnt lines surrounded his eyes hooded under a brow drawn sharply over his nose. Jolie almost reached up to smooth them.

"Put your skirts on, Jolie." He used the soft 'J' again. She noticed a hint of a southern accent in his speech now, too. "I won't molest you anymore. Could I stop at your father's house for a bite before going on to Ma's?"

He waited while she tore on the rest of her clothes. As they led the horse up the path, Kane said, "Early this morning I jumped ship a few miles up the coast. I had to hide most of the day. Didn't want to get picked up and enlisted. Not yet anyway."

Jolie had to run to match his stride.

"The *Lady Loraine* flies the Stars and Bars now," he sighed. "We were about to sail home when she was seized."

At the top of the bluff Kane looked reluctant to go on. "I need your father's help. And Garner's."

"Garner's gone to sea. We haven't seen him in months. Papa's home today. He's been working overmuch."

"He won't be glad to hear what I've come to tell him then. Can I wait and say it all in a piece? It's a long story." At her look of dread Kane made a small smile. "He's not dead. He's just lost."

Jolie groaned.

They went in the house through the terrace doors. Jolie opened the library door to Papa nodding in his chair, the daily newspaper open across his chest.

Adam opened his eyes. The moment he saw Kane, alone, his face fell.

"Get Kane a brandy," Adam said rising quickly. The paper fell to the floor, open to the lists of dead and still missing from the battle of Bull Run lost to the Confederacy only weeks before.

As Jolie poured she covered the credenza with spills.

"I take it the *Lady's* gone," Adam said offering Kane his chair. He looked at Kane's sandy bare feet and seemed touched.

"I need money, sir. To go back. We ran into a bit of trouble. If the Union doesn't draft me and the Confederates hang me for a spy, I'll find Clay, sir."

Jolie ran to get her mother and Hope. Moments later they gathered around Kane, their faces strained and anxious.

"As I told Jolie, just before we were to sail—this was about Christmas—the *Lady* was boarded and seized. Clay and I waited, hoping to find passage back before it came to war. No ships were going north, though, and the river was blocked. We stayed at a hotel thinking Captain Graves would help us get back." Kane looked uncomfortable suddenly. "We had plenty of money. If we'd lived easy we could've lasted a good while. I have to confess, sir, I grew short with Clay. He was used to finer things and went through his money as if…" Kane shook his head. "I warned him. I told him two Yankees throwing around money would draw attention. He just kept drinking—plenty of pretty young belles helped him there. Finally one night I had my fill."

"You quarreled?" Loraine whispered. To Jolie she looked as if at any moment she might attack Kane. Since the fall before she'd done a magnificent job of trying to accept this Mercedes everyone told her was such a good man. Now her worst fears had come true.

"Worse than that," Kane said. "I walked out on him."

Adam looked away. One hand massaged the other balled into a fist.

"By then it was March. I took a room and rationed the cash I had left. When news of war reached us, I figured getting home was useless. Then the blockade made things impossible. I did meet a fellow then, a rum runner who agreed to take us out. I had just enough to pay him."

"Then what *happened?* Where's Clay now?" Hope cried stepping forward.

"I went back to his hotel," Kane said. "It was already too late. He'd been arrested—as a spy. I took what I could spare and paid for information. When I found where he had been taken I had to pay even more just to see him. I hatched a plan to get him out, but it took all the money I had left. The escape went well, but then the guards followed us through the streets. I finally lost them, but when I turned, I saw I'd lost Clay too."

"He wasn't hurt?" Loraine said turning to Adam for support.

Kane shook his head. "I don't think so. I stayed and looked as long as I could, but…" He shrugged. "I didn't know where he might have gone. After Bull Run I feared if I didn't get out then I never would. I'd be no good to Clay, or you, dead, or in some prisoner of war camp."

"The plantation!" Jolie cried.

Loraine stopped her. "He didn't know where it was. Besides, he knows how I feel about my aunt. He wouldn't go there."

"But the letter, Mama! If he was desperate…"

"The letter means nothing!" Loraine shouted. "Aunt Fabrienne is asking for legal help. Money. Someone is claiming a share of my inheritance from her. Every time one of her letters arrives I feel all over again her evil. She's a crazy old woman. I wouldn't want Clay there, even if his life did depend on it. She wouldn't help him anyway. I've refused to help her." Loraine covered her face and wept. "This is what *my* selfishness and bitterness have brought us."

"You can't blame yourself," Adam said drawing her close. Then he turned to Kane. "How do you propose to get back to New Orleans?"

"The runner leaves again in two days. I owe him, and I'll need all the money I can carry to get information about Clay. You'll have to trust me…"

"Of course we do," Adam said putting Loraine away from him. He went to his desk and drew out a bulging packet. Counting through a stack of greenbacks, he looked up frowning. "We'll have to go to the bank for gold. You'll need clothes…"

"I won't come back without him," Kane said, turning to them all, his voice full of his burden.

"I'll go with you," Hope said lifting her chin defiantly.

Adam looked at her. "You know I can't spare you now. You're too good at what you do."

Jolie could go, she thought, but no one looked to her.

As everyone talked at once, Jolie watched Kane. What had really happened to Clay? Why wouldn't Mama open that letter from the plantation?

Kane was ready to go on to his mother's when suddenly he ran his fingers through his hair and sank back into the chair. "This won't work."

Hope drew up her arms. "What is it *now?*"

"The men on that runner's ship took everything I had including my boots. I wouldn't last an hour if I carried the cash necessary to find Clay. The Confederates hold the Mississippi. I'd never make it across enemy lines. I thought if I could just get back the rest would work itself out."

Adam's eyes narrowed as if his face hurt. Painful thoughts formed in Jolie's mind, too.

"I'm outfitting a small clipper barque for the navy," Adam said looking down at Kane. "Could *you* sail it?"

• • •

Three days later the Roeblings, and Maddie Horn, gathered again to watch Kane Mercedes sail. This time, however, he was alone. Two nights before his ship had "disappeared" from the Roebling docks. Adam had renamed her the *Petit Noir.*

An hour before dawn the family waved from the beach north of Union Harbor. Kane would hide in the fog most of this day for he was now a runner in his own right, carrying goods enough to free Clay from the whole of the Confederacy if necessary.

They had all said their farewells. Now Kane climbed in an old dingy to be rowed out to the *Noir* and his loyal Roebling crew. He looked magnificent dressed to his task, his red beard a dashing addition to his charming grin. Hope wept openly as he waved. Adam and Loraine clung to each other. Only Maddie stood stiffly erect, dread written on her face.

Jolie turned away unmoved.

What a clever rogue Kane Mercedes was! Captain of the *Petit Noir.* Didn't anyone *see* what he had accomplished? They had all been taken in, just as she had that first rainy afternoon more than a year ago.

Not only had he managed a satchel full of gold, a fine new suit of clothes *and* the heart of the Roebling clan, he had a ship. Had everyone forgotten what his father had always wanted?

Jolie sat up from her bed. She wiped sweat from her brow and looked at it in surprise. Long afternoon shadows filled her bedchamber. Her skin felt clammy, but in her dream she'd been miserably hot. She'd been stumbling through a green mist, the sounds of oars behind her in dark muddy water.

Going to the window, Jolie watched rain pound the lawns into muddy lakes. How far had the *Petit Noir* gotten in such weather? Had she passed the harbor undetected? If she was seen, Kane might be arrested for stealing her.

Jolie sighed. No matter where the Mercedes went, and no matter their purpose, they courted trouble.

Rubbing her sleepy eyes, Jolie ventured into the hall. She paused long enough to determine her parents were in the hall below on their way to the parlor for a dinner drink. "...Miranda has gone away, but he doesn't say where. What will become of her?" her mother was saying. Jolie assumed she had just received a letter from Uncle Conrad.

"Maybe she'll come back to James," Adam said as they moved out of Jolie's hearing.

The drumming rain masked the rest of the sounds common to the vast Roebling house. Though hushed, it wasn't the same cold silence that had pervaded the rooms since Yolanda's arrival the year before.

Jolie would never again be the wide-eyed child Clay had once teased. For that matter, Clay would never again be the quiet dutiful young man she'd tried to protect.

Standing in the upstairs hall, Jolie wondered again if Clay still lived. How much of what Kane had told them was true? What guarantee did they have that Kane would *really* go back to the south where he'd be in danger? Wouldn't it be far easier for him just to sail away with his ship and his gold?

No one questioned Kane's honesty. No one doubted his success. Jolie was so afraid Kane was doing just what came to him naturally, charming, lying, and spoiling.

The door to her mother's drawing room stood ajar. A torn envelope lay on the carpet—the one from Conrad. Quickly, Jolie slipped into the room. She found the letter from Gautier Plantation still hidden under her mother's jewel case. She tore it open.

"Dear Niece, My slaves ran off. The army agents took my food. That so-called gentleman, Raymond Brown, is still after our land. I beg of you, send help. We must denounce this factor for what he is. A fraud! Only last night he sent a robber to my door claiming to be your son. I took my pistol to him. Can you leave an old woman to this? I suppose I should not expect so much of Florie's daughter but I am desperate. Think of your duty, Loraine. Your humble, Aunt Fabrienne."

Jolie clasped the brittle stationery to her breast. The old woman sounded frightened and lonely. And Clay *had* been there! He might have been wounded.

Noticing the March date, Jolie groaned. It was September now. If Clay could have gotten home by any means, he would have arrived by then. He must still be near the plantation—if he was still alive.

The *Noir* couldn't have gotten far in the storm. If she could get this information to Kane, and satisfy herself that he was, indeed, returning to search for Clay, Jolie might be able to sleep again.

Stifling a cry of hope, Jolie threw the letter down and dashed to her room. She tore off her crinoline and slippers. With her heaviest cloak as protection against the rain, she dashed down the servants' stairs and out the terrace doors.

The dense cloud cover made the afternoon seem more like evening. Jolie relished the feel of the cool rain-wet grass on her bare feet. By the time she reached the stable, the rain had soaked the hem and shoulders of her cloak.

She led Thunder into the gray afternoon darkness. As she swung up on his broad back and clutched his mane between trembling fingers, she thought of Kane. Just as quickly she put him from her mind. She forced away the memory of his hands on her waist with only the sheer lawn of her camisole between his warm flesh and hers. She wouldn't allow herself to remember the feel of his smooth warm lips on hers. The kiss had meant nothing. Nothing! She was going after the *Noir* for Clay's sake!

Guiding Thunder down to the beach, Jolie approached the harbor from the north. When her absence was discovered, they'd expect her to go to town by the road. She'd beat them. She'd find the *Petit Noir* before they dragged her home scolding all the way. She'd prove one way or another Kane's true character.

Just what did she hope his character to be? Wiping rain from her eyes, she urged Thunder on. How nice it would be to say, there, you see, he *is* a rogue! But then her own heart would break, for beating in her breast was a traitor!

How could she hope to find a small ship in a storm when that ship's very purpose was to remain hidden? She was an absolute fool, and she knew it. For the hundredth time she cursed Kane Mercedes and his name. And she cursed her heart.

Moving through the yards and between narrow lanes lined with taverns was no easy task, but thanks to the rain Jolie was quickly beyond the wharves and docks. Once again she followed an open stretch of beach to the south.

Now and again she stopped. Thunder stood silently as she strained to see through the rain to the fogbank a mile or more offshore.

Turn back, she thought again and again. This is hopeless. Impossible. I'll never see him again.

Yet she went on. The rain soaked through to her clothes, then to her skin. Ahead, breakers crashed high and white against an arm of rocks reaching from the bluff to the sea. She could ride no farther.

Dismounting, Jolie knew she *must* turn back now. Aside from the wind's howl and the ocean's fury, the only sound was her chattering teeth and...Did she hear a bell? A shout? Was that faint yellow glow just beyond the rocks lantern light?

Twice she gashed her shins as she scrambled over the rocks. On the other side she saw an old man limping toward a smoky fire built under the protective overhang of the bluff. He set down his lantern and was about to douse his campfire when he heard Jolie's groan.

"What brings you out in this storm, lassie? Are you daft?"

Jolie paused, holding fast to her throbbing shin. "I'm looking for the *Petit Noir.* I have a message for her captain, Kane Mercedes."

Jolie explained who she was and how she came to know Kane was following the safest and most secret way south to find her brother.

"She just passed by, my girl. I'm taking a message to your father and Kane's ma that he got this far."

Jolie hobbled to the waves and squinted into the gray rain. She was sure she could still hear the rush of the waves against the *Noir's* hull. The creak of ropes and timbers was ever so faint in the wind, but it was there!

Then she saw the battered skiff tied among the rocks. "Row me out! Please! I'll pay when we get back. He might miss Clay unless he knows Clay went to the plantation! Please!"

The old man chuckled. Then, shaking his head, he pulled his hat low over his bushy brows.

"I'll row myself then!"

"Now, now, lassie. I'll take you. These old arms will try, anyway. Hop in, and mind you, lay low. I don't want you falling out."

The old man put his back to his work. Quickly they dipped and leaped over the waves like flotsam. "She's moving fast now," the old man shouted over the wind, pointing at the lumbering shadow of the *Noir* ahead of them.

"Hello!" Jolie screamed. "Can they see us?"

"Not likely."

"Hello!" she called again. The gap between them and the *Noir* narrowed. "Keep going! I see someone at the rail!"

The old man paused for breath. The oars seemed to come alive in his hands and fight him. Finally he sagged over them, gasping. "Give me a moment, lassie. I'm older than I thought."

The wind came up sharply, whipping the sea to a froth that stung Jolie's eyes and burned her lips. They were so close! So close. She threw off her heavy cloak.

"Sit down! You'll land us both in the sea. Give it up, lassie. He's a good smart lad. He'll find Clay."

The *Noir* seemed to turn away then, an indifferent black mass hidden in the rain and wind. "Wait!" Jolie called, feeling her tears mix with the salt spray. Then without thinking, she arced into the water. She sank beneath the surging waves stunned by the cold. As she went under she heard a shout.

Surfacing to get her bearings, she ducked under again and drove herself toward the *Noir* several hundred yards away. She swam for the full length of her breath, her skirts feeling like cold hands holding her back. If she was naked she could swim rings around the *Noir!*

When she surfaced again, the *Noir* looked miles away. She drew in all the air her lungs would hold and swam for another full breath until her lungs threatened to burst. Her arms ached. Her temples throbbed. When she surfaced again she was only a little closer.

Several men were at the rail now. They called to her and threw a rope ladder over the side. Behind her the old man rowed frantically. He thought she was floundering.

Abruptly, Jolie sank, the pull of the seawater on her skirts dragging her deep. She struggled against the cold, wet darkness. Her arms moved as stubbornly as the old man's oars.

With one quick jerk, she released her skirt ties. The linen fell away, and she fought for the surface and air. The calls were louder now, sharp with alarm. With one last breath she dove deep, the water like cold silk against her arms and legs, and swam with all her strength. She kept one thought before her—Kane. She would reach him. She would never let him escape.

Her hand touched the slippery barnacled hull of the *Noir!*

Hand over hand, she found her way to the crashing, dashing surface. Those watching over the rail looked beyond to where she'd last disappeared under the waves. She twisted her trembling arms through the rope rungs and hung gasping, almost laughing. Above, Kane tore off his shirt. He climbed to the rail.

"Here!" Her voice was swallowed by the howl of the storm. "Here I am!"

The deckhands looked straight down. She could see their shadowy faces, hear their grunts of surprise. And she laughed.

In seconds they hauled her up and over the rail. They steadied her and then backed away ogling her clinging bodice and pantalettes.

Kane's eyes were almost black in the darkness. His teeth were clenched white and fierce like a shark's. He yanked her to his bare chest and held her. "Get her a blanket. Heat coffee. You damn fool!" he shouted, holding her at arm's length. His fingers bruised her arms as he shook her. "You damned crazy fool!"

For a moment all Jolie knew was that she had survived the sea. She took Kane's bewhiskered face in her numbed hands and kissed him. His warmth flowed into her body like radiant fire, melting her fears, igniting her desire. She wanted nothing more than to be surrounded by his arms for the rest of her days.

"What are you doing here?" he shouted more furiously than before.

Jolie began to hear the chuckling and sniggers around them. Cold reason washed over her. She had come because of Clay. Only Clay!

"Clay was at the plantation," she panted pulling free. "Look there first."

"Captain, Irish turned back," one of the deckhands said. "I don't know if he'll make it."

Someone slipped a blanket around Jolie's shoulders. They stood watching as the gray speck of the skiff inched back toward the rocks and was thrown to the safety of the beach.

Kane ran his hand over his dripping face then. "I can't turn back, Jolie. What am I to do with you?"

Jolie folded her arms against her violent shivers and looked around with delight. "I'm going with you!"

# Thirty-Seven

"Drink this!"

"I don't want any more of your poison brew!" Jolie came awake grumbling. She'd been sleeping peacefully for the first time in it seemed like years.

"You'll drink it and be glad for it. You'd be dead otherwise."

Jolie dashed away the broad hand hovering over her face. The hot liquid spilled across her cheek.

"You must be better," Kane said straightening with a scowl. "You've been far more trouble than you're worth."

"You should have thrown me overboard then. It would've been a kinder death. Let me sleep."

Kane seated himself at the desk bolted to the floor across the cabin. Now and again he looked up at Jolie lying in his bunk. His beard had grown ragged, but his eyes were still sky bright.

Jolie tried getting up. Finally she fell back trembling. "How long have I been sick?"

"Too long. Are you hungry?" He closed the log and corked his ink bottle.

"I suppose. Where are we?"

"Some fifty miles from the coast. We spotted a Yankee gunboat a few hours ago. I don't know how long it'll take to get by her. I'll rouse Cookie, and you can…tidy up. The chamberpot's over there in the cupboard."

He stooped and disappeared out the hatchway, closing Jolie in with her own sour smells. She rose and washed. She was wearing only a loose boatman's shirt and felt scrawny and light as thistledown. When she emptied the chamberpot out the porthole moments later she paused to wonder and then her cheeks burned with embarrassment.

She found a mirror hanging near a row of pegs. She looked older, thin and sallow, and her hair was matted into a dull gold mass. She was trying to brush it out when Kane returned with a bowl and mug.

340

His face brightened.

She wrinkled her nose at the fish broth. "Somewhere in my grandmama's diary is an account of her voyage north," Jolie said. "I don't recall her saying she ate during that time." Jolie's stomach rolled. "Have you cared for me all along?"

"Um-m, when I had the time. We've only been out a week. It's slow going, and the weather's been bad."

Jolie couldn't imagine that bearded man spoon-feeding her or...
"My poor mother," she said struggling with the massive knots in her hair. "She'll think I'm dead."

"Irish would have told her you boarded the *Noir*. She'll know you're safe." Kane put the bowl and mug down.

"Will she?"

"If you're with this Mercedes, you're safe." He went to a small chest. "I have only these to offer you. You came aboard half..." He turned and looked long at her.

"We've been sighted, Captain! The gunboat's headed this way!" came a cry from the hatchway.

Leaving Jolie holding a pair of trousers, Kane dashed out.

She gulped a few swallows of bitter thick coffee and then pulled the rough linen over her legs. Through the port she could see a man-of-war approaching. Old Glory flying from the main mast snapped in the breeze. She felt very weak suddenly and wanted to hide. Would they put her in prison, too?

The ship's log lay on the desk, the ragged quill across it. Shamelessly, Jolie opened at random and read the entries—details of wind, current and headings; Kane's thoughts of his mother's failing health; the Roeblings' trust in him; ideas on how to find Clay. She found brief sentences like, "She's worse this morning. Fever. Chills. Crying in her sleep. God help her."

Blinking back tears, Jolie closed the log and sighed. The gunboat was close in now. Sailors rowed across in a dingy. Taking Kane's ragged blue jacket from the peg, she went topside. In the blinding sunlight her eyes ached.

Kane was explaining his presence in captured Confederate waters. Shielding her eyes, Jolie looked at the Union sailors clambering up the side.

"And who's...what's this?" the naval lieutenant said lifting his cap when Jolie's hair fanned out in the breeze.

"I'm Jolie Roebling, sir. Excuse my appearance. Captain Mercedes rescued me from the sea and I've been very ill."

"My apologies, Ma'am." The lieutenant's gray eyes flashed suspiciously. "Roebling, you say? Captain Roebling spoke of no wife."

"Is Garner near here? I'm his sister! Please, let me speak to him!"

"Sister? Why do so many well-born captains have so many sisters? I think we'll just take you to the island and see whose sister you really are. It's a day's sail from here."

"We need fresh water," Kane said looking none too pleased. "And you need a doctor."

Jolie nodded, her head whirling. Kane looked eager to be rid of her. "But I'm going on with you then," she said as the lieutenant assigned men to remain aboard the *Noir*. Together they watched him go back to the man-of-war.

Scowling, Kane ordered sails to be hoisted. Over the next several hours the *Noir* followed the man-of-war to a small island recently captured by the Union navy.

Jolie rested and then washed her hair bracing herself to face Garner. When the time came she'd scold the socks off him for enlisting the way he had!

"Are you sure you must go on with him to New Orleans?" Garner said three days later as Kane's dingy approached from the *Noir* anchored offshore.

"Stop worrying!" Jolie laughed. She felt a good deal better wearing a yellow calico dress Garner had commissioned from the village his men occupied. "Just get word to Mama for me. Tell her we're still looking for Clay."

Garner squinted into the sun, his dark eyes alive and bright. Jolie had never seen him look so well. His uniform made him seem even taller than Papa. His face was tanned now, and his lovingly cultivated mustache made him appear older. He carried his authority with pride, smiling every time Jolie's eyes went over him. They had had a happy, if somewhat stormy, reunion.

"You've found your place, haven't you, Captain Roebling?" she said kissing him goodbye. "I hope I find mine soon."

"Take care," he said. "The weather won't get any better. And the runners and gunboats are everywhere. You're damn lucky *I* was here to receive you, or you'd be in irons right now. Or worse. You realize, of course, after this voyage your reputation won't be worth a Rebel dollar."

"What was it worth before?" she snapped. Then she laughed a little. Garner hadn't changed that much and neither had she. Her heart ached for those lost days of their childhood.

She stepped into the dingy and waved. As one of Kane's men rowed her back to the *Noir* she watched Garner shrink to nothing. Like a vision, the island shimmered in the early December sun. The voyage, her illness, now the garrison on the island were all like jumbled parts of a dream.

In a few hours the *Noir* was under sail, slipping through the water around the Florida peninsula toward the Gulf. Jolie took her evening meal alone while Kane told his men of their new secret mission, one conceived by Captain Garner Roebling. They were to find the weak points in New Orleans' defenses. Soon the blockade would squeeze the life from the South. With New Orleans and the Mississippi in Federal hands, the South would be cut in two. The war could end in a matter of months!

After Jolie went to bed, the sea grew rough. She lay listening to the ship's timbers creaking. Cargo shifted heavily in the holds. Her stomach threatened to erupt and finally she put on a thin cape Garner had given her and went topside.

The ship seemed eerie in the darkness, like a great spirit adrift, massive white wings spread to tame the wind.

Jolie clutched the rail, her nerves steadying. At the sight of the waves slipping by she forgot her stomach. She sucked in the moist sea air and lifted her face to the salt spray. Heavy weather huddled like sea monsters on the horizon in every direction.

At the sound of voices, she turned to see Kane talking to the man at the helm. He came toward her then. Whether waking or in her dreams she always saw him in shadow. Would she never see him in the light, as he really was?

"Are you all right?" he asked in that deep, rich voice.

"I don't fare so well in your cabin, Captain Mercedes. I needed some air."

"We're running at full sail tonight. I don't like the looks of those thunderheads. If we run into foul weather you'd best stay below."

"You learned a lot since sailing on the *Lady Loraine*," she said not bothering to mask the suspicious harshness in her voice.

"My men still have to help me sometimes, and I did read before I met Clay and your father."

"Did you always want to sail?"

"What boy raised in Union Harbor doesn't?"

"For that matter, what girl?"

"You've always known what you want, haven't you?" Kane said, his own feelings betrayed in his tone.

"No, I never thought about it."

"No goals? No dreams? That doesn't sound like a Roebling."

"What do *you* know of Roeblings?" Jolie asked turning from the boiling black fury on the horizon.

Kane didn't answer. He turned up his collar and hunched his shoulders. "Clay and I…" He shook his head and laughed a little. "We're too much alike."

"Money," Jolie said thinking Kane was finally going to make excuses for losing Clay.

"I've had more time than I like to think over what happened between me and Clay in New Orleans. I told your family I'd had my fill of him, and his ease with money. But that wasn't why I really left."

"Does sailing make you so thoughtful, or darkness?"

"The Roeblings waiting back in Union Harbor make me see myself for what I really am," Kane said. His face moved into mysterious lines of sharpness and shadow. "I discovered traits in Clay I didn't like. Those traits were in me, too."

Jolie's breath came faster. "What traits?"

Kane shook his head as if it didn't matter. "Dreams, I suppose. Fancies, desires for…ships and adventure…and love." His voice grew soft. "Like my father."

"Sometimes I worry, too," Jolie said just as softly. "My grandmama was once mad, you know. My mother was dangerously impetuous."

"Together we are tied by these things we can't change," Kane said.

Jolie looked up sharply. He stared at her, his eyes hidden, his face shadowed. She couldn't judge him by what other men had done, could she? She didn't want to be condemned for her grandmother's or mother's faults. She had enough of her own. "Why did you let me come back aboard the *Noir?*"

"You were my passage on to New Orleans."

"Why didn't you just sail away?"

"Gunboats could easily catch me."

"I mean before, when Papa gave you the *Noir?*"

The wind ruffled Kane's hair. "You don't think much of me, do you?"

She wanted to tell him he had hurt her that night in the woods. He had thought little of her then, but the words stayed knotted in her throat.

After a moment she said, "Garner tells me I'll have no reputation after this voyage."

"Ah!" Kane turned away with a small smile. "I wondered why he let you come back aboard. He thought I must've already done my worst by you. At first I didn't expect any of you Roeblings to trust me. But I'd hoped…It's always been hard, all my life, seeing the look in men's eyes." He looked at her quickly. "And women's."

Jolie shivered. Every day of his life Kane defended himself against the reputation his father and grandfather had forged. Now he battled even himself. He was going back to get Clay, holding on when he could so easily let go. She must not judge him. Not yet.

In the past hours she'd felt safe aboard his ship. The weeks ahead, alone with him, hadn't worried her. Her hate for his name and suspicion of his motives had held her heart in check.

Now she saw a *man* before her, a warm and human man struggling to be more than he'd been born to. That very struggle might prove he wanted the wrong things. Or it might prove…

Jolie shook her head to clear it. Her own fight had just begun. Would *she* go mad or make foolish mistakes? This man was the madness and disaster she feared most. Yet if he could face his legacy, could she do any less?

"Sometimes when you look at me like that, Jolie," Kane said, his voice growing husky, "I forget everything I know. I think you bewitch me."

She tried to laugh. Some evil alchemy lived between the Mercedes men and the women of the Gautier Line. Who bewitched whom? Where did the hate end and the love begin?

Her laugh came from her throat more like a cry. She walked away, befuddled and trembling. She had no escape from the enchantment here. On the sea she couldn't battle Kane's magic, and win.

Surrender filled her heart. And if she surrendered, what did that mean for her future? What *was* her future? What *were* her dreams and goals?

Grandmama had hoped only for escape. Her escape had been her prison sentence. Mama had longed to escape, too, and though she eventually found freedom, she paid with many, many tears.

Jolie couldn't dream of running away. She must face her life, her heritage, her destiny and shape it with all her might.

Kane's hands closed over her shoulders. He turned her to face him. She knew what she felt yet dared not trust it. When he drew her close, she let herself curve against him, soft and pulsing like the life force of the sea. His lips moved over hers filling her with fire. The bewitchment was complete. They had been born to it.

Kane swept her into his arms and carried her to the hatchway, pushing it open with his boot. Jolie didn't say anything. It was no use. If she had cared to look she was sure the helmsman's eyes would be on them, laughing, knowing what lay ahead. The crew was no barrier. On the sea Kane and Jolie were free. She could follow her heart this one time and take up the fight again later.

Setting her on her feet in the dark cabin, Kane loomed over her all heavy breathing, warmth and need. He pulled her close again. His body arched against hers, urgent and warm, powerful and demanding.

He had quickened her soul. Now he expected her womanhood to flower at his touch. She wanted to fall open and willing to his kisses, melt in the heat of his embrace, but somewhere in her mind, in her heart, was a small voice crying, Grandmama! Mama!

Dreams melted as quickly as reason. Lifetimes were altered by kisses. She was afraid, afraid to make a mistake! Her life and her future trembled, not in Kane's open palms searching out the warmth of her upturned breasts and her quivering aching loins. The future was hers to shape.

The heat of her response jelled in her heart like unshed tears. Kane lifted his face and opened his eyes. He didn't look angry or even disappointed. He understood.

They couldn't be together until the fear had been conquered, and for a Mercedes and a Roebling, the fear lived virulent between them, and within them.

Jolie had come this far. She must go on, not just in search of Clay, but in search of herself.

Kane turned away, his cheeks flushed, his eyes tight at the corners. He went to the adjoining cabin where a narrow bunk meant for a small cabin boy welcomed him. Jolie crawled into Kane's bunk and listened to him try to settle himself in the cramped space.

Fog settled over the *Petit Noir* like a velvet cape. The sea rose. All night long, and for those many to follow, Jolie and Kane slept apart, one ear cocked for the other's call, muscles twisted into aching denial.

Circumstance had defeated Grandmama Gautier and John Roebling. Pride had nearly destroyed Jolie's mother and father. For Jolie, the strongest barrier of all lay ahead. Herself.

# Thirty-Eight

Like in a dream, the shore of Louisiana greeted Jolie with the languid moist hand of a mild winter. The dawn came sleepily to the moss-laden oaks and poured a wet yellow light across the grasses.

This wasn't the land described in Grandmama's diary. The only evil lingering here was the threat of war. And for Jolie safely relegated to the captain's cabin of the *Petit Noir* it seemed as remote as her brother Garner hunched over his charts in that island village a thousand miles away.

For several nights Jolie had watched Kane slip away in the dingy to the shore. He searched for information, and each time he returned he was more surly. The spark in his eyes grew dull, the tension between them unbearable. Jolie was ready to swim ashore and take her chances finding Clay alone.

The first night Kane didn't return from his skulking about in the city's underworld, Jolie couldn't sleep.

"We'll wait him out," his first mate said when she insisted she be rowed ashore. The crew was anxious, too, for they often had to weigh anchor and slip out of sight when a warship appeared on the horizon.

The second night Jolie stood at the rail with Kane's men, straining to see the dingy appear from the fog.

"He's been captured," she said for the dozenth time, always meeting with stony Yankee silence.

When she was about to jump overboard, they saw Kane approaching. Jolie was alarmed at how glad she was to see he was safe. He climbed up the side, mud caked in his hair, his clothes unrecognizable. Without a word he went to the cabin and stripped off his shirt. Relieved to have him back, his men set sail for a point farther west to await the dawn.

"Are you going to tell me where you've been?" Jolie demanded, following him to the cabin and watching him wash.

"Hiding in mud up to my ears," he said, his voice hoarse. "There's been fighting upriver. I nearly didn't get back." Beneath the dirt, his chest muscles swelled. His arms were like yardarms, thick and powerful.

"When are we going into New Orleans to see that Raymond Brown? When are we going to the plantation? I'll be old and gray if I wait for you!"

Wearily Kane looked at her and then turned to the task of lathering his scraggly beard. "I wondered if you'd still be here when I got back."

"Your men did a fine job of warning me of sucking mud and snarling alligators. Will you *please* tell me if you learned anything?"

Kane stropped his razor and began exposing careful strokes of his bare cheeks and throat. Jolie had forgotten the special curve of his full jaw, that stubborn lump of a chin. A certain hardness had replaced some of the boyish quality of his face. Like that first time, Jolie's heart stopped at the sight of him. And it ached in a new and lonely way.

Kane met her eyes in the mirror. A flattering flush reddened his skin. Then he lathered again. The razor flashed away the leftover stubble. Compared to his forehead and nose his cheeks were baby pink. Finally all that remained was a full mustache which he spent several minutes clipping into a good Rebel droop.

"Before you tell me I should've left the beard," he said rubbing the raw skin the sun hadn't touched in months, "I'll tell you it was either that or be hanged. They know me by that beard now. If we find Clay it'll be one kind of miracle. If we all get away alive, it'll be another still."

"What *happened?*"

"The details aren't important. What is, is: I found Brown, and he knows nothing of Clay. But he did say he would take us to the plantation. That was two days ago. He also has a brother upriver who might be able to tell us something. In between time I met with a band of renegades fighting their own war. Deserters mostly. I don't want to take you ashore, Jolie, but...Wait, and let me finish! Knowing you, I'll *have* to take you just to keep you in line."

He turned from the mirror and grinned. "Be a good girl and have Cookie bring me some chowder. I haven't eaten in days."

Not knowing whether she should be angry or not, Jolie went out. The men were opening a satchel they'd hauled up from the dingy. One was laughing as he lifted up a petticoat and lacy drawers from it—mud-stained and still dripping.

"These must be for you, Ma'am!"

"The captain's hungry," she said snatching away the satchel.

She stormed back to the cabin just in time to see Kane pulling on a clean pair of trousers. He turned and grinned as she kicked the hatchway shut, her cheeks crimson. "What's *this* for?"

"How far do you think you'd get dressed in a slave's housedress?"

Jolie plucked at her yellow calico skirts. "This dress is the most comfortable I've ever worn."

"And the most flattering." He eyed the uncorseted softness beneath her bodice. "I understand your aunt's an odd old lady. She might turn you away if you look too much like white trash."

"Trash!" Jolie gasped advancing on Kane.

"Spare me your temper, Miss Roebling. To me you look like quality, with or without your calico, but we'll soon be in enemy territory. You'd best hold your Yankee tongue. You could get us both killed."

Jolie sat on the bunk and huffed. "Where did you get these things?"

"You'd rather not know. Sorry I got everything wet. Can you wash out the mud?"

Jolie fingered the drawers. "I'll try. What did you think of Raymond Brown? Mama told me his father managed the plantation for years. How can he think *he* has a right to inherit?"

"Because Raymond Brown's father was Pierre Gautier's son."

"Grandmama had a brother?"

"An unrecognized one, by a mistress who lived in New Orleans. Odessa Brown was what is known hereabouts as a 'quadroon.'"

Above the line of oaks the morning sun sent a feeble wash of light. For a moment the riverbank lit with gold. Then the clouds closed in, and a chilly breeze rippled the muddy river.

"It stands just beyond a curve to the west," Raymond Brown said pointing the way upriver. "On the right. You can't miss the red brick house."

Raymond Brown was a compact man who looked dignified in a full-skirted frockcoat and trousers tucked in glossy black boots. His coffee-colored skin glowed when he smiled, as he had from the moment he shook hands with Jolie the night before. She and Kane had arrived at the Browns' townhouse muddy and cold from their miserable trek upriver from the sea.

Raymond came back to Jolie then and helped her aboard the pole barge he'd hired. "Remember now. Don't tell your grandaunt you saw me, or she'll use her papa's pistol on you. I'd take you up myself, but I'd best not just now." He nodded toward his pregnant wife and two saucer-eyed daughters clinging to her cotton skirts. "This town's no place for a lady in her condition. I'd take her someplace safe, if I knew of one. My people and hers are scattered as far as Georgia."

"Have your girls ever seen Gautier Plantation?" Jolie asked huddling in a shawl Mrs. Brown had lent her. She liked Raymond and admired her cousin's intelligent butternut brown eyes.

"No use getting their hopes up," he said. "It means a lot to us though that you'd come to us for help."

"Thank you so much, Raymond," Jolie said shaking his hand.

"No trouble. You both take care now. That river's crawling with riffraff."

"We should be back in a few days," Kane said taking the pole and stepping aboard.

In moments they were moving upriver. Raymond and his family turned back down the river road toward the city.

"He took a chance helping us, didn't he?" Jolie whispered, watching the marshy banks slip by. They were already advancing on the charred ruins of a stately old house standing back from the river among blackened willows.

"I think he's got a fair claim to your great-grandfather's land."

"Mama will think so, too."

Kane waved her quiet suddenly and poled them to the safety of a bank of tall rushes. Moments later a small paddlewheeler running over with soldiers and wounded splashed by. They crouched among the rushes until it was passed.

They fell silent as Kane concentrated on moving upriver again. A few hours later Jolie was nodding, lulled by the rhythm of Kane's lift and push. A cool drizzle was soaking through her bonnet.

Jolie came awake with a start. The sound of the push-pole reminded her of the dream she'd had just before leaving Union Harbor. The hair under her bonnet prickled.

Kane eased them to a stop along a denuded bank. Some pilings that had once supported a dock now torn away and long since burned in Confederate campfires poked up from the slow-moving water.

He scrambled up the muddy bank and stood looking around. He was dressed once again in his "gentleman's" clothes, gray frockcoat, ruffle-breasted shirt with lacy cuffs. Even in that gloomy light his blue eyes still burned. Jolie looked away.

"This is the place," Kane said, his voice hushed. He helped Jolie climb ashore.

This was the river curve Grandmama had written of, the broad sweep of brown water cutting through the dense green world. There were the oaks, the cane fields. The house was faded now to a dusky rose. The vast roof sagged worse than a sway-backed mule.

"It must have been so beautiful once," Jolie said sighing. The lawns had been recently cut into twin tracks of upturned mud where horses, men and artillery had crossed. Not a fence post or outbuilding remained, just the house, a sore reminder of a time long past. This was where her grandmama had been born.

Kane tied the pole barge to a stump and helped Jolie pick her way across the ravaged lawns toward the house.

"Do you suppose she's still here? The place looks deserted."

"Brown said she was."

A massive oak in the front yard had been charred to a stump. The magnolias across the veranda had been trampled. Jolie tried to imagine her grandmama playing there as a child, her sisters living out their lives on the other side of those cracked and filmy windows. The house looked dead, and Jolie wondered if it had ever been a place of life.

The scarred front door opened a few inches. The long silver muzzle of a French flintlock duelling pistol greeted them. "There's nothing for you here," came a high feeble voice, thick and slow. "Get off my land, you damnable jayhawkers."

"Grandaunt Fabrienne, I'm Jolie Roebling, your sister Florie's granddaughter. I've come to help you. This is…my…escort, Kane Mercedes. He's a sea captain."

"Sea captain, are you?" A white hand appeared and cocked the pistol.

"It's all right," Kane whispered as Jolie jerked back. "She's forgotten the charge. Ask her about Clay. Offer her money."

Jolie shook off Kane's hand. "You wrote to my mother and asked for help. Remember? I've come all this way to help you. May we come in?"

"Who'd you say you were?" The door opened a little wider. A disembodied white face emerged from the darkness. Now a slight figure appeared, one shoulder dragged down by the weight of the pistol. Her grandaunt's face was bloodless, the skin like paperbark birch, and without a wrinkle. Two eyes the exact color and size of a snake's stared at them.

"She looks dead," Kane muttered under his breath.

"How do you do, Grandaunt Fabrienne," Jolie said extending her hand and smiling though her face twitched with terror.

How old was this apparition? She had been ancient when her mother visited more than twenty years before!

Fabrienne was like the house and land, existing from a bygone age. Her black morning gown was a good forty years out of date. The empire line covered with a fine spider-net was worn to nothing in places so that the dull dark silk showed beneath.

"Away with you," Fabrienne said wagging the long muzzle at Kane. "I don't allow men on my land. Drove off my own overseer the thieving snake. Away with you, I say!"

"We'd better go," Kane said. "She won't remember…"

"Did a man come here last spring, a man with yellow hair? He was my brother. We're looking for him."

"No men come here! You come inside out of the sun, young lady. Turn your eyes from that rake. Off my land, you Yankee beggar!" Fabrienne shouted.

Jolie went to her grandaunt and turned the pistol away. "Look! She means no harm," she said back to Kane. "May I stay the afternoon, Grandaunt? What about this fuss over the inheritance?"

"The very idea!" Fabrienne declared, showing Jolie into the dark entrance hall. "A man of color claiming to be my brother! My father was an upstanding man, an aristocrat from Paris. He would never have had relations with a…with a…" Fabrienne toddled out of sight, talking in a high singsong of the proud Gautier line which could be traced, if one had the intelligence, all the way back to the Venetian royal court.

"I could go on ahead and look up Raymond's brother," Kane said looking uneasily at the doorway. "If Clay is still around here, he'll know." He ran his hand over his shaven cheeks. "I don't like leaving you though."

"She's a tottering old baby," Jolie said, though as she spoke she remembered how desperately her grandmama had wanted to escape this place.

Fabrienne had been younger then, and even if she had been as evil as Florie and Loraine had believed, she was no match now for a girl who could swim the sea in a gale!

"By tonight we'll be friends," Jolie said. "Old people have always liked me."

"I'll be back before dark then," Kane said. He took a few steps away, paused and then went on. He went all the way to the riverbank before Jolie turned and closed the door.

The house inside had been built on a cosier scale than her own back in Union Harbor. Once it had been a warm and lovely place. Jolie crept down the hall feeling a sandy grit under her shoes. She found her grandaunt waiting in a rear parlor.

"Won't you sit down?" Fabrienne said indicating a slashed silk-cushioned chair drawn up before a blackened white marble chimneypiece. No fire burned in the grate. The room was chilly and damp, and bare except for a shattered harpsichord near a huge naked window. "Forgive the state of affairs in Papa's home. Between the thieving soldiers and murdering, raping jayhawkers, I've had my hands full trying to keep a roof over my head."

"What are jayhawkers?"

"Deserters. Runaways. Criminals on the loose. Why, a white person isn't safe anymore. I never thought I'd live to see the day!"

"Did they do all this?" Jolie waved her hand about the vandalized room.

"Soldiers did this. Jayhawkers wouldn't dare set one foot in Papa's house. They know better." She revealed the duelling pistol hidden in her skirts.

A while later Fabrienne brought two delicate teacups containing warm water. "I have no more tea, my dear. Even if I had some of that so-called Confederate money, I wouldn't know where to buy provisions myself."

"You're all alone?"

"Helpless," Fabrienne said shaking her small old head. "All my life I cared for my family. I never once gave a thought to myself. When my poor mother died...I couldn't possibly think of marrying. I had to manage the house for Papa. I raised my sisters singlehandedly, but they turned out to be the most ungrateful girls. They caused me *untold* grief. Then, one by one, they deserted me. Florie was the youngest. *She* married a Yankee." Fabrienne's lip curled. "Dulcine and Lalange just grew old, and then they died." She leaned closer, her eyes like coals. "You *look* like Florie."

"I never met Grandmama. She died before I was born."

"*My* only children were my sisters. Selfish, the lot of them. You remind me of Mother too. She had that look." Fabrienne's eyes grew misty. "She was the loveliest woman on this earth."

"You must have loved her very much."

"I was born in France, you know. Mother carried me through the whole terrible long voyage across the ocean in her very own arms. And she was a frail, frail woman. Like me. I remember coming to this house when it was new. Such a house I'd never seen. So small! Our life was good, though. Papa, of course, wanted a son to carry on our proud name. The Gautier were very rich in France, until the revolution, a respected, honorable family." She spoke so slowly Jolie felt mesmerized.

"When Dulcine and Lalange were born they weren't *too* much of a disappointment to Papa. After Florie, however everything changed." Fabrienne's eyes began to snap.

Drinking the warm water made Jolie feel vaguely ill. She wished Kane would hurry. She wished she could have gone with him to find Raymond Brown's brother who lived in a settlement upriver. Her grandaunt's voice droned on and on about all the years lived in this house. Jolie could feel the weight of them pulling on her eyelids.

Jolie felt drawn into the languid life her grandmama had known here. Days on end went by with nothing to do unless someone was visiting, which for the newly settled Gautier family was seldom.

Fabrienne detailed the lives, genealogies, and gossip about each of her neighbors on adjoining plantations until Jolie ached with boredom. The hour for midday meal passed. Jolie grew faint and cranky, but still Fabrienne talked. At last her grandaunt offered a tour of the ravaged house and Jolie eagerly accepted the chance to stretch the muscles in her back.

"I always kept Papa's house in perfect order. He was a very particular man." Fabrienne led Jolie up the groaning staircase walking as slowly as she spoke. There the damage was less evident. The rain was louder drumming over their heads like impatient callers.

"When Papa was alive he never would have allowed the house to remain like this. He punished me severely for neglecting even the smallest chore."

*"How* did he punish you?"

Fabrienne opened door after door to faded mildewed bedchambers still containing much of the old furniture brought from France. "He went away. Sometimes for months. Sometimes I feared…But oh, Papa was the most wonderful man. So elegant. He could speak French and English perfectly. And he raised the best horses. We still had one at stud until that reprobate Mr. Pace stole him away last year. Papa's cane fields were coveted by all. I would have done anything for him. It was my privilege to care for him until he died."

"What about your sisters?"

Fabrienne reached a door and decided against opening it. "Let's find a bite of supper now. I allow myself one meal a day. It's so nice having someone to talk to. Yes, you remind me very much of Florie. What did you say your name was?"

"Jolie."

"Oh, yes. I remember that means pretty. Of course it can also be used as, 'You've gotten yourself in a pretty mess,' but I can see you're a lovely young woman. You wouldn't cause a body grief. It's good of you to come all this way to help save the plantation."

"I do want to talk to you about that. It's so big and run down. And I am looking for my brother too, you remember. Do you remember him coming here last spring? You wrote my mother and said you drove someone away because..."

"No *men* ever come here," Fabrienne said. "Not since that Yankee Florie married. She killed Mother, you know, and drove away all our beaus with her wickedness."

"I thought your mother died of a fever!"

"That is true enough, but she wouldn't have grown so weak if she hadn't tried that one last time for a son. Papa had *me*, didn't he? She wouldn't have gotten so tired and old if she'd gotten out of her bed and tended her household and the rest of her daughters. Even then I did most everything for her. When *I* tended my sisters they stopped whining. I made sure of that."

Fabrienne led Jolie down the stairs and back through a broad hall to the cookhouse. There she took an enormous pot filled with some mysterious white goo and put it atop a bank of iron cookstoves. She fed a low fire with twigs and dry grass until a flame began to heat the gruel. The kitchen was huge, lined with doors to larders and pantries, cluttered with pie tables, hutches and dough bins—all now empty.

"You cannot imagine the torment three small sisters can bring upon a person," Fabrienne went on. "Dulcine and Lalange were expert at teasing Florie into one of her rages. And always they did it just when Papa was due back from New Orleans. He wouldn't tolerate a fuss, of course. Florie would fly to him with her tales. Dulcine and Lalange would then behave like angels. *I* would be punished for the disharmony. Quickly enough I put a stop to that nonsense. I beat Dulcine and Lalange into obedience, and if Florie insisted on crying..."

"You'd lock her in a wardrobe."

"How *did* you guess? It was the one place where she'd remain quiet. That worked quite well until she was older and grew still more clever. Do you know, that girl used to run away into the swamp? Papa would get *so* upset!"

"And blame you?"

"Of course. She was my responsibility!"

"What did you do to her then?"

"It's not to be believed what that girl would do to bring down

Papa's wrath upon my head." Fabrienne spooned hot globs of mush into chipped china bowls and set one before Jolie. "It's growing dark," she whispered as if darkness was a dangerous new phenomenon.

"Kane should be coming back for me soon," Jolie said, her mind torn, and weary of being torn, between suspicion and pity. "Don't you think you should move someplace more safe? You could be killed if you stay here."

"Leave Papa's home?" Fabrienne looked incredulous. "He'd never stand for it."

Jolie was confused. Did the woman have all her wits?

"I think you'd best stay the night, Jolie. You can't possibly travel about unchaperoned. Now that you're here, I'll look after you." They finished their meal and went back upstairs.

"I appreciate your offer but…"

"You'll sleep in the guest room. I still keep up the best rooms. Soon this house will look as it once did. Papa will be so proud."

Jolie saw no candle standing about on the tables and decided she might as well rest a while. She and Kane had left the *Noir* early the night before to travel by darkness. She looked in the room Fabrienne offered and welcomed the chance to lie down.

"Sleep well. Why, it seems like only yesterday Florie spent her wedding night in this very room."

"Did you really make her wear false bosoms under her wedding gown?"

"Of course! She was marrying a Yankee, and everyone knows they're little better than animals."

"Well, I understand that was true of my grandfather," Jolie muttered. "You realize, of course, I'm a Yankee."

"Nonsense. You're a Gautier."

Shaking her head with weary amusement, Jolie closed herself in the musty bedchamber. Compared to the others, it was in better condition, but only slightly.

She made a thorough investigation of every drawer and cupboard and, finding her heart pounding in rhythm with the rain, she peeped under the tester for lurking jayhawkers before lying gingerly on the bed. Moments later she leaped off, her skin crawling and twitching. The bed was alive!

Swallowing a scream, she was halfway to the stairs when Fabrienne appeared in one of the chamber doors. She wore a white gown in tatters at the hem. "I can't allow you to wander about in the dark."

"I've decided to go on and find my brother. Kane should have been here by now."

"Who?"

"The man I arrived with. You remember. He had brown hair and blue…"

"No men come here," Fabrienne said with perfect certainty.

What was the use? Jolie went back to her room and curled into a chair to wait. She didn't think she could convince her grandaunt to leave. What would she do with her if she could? Maybe Grandmama had provoked the tortures she hinted at in her diary. Jolie couldn't decide. Fabrienne seemed sincere enough now in her efforts to raise her sisters. But Jolie, too, longed to escape the old tomb of a house.

Thinking of Kane, she drifted to sleep, starting now and again as her muscles cramped. During the night she thought she saw a ghost glide across the bedchamber.

She shut away her foolish dreams and went on listening and waiting. Toward dawn she woke sweating and aroused by a dream; undulating dark currents, white mist, whispering voices. She nearly fell backwards trying to unfold her numbed legs from the chair. Then she stood gasping and trembling, certain she had not only been watched while she slept, but touched!

# Thirty-Nine

"The rain's let up."

"Thanks for the shelter," Kane said shaking Lester Brown's hand.

"Are you sure you won't wait out the storm? By the looks of those clouds it could be a bad one."

"I've been gone too long already." Kane ducked into the gentle patter and climbed aboard his pole barge.

"Keep to the right now," the small black man said pointing into the swamp from the doorway of his cabin. "Otherwise you'll be lost for sure. I ain't certain for sure that fella I heard about is your brother."

"You've been a great help," Kane said. "I'll tell Raymond I found you safe when we get back to New Orleans."

Kane jabbed the forked pole into the soft river bottom and slipped away toward the reeds and willows forming a living labyrinth into the swamplands. Here, Raymond's brother said, lived a trapper who had taken in a sick man a few months before.

He should've gone back for Jolie first, Kane thought gliding soundlessly into the darkness. But if Clay had swamp fever like Lester said, he might now be dead. Kane didn't want to bring Jolie, if that was all that awaited her. She was safe with her grandaunt.

"Where are you going now?" Fabrienne said.

Jolie jumped and whirled. She tried to laugh away her fright. "I thought I'd look upriver to see if Kane is coming yet. He should've been back last night."

"Close that door. You're letting in all the heavy air. Do as I say, now. Just look at this floor! Papa will have my ears for this. Lula! Shareen! You lazy wenches, come do up this floor. I can't tolerate this mess. Come away from that door now!"

Fabrienne's claw-like hand closed around Jolie's arm and bit surprisingly deep as she guided Jolie back toward the stairs. "Up to your room. Don't give me that look. I know what's best for you. It's much too early to be up running about. These girls," she said to herself. "Always trying me so. I was meant for better things, you know. I was once a belle, much sought after by the gentlemen from New Orleans. But here I am doing my duty, you ungrateful child. Back to bed!"

"I can't go back in there, Grandaunt! I've got to get out of this house! Won't you come with me? Please! You're hurting me!"

Fabrienne turned her yellow eyes on Jolie, her face cut into shadowed bony hollows.

Jolie swallowed hard. "Let me go."

"Back to your room or I'll take my switch to you."

"Like you did to my grandmother? On her bare thighs? Was *that* how you made a child mind you? I should never have felt sorry for you!"

Fabrienne pushed her toward the stairs. "You'll never be too big that I can't cane the skin right off your back, just like Papa did his slaves. Only one way to make an animal mind. Get on up those stairs."

"All right, but let me go!" Jolie tore free and rubbed her bruised arm. "I'll go up, but when Kane gets here…"

"Willful child!"

Jolie raced up the stairs back to the horrible room and its penetrating chill. How was she going to get away?

She looked a long while out the tall fly-specked windows that overlooked a jungle-like garden littered in the dawn pale with broken marble benches and fountains. Beyond the blackened cane fields the river lay beneath an iridescent mist. The oaks bent to the wind as it rose anew. Heavy rain began pummeling the house.

Jolie drew her shawl tight and fought a lump of tears in the back of her throat. "Kane, where are you?" She watched the sky attempt to brighten. Then the clouds closed in dampening the day to a gray gloom.

The hair on the back of her neck suddenly arose. She turned, looking about automatically for a weapon. Then her heart squeezed to a stop. She watched her grandaunt enter the bedchamber. In her hand was a riding crop.

"By God, it *is* you!" Clay said opening hot eyes to see Kane bending over him. His heart leaped for joy. "I figured you were dead!" Kane's hand felt so warm! Clay clasped it with all his strength.

"How long have you been here?" Kane asked. He looked about the shanty cluttered with piles of muskrat pelts and wiped his mouth.

"Don't know. God, I'm glad to see you! Sit down and have some of Raoul's gumbo. It's the best I ever tasted. Damn near saved my life. Just don't ask what he puts in it. Raoul, this is my brother Kane."

"Another Yankee," a middle-aged Cajun with a wry black-toothed grin muttered. "When he have zee fever, this boy talk of nothing but his brother. Always his brother and this home far away. This bayou zee best home *I* know."

Clay laughed with the old man. Clay didn't know what would have become of him if Raoul hadn't found him in the mud and cared for him like a son all those weeks.

"How did you find me?" Clay asked turning back to Kane. "Damn, but you look good. I like the mustache. Makes you look like a good ol' southern boy. And the coat! Come on. Tell me where you've been!"

"Home," Kane said grinning.

Clay's jaw dropped. "But how?"

Pulling up a stool, Kane plunged into his story, recounting his escape back to Union waters, his visit at the estate and then Jolie's mad swim for the *Petit Noir.*

"*Jolie's* with you?" Clay pushed back his hair wondering if his appearance would shock her.

"She's back at her aunt's plantation. The weather looked bad, and the old lady didn't think so much of my looks. I guess there's some question of who has the right to inherit. Jolie's trying to clear that up. The place doesn't look like much to me."

"That old woman nearly took my head off!" Clay said. "It took me a week to get upriver and find that place. Asking people, hiding in barns, dodging rebels. Then she pulls out this old flintlock pistol and waves it in my face! Is Jolie safe there?"

"She's safe anywhere," Kane grinned.

"What old woman you talking about?" Raoul asked. "Not that witch what canes her slaves. She's no better than her papa." He shoved a steaming bowl into Kane's hands. "As cold as the devil's own heart."

With one eye on the window, Kane began to eat. Though it was dawn, the sky scarcely lightened. "I'll go get her now," he said. "Then we'll come back for you. I can't leave the *Noir* too much longer either. If I lost that ship…" He shook his head as he rose and brushed at his wet shoulders. "I'm already indebted to your father more than I like."

"I doubt he considers it a debt. If he gave you a ship it meant only one thing." Clay watched his brother's face darken. "It means he trusts you, you damn fool! You remember how he used to feel about *me* sailing."

Kane sighed. "We can talk when I get back with Jolie."

"Do I detect a note of softness in your voice when you say that name?" Clay grinned at Kane's discomfort. "She's a wonderful girl."

"Damned headstrong one."

"Zee best women are zee ones with heart!" Raoul said striking his chest with his fist. He chuckled as he spooned another mouthful of the gumbo behind his teeth.

Clay laughed. He eased up on his elbow. Strength was flowing back into his arms. All the weeks of worry and brooding were over now. He'd soon be home again! He had so much to tell everyone, so much to make up for. "Get my boots, Raoul. I want to be ready when Kane and Jolie get back. Help me up, Brother. Remember what an ass I was at the hotel?"

"About that..." Kane began.

"You were right, though. I didn't have to spend all my money to prove I was a man."

"And I didn't have to starve to do it either."

"Looks like we both have come to understandings with ourselves," Clay said, resting on the edge of his cot, his heart pounding with the exertion. The shanty was a dismal place, but warm, and Raoul, for all his foul odors, had been a good friend. Now though, Clay was ready to take up his life again. He wished he could leave with Kane right then. He knew just what he was going to do when he got home—work side by side with Hope. The Roebling Line would belong to them both!

Kane looked impatiently out the window again. The wind had grown fierce.

"Go on!" Clay said pushing himself to his feet even though he felt a bout of tremors coming on again. Damn the malaria! He saw Kane to the door. "I can wait a few more hours. Can you give the old man some money? He saved my life."

Kane removed a packet from inside his shirt. "I guess they did trust me. I wish Jolie did."

Clay held him back a moment more. "When you were back, did you see Hope? I've been worried about her."

"She looked fine. She's all but taken over the yards. I think she was worried about you, too. If you want to hear softness in someone's voice, you should hear her say *your* name."

"Hurry back!" Clay said then fairly pushing Kane out into the rain. "Union Harbor's going to keel over when you and I get back. The Mercedes men and the Roebling women!"

Kane turned with a look of surprise that fell softly as the rain washed down his cheeks. "Maybe it'll work for you. I don't know about me."

Kane dashed for the barge and pushed off once again. *Did* he understand himself now? Did he dare hope…He had dreamed all his life of sailing without ever believing he would do it. He had dreamed of a great love, too, and always held himself back.

Now he had a ship! He could have Jolie, too, if he really wanted her. He was afraid he did. Yet he could be—he might already be *all* his father had been.

He pushed on through the water fighting the wind and current, blinded by the rain. The wind whistled through the trees setting his nerves on edge, filling him with impatience. He shouldn't have left her alone with that old woman. Had he really been running from Jolie?

He pushed the pole so deep he nearly threw himself into the swirling water.

She had wanted him, there on board the *Noir*. He knew that. She had tried to overcome her fear and hate for his name. If he had been any other kind of man he would have…

Kane let the barge drift into the wide flow of the dark Mississippi. There the wind was so strong he had to crouch to avoid being blown overboard. The current caught the barge and dragged it southward. Could he reach the plantation or would he be dragged past?

Jolie was so very lovely, so strong and sure of herself, except when she looked up at him with those soft, full eyes. He filled with longing at the thought of her. The ache was sweet and pure, and felt so good and hurt so cleanly all at the same time, it was like the thrust of a perfectly formed blade.

What could he hope to offer a girl like Jolie? Until she fastened those warm brown eyes on him and pulled his heart out by the root with her kiss, he had been perfectly content. He had been a bastard, a plain and simple man with plain and simple plans.

Now the contentment was gone. In its place was a dream, a dream of salt wind in his face, the well-worn helm of his own ship in his sure hand.

Jolie was in his dream, too, in his arms, her breath quick on his lips. If he had been any other kind of man he would have ignored her fears and taken her.

But he was not.

He was Kane Mercedes and in spite of thirty years of hard-fought wisdom, he loved Jolie Roebling.

Fabrienne could move with frightening speed.

She was halfway across the bedchamber before Jolie darted from the window for the door. Jolie took two running steps across a small carpet and was flying headlong into a table before she even realized she had slipped.

Double images of Fabrienne's unwrinkled white face appeared above her as she tried to rise from the floor.

"Get up," Fabrienne hissed. "Someone's coming. You must hide. Think what they would do to a pretty young girl like you."

"I'll fight…" Jolie said sitting up and feeling the welt growing on her forehead. She felt sick and dizzy. Was Fabrienne chasing her or helping her? Couldn't the old woman just leave her alone?

Fabrienne lifted her and guided her down the hall with the tip of the crop. At the door she hadn't opened before, Fabrienne stopped. "You'll be safe in here. Hurry! They're coming!"

Her grandaunt didn't look dangerous or evil. She looked small and helpless. She was so very old.

The door opened to a lovely room decorated all in white. A massive canopy bed stood between twin windows draped in white velvet. Though gray now, the carpet had once been pastels and creams, obviously all the way from Persia.

"Back here," Fabrienne said urging Jolie toward a corner beside a wardrobe that reached to the ceiling.

Jolie followed, listening for intruders and hearing only the fury of the storm. Then before she could struggle, Fabrienne opened the wardrobe door and pushed.

Jolie fell backwards into a dozen gowns covered with dusty paper wrappers. Her head hit the rustling softness and then the back board. Both her arms scraped against the edges of the doorway as she fought for balance.

"You can't make me stay in here!"

A flurry of pain rose from Jolie's legs. She fought the tangle of gowns until she could see Fabrienne's arm rising and falling, the riding crop hitting and hitting so that Jolie would draw her legs inside.

Jolie did just that. The door slammed. A tiny rattle told her Fabrienne had turned the latch. She was trapped!

After a moment she struggled to her feet, beating away the gowns, sneezing from the dust. She pounded the panels, unnerved by the solid feel of the old closet. Then she almost laughed. Almost.

"I told you before, get off my land!" Supporting her right arm with her left hand, Fabrienne lifted and aimed her papa's pistol. The man advancing toward her front door didn't turn away. She stepped back out of the wind and sifted the last of the powdered charge she'd saved into the pan and cocked the flintlock pistol. "Go!" she screeched.

He came right to her and turned the muzzle away! She released her hold as if the pistol handle had burned her hand.

"Don't you *dare* come into Papa's house!"

"Where's Jolie?"

He was letting the rain pour in all over the parquet floor! Papa would be so angry! Now that jayhawker was stepping inside! If anything happened...Fabrienne backed away even more. "Don't you touch me. Papa will hunt you down!"

*"Where is Jolie?"*

They never asked for her, Fabrienne thought. *She* was eldest, but they never asked for her. Always they wanted the young one with the big soft eyes, full breasts and slim strong thighs.

"Don't come any nearer! There's no one here but me. Get out. Get out!" Fabrienne crossed her arms over her chest.

Mother of God, he must not touch her or...In her mind the man in the doorway came swiftly and tore away her clothes.

"No!" she screamed at the startled face by the door. "Mama will hate me! Papa will beat me!"

"Did Jolie leave? Where did she go?"

"North!" Fabrienne said, her heart filling with rage.

She had gone north with that fat Yankee to be his wife and lie in his bed. She went to have all the things Fabrienne could never hope to have, not even by force.

"How long ago?" Kane Mercedes asked looking puzzled and hurt.

"Long ago!"

So many long, empty years with nothing, nothing! to ease the pain, the ache, the nagging wicked, wicked ache. They had all left her long ago. She had only death to look forward to and even he, in his long black robes, even *he* never came!

Kane's face twisted. "North?" He looked back into the driving rain, lifted his dripping hat and scratched his head. "I must have passed her."

He turned and went back out.

Jolie had settled herself on the cluttered floor of the wardrobe to think. It was so close within the narrow chamber, and warm, she began to doze. The sleep that had eluded her in the night came quickly now. The morning hours passed in stuffy silence. The storm rose ever louder and more violent. Jolie wandered in the mists of her dreams searching for her brother Clay. His face, however, always changed into Kane's. Kane would come to her, his warm lips quickly on hers, his hands searching out her secrets, but then she would cry and run. Yolanda would appear holding a riding crop and shrivel quickly into a witch with yellow eyes.

With a shuddering throat-tearing scream, Jolie came awake. She fought her way to her feet, shrieking as she kicked at the door. Where was she? She couldn't breathe!

The thinner center door panel splintered in the middle. Jolie tore open her arm reaching through the hole to twist the latch. The door fell open. Jolie vaulted out, catching both her shins on the high sill as she scrambled to the floor. Gasping with disgust, her skin crawling, she stood up brushing herself all over. Several spiders dropped to the floor and skittered away leaving Jolie shaking with revulsion.

What a horrid, horrid place!

She couldn't stop twitching and shook out her shirts once more to make sure all the spiders were gone. Had there been spiders in the wardrobe when her grandmama was locked in it as a child?

Her shins smarting, her forehead and crown aching, arms scraped and bleeding, Jolie opened the chamber door determined this time to escape. She came face to face with Fabrienne. They both let out a cry. Fabrienne raised her fist. Jolie threw up her arms to protect her face. "Let me out of here!"

A sudden gust of wind moaned through cracks around the windows lifting the tattered curtains and swirling dust across the floor. Jolie knocked away Fabrienne's first blow and fell back hoping to get a clear path through the door. When Fabrienne didn't move, Jolie dashed across the chamber to draw her away.

"Always they come for the young one," Fabrienne said turning toward a table. She pulled a length of cord from the drawer, uncoiled some between both hands and started forward. "I'll show you what he'll expect, Florie," she said, her eyes narrow and yellow, her white face lowered and sharp.

Rain slashed against the window cutting what little afternoon light was left to a pale shade of brownish black. Jolie forced herself not to look. She must keep her eyes on the old woman snapping the cord between her hands. On the ceiling over Fabrienne's head a great dark circle appeared. Jolie noticed several other smaller stains now. Drops gathered and oozed from the center.

"You know I'll catch you," Fabrienne said softly. "It'll be worse if you run. Wicked, willful child. You *must* be punished."

"You can't do anything to me!"

Like a hawk, swift and black, Fabrienne lunged. Jolie dove across the huge bed expecting to escape on the far side. Her weight crushed the time-brittle legs and brought the posts crashing down upon her. She rolled, coughing and screaming and flung up her arms to protect her face.

The lace canopy dropped over her like a heavy dirty web. The old woman clawed at her legs, pulling and dragging her from under the tangle. Jolie grabbed at air. Something twisted around her wrist.

"Don't!" She couldn't wiggle free. She hated to push or kick the old woman but finally she lashed out. Her foot sank into a fragile collection of flesh and bone.

Fabrienne howled. Now she was on Jolie's back, scratching, jabbing, tearing at her other arm. Jolie clutched at the coverlet and it came away in shreds. Then her arm was wrenched back. Pain twisted and flashed at her shoulder. The cord went around her wrist sharp and tight. She lay face down in the ancient bed, covered with rotting lace work and fallen bedposts, helpless.

"I'm not your sister!" Jolie shouted.

She struggled against the cords. Though a foot or more was between her wrists, she was too tangled to break free.

Fabrienne rolled her over and glared into her eyes. "You took everything from me. Now I'll take what you have." She slapped Jolie silent.

Jolie was still seeing stars when she felt her bodice tearing. Something cold and hard touched her throat, now her breasts. Fingers! Crusty old fingers!

Jolie let out a shriek and erupted with both legs flailing. She arched up and down fending off the violation. She screamed, not for herself, but for her grandmama who had had to endure this madwoman's torture. Bringing up her knee, she caught her grandaunt sharply under the chin. With a grunt, Fabrienne staggered back.

Now the ceiling was a mass of dripping circles. A terrible crash came from below. The wind howled through the house like unleashed devils. One after another, windowpanes shattered. Walls bowed. Rafters shifted. Fabrienne looked up in terror.

Her hair had come loose and fluttered about her shoulders like yellowed gray feathers. When another crash sounded below, a smaller one, as if a chair had been dashed to the floor she stumbled from the room leaving the door wide.

Jolie fell back panting and sobbing. The old witch was gone! Thank God! She slid to the floor and struggled against the cords. She rested and struggled some more. Her hands were growing numb. The cold seeped up from the floor through her shoulder blades and twisted arms like death. She could feel cold wind on her breasts.

Where was Kane?

She heard a high thin scream.

Sweating, Jolie began struggling harder. The cord seemed to be coming apart as if it, too, was old and rotten.

She heard another cry. Now another crash and some distant laughter. Renegades really were in the house now! She lay in plain view of the door. If they came upstairs...

The cries became continuous. Jolie's hair stood on end. Her stomach curled. How many were there? What were they doing to Fabrienne? Could she help her grandaunt? Did she want to?

One loop slipped over her purple fingers. She jerked and tugged. Her other hand tore free! She flung the cord away and stood. She'd *have* to help Fabrienne. She couldn't listen to her being murdered.

Heavy footsteps sounded on the staircase, now along the upper hall. Closer. Closer.

More deep laughter.

Jolie backed into a corner, cowering. Should she draw them away from the old woman?

Softer cries. Cries of pain, cries of terror. Flickering yellow light crept toward the door.

She couldn't crawl under the broken bed. She wouldn't climb back into the wardrobe! God help her!

The men laughed as they tore through each room dashing Fabrienne's last treasures. There was no time to think, no time to wonder if Kane would have her after…

Jolie backed farther into the corner. Afraid.

The wind rose even higher. The old house took its force like death blows. From somewhere in the house came a deep rumble that shook the floorboards. The voices suddenly faded, down the stairs to the outside. The screams and moans stopped.

Jolie covered her mouth to hold back a hysterical laugh. Holding her breath, she crept to the door. She saw no movement. She heard nothing but the wind tearing freely through the house.

Another rumble shook the walls. A hairline crack like lightning in the plaster raced toward the ceiling. The ceiling shifted and sagged. Another crack spread across it and suddenly it exploded. Water gushed onto the bed.

Jolie dashed down the hall as water plaster and rotted beams crashed to the chamber floor. Everywhere she ran water dripped, plaster fell. The great expanse of ceiling over the staircase and lower hall was lively with drops. The walls ran with water seeping through cracks.

The house shuddered under another savage stormy blow. Jolie flattened herself against the wall wondering if more ceiling would fall. Except for the storm, the house was silent, throbbing like something dying. One at a time she took the steps, lower and lower looking into dark corners, glancing back at the swelling ceiling.

The rain drove in through the open front door and oozed around shreds of black silk lying scattered on the floor.

The house rumbled again. New cracks appeared. A fat drop hit Jolie's cheek.

She heard a moan.

Beyond an open doorway down the hall, a bony foot was visible. Oh, no. No, no, Jolie thought creeping closer. She didn't want to look.

More sodden plaster fell just behind her. Jolie's elbow hit the doorjamb as she jerked out of the way. She couldn't look. She couldn't! "If you can get up…" she whispered, her eyes closed.

She heard no reply. She had to get out. She had to open her eyes. More plaster fell. She turned, and groaned.

Fabrienne lay on her back, her arms crossed over her shriveled breasts. The hollow of her belly looked like a bowl.

Jolie closed her eyes again. Lord have mercy. The image engraved on her eyes wouldn't go away. The white legs askew like the fallen rafters in the upstairs bedroom…would she ever forget?

The house gave another deep shudder. Fabrienne moaned again, softly. The wind broke through another window somewhere and swirled in with a high-pitched wail. Jolie heard a tortured creak as if supporting timbers were failing.

She knelt beside her grandaunt and cradled her head in her lap. The old woman felt feather-light, and cold. "You poor old thing," Jolie said bowing her head. She couldn't think of a prayer.

Fabrienne clutched her arm. "Mama?" Her voice was a raw whisper like a sick child's. "Mama?"

Jolie began to cry. She felt so helpless. She wanted to have done some good, and she could do nothing. Nothing!

"Mama?" Fabrienne whispered.

Jolie smoothed back her sparse hair. "It's all right. You're all right."

"Let me sit on the bed with you. I'll be quiet."

Jolie made soothing noises. The old woman's face softened. Her skin was remarkably unlined, as if she had never really grown old. Where had Fabrienne been while Grandmama lived her happy years with her mother, Jolie wondered. What had it been like to try pleasing a father who was always preoccupied? Or a mother who favored another? What had it been like to see Florie go away a wife and have no hope, ever, of having a man of her own? Fabrienne had been, after all, a woman.

Now, this.

Jolie stroked the old woman's cheek. Fabrienne had let her envy rule her cold, cruel life and now she was dying a cold, cruel death. If she had just once done something other than her duty...

"But you did, didn't you?" Jolie whispered more to herself than to her grandaunt. "You did take hold of your life, but you hurt when you could have helped. We all have that choice."

As Fabrienne's body grew heavy, Jolie could still hear her whispering, "Mama?" The dull amber eyes stared up at nothing now, but Fabrienne's thin lips had curved into a faint smile.

Jolie let her slip back to the floor and covered her ears to shut out the wind. She had to think! She had to take hold of her own life and...

The floor began to tremble. It didn't stop. Jolie scrambled for the front door. She dove across the veranda and fell onto her face in the mud, crawling as far away as she could. She finally rested by the charred oak stump.

The house heaved. Bit by bit, it flew apart. The roof was gone now. One side wall had collapsed, and now the other corner sank as if exhausted to the ground.

She would take hold of her life. If she had stayed home brooding over Mama's neglect and Hope's brightening future, she would have become a bitter old crone just like Fabrienne!

Jolie rose to her feet and wiped her eyes. She'd go back to New Orleans and wait for Kane there. Yes! She'd follow the river's curve south to safety.

She began running across the rutted muddy lawn toward the reeds and brush along the river's edge. She'd take hold of her life, her heart and her love and forge something strong and good. She'd never sink into madness, or be driven to foolish deceptions. She'd take what she wanted. And what she wanted was Kane!

Her feet grew light. She threaded her way through the marshy land until she reached an inlet. She was almost laughing. She wanted Kane! She loved him!

Should she swim across the inlet or follow the edge around? She didn't want to get lost. Not now.

The wind faded. The deep angry sky lifted. Jolie tested the water with her toe.

Her eyes jerked to the left.

They were huddled in three canoes just beyond the reeds—two bearded men in gray in the first canoe, a scarred blond man in his forties with a black in the second canoe, and another huge black with a young white man wearing the ugliest grin Jolie had ever seen in the third. He looked like the kind of man who could rape an old woman.

Jolie didn't scream. She twisted around to run and slipped in the soft mud. She went down and in seconds the men scrambled from the canoes.

"What a treasure!" the ugliest said as the big black lifted Jolie with one massive arm.

"Put me down!"

She beat the arm and kicked at the other.

"Put her in this one," one said easing his canoe closer. Jolie felt herself lifted and then dumped. The canoe wobbled dangerously as the big black and the man with the ugly grin climbed in with her. "This is more like it."

They pushed into the river and caught the current. Jolie lunged to the side trying to fall into the muddy water. The ugly one caught her ankles. The black laughed as she fought the vile hands moving up her thighs.

With all her strength, Jolie threw her weight to the side. With the help of the wind, the canoe tipped. The three of them plunged into the river. Under the dark water Jolie could feel hands groping at her hips.

Kicking, she swam deep and far to the limit of her breath. Her heart swelled and slowed. Her chest began to ache. She longed to breathe, but held on longer, longer longer still, until blackness filled her mind. She could stay under forever she thought. It was easy!

Then suddenly she fought for the surface. It seemed impossibly far. She broke the surface gasping and crying. The rain was coming harder. The wind whipped the river water into her face. She couldn't see the men or canoes anywhere.

Then they appeared, bearing down on her, their teeth gleaming. She dove to avoid them. Had she seen a small pole barge, too?

She let herself sink again and felt the current drag her downstream. She had reached the last of her strength. Her muscles had turned to butter. Her head throbbed. She began to flounder swallowing great horrible gulps of the gritty water. She couldn't go on. She couldn't!

But she did go on. Stroke by weary stroke Jolie fought her way to the riverbank. When her hand touched muddy grass, she held on even though it kept coming away in her hands. She hung there with the water pulling at her legs. When a hulking shape appeared over her she couldn't even cry out.

She closed her eyes and let herself slide back into the water.

A hand caught her wrist. Slivers of pain shot from her shoulder as she was pulled from the water and laid on the wet grassy bank. Tender hands rolled her over. She must be dreaming. It was too much to hope...

"I thought I'd lost you," Kane whispered, his voice thick.

Jolie opened her eyes. It was true! Kane bent over her, his dark hair dripping in his eyes, his proud handsome face framed by flying clouds streaked with weak but beautiful afternoon sun rays.

She put her arms up and moaned as he drew her to his chest. "Hold me!"

He pulled her to her feet but her knees buckled. Then he scooped her up like he had that night on the *Noir* and carried her through the marsh grass, slipping and stumbling in the mud. He carried her to a shelter of a hollow among some bedraggled willows where the rain didn't reach. The wind rushed over them and away leaving them to shiver in each other's arms.

"I found Clay," Kane whispered smoothing her hair out of her face. "He's safe. As soon as the storm lets up, we'll go back for him. Then we go home."

Home, Jolie thought curling against his chest. She wanted to think only of his warm arms across her back. How broad and solid his chest felt. She snuggled closer, curving her body against his, breast to chest, thigh to thigh, warm and solid and so alive.

The sky changed from gray to pink. From the drooping branches silver drops fell to the mud like kisses, and beyond, the river stole away softly to the sea.

Kane lifted Jolie's face and kissed her. When she looked into his eyes, full and deep, she felt peace penetrate to her soul. With that peace was heat and strength and desire.

As he pushed away the shreds of her torn muddy bodice to the tender waiting breasts beneath, Jolie gave herself up fully to the truth in her heart. Whatever the Mercedes name had stood for in the past, it was now cleansed. Whatever mistakes the Gautier, DeMarsett and Roebling women had made, they had been forgiven.

Jolie lay back in the cool soft hollow freed of all fears. She spread her hands across Kane's broad bronzed chest and then drew him to her, wanting now the full measure of his love. She was part of him, and he part of her, one breath, one life, one flame with the brilliance and reach of generations.

There in the sunlight they were together bound into one pulsing current, so strong, so pure it would forever stand, even against the winds of a hurricane sweep.

# PART THREE

# 1869

# Epilogue

*Dear Mama,*

*Kane tells me if the wind holds we'll sight the Sandwich Islands by the end of the week. Our voyage has been good this time, no fever and not many storms.*

*I have happy news! Last night I safely delivered your first granddaughter. I haven't named her yet. She is such a little mite, loud and red. I think she looks like her father. Kane was with me last night. He made a proud, if somewhat nervous, midwife.*

*I know having us sail again with me expecting worried you, but you know how I love sailing with Kane. He gave me the package you entrusted to him just before we sailed. I must admit I was surprised! I can only say, thank you, Mama, for your faith and trust! The christening gown is lovely. I'm so proud to have it. This afternoon, after my rest, I'll embroider a new name on it. I know once you could not have borne the idea of putting the name Mercedes with the rest, but because you sent it I know, at last, you accept Kane with all your heart.*

*Thank you, too, for the little wooden sailor boy. Our little sailor girl will love playing with it.*

*It'll be some time before we set sail again for Union Harbor. I trust you'll give my love to all. Kiss Papa and bid him take care of his old heart. Thank Uncle James for the text on childbirth, and bid him take care of himself, too. Most of all, give our love to Hope and Clay.*

*I share motherhood with you now, Mama, and understand more with every hour* the love and care that has come to me through the generations. My baby girl is going to be very happy for I feel love swelling in me like the tide. To see Kane's pride shining in his eyes makes me know it was worth the fight.

Until I see you then, Mama. All my love,

Jolie Mercedes

## CACTUS ROSE

In the heat of the southwest, desire is the kindling for two lost souls—and the flame of passion threatens to consume them both.

Rosie Saladay needs to get married—fast. The young widow needs help to protect her late husband's ranch, but no decent woman can live alone with a hired hand. With the wealthy Wesley Morris making a play for her land, Rosie needs a husband or she risks losing everything. So she hangs a sign at the local saloon: "Husband wanted. Apply inside. No conjugal rights."

Delmar Grant is a sucker for a damsel in distress, and even with Rosie's restrictions on "boots under her bed" stated firmly in black and white, something about the lovely widow's plea leaves him unable to turn away her proposal of marriage.

Though neither planned on falling in love, passion ignites between the unlikely couple. But their buried secrets—and enemies with both greed and a grudge—threaten to tear them apart. They'll discover this marriage of convenience may cost them more than they could have ever bargained for.

## ANGEL

When her mother dies, fourteen-year-old Angel has no one to turn to but Dalt, a gruff-spoken mountain man with an unsettling leer and a dark past. Angel follows Dalt to the boomtowns of the Colorado territory, where she is thrust into the hardscrabble world of dancehalls, mining camps, and saloons.

From gold mines to gambling palaces, *Angel* tells the story of a girl navigating her way through life, as an orphan, a pioneer, and ultimately a miner's wife and respected madam…a story bound up with the tale of the one man in all the West who dared to love her.

## AUTUMN BLAZE

Firemaker is a wild, golden-haired beauty who was taken from her home as a baby and raised by a Comanche tribe. Carter Machesney is the handsome Texas Ranger charged with finding her, and reacquainting her with the life she never really knew.

Though they speak in different tongues, the instant flare of passion between Firemaker and Carter is a language both can speak, and their love is one that bridges both worlds.

## KISS OF GOLD

From England to an isolated Colorado mining town, Daisie Browning yearns to find her lost father—the last thing she expects to find is love. Until, stranded, robbed, and beset by swindlers, she reluctantly accepts the help of the handsome and rakish Tyler Reede, all the while resisting his advances.

But soon Daisie finds herself drawn to Tyler, and she'll discover that almost everything she's been looking for can be found in his passionate embrace.

## SNOWS OF CRAGGMOOR

When Merri Glenden's aunt died, she took many deep, dark secrets to the grave. But the one thing Aunt Coral couldn't keep hidden was the existence of Merri's living relatives, including a cousin who shares Merri's name. Determined to connect with a family she never knew but has always craved, Merri travels to Colorado to seek out her kin.

Upon her arrival at the foreboding Craggmoor—the mansion built by her mining tycoon great-grandfather—Merri finds herself surrounded by antagonistic strangers rather than the welcoming relations she'd hoped for.

Soon she discovers there is no one in the old house whom she can trust...no one but the handsome Garth Favor, who vows to help her unveil her family's secrets once and for all, no matter the cost.

## SUMMERSEA

Betz Witherspoon isn't looking forward to the long, hot summer ahead. Stuck at a high-class resort with her feisty young charge, Betz only decides enduring her precocious heiress's mischief might be worth it when she meets the handsome and mysterious Adam Teague.

Stealing away to the resort's most secluded spots, the summer's heat pales against the blaze of passion between Betz and Adam. But Betz finds her scorching romance beginning to fizzle as puzzling events threaten the future of her charge. To survive the season, Betz will have to trust the enigmatic Adam…and her own heart.

## SWEET WHISPERS

Seeking a new start, Sadie Evans settles in Warren Bluffs with hopes of leaving her past behind. She finds her fresh start in the small town, in her new home and new job, but also in the safe and passionate embrace of handsome deputy sheriff, Jim Warren.

But just when it seems as if Sadie's wish for a new life has been granted, secrets she meant to keep buried forever return to haunt her. Once again, she's scorned by the very town she has come to love—so Sadie must pin her hopes on Jim Warren's heart turning out to be the only home she'll ever need.

## TIMBERHILL

When Carolyn Adams Clure returns to her family estate, Timberhill, she's there to face her nightmares, solve the mystery of her parents' dark past, and clear her father's name once and for all. Almost upon arrival, however, she is swept up into a maelstrom of fear, intrigue, and, most alarmingly, love.

In a horrifying but intriguing development for Carolyn, cult-like events begin to unfold in her midst and, before long, she finds both her life and her heart at stake.

## VANITY BLADE

Orphan daughter of a saloon singer, vivacious Mary Lousie Mackenzie grows up to be a famous singer herself, the beautiful gambling queen known as Vanity Blade. Leaving her home in Mississippi, Vanity travels a wayward path to Sacramento, where she rules her own gambling boat. Gamblers and con men barter in high stakes around her, but Vanity's heart remains back east, with her once carefree life and former love, Trance Holloway, a preacher's son.

Trying to reclaim a happiness she'd left behind long ago, Vanity returns to Mississippi to discover—and fight for—the love she thought she'd lost forever.

9 781682 300886